THE FULLER MEMORANDUM

Ace Books by Charles Stross

SINGULARITY SKY

IRON SUNRISE

ACCELERANDO

THE ATROCITY ARCHIVES

GLASSHOUSE

HALTING STATE

SATURN'S CHILDREN

THE JENNIFER MORGUE

WIRELESS

THE FULLER MEMORANDUM

THE
FULLER MEMORANDUM

CHARLES STROSS

ACE BOOKS, NEW YORK

THE BERKLEY PUBLISHING GROUP
Published by the Penguin Group
Penguin Group (USA) Inc.
375 Hudson Street, New York, New York 10014, USA
Penguin Group (Canada), 90 Eglinton Avenue East, Suite 700, Toronto, Ontario M4P 2Y3, Canada
(a division of Pearson Penguin Canada Inc.)
Penguin Books Ltd., 80 Strand, London WC2R 0RL, England
Penguin Group Ireland, 25 St. Stephen's Green, Dublin 2, Ireland (a division of Penguin Books Ltd.)
Penguin Group (Australia), 250 Camberwell Road, Camberwell, Victoria 3124, Australia
(a division of Pearson Australia Group Pty. Ltd.)
Penguin Books India Pvt. Ltd., 11 Community Centre, Panchsheel Park, New Delhi—110 017, India
Penguin Group (NZ), 67 Apollo Drive, Rosedale, North Shore 0632, New Zealand
(a division of Pearson New Zealand Ltd.)
Penguin Books (South Africa) (Pty.) Ltd., 24 Sturdee Avenue, Rosebank, Johannesburg 2196,
South Africa

Penguin Books Ltd., Registered Offices: 80 Strand, London WC2R 0RL, England

This is an original publication of The Berkley Publishing Group.

Copyright © 2010 by Charles Stross.
Text design by Kristin del Rosario.

ISBN 978-0-441-01867-3

PRINTED IN THE UNITED STATES OF AMERICA

IN MEMORY OF
CHARLES N. BROWN AND JOHN M. FORD.
WE MISS YOU BOTH.

ACKNOWLEDGMENTS

Writers build on the shoulders of others. In particular, I'd like to single out three other writers, without whose work this book would not be as it is: Ferdinand Ossendowski, for his memoirs of events during the Russian civil war; James Palmer, for his portrait of the Bloody White Baron; and Anthony Price, who gave this book a skeleton.

Prologue

LOSING MY RELIGION

THERE CAN BE ONLY ONE TRUE RELIGION. ARE YOU FEELING lucky, believer?

Like the majority of ordinary British citizens, I used to be a good old-fashioned atheist, secure in my conviction that folks who believed—in angels and demons, supernatural manifestations and demiurges, snake-fondling and babbling in tongues and the world being only a few thousand years old—were all superstitious idiots. It was a conviction encouraged by every crazy news item from the Middle East, every ludicrous White House prayer breakfast on the TV. But then I was recruited by the Laundry, and learned better.

I wish I could go back to the comforting certainties of atheism; it's so much less unpleasant than the One True Religion.

The truth won't make your Baby Jesus cry because, sad to say, there ain't no such Son of God. Moses may have taken two tablets before breakfast, but there was nobody home to listen to the prayers of the victims of the Shoah. The guardians of the Kaaba have got the world's best tourism racket running, the Dalai Lama isn't anybody's reincarnation, Zeus is out to lunch, and you *really* don't want me to start on the neo-pagans.

However, there *is* a God out there—vast and ancient and infinitely powerful—and I know the name of this God. I know the path you have to walk down to be one with this God. I know his secret rituals and the correct form of prayer and his portents and signs. I have studied the ancient writings of his prophets and followers in person, not simply relying on the classified digests in the CODICIL BLACK SKULL files and the background briefings for CASE NIGHTMARE GREEN.

I'm a believer. And like I said, I wish I was still an atheist. Believing I was born into a harsh, uncaring cosmos—in which my existence was a random roll of the dice and I was destined to die and rot and then be gone forever—was infinitely more comforting than the truth.

Because the truth is that my God is coming back.

When he arrives I'll be waiting for him with a shotgun.

And I'm keeping the last shell for myself.

A COUPLE OF YEARS AGO, ANGLETON SUGGESTED I START WRITING my memoirs. It seemed a pretty weird idea at the time—a thirty-year-old occult intelligence officer should take time off on the job to work on his autobiography?—but he had a point. "Bob," he said, in his usual frighteningly avuncular tones, with a voice like dry sheets of parchment rubbing, "like it or not, that thick little skull of yours contains valuable institutional knowledge that has been acquired over years of service for H. M. Government. If you don't start now, you may never catch up with the job. And if you don't catch up with the job, part of the Laundry's institutional memory might vanish for good." He gave a curious little chuckle, as if he regretted having had to admit that there was any value to my meager contribution. "You might die on your next field assignment, or be turned by the enemy. And that'd be nearly ten years of work down the drain."

Then he pointed me at the rule book that explained how all officers above OC2 rank are required to either keep a classified journal or to periodically update their memoirs, which would be stored under lock and key—automatically classified under the various keywords they'd been cleared for during the time period covered—the books to be opened only in event of their author's death, retirement, or permanent disablement in the line of duty.

You know something? I *hate* writing. I keep having to distract myself, hence all the little jokes. It's actually not as if the job is all that funny, when you get down to it. Especially as I have to write everything either in longhand or on a 1962 Triumph Adler 66 manual typewriter, and burn the ribbons and carbon papers afterwards in the Security Office incinerator in front of two witnesses with high security clearances. I'm not allowed to use rubber bands or paper clips to hold the papers together (although string and, ye horrors, traditional red sealing wax—and *don't* get me started on how difficult it is to melt the stuff in a smoke-free building with fire detectors in every office—is permitted). My fingers are hardwired for the Emacs programmers' editor and a laptop; this historic office reenactment stuff gets old real fast. But I digress.

This is the story of how I lost my atheism, and why I wish I could regain it. This is the story of the people who lost their lives in an alien desert bathed by the hideous radiance of a dead sun, and the love that was lost and the terror that wakes me up in a cold sweat about once a week, clawing at the sheets with cramping fingers and drool on my chin. It's why Mo and I aren't living together right now, why my right arm doesn't work properly, and I'm toiling late into the night, trying to bury the smoking wreckage of my life beneath a heap of work.

It's the story of what happened to the Fuller Memorandum, and the beginning of the end of the world.

Are you sure you want to carry on?

1.

GOING TO SEE THE ELEPHANT

Summer in England

THOSE WORDS ARE SUPPOSED TO CONJURE UP HALCYON SUNNY afternoons; the smell of new-mown hay, little old ladies on bicycles pedaling past the village green on their way to the church jumble sale, the vicar's tea party, the crunching sound of a fast-bowled cricket ball fracturing the batsman's skull, and so on.

The reality is, of course, utterly different.

It's an early summer afternoon in June, and I'm sharing an overcrowded train carriage with an assortment of tired commuters heading back to their dormitory suburbs, and a couple of angry wasps trying to drill their way out through the toughened glass. The hamster-powered air conditioning is wheezing on the edge of a nervous breakdown, it's twenty-eight degrees and ninety percent relative humidity out there, and the asshole behind me is playing something very loud on a pair of tinny headphones.

I'm having second thoughts about having paid fifty pounds to sit on this train, expenses or no expenses. But I don't see what alternatives there are. I need to get from London to RAF Cosford, just outside Wolverhampton, and I don't have a car and the Laundry certainly isn't going to hire me a helicopter for a job that isn't time-critical. They won't even pay for me to take a taxi the whole way. So I'm stuck with a choice: train or coach. At least this way I get to avoid the M6 motorway . . .

And at least I've got a seat with a table. I reread my instructions as the train shudders and lurches through the parched countryside. It's a low-priority field job: to investigate reports of eerie manifestations of a disturbing nature from one of the airframes stored in the hangar annex to the Royal Air Force Museum. The museum houses a lot of historic warbirds. Violent death tends to go with the territory, and a few ghosts—echoes in the informational substrate of reality—wouldn't be anything out of the ordinary. My job is to dispel any annoying manifestations, reassure the locals, close out the case, etcetera. It's sufficiently routine and predictable that I'd normally send the office junior, but for some reason, Angleton pulled me into his office this morning. "Bob, I'd like you to deal with this one yourself," he said, handing me the brief. "It'll get you out of the office for a day."

"But I'm busy!" I protested, a tad limply—the lack of aircon was getting to me, and I'm not good at standing up to Angleton at the best of times. "I've got to respond to the RFP on structured cabling requirements for the new subbasement extension in D Block"—don't call it a crypt, *the government* doesn't do crypts, *the Spanish Inquisition* does crypts—"and go over Claire's training budget. Can't Peter-Fred do it? He's finished Exorcism 101, it's about time he had a field trip . . ."

"Nonsense!" Angleton said crisply. "You can take the paperwork with you, but I specifically want *you* to go and look at this one."

There's a warning gleam in his eyes: I've seen it before. "Oh no you don't," I replied. "Not so fast!" I raised an eyebrow and waited for the explosion.

Angleton is old school—so old school that I'm pretty sure I've seen his face in a departmental photo taken during the war, back when the Laundry was an obscure department of SOE, the Special Operations Executive, tasked with occult intelligence gathering and counter-demonology. He doesn't look a day older today than he did back then, sixty-five years ago—dress him in a bandage and he could star in a remake of *The Mummy*. Ice-blue eyes with slightly yellowish scleras, skin like parchment left out for too long in a desert sandstorm, dry as bone and twice as chilly as ice. And I never want to hear his laugh again. But I digress. The thing about Angleton is that, despite (or in addition to) being the honorary departmental monster, he has a sense of humor. It bears about the same relationship to mirth that his cadaverous exterior does to Paris Hilton's—but it's there. (He has the heart of a young boy: keeps it in a reliquary under the coffin he sleeps in.) And right then, I figured he was winding me up for the punch line.

But: no. He shook his head slowly. "Not this time, Bob." The gleam in his eye guttered out, replaced by dead-cold sobriety: "While you're up there to do the business, I want you to take a look at one of the other museum exhibits—one that's not on public display. I'll explain it later, when you get back. Take your warrant card. When you're through with the job on the worksheet, tell Warrant Officer Hastings that I sent you to take a look at the white elephant in Hangar 12B."

Huh? I blinked a couple of times, then sneezed. "You're setting me up for another working group, aren't you?"

"You know better than to ask that, boy," he grated, and I jumped back: Angleton is nobody you want to stand too close to when he's even mildly irritated. "I'll give you the background when you're ready for it. Meanwhile, get moving!"

"Whatever." I sketched a sarcastic salute and marched off back to my office, lost in thought. It was a setup, obviously: Angleton was softening me up for something new. Probably a new game of bureaucratic pass-the-parcel, seeing if some poor schmuck—I was already in charge of departmental IT services, for my sins—could be mugged into taking on responsibility for exorcising hovercraft or something.

Back to the here-and-now. The carriage is slowing. A minute later I realize it's pulling into a main line station—Wolverhampton, where I get to change trains. I shove my reading matter back into my messenger bag (it's a novel about a private magician for hire in Chicago—your taxpayer pounds at work) and go to stand in the doorway.

The air in the station hits me like a hot flannel, damp and clingy and smelling slightly of diesel fumes. I take a breath, step down onto the concrete, and try to minimize my movements as I go looking for the Cosford service. I find the platform it stops at: a crumbling concrete strip opposite a peeling wooden fence. The rails are rusty and overgrown, and a couple of young trees are trying to colonize the tracks; but the TV screen overhead is lit up and predicting a train will be along in ten minutes. I take a shallow breath and sit down, hunching instinctively towards the nearest shade. Fifteen minutes later, the TV screen is still predicting a train will be along in ten minutes; then my mobile rings. It's Mo.

"Bob!" She sounds so cheerful when she says my name: I don't know how she does it, but it cheers me up.

"Mo!" *Pause.* "Where are you?"

"I'm back in the office! I spent most of the morning in the stacks, I only just got your text . . ." The one telling her I was off on a day trip to Cosford. The Laundry's deep archives are in a former underground tunnel, way down where the sun doesn't shine, and neither do the cellular networks.

"Right. I'm on a railway platform waiting for an overdue train. It's about two hundred degrees in the shade, the pigeons are falling out of the sky from heatstroke, and nobody will sell me a beer." (Well, they might if I'd asked for one, but . . .)

"Oh, good! When are you going to be back?"

"Sometime late this evening," I say doubtfully. "I'm due to arrive in Cosford at"—I check the lying timetable—"two thirty, and I don't think I'll get away before six. Then it'll take me about three hours—"

"Angleton did this? He did, didn't he!" Suddenly Mo switches from warm and cuddly to spiky as a porcupine: "Didn't you tell him you couldn't? We're supposed to be having dinner with Pete and Sandy tonight!"

I do a mental backflip, re-engage my short-term memory, and realize she's right. Dinner for four, booked at a new Kurdish restaurant in Fulham. Pete was at university with Mo years ago, and is a priest or a witch doctor or something; Sandy is blonde and teaches comparative religion to secondary school kids. Mo insists we stay in touch with them: having friends with ordinary jobs who don't know anything about the Laundry provides a normative dose of sanity for the two of us, to keep us from drifting too far out of the mainstream. "Shit." I'm more mortified for having landed Mo in it than anything else . . . "You're right. Listen, do you want to go on your own, tell them I'll turn up later—I'll come straight from the station—or do you want to cancel?"

There's silence for a second, then she sighs. "Sandy doesn't have flexitime, Bob, she's got classes to teach. *You* cancel."

"But I don't have their mobile numbers—"

I'm bluffing, and Mo knows it. "I'll text them to you, Bob. Maybe it'll help you remember, next time?"

Bollocks. She's right: it's my fault. "Okay." It's my turn to sigh. "I'll be claiming some hours back. Maybe we can use them for something together—" The tracks begin to vibrate and squeal and I look up. "It's my train! See you later? Bye . . ."

The train to Cosford is about as old as Angleton: slam doors, wooden partitions, and high-backed seats, powered by a villainously rusted diesel engine slung under its single carriage. Air conditioning is provided by the open louvered windows. I swelter in its oven-like interior for about forty minutes as it rattles and burbles through the countryside, spewing blue smoke and engine oil behind it. Along the way I furtively leave my apologies on Pete and Sandy's voice mail. Finally, the train wheezes asthmatically to a halt beside a station overlooking a Royal Air Force base, with a cluster of hangars outside the gate and some enormous airliners and transport aircraft gently gathering moss on the lawn outside. Breathing a sigh of relief, I walk up the path to the museum annex and head for the main exhibit hall.

It's time to go to work . . .

* * *

PAY ATTENTION NOW: THIS BRIEFING WILL SELF-DESTRUCT IN fifteen minutes.

My name is Bob, Bob Howard. At least, that's the name I use in these memoirs. (True names have power: even if it's only the power to attract the supernatural equivalent of a Make Money Fast spammer, I'd rather not put myself in their sights, thank you very much.) And I work for the Laundry.

The Laundry is the British Government's secret agency for dealing with "magic." The use of scare-quotes is deliberate; as Sir Arthur C. Clarke said, "Any sufficiently advanced technology is indistinguishable from magic," so "magic" is what we deal with. Note that this does not involve potions, pentacles, prayers, eldritch chanting, dressing up in robes and pointy hats, or most (but not all) of the stuff associated with the term in the public mind. No, our magic is computational. The realm of pure mathematics is very real indeed, and the . . . *things* . . . that cast shadows on the walls of Plato's cave can sometimes be made to listen and pay attention if you point a loaded theorem at them. This is, however, a very dangerous process, because most of the shadow-casters are unclear on the distinction between *pay attention* and *free buffet lunch here*. My job—applied computational demonologist—comes with a very generous pension scheme, because most of us don't survive to claim it.

Magic being a branch of pure mathematics, and computers being machines that can be used to perform lots of mathematical tasks very fast, it follows that most real practicing magicians start out as computer science graduates. The Laundry, the government agency for handling this stuff, started out as a by-blow of the Second World War code-breakers at Bletchley Park, the people who built the first working programmable computers. And the domestic side of our work—preventing accidental incursions by incomprehensible horrors from beyond spacetime—has been growing rapidly in recent decades. You may have noticed there are more computers around these days, and more computer programmers. Guess what? That means more work for the Laundry!

I have a somewhat embarrassing relationship with Wolverhampton. Back when I was at university in Birmingham I nearly landscaped it by accident. I was trying to develop a new graphics algorithm. Planar homogeneous matrix transformations into dimensions dominated by gibbering horrors tend to attract the Laundry's attention: they got to me just in time—just before the nameless horrors I was about to unintentionally summon into this world—and made me a job offer I wasn't allowed to refuse.

(Mo's history is similar—indeed, I was involved not only in recruiting her, but in keeping her alive until she could be recruited. That was some years ago. Mo and I have been together for, oh, about six years; we tied the knot nearly three years ago, using the urgent need to break a behavioral geas as an excuse to do something we both wanted to do anyway.)

So, I'm here at RAF Cosford, an active air force base which is also home to the Royal Air Force Museum annex, where they keep the stuff that's too big to fit in their North London site at Duxford. Ostensibly I'm here to examine an aircraft that has been the locus of some disturbing incidents (and to stop those incidents recurring). Also, thanks to Angleton, I'm supposed to take a look at something in Hangar Six.

One of the things you learn fairly fast in the Laundry is that most people in the British civil service and armed forces don't know you exist. You—your organization, your job, the field you work in—are classified so deeply that the mere knowledge that such a classification level exists is itself a state secret. So, to help me do my job, I carry something that we laughably call a "warrant card." It's a form of identification. It comes with certain Powers attached. When you present your warrant card for inspection, in the course of official business, the recipients tend to believe you are who and what you say you are, for the duration of that business. Not only that: you can bind them to silence. Of course, trying to use your card *outside* official business tends to attract the attention of the Auditors. And having attracted their attention once or twice, I've never been too keen on finding out what happens next . . .

The RAF Museum is fronted by a shiny new glass-and-steel aircraft hangar of an exhibit hall. I march right up to the front desk (there's no queue), present my warrant card, and say: "Bob Howard. I'm here to see Mr. Hastings."

The wooly headed volunteer behind the cash register puts down her knitting and peers up at me over the rim of her bifocals. "Admission is five pounds," she chirps.

"I'm here to see *Mr. Hastings*." I force a smile and adjust my grip on the warrant card.

"Is that a season pass?" She looks confused.

What? I shove the card under her nose. "I have an appointment with Warrant Officer Hastings," I repeat, trying to keep a note of impatience out of my voice. "I'm from the Department of Administrative Affairs." It's a thin bluff—jeans and tee shirt aren't normal office attire for the civil service, even in this weather—but I'm crossing the fingers of my free hand and trusting my card to untangle enough of her neurons to get the message across. "A meeting to discuss the, ah, business in Hangar Six."

She blinks rapidly. "Ooh, Hangar *Six*! That's a bad job, it hasn't been the same since Norman had his Health and Safety inspection . . . They used to keep the Whirlwind in there, did you know? You're wanting Geoffrey, aren't you?"

"Would that be Warrant Officer Hastings?" I ask, hopefully.

"Oh yes." She pushes her knitting aside with one liver-spotted hand and picks up the telephone with another. "Geoffrey? Geoffrey? There's a man here to see you! Who did you say you were? A Mr. Howarth! Yes, to see you now! He's out front!" She puts the phone down. "Geoffrey will be here in a couple of minutes," she confides, "he needs to scrub up first."

I tap my toes and whistle tunelessly as I look around the entrance hall. There's something casting a weird shadow overhead; I look up, and find myself staring at the bulging ventral fuel tank of an English Electric Lightning interceptor, dangling from the ceiling like a demented model-maker's pride and joy. It's enough to stop the foot tapping for a moment—if the cable fails, I'll be squashed like a bug—but a moment's consideration tells me that it's highly unlikely. So I stare wistfully at the Lightning for a couple of minutes. Two missiles, sharply raked razor-thin wings, a huge, pregnant belly full of fuel, and the two screamingly powerful engines that once rammed it from a cold start to a thousand miles per hour in under a minute. Life would be so much simpler if our adversaries could be dealt with by supersonic death on the wing—but alas, Human Resources aren't so easily defeated.

"Mr. Hogarth?"

I turn round. There's a bluff-looking middle-aged man in blue overalls standing by the front desk: sandy receding hair, a gingery regulation mustache, and a face creased with questions. I hold up my warrant card. "Mr. *Howard*," I say. "Capital Laundry Services. I believe you asked for a visit."

He does a visible double take. "Eh, yes, I did—" He's clocking the jeans, tee shirt, and casual linen jacket, and I can see the gears whirring in his head as he wonders if I'm some kind of impostor. Then his eyes reach my warrant card and something clicks behind them and he's slightly less human than he was a moment before—"sir."

"I was told your problem is in Hangar Six. Why don't you take me there? You can explain along the way."

I put the warrant card back in my pocket. No point in frying him.

"If you'd follow me, please, sir." He has a pronounced borders accent. He turns and opens a door marked AUTHORIZED PERSONNEL ONLY. "Sorry about Helen on the front desk," he murmurs. "She's a little slow, but she means well. Only see you, she's been helping out here since forever, and we run on volunteers." He shrugs. "I suppose it's better for her than sitting around an old-age home waiting to die—" He lets the door close behind us before he says anything more. "Bloody rum business, Hangar Six."

"Tell me about it. In your own words," I add.

"It's another of the Lightnings—hull number XR727." He glances over his shoulder. "It's been sitting in Hangar Six for years while we were waiting for funding to come through—plan was to restore it for static display in Hall Four when it's ready. It's an F. Mark 3, upgraded from F.2A like the one over the front desk." I'll take his word for it: I'm not au fait with the model numbers. "We've had a few odd incidents."

Odd incidents? "Define odd."

"Frosty patches on the hangar floor, mysterious oil leaks—under hydraulic pipes that were drained more than twenty years ago when it was taken out of service—nothing really unusual, seeing where it came from, if you follow my drift. But then there was the business with Marcia and the instrument panel, and I thought it might be a good idea to call you chappies directly."

Clunk. A domino slips into place in my mental map. This enquiry didn't come through the RAF, this came direct from Hastings. "You've worked with us before."

"Not exactly . . ." He pauses beside an anonymous door, and extracts a fat key chain: "But I was with the Squadron, on ground crew. Once you're in, you never really leave." *Click.* "They like to stay in touch."

What squadron? I wonder, annoyed but afraid to display my ignorance. "Tell me about Marcia," I prompt, as he opens the door to reveal another prefab tunnel between buildings, this one windowless and stifling.

"Volunteer airframe conservator Marcia Moran. Age twenty-nine, completed her short service enlistment, then signed up with BAE Systems maintenance division when the defense review came down—she's solid. *Was* solid."

He took a deep breath. "She should never have been allowed to work on XR727's cockpit instruments. We had them round the back, under padlock and warded by a class two repulsion geas. She shouldn't even have been able to *see* them. She'd have twigged straight off that it wasn't a normal F.3 integrated flight system and weapons control board. She wasn't qualified to work on it."

He falls silent as he trudges along the passage.

"What happened to her?" I repeat.

14

Hastings shook his head. "You'd have to ask the doctors. I'm not sure they know; they say she might be safe to release next month, but they said that last month too."

Another domino. "XR727 was one of the, uh, Squadron's planes. Yes?"

"They didn't brief you?" He doesn't sound surprised. "In here, Mr. Houghton." I don't bother to correct him as he shoves open a side door and steps into an echoing, gloomy cavern of a room. "See for yourself."

The room we're in resembles an aircraft hangar the way a mausoleum in a graveyard resembles a bedroom. It's dimly lit, daylight filtering through high windows, and the light reveals the mummified skeletons of half a dozen fast jets littering the oil-stained concrete floor. Their severed limbs are stacked in jigs and frames, their viscera embalmed in the canopic jars of parts bins—patiently awaiting resurrection, or at least reassembly into the semblance of life. There's junk everywhere, toolboxes, rodent control traps, workbenches piled high with parts. Closest to the door hulks the fuselage of a Lightning. Its tail is missing, as are its outboard wing segments and the conical spike of its nose radar, but it's substantially intact. Close up, the size of the thing is apparent: a pit bull to the chihuahua of an old Russian MiG—squat, brutal, built for raw speed. It's big, too—the wing root high enough overhead to walk under without stooping.

Something about it makes me feel profoundly uneasy, as if a black cat has walked half the length of my grave, paused furtively, taken a crap, and been about its business before anyone noticed.

"This is Airframe XR727. According to the official records it was scrapped in 1983. Unofficially . . . it ended up here, because of its history: it's a ringer, it was on the books with 23 squadron and 11 squadron, but they never saw it. It was working for you people. In the Squadron." I shiver. The hangar's weirdly, incongruously cold, given the bright summer afternoon outside. "It logged 280 hours on the other side, escorting the white elephants."

Angleton mentioned a white elephant, didn't he? I glance at the shadows under XR727's belly. The concrete is stained and greasy with fluid, whorls and lines and disconnected nodes that swim before my eyes. *Clonk*. The final domino slides into place.

"Jesus, Angleton," I mutter, and pull out my PDA. *Tap-click-boing* and I pull up the thaumograph utility running on the rather nonstandard card in its second expansion slot. I point it at the swirling directed graph that the phantom hydraulic leak has dribbled across the concrete apron and the display flashes amber.

I take a slow step back from the airframe, and motion Hastings over. "I don't want to alarm you," I murmur. "But did you know your airframe is hot?"

Hastings shakes his head sadly. "Figures." He shrugs. "Do you want to look at the cockpit instrumentation?"

I nod. "Just point me at it. Is it still where Marcia had her incident?"

"I haven't moved it." He gestures towards a canvas screen, surrounded by a circle of traffic cones with hazard tape strung between them. "Do you need any help?"

"I'm afraid I'm probably beyond help . . ." I advance on the traffic cones, PDA held in front of me. It begins to bleep and warble immediately. Edging sideways, I look round the canvas screen. There's a workbench bearing a stack of black metal boxes, wires dangling, needles and dials glowing eerie blue—*blue? Glowing?* I check my PDA and swear under my breath. If this was a radiation leak I'd be backing away and reaching for the lead-lined underwear right now: but it's not, it's just thaumic resonance, albeit at levels you don't usually see outside of a summoning grid—what the ignorant persist in calling a pentacle. "Scratch that. Do you have any conductive tape? A soldering iron? Some blue chalk?"

"You're going to exorcise it," states Hastings. "Right?"

"Right—"

"Got a field exorcism kit in the mess hut. Squadron issue, rev three, and I keep everything in date. Want me to fetch it?"

"I think that would be a very good idea," I say with feeling, thinking,

Field exorcism kit? Squadron issue? "By the way, what was the Squadron's unit number?"

Hastings stares at me. "Triple-six. Didn't they tell you *anything?*"

HERE IS HOW YOU GO ABOUT EXORCISING A HAUNTED JET fighter, latterly operated by the more-than-somewhat-secret 666 Squadron, RAF:

- You can explosively disassemble the airframe, if it's in the middle of a desert and there are no neighbors within a couple of miles.
- You can violate any number of HSE directives and outrage public opinion by dumping it at sea—shallow waters only, we don't want to annoy the owners by violating the Benthic Treaties—and wait for time (and electrolytes) to wash the memories away.
- You can truck it to a special hazardous waste certified recycling site in Wales, where they have a very special degaussing coil for exactly this purpose.
- Or, if you believe in living dangerously, you can do it with a soldering iron, a stopwatch, a grounding strap, and a good pair of running shoes in case you screw up.

Guess what Muggins here does?

Look, it's a *museum piece.* They don't exactly grow on trees: blowing it up and drowning it aren't on the menu; shipping it to Wales would cost . . . Well, it wouldn't fit on my discretionary expense worksheet: too many zeros (more than two). That leaves the grounding strap and the running shoes. So if you were in my place, what would *you* do?

I approach the anti-static point beside the nosewheel bay very cautiously: holding one end of a grounding strap at arm's length in front of me, the other fist clutching the stopwatch behind my back, legs tensed, ready to run. The grounding strap is basically a long conductive wire; the other end is attached to a villainous black signal generator Hastings pulled from the field exorcism kit—all bakelite and flickering needles on dials, like something out of a 1950s Hammer Horror flick. There's a small but bizarre diorama occupying the middle of the hastily cleared workbench it sits on: a model airplane from the souvenir shop, a rabbit's foot, a key-ring fob skull pendant, and a diagram carefully sketched in conductive ink.

Look, this isn't quite as spontaneously suicidal as it sounds. I don't go anywhere these days without a defensive ward on a chain round my neck that'll short out a class three offensive invocation, and Hastings is safely tucked away inside a grounded pentacle with Thoth-Lieberman geometry—he's safe as houses, at least houses that aren't sitting on top of a fault line wound up to let rip with a Richter 6.0 earthquake. As it happens, I do this kind of thing regularly, every week or so. It's about as safe as a well-equipped fireman going into a smoldering inflammables store to spray cooling water across the overheating propane tank in the corner next to the mains power distribution board. Piece of cake, really—as long as somebody's shut off the power.

"Are you centered?" I call over my shoulder to Hastings. "In the safety zone?"

"Yes." He sounds bored. "How about you?"

"I'll be okay." I keep my eyes peeled as I shove the plug on the end of the strap into the anti-static point, and twist. I've plonked my PDA down on the floor a couple of meters away and set it to audio, beeping like a Geiger counter in the thaum field. It ticks every few seconds, like a cooling kettle. The airframe itself is probably safe, unlike the blue-glowing instrument panel on the workbench, but it's a bigger physical hazard, which is why I'm tackling it first.

I take a couple of steps back, then straighten up and walk over to the signal generator. *Where was I? Ah, yes.* I flip a couple of switches and there's a loud chime, almost like a bell ringing, except slightly off-key. It sets my teeth on edge. "Degaussing resonator on," I say aloud. Continuing the checklist from memory: "Exclusion field engaged." I pick up my PDA, fire up the ebook reader, and shuffle round the airframe slowly, reading aloud as I go: words in an alien tongue not suited for human lips. The signal generator chimes periodically. There's your exorcism in a nutshell: *bell, book, and candle*—although the candle is strictly optional if you're reading from a backlit screen, and the bell's a synthesized tone.

Finally, after squeezing between the Lightning and a tarp-shrouded jet engine on a trolley I fetch up where I started from, back by the workbench. "Last words." I pick up the microphone that's plugged into the signal generator, flip the switch, and say, "Piss off."

There's a bang and a blue flash from the grounding point on the airframe, and my PDA makes an ominous crackling noise. Then the thaum field dies. "You nailed it," says Hastings.

"Looks that way," I agree, turning to face him.

He looks past me. "What about the— *Hey, what are you*—"

Now here's where things go wrong.

Muggins here didn't bother to set up a ward around the workbench with the contaminated cockpit console before he sorted out the airframe, because he thought that he could do the two jobs separately. But they're not separate, are they? The law of contagion applies: the cockpit instruments had been physically bolted to the airframe for a number of years, and things that form a unitary identity for a long time tend to respond as one.

More importantly, nobody had thought to tell Muggins precisely *what* Squadron 666, Royal Air Force, did with its planes. *Escorting the white elephants*. Muggins here still thought he was dealing with a simple spontaneous haunting—bad memories, terrified pilot in near-death experience, that sort of thing—rather than secondary activation caused by overexposure to gibbering unearthly horrors; the necromantic equivalent of collecting fallout samples by flying through mushroom clouds.

But I'm second-guessing the enquiry now, so I'll shut up.

Warrant Officer Hastings survives the explosion because he is still inside his protective pentacle.

Muggins here survives the explosion because he is wearing a heavy-duty defensive ward around his neck and, in response to Hastings's call, has turned to look at the open doorway where little old Helen with her tightly curled white hair is standing, clutching a tea tray.

Her mouth is open as if she's about to say something, and her eyebrows are raised.

I will remember the expression on her face for a very long time.

Beauty may be skin-deep, but horror goes all the way down to the desiccated bone beneath, as the eerie purple flashbulb glow rises and her eyes melt in their sockets and her hair and clothes turn to dust, falling down and down as I begin to turn back towards the airframe and reach for the small pouch around my neck, which is scalding hot against my skin as the air heats up—

There's a dissonant chime from the signal generator on the bench, unattended, then a continuous shrill ringing alarm as its safeties trip.

The hideous light goes out with a bang like a balloon bursting, a balloon the size of the Hindenburg.

"*Shit*," I hear someone say as I grab the ward and feel a sharp pain in my hand. I blink furiously as I yank, breaking the fine chain. There's a clicking in my ears and I blink again, see white powder everywhere—like snow or heavy dust on the floor, a patina of corrosion on the aircraft wings stacked in their jigs around me, white on the workbenches—

"Helen!" shouts Warrant Officer Hastings, stepping over the boundary of his protective perimeter.

I don't need to look round to know it's too late for her but I still cringe. I drop the ward and gasp as air touches the palm of my hand and the spot on my sternum that's beginning to sting like a kicked wasps' nest. My ears are ringing.

I turn back to the bench with the signal generator to check my PDA for the thaum field. Unwelcome surprises come in threes: Number one is, the bench is a centimeter deep in white dusty powder. Surprise number two is, my PDA has gone to meet its maker—it's actually scorched and blackened, the case melted around one edge. And surprise number three—

A thin, wispy trickle of smoke is rising from behind the (scorched, naturally) canvas screens around the Lightning's cockpit instruments—ground zero for the pulse of necromantic energy that has just seared through the hangar like a boiling propane vapor explosion.

Here's Hastings, kneeling and clutching a dented steel teapot that looks as if it's been sandblasted, sobbing over a pile of—

The ringing in my ears is louder, and louder still, and the big hangar doors crack open to admit a ray of daylight to the crypt and the howl of the airfield fire tender's siren, but they're too late.

I GET HOME LATE. REALLY LATE: SO LATE I END UP EXPENSING a taxi to take me into Birmingham to catch the last train, and another taxi home at the other end. Iris will probably give me a chewing out over it but I'll cross that bridge when I come to it. The emergency response team kept me at the first aid post for a couple of hours, under observation, but I'm okay, really: just scooped out and full of a numinous sense of dread, looping on the bright purple flash as I looked round and saw the door opening, Helen standing there for a moment as the thaum field on the instrument console collapsed, sucking out the life from anything within a fifty-meter radius that wasn't locked down and shielded.

(Hangar Six isn't going to have a rat problem for a while.)

The unshielded instrument console entangled with the shielded airframe I'd just exorcised. And the seventy-something lady in the pink slippers, shuffling forward with a tea tray and two mugs she'd carefully poured for us—

Too clever by half.

As I open the front door, I can feel the house sulking. I switch on the lights and hang up my coat in the hall, fighting the urge to hunch my shoulders defensively. It's Mo, of course. This is her house as much as it's mine—okay, it's our maisonette, two civil servants can't possibly afford a house in London even if they're both management track—and it reflects her mood. I canceled Pete and Sandy but I can't cancel Mo. She's got a snit on, perfectly justifiable. I really ought to go upstairs and apologize, but as I bend down to untie my shoelaces I find my hands are shaking.

An indeterminate time later I open my eyes. I'm sitting at the kitchen table with an empty glass in my hand. The quality of the light just changed.

"Bob?" It's Mo, wearing a dressing gown, rubbing her eyes. "Shit. Bob"—her tone of voice changes, softening slightly—"what's wrong?"

"*I—*" I clear my throat, force air through my larynx: "I screwed up."

The bottle of Talisker sitting beside my left hand is half-empty. Mo peers at it, then takes a step closer and peers at me. Then she picks up the bottle, pops the cork, and pours a generous two fingers into my glass, bless her.

"Drink up." She pauses with a hand on the back of the other kitchen chair. "Am I going to need one too?"

"Dunno. Maybe."

She goes to the cupboard and takes out another glass before she sits down. I blink at her, red-eyed and confused.

"Talk." She pours a shot into her own glass. "In your own time."

I glance at the kitchen clock. "It's one a.m."

"And it'll be one a.m. again, at least once a day for the rest of your life. So talk, if you want. Or drink up and come to bed."

I sip my whisky. "I screwed up."

"How badly?"

"I killed a bystander."

"A by—" She freezes with her glass halfway to her lips. "Jesus, Bob." *Pause.* "How did you do *that*?"

She looks appalled, but probably much less appalled than *your* spouse would look if you confessed to killing someone over the kitchen table. (Mo is made of stern stuff.)

"Angleton sent me to do a routine job. Only I missed something and fucked up my prep."

"But you're still—" She bites her lip, and now she looks shaken; my ears sketch in the missing word: *alive.*

"Oh, I *almost* got it right," I explain, waving my glass. "Warrant Officer Hastings wasn't hurt. And I'm here." But then I remember the purple flash again, and the door opening, and the sight of Helen's face aging a hundred years in a second right before my eyes. "Only the tea lady opened the door at the worst possible moment . . ."

Mo is silent for a while, so I take another sip.

"Fatal accidents never happen because of just one mistake," I try to explain. "It takes a whole chain of stupids lining up just *so* to put a full stop at the end of an epitaph."

"So what did you do afterwards?" she asks quietly.

"Afterwards? It was too late to do anything." I shrug. "I told 'em not to disturb the scene and called the Plumbers. Then I had to wait until they arrived and hang around while they logged the scene and filed a preliminary report and bagged the body, which took all evening. They had to use a Dyson—there wasn't enough left of her to fill a teacup, never mind a reanimator's workbench. It's on the books as a level four excursion, incidental unintended fatality. The desk officer was very understanding but I've got a ten o'clock appointment with someone in Operational Oversight to file an R60." An official incident report. "Then I suppose there'll be an enquiry."

And the juggernaut of an internal investigation will start to roll, bearing down on my ass like hell's own lawn mower in search of an untrimmed blade of grass, but it's not as if I don't deserve it. I take another sip of the whisky, wishing I could drown myself in it. This isn't the first time I've killed someone, but it's the first time I've killed a civilian bystander, and I lack the words to express how I feel.

"I was going to dump on you," Mo tells me, "but . . . forget it." She empties her glass and I realize that while I was seeing that purple light the whisky has evaporated from my tumbler. "Come to bed now."

I push myself to my feet, neck drooping. "It won't make things better."

"No."

"I feel like shit."

"No, Bob, you need to get some sleep."

"I am a shit."

"You need to get some sleep. Come to bed."

"If you say so."

I follow her upstairs. Today's been shit, and tomorrow is quite possibly going to be worse—but it can wait for a while.

2.

POINTING THE FINGER

I GO TO WORK IN A NONDESCRIPT OFFICE IN CENTRAL LONDON,
south of the river and east of the sun—I can't say precisely where—located
above a row of shops. It's a temporary home for the department, and it's
officially called the New Annexe, probably because it was thrown up in
1964. It consists of three floors of characterless sixties concrete piled up
above a C&A and a couple of other boring high street stores like a bad
perm on a grocer's granny; it used to belong to the Post Office, back in
the day. And nothing you can see through the windows from outside is
really there.

The weather is just as unpleasant as yesterday, if not worse—muggy
and humid, warm enough to be annoying but not hot enough to provoke
businesses into paying for air conditioning—and there's a stale tang of
vehicle exhausts and fermenting dog shit underlying every noisome breath
I take. Wasps buzz around the overflowing litter bins on the street outside the office as I nip into the staff entrance to the store, then push
through a plywood door labeled BUILDING MAINTENANCE ONLY
and up a whitewashed stairwell with peeling linoleum treads. (A lot of
people go through that door every day, and they don't look much like store

employees, but for some reason nobody seems to notice. Or more accurately, they *can't* notice.)

At the top of the stairs there's another door. This one's a bit more substantial. The wards make my skin crawl and send pins and needles singing up my arm as I push it open, but they recognize me as someone who belongs here, for which I am profoundly grateful. (A couple of years back a gang of thugs decided to ram-raid us and steal the office computers. Boy did they get an unpleasant surprise . . .)

I slouch over to reception. "Are there any messages for me today?" I ask Rita.

Rita, who is about a year younger than my mother and about as maternal as an iron maiden, stares at me in brassy-eyed surprise. "Iris said she wants to see you, if you showed up today!" she declares. "Are you signed off sick or something?"

"No, but I might be contagious."

"Be off with you." She turns back to her web browser, dismissing me, and I take a deep breath and head for Iris's office.

Iris is my (How to describe our relationship accurately? Person from Porlock? Morlock?) latest line manager. I seem to get through about one a year. It wasn't always so: but Andy got moved sideways into Research and Development, and before him, Harriet and Bridget are, ahem, long-term indisposed. They took on Angleton and lost, epic level. I actually work directly for Angleton these days, but Angleton isn't a manager according to our org chart; he's a DSS, and DSSs are too important to burden with boring administrative duties like overseeing staff performance appraisals. So although I work for him, I have to have an actual manager to report to, at least in theory, and that's where Iris comes into the frame. She handles my interface with Human Resources, Payroll, and general admin stuff. She doesn't know everything I do, but she knows I work for Angleton and it's her job to be my manager-on-paper. And she's good at it.

Her office door is ajar as I turn the corner between the reception area and the coffee station: she's the kind of manager who's happy to sacrifice an outside office with a window in return for an interior one that lets her keep an eye on everyone entering and leaving her little fiefdom, which should tell you something. Her attitude is one of those irregular verbs peculiar to bureaucracies: if you like her she's attentive, and if you don't, she's paranoid.

"You wanted to see me, boss."

Iris waves me at the seat opposite her desk. She's leaning back with feet up and phone clamped between ear and shoulder, nodding along unconsciously to the beat of her unseen caller's narrative.

"Yes, I understand. You can use his office, I think. When? . . . Half an hour? Excellent, thanks. Yes, and you too. Bye." She puts the receiver down, then hits the divert to voice mail button on her handset. "How are you feeling, Bob?" She looks concerned.

"Like shit." I don't see any need—or room—to dissemble. "I came in because I've got a report to file."

"Are you sure that's wise?" She raises a penciled-in eyebrow. "I've given you my presenteeism lecture, haven't I?"

Bless her, she has: she's the first manager I've ever had who explained to me in words of one syllable that she'd be really pissed off if she caught me skulking around the office while I'm feeling ill. (This is the Laundry; they don't fire you for calling in sick, in fact, they *can't* fire you: all they can do is give you scut work. Back in my first year I took two weeks off, once, just to try it on—I ended up going back to work when I got bored with counting the cracked tiles on the bathroom wall. We still maintain this endless pretense that we're the same as any other government department, clock-punching time misers all, but it's not true: we do things differently in the Laundry. And so does Iris, and for a blessing, she *admits* it.)

I nod.

"Good," she says briskly, her accent so clear she could get a job as a BBC news anchor. "So." She pauses. "Something went wrong yesterday, and you've got a report to file. Want to fill me in on it? So I know what to expect?"

So I know what to expect is Iris-speak for *so I can cover your ass.*

"Yeah . . . I fucked up a routine out-of-the-office job for Angleton." I take a deep breath. "One dead bystander, in front of witnesses—luckily the only direct eyewitness is already sworn to Section Three." (Section Three of the Official Secrets Act, which covers our activities, is itself classified Top Secret under the terms of Section Two, making knowledge of it by unauthorized persons an offense—and we enforce it ferociously.)

"I've got to file an R60 and then Operational Oversight are going to be calling the shots. There'll probably be an enquiry. I may be suspended pending the outcome." Oddly, it's a lot easier to say this to Iris than it was to Mo.

Iris watches me for a few seconds. "Oh, you poor thing." She nods to herself. "Was it bad?"

"It was *stupid,*" I say between gritted teeth. "Stupid, stupid. If I'd noticed the entanglement channel between the airframe and the control panel, or warded both artifacts at the same time, it wouldn't have happened. And if she'd opened the door five seconds sooner, or later, it wouldn't—shit. If I'd been told what the airframe had been used for I wouldn't have . . ." I trail off.

"Save it for the Auditors," Iris says tiredly. She takes her booted feet off the desk, then leans forward. "That phone call I just took was your case officer, Bob. I think you should go and get yourself a nice cup of tea or coffee or whatever pleases you, then go and wait in your office. Business as usual is canceled for the day, and if I catch you doing your time sheet or answering support queries I will personally kick you around the block, okay? Go play games on Facebook or something. I'll bring your case officer round and sit in with you while you fill out the R60, so you've got a witness. If you think she's giving you grief, let me know and I'll handle it. Then"—she takes a deep breath—"I'm signing you off sick for two weeks. You don't have to take it, I mean I can't *force* you, hell, maybe you'd rather do some light admin and filing than sit at home or go for a week in York—that's my suggestion—but you're overdue for a slowdown, and I'm going to make sure you get it."

"But Angleton—"

"Leave him to me," she says brightly, with a smile that shows me her teeth: "He'll do as I say."

Oh.

Before I can open my mouth and insert any feet, she adds, "It's Angleton's job to point you at the enemy, Bob, but it's my job to keep you from breaking. I take my job seriously. If I tell Angleton to back off, he will."

Oh. I hadn't looked at it quite that way before. I manage to nod, then close my mouth.

"Why?" I ask.

"Fatal accidents never have just a single cause," she tells me, "they happen at the end of a whole series of errors. What the enquiry is going to ask is, how far back did the chain start? And I'll tell you this right now, it started before Angleton shoved you out to go and do that job yesterday. But I'd better not say any more for now. Go and get that coffee: we've both got a tough morning ahead."

I'M SITTING IN MY OFFICE, SHIVERING OVER A COOLING CUP of coffee and reading *The Register*, when my door opens without warning. I look up: it's Iris, which is no surprise, but the other visitor—"Jo?" I say, standing: "Long time no see!"

"Not long enough, under the circumstances," she says with a twitch. Jo is short for Josephine, as in Detective Inspector Josephine Sullivan, formerly of Milton Keynes but working for us in Operational Oversight these days. (That's my fault; on the other hand, so is her still being alive after the SCORPION STARE business, so I suppose they cancel out.) Looks a bit like Annie Lennox, if she'd taken up a second career as a nightclub bouncer. "How are you keeping?"

"Badly." I look round at the mounds of paper, the padlocked secure cabinet covered in *Dilbert* cartoons, the cubicle-farm-sized novelty dartboard with a picture of the Prime Minister's face over the bull's-eye: "Uh, I wasn't expecting you."

Iris gives Jo a sidelong look: "You've met?"

"Yes." Jo gives her one right back. "I won't let it influence me."

"You're here to take my statement?" I ask.

"Yes." For a moment Jo looks haggard. "Bob, what have you gotten yourself into?"

"I'll fetch another chair." Iris catches my eye and shakes her head pointedly as she backs through the door.

"A mess. How long have you been working for Oscar-Oscar?"

Jo sits down on the squeaky chair with no arms, and opens her attaché case. "Two years now," she says quietly. "Please tell me before we begin, while we're not under oath, you didn't do this deliberately?"

I shake my head. "Cross my heart and hope to die, it was an honest fuck-up."

"Okay." She takes a deep breath. "I'm just here to fill out the forms with you and ask you the questions. If a decision is made to pursue an enquiry I will declare a conflict of interest and withdraw. Are you happy with that?"

For a moment I feel a flicker of gratitude amidst the gloom and dread. "Fair enough."

Iris returns, pushing another rickety office chair through the door. (I approve. Most of my previous managers would have sent a minion to do that for them; actually mucking in and getting stuff done was beneath the dignity of their station. I'm still taking notes on Iris's style, although right now my career doesn't exactly look to be on course for promotion.)

"Are you ready to begin?" Jo asks.

I nod.

Jo pulls out a notepad and a voice recorder, then her official warrant card. She holds it up and my eyes are drawn to it, with a swelling, stabbing sensation in my forehead as if a swarm of bees have taken up residence between my ears. "By the power vested in me in the name of the state, by the oath of service you have sworn under penalty of your mortal soul, I bind you to tell the truth, the whole truth, and nothing but the truth."

Not *ask*, or *order*, but *bind*. My tongue feels swollen, as if I'm having an allergic reaction. I manage to nod.

"State your name, rank, and date of birth."

I feel my lips move and hear a voice reciting. Iris is watching me closely, her expression hard to read. It's okay: I feel comfortably numb. I want to tell her, but my voice isn't having anything to do with my mind right now.

"Yesterday morning, June fourteenth, you met with Detached Special Secretary Angleton in his office. Describe the meeting."

It's funny, I didn't realize I could remember that much detail. But the geas drags it out of me over the course of an hour and a half, and by the end of it Jo is grimacing and wincing as her hand spiders back and forth across the pages of her report pad, filling it in verbatim—I'm not the only one whose muscles aren't under my own control while the report field is in force.

Finally she draws breath again. "Is there anything you'd like to add for the record?" she asks, turning over a new page.

My mouth opens again, almost without me willing it: "Yes. I'm very sorry." My jaw shuts with an audible *click*.

She nods sympathetically: "Yes, I suppose you would be." She closes the report pad with a twitch, says, "The report is now over," and switches off the voice recorder.

Iris sags. I follow suit a moment later, then Jo makes it a threesome. The wards on the cover of her R60 pad and voice recorder are glowing almost as brightly as the haunted instrument panel in Hangar Six. "Wh- what happens now?" I ask. My throat feels gravelly.

Jo glances at Iris, who raises that eyebrow again—the one that can shut down committees or terrify demons to order.

"I take this back to Oscar-Oscar, and have copies created under seal. One goes to Human Resources"—I try not to cringe—"one goes to the Auditors, and one goes to Internal Affairs. Everyone else involved in the incident gets the same treatment. IA put the collected transcripts—and the special coroner's report on the victim—in front of the Incident Committee, who investigate and determine the cause of the event."

I lick my lips. "And then?"

Jo shrugs uncomfortably. "If they find that the cause was negligence they throw it back at HR for an administrative reprimand. If they attribute it to malice they may action Internal Affairs to prosecute the case before the Black Assizes, but that requires evidence of actual criminal intent. Oh, and they copy Health and Safety on their findings, so H&S can issue guidelines to prevent a recurrence. Meanwhile the Auditors get a chance to muck in if anything catches their eldritch eye. But that's basically it."

She delivers this with her best poker face.

"And in practice . . . ?" Iris nudges.

"Do you really want to . . . ? Well, hmm." Jo looks at me sidelong. "I'm not going to try to second-guess the Incident Committee, but it sounds to me like a straightforward mistake made by an overworked employee who hadn't been fully briefed and was in a hurry to get back to his other duties. If it turns out that the victim wasn't authorized to be in Hangar Six, the employee in question would be off the hook—up to a point. But Jesus, Bob!"

Her composure cracks; I hang my head before her dismay.

"I'll not make that mistake next time," I mutter, then try to swallow my tongue.

"There won't *be* a next time," Jo says vehemently. "What were you *thinking*, Bob?"

"I don't know!"

Iris stands up. "Thank you for your time, Ms. Sullivan." She angles herself towards the door, transparently urging Jo out.

"I'm out of here," Jo says defensively as she stands up. "I'll see you around, Bob. Hopefully under happier circumstances."

I nod as she leaves. Iris sits down again and looks at me, frowning. "What are we going to do with you?" she asks.

"Um. I don't understand?"

"To start with, you're taking the rest of the week off work," she says, and her expression tells me not to even think about arguing. "And when you come back in next Monday and not a day before, you're off active duty for the rest of the month."

"But Boris is shorthanded and Angleton needs—"

"They need you sane and fit for duty next month as well," she says sharply. "And next year. You can pick up the cabling job you were speccing out, and the routine server upgrade, but you're not to go tearing around banishing demons and shooting up cows until further notice. A couple of months of boredom won't do you any harm, and more importantly, if it takes the stress off your shoulders so you're less likely to make mistakes I'd call that a win. Wouldn't you?"

I wince, but manage to nod.

"Good." She unwinds a fraction. "You're probably wondering why I'm giving you the velvet glove treatment. Well, in case you hadn't noticed, you're now the focus of a fatal incident enquiry. You may or may not come out of it with your honor intact, but it *is* going to place you under stress. When people are under stress they're more likely than usual to make mistakes, and I don't think you're any exception. So I'm not going to let you take on any hazardous jobs until this is sorted out. If you screw up and get yourself killed then—speaking as your line manager—I will follow you all the way to hell and kick you around the brimstone pits. Because letting you make further screwups due to stress would not only be an avoidable, hence senseless waste—it would be a black mark on *my* record." There's a peculiar, dangerous gleam in her eyes. "Are we singing from the same hymnbook yet?"

I nod again, slightly less reluctantly.

"Good. Now piss off home and leave the damage control to me." She pulls up a strained smile, and I could cry. "Go on, it's what I'm here for. Scram!"

I can take a hint: I scram.

* * *

IT IS A TRUTH UNIVERSALLY ACHNOWLEDGED THAT A SANE
employee in possession of his wits must be in want of a good manager.

Unfortunately it's also true to say that good management is a bit like
oxygen—it's invisible and you don't notice its presence until it's gone, and
then you're sorry. The Laundry has a haphazard and inefficient approach
to recruiting personnel: if you know too much you're drafted. The quid
pro quo is that we have to make do with whatever we get; consequently
it should be no surprise to learn that our quality of management is famously random, governed only by the tiny shred of civil service protocol
that sticks to the organization, and Human Resources' spasmodic attempts
to cover up the most egregious outrages.

As I already noted, I've had an unfortunate history with managers. I'm
not a team player, I don't suffer fools gladly, and I don't like petty office
politics. In a regular corporation they'd probably fire me, but the Laundry
doesn't work like that; so I get handed from manager to manager as soon
as they figure out what I am, like the booby prize in a game of pass-the-
parcel.

Iris showed up one morning and moved into the interior corner office
that Boris had temporarily vacated—he was on assignment overseas,
doing something secretive for MI5—with her bike helmet and a framed
photograph of her husband on his Harley, and a bookshelf consisting of
The Mythical Man-Month and a selection of mathematics texts. It was a
whole week before she told me over coffee and a Danish that she was my
new line manager, and was there anything she could do to make my job
easier?

After she put the smelling salts away and I managed to sit up I confessed that yes, there were one or two things that needed minor adjustment. And—who knew?—the trivial annoyances fucked right off shortly
thereafter.

Iris couldn't do anything about my biggest headaches—as Angleton's
secretary, I get to carry his cans all the time—but she even managed to

make *him* ease up a little in April, when I was overbooked for two simultaneous liaison committee meetings (one in London, one in Belgium) and he wanted me to go digging in the stacks for a file so vitally important that it had last been seen in the mid-1950s, slightly chewed on by mice.

I don't know where in hell they found her, but as managers go she's all I can ask for. I don't know much about her home life—some Laundry staff socialize after work, others just don't, and I guess she's one of the compartmentalized kind—but she seems like the type of manager who learned her people skills in the process of steering a big, unruly family around, rather than in business school. The iron whim is tempered with patience, and she's a better shoulder to cry on than any member of the clergy I've ever met. People who work for her actually *want* to make her happy.

Which goes some way towards explaining, I hope, what happened later—and why, when Iris ordered me to scram, I hurried to obey.

But not what I did on my way out of the office.

ANGLETON'S OFFICE IS DOWN A STAIRCASE AND ROUND A bend, in a windowless cul-de-sac that I'll swear occupies the fitting rooms at the back of the M&S opposite C&A—I've never been able to make the geometry of this building line up. But that's not surprising.

When the rest of us upped sticks and moved to the New Annexe two years ago (to make way for redevelopment of the old Service House site under some kind of public-private partnership deal), there was much headless-chicken emulation, and many committee meetings, and probably several stress-induced heart attacks due to the complexity of the relocation. Angleton didn't show up to any of the planning meetings, ignored the memos and pre-uplift checklists and questionnaires, and cut the woman from Logistics and Relocation dead when she tried to shoulder-barge his office. But when we got to the end of it, what do you know? His office was at the bottom of the rear stairwell in the New Annexe, just as if it had always been there, green enameled metal door and all.

I could easily go home without passing his door, but I don't. Now that the worst has come to pass, a gloomy curiosity has me in its grip. Why did he want me to go to Cosford? What was that guff about a white elephant? It'll bug me for the rest of the week if I don't ask the old coffin-dodger, and Iris told me to go home and relax. So I curve past the crypt on my way to the lich-gate, so to speak, and steel myself to beard the monster in his den.

(See, I'm calling him rude names. That's to prove to myself that I'm not scared of him like everybody else. See? I'm not terrified!)

The dark green metal door's shut when I come to it. But the red security light isn't on, so I knock. "Boss?" I ask softly.

I hear a muffled noise, as of something very large and massive shuffling around in a confined space. Then there's a grunt, and a heavy thud. I rest my palm lightly on the pitted brass door handle. "Boss?" I repeat.

Heavy breathing. *"Enter."*

I push the door open, with trepidation.

Angleton's office feels like it's the size of a self-respecting broom closet, even though it's actually quite large. All four walls are shelved floor-to-ceiling in ledgers—not books, but binders full of microfiche cards. In the middle of the room sits his legendary desk, an olive-drab monolith that looks like it came out of a Second World War aircraft carrier; a monstrous hump like a 1950s TV set sits on top of it, like a microfiche reader. Except that it isn't. Microfiche readers don't come with organ pedals and hoppers to gulp down mountains of cards. Angleton's desk is a genuine Memex, the only one I've seen outside of the National Cryptologic Museum run by the NSA in Maryland.

To those who don't need to know, Angleton is just a dry old guy who rides herd on the filing cabinets in Arcana Analysis and does stuff for the Counter-Possession Unit. His job title is Detached Special Secretary, which doesn't mean what you think it means: scuttlebutt is that it's short for *Deeply Scary Sorcerer*.

He's nearly bald, his chin is two sizes two small for his skull, and his domed scalp gleams like bone: with his wizened mannerisms—like a public school master from the 1930s, Mr. Chips redux—people tend to underestimate him on first acquaintance. It's a mistake they only make once. Whether or not they survive.

"Ah, Robert." He looks up from the Memex screen, his face stained pale blue by its illumination. "Please be seated."

I sit down. The chair, a relic of the cold war, squeaks angrily. "I fucked up."

"Hold it for a minute, please." He peers at something on the screen again, twisting a couple of dials and adjusting a vernier scale. Then he lifts a hinged lid covering the front of the Memex and begins to type rapidly on a stenographer's keyboard. Paper tape spools out and over into a slot behind the keyboard. He inspects it for a moment, then reaches over to a panel and pulls out two organ stops. There's a bright flash and a click, and he closes the lid over the keyboard with a look of satisfaction. "Saved."

(The Memex is an electromechanical hypertext machine, running on microfiche: it's fiddly, slow, lacks storage capacity, and needs a lot of maintenance. I once asked him why he stuck with it; he grunted something about Van Eck radiation and changed the subject.)

"Now, Robert. What did you think of the elephant?"

"Never got to see it." I shake my head. "I said I—"

"Oh dear." Angleton looks mildly irritated: I shiver.

"That's what I came to tell you; I've just finished filing an R60 and Iris told me to sign off sick for the week. I killed a bystander by accident. It's a *real* fuck-up."

"So you didn't see the white elephant."

I do a double take. "Boss? Hello? Major FATACC incident while carrying out the primary assignment! What's so important about a museum piece?"

"*Harrumph.*" He reaches out and flicks a switch: the Memex screen goes dark. "I thought it was high past time you were briefed on the Squadron."

"The Squadron? That would be 666 Squadron RAF, right? I looked them up on the web—they were deactivated in 1964, weren't they?"

Angleton's thin smile tells me exactly what he thinks of the world wide web.

"Not exactly. They were just redeployed in support of a higher mission."

I remember the blue-glowing instrument panel lighting up the hangar from behind canvas screens, and shudder. "What kind of . . . ?"

"They're part of the contingency planning for CASE NIGHTMARE GREEN, boy." He looks momentarily annoyed, as if the impending end of the world as we know it is a minor inconvenience. "Bystanders," he murmurs: "Whatever will they think of next?"

"The white elephant," I prompt, but I'm too late.

"Never mind that now, boy, you can go back and look at it later." He looks at me, concern and irritation wrinkling his face further, and this time he's actually *looking*, studying me with those merciless washed-out eyes as if I'm a sample on a dissection tray: "Hmm. If Iris told you to take the rest of the week off, I suppose you ought to do as she says. A bystander, eh? What was a bystander doing there?"

"She was a volunteer at the museum—she was bringing us tea."

Angleton's eyes narrow. "Was she indeed?" He picks up a pen and a pad and scrawls a list of numbers on it. "Well, when you feel like getting back to work, you might want to go down to the stacks and retrieve these documents from the dead file store. I think you'll find them *very* interesting." He signs the note and slides it across the table at me. The document references are just catalog numbers identifying files by their shelf location, no actual codewords referring to named projects. Typical of Angleton, to be so elliptical about things. "And I'd like you to deputize for me on the BLOODY BARON committee."

"Iris is putting me on light administrative duties," I protest.

Angleton smiles humorlessly. "Then you'll have something to do when you're bored," he says. "Be off with you!"

3.

THINGS THAT GO BUMP IN THE DAYLIGHT

I EMERGE FROM THE STAFF ENTRANCE TO THE C&A ON THE
high street, blinking like a groundhog caught in the headlights of an onrushing Hummer.

It is a Wednesday, just before the lunchtime rush, and the pavements
are full of shoppers and people with nowhere better to go. A herd of buses
rumble past, farting clouds of sulphurous biodiesel and lunging at cyclists. But I am not at work. Something is wrong with the world, something is broken: a wire has come loose in my soul.

I start to walk.

I don't want to go home just yet: it's sixty to seventy minutes of riding
on two buses, but then I'll have nothing to do but sit staring at the walls
for the rest of the afternoon. If it was a normal summer's day I could go
for a walk on Wandsworth Common—it's only about a mile or two from
here—but the sky is overcast and gray, threatening rain later on. Or I
could go into town. Maybe get the tube to Euston and visit the British
Library. I've got a reader's card, and there are some interesting manuscripts I've been meaning to look at for a while, relevant to the job . . .

No, I can hear Iris ticking me off in the back of my head, telling me that's not what I ought to be doing when I'm on medical leave.

In the end, I walk to the next bus stop just in time to see the tail end of the herd vanishing round the corner, and wait nearly ten minutes for the next bunch of buses to arrive, with only my iPod for company—that, and a couple of students, a pensioner pushing a shopping bag on wheels, and an Uncle Fester type in a dirty trench coat who is pointedly not making eye contact with anyone.

I sit on the top deck for forty minutes as it slowly migrates towards Victoria, then hop off and head for an all-you-can-eat Chinese buffet for lunch. It's stowed out, as you can imagine, because I've hit peak lunch time; but it makes a welcome change from the dismal little pie shop round the corner from the New Annexe. I emerge into daylight with a full stomach and my sense of well-being marginally restored. It's trying to rain, lonely drips spattering the pavement and evaporating before they can join up. I shuffle along with the tourists and foreign language students and shirking office workers, staring into shop windows and feeling faintly wistful, something nagging at the back of my mind.

The penny drops. My PDA! Okay, it's Laundry-issue. But it's toast! Sure I have a cheap, dumb mobile phone as well, but I relied on that PDA; it had my life embedded in its contacts and calendar. Yes, there's a backup, but it's on my office PC, which is most definitely not a laptop and most definitely not allowed to go home with me—the last thing the Laundry needs is headlines like CIVIL SERVANT LOSES LAPTOP: ENTIRE POPULATION OF TOWER HAMLETS EATEN BY GIBBERING HORRORS FROM BEYOND SPACETIME—so for the time being, I'm adrift. If Mo called me right now I genuinely *couldn't* phone Pete and Sandy. Help, it's a crisis! Well okay, it's a minor crisis, but I rationalize: obsessing over my lost address book is a lot healthier than obsessing over a blinding purple flash and an imploding face—

Besides, shopping is therapeutic. Right?

I pull out my phone and look at it in distaste. It's a cheap Motorola jobbie with a pay-as-you-go SIM, and its major virtues are that it's small and it makes phone calls. I bought it a year and a half ago when word went round that IT Services were threatening to inflict Arseberries on us along with a centralized work directory, and start billing for personal calls. The rumor turned out to be unfounded but I kept the phone (and the PDA I wangled Andy into signing off on) because between them they did a better job than the old Treo, and besides, all smartphones are shit these days. It's the one industry where progress is going backwards in high gear, because the yakking masses would rather use their phones as car navigation systems and cameras than actually make phone calls or read email.

About the only smartphone that doesn't stink like goose shit is the JesusPhone. But I've steadfastly refused to join the Cult of Jobs ever since I first saw the happy-clappy revival tent launch; it brought back painful memories of a junior management training course the late and unlamented Bridget sent me on a few years ago. Nothing can possibly be that good, even though the specifications look rather nice on paper, right?

You know how this is going to end . . .

I spend an hour shuffling around mobile phone shops, comparing specifications and feeling my brains gently melting, which confirms what I already knew: all mobile phones are shit this year. Then I allow my feet to carry me into the O2 shop and plant me in front of an austerely minimalist display stand where halogen lights play their spotlight beams across the polished fascia of a JesusPhone, a halo of purity gleaming above it.

"Can I help you, sir?" beams one of the sales staff.

"That thing." My finger points at the JesusPhone as if drawn to it by a powerful geas. "How much?" (That's the only question that matters, you see: I've already memorized its specifications.)

"The 64Gb model, sir? On an eighteen-month contract—"

The JesusPhone, I *swear* it is smiling at me: *Come to me, come to me and be saved.* The luscious curves, the polished glissade of the icons in the multi-touch interface—*whoever designed that thing is an intuitive illusionist,* I realize fuzzily as my fingertip closes in on the screen: *That's at least a class five glamour.*

The next thing I think is, *I shouldn't have let myself get so close.* But by then I'm on my way out of the store, clutching a carrier bag and a receipt that says I've put a dent in my bank balance big enough that Mo's going to have something new to swear about this month, to the benefit of Apple's shareholders.

I slink home with my metaphorical tail between my legs, clutching my shiny new JesusPhone like a consolation prize for my lack of a real life.

IT IS 4 P.M., THE COOL RAINS HAVE BROUGHT THEIR GURGLING freight of water to the overflowing gutter above the kitchen window, and I am sitting at the table with a laptop and a freshly jailbroken JesusPhone when the doorbell chimes.

(You didn't expect me *not* to jailbreak an iPhone so I can run unsigned applications on it, did you? That would be no fun at all!)

I get up and slouch towards the front porch.

"Surprise party!" It's a pair of familiar faces. Pinky is holding the umbrella while Brains hefts a pair of beer casks at me.

I take a step back. "Hey, what's the big deal?"

"Beware of geeks bearing beer." Pinky cocks his head and looks at me madly as Brains makes a beeline for the kitchen and clears some counter space. "We heard about the whoopsie and figured you might want some company."

Pinky and Brains: the (ex-)flatmates from heck, if not hell. I used to share a house with them, back in the days when I was still seeing Mhari. They're a matched couple of geeks, working for Technical Support these days (Gizmos department, Dirty Tricks directorate). Brains does the hardware, Pinky does human factors and delivery flourishes, and both of them do the Pride march around Regent's Park every summer even though they don't need to be publicly out to maintain their security clearances these days.

A voice calls from the kitchen, "Hey, who let *that* thing in here?"

I go back inside hastily. "It's mine. As of this afternoon."

"Mine, *precioussss*." Brains is bending over my new phone. "Jailbroken it yet? I've been doing some evaluation work on these too, they look promising . . ."

"Don't be silly." I peer at the beer casks. He's lined them up next to the sink. "Hey, that's not nitro pressurized."

"That's right; they're cask-conditioned!" Brains says proudly. "Normally you have to leave them twenty-four hours to drop bright after you tap them, but with *this*—he produces a home-brew box of electronics from one waterproof pocket—"you can cut the wait to sixty minutes."

"What is it?" I pause. "If it's a temporal multiplexer I've got to warn you, last time we had one in here Mo had to beat the fridge contents to death with a cricket bat—she was most annoyed—"

"Nope, it's ultrasonic." He switches it on as he plants it on top of the first cask, and I feel my jaw muscles clench. Ultrasonic it may be, but it's got some low frequency harmonics that remind me unpleasantly of a mosquito the size of a Boeing 737.

"Switch it off, please."

Pinky is doing something bizarre to the umbrella, turning it inside out through its own center—I do a double take: *Is that really a Möbius strip umbrella?*—and it vanishes, except for a stubby handle, which he hangs on the inside doorknob. I blink. "To what do I owe the honor?"

"Iris said you could do with some company," Brains says blandly as my phone chirps and does an incoming-text shimmy on the counter. I grab it. It's a message from Mo: UNAVOIDABLY DETAINED BY WORK, DON'T STAY UP.

I might not be wearing a ward around my neck right now—I didn't stay in the office long enough to sign out a replacement for the one I toasted yesterday—but it's not my only defense, and right now my this-is-a-setup gland is pulsing painfully. "This is a put-up job, right? What's going on?" I glance at the front hall, half-expecting the doorbell to ring again and Boris and Andy to be standing there, along with a briefing on some kind of harebrained operation—

"Don't be silly, Bob," Brains says crisply: "Iris just got word that your fragrant wife has been called away to an incident in Amsterdam and she thought someone ought to keep you company today. The saintly Mo should be back tomorrow; until then, we drew the short straw." He gestures at the beer: "Just like old times, huh?"

"No, it's not just like old times," I snort. Then the penny drops: "Job in Amsterdam . . . ?"

"They needed a lead violin."

"Oh," I say, feeling very small.

There is this about being married to Mo: every few months she gets called to an unexpected job somewhere in Europe, at short notice, with her violin. A philosopher by academic training and a combat epistemologist by subsequent specialization, she doesn't talk about what happens on those trips; but I get to hold her shoulders and calm her when she wakes in the pre-dawn gloom, shuddering and clammy. Years ago, shortly after we first met, we got into a situation where I ended up rescuing her from— well, it wasn't nice, and she overcompensated, I think. The violin's an Erich Zahn original, refitted with Hilbert-space pickups. There's a black-on-yellow sticker on its case that says THIS MACHINE KILLS DEMONS. And sometimes she sits up late into the night, playing music on it that I don't want to think about.

I pick up my phone and thumb-tap back at her: ENJOY AMSTER-DAM AND TAKE CARE XXX. Then I put it down carefully, as if it might explode.

Now I've got something to worry about, something to distract me from feeling sorry for myself because of the enquiry, or gnawing over the hollow sense of gnawing wrongness as I see Helen's face melting away in front of my eyes again and again—something tangibly threatening to be upset about. If anything happens to Mo I don't know what I'll do. It's not as if my parents or elder brother know what I do for a living: they think I'm just a junior civil servant. The same goes for Mo, only more so—her dad's dead, Mum's a ditz, and her kid sister's married to an engineer in Dubai. We're isolated, but we can confide in each other, do the mutual support thing that so many couples don't seem to do. We understand each other's problems. Which means that right now I'm drinking for two.

"In the fridge, top shelf on the left, there's an open bottle of wine," I say, standing and making for the cupboard to root out some glasses. "You guys didn't drive, did you?"

"That would be irresponsible, Bob," Pinky says soberly. "Is this the right bottle . . . ?"

"Give it here." I pause for a moment, bottle poised over an inviting glass: "Boris doesn't have anything to do with this, does he? You're quite sure it was Iris's idea?"

"Don't be silly, Bob," says Brains, taking the bottle (and the glass). "Boris is on detached duty with the Dustbin this year. Here, take this. How about a toast? Confusion to the enemy!"

I raise my glass. "What enemy?"

He shrugs: "IT, Human Resources, the grim march of time—whoever you want, really."

"I'll drink to that!" says Pinky, and I nod.

It's going to be a long evening, but it was going to be a long evening anyway and at least this way I don't get to spend it brooding on my own.

THE NEXT MORNING. I AWAKEN TO FIND THAT MY MOUTH TASTES as if a rat used it for a bed and breakfast, and Mo still isn't here. I roll over, reaching across her side of the bed. Empty. It's early but I yawn and sit up, then visit the bathroom to change the rat's bed linen before stumbling downstairs. The kitchen sink is full of empty bottles, and someone left a JesusPhone on the kitchen table, plugged into my laptop—

Oh. Shit. It wasn't a dream, then.

I switch the kettle on and run a comb through my hair, wondering if I can take the bloody thing back. *I haven't activated it, have I—oh.*

There's a handwritten note next to it. I read it with a sinking heart: HI BOB HOPE YOU LIKE THE EASTER EGGS BRAINS.

No, I can't take it back. Not until I find out what Brains did to it. I rack my memories for any hint of details, but it's all a bit of a blur. I remember him saying something about evaluation work. *Jesus, he could have put* anything *on it*. Not that Brains would install classified experimental work-related software on an agent's personal mobile phone, oh no, but if he thought it had been issued to me by work that would be another matter *entirely*.

I turn the radio on just as the kettle rises to a rattling, rolling boil and shuts off. I pull the cafetière out of the cupboard and spoon coffee into it, pour water and stare at it, as if that'll make it brew faster.

It is just occurring to me that today is a Thursday and I am not expected to—no, scratch that, I am expected *not* to—go into the office today, and I haven't the foggiest idea what to do with myself. It's not like a holiday, meticulously planned fun'n'frolics on a beach with Mo, or even a weekend of vegging out in front of the TV at home. It feels more like I'm under house arrest. Sick leave is no fun at all when you're doing it on instructions from management.

The radio is blatting on about the news: Prime Minister talking about the need for faith schools, something about a UN Population Fund meeting in the Netherlands, an idiot footballer getting an idiot multimillion-pound handshake from an idiot football team . . . all the usual cheerily oblivious rubbish we listen to in order to feel connected. Right now it sounds like it's bleeding in from another world.

I carefully lower the plunger on the cafetière—it's balky, and has a tendency to squirt hot coffee grounds everywhere if you don't do it *just* right—then pour myself a mug and sit down in front of the JesusPhone. Gosh, that thing's *shiny*. Now, what can Brains have done?

It doesn't take me long to find out: the icon that looks like a tumble drier is a bit of a giveaway, come to think of it. I groan and stab the thing with my thumb, and a whole bunch of new icons show up. *What the fuck . . . ?* I swear quietly: there's a lot more to this than just *evaluation work*. Those of us who do fieldwork have a whole suite of specialized software tools we need to carry about—most of them don't require any particular hardware, they just need a general-purpose processor that can do some rather unusual number-intensive calculations, and the new phone's got plenty of grunt in that department. *This* looks like a first pass at porting the entire Occult Field Countermeasures Utility Trunk to run native on JesusPhone, which means I can forget about returning it to the shop, for starters.

Brains has unintentionally taken a huge stinking shit all over our security frontline, installing classified software on an unapproved and unauthorized device. It was just an obvious misunderstanding and no harm's come about, and as soon as I can smuggle the phone back into the New Annexe and get him to wipe the fucking thing back to factory condition we can pretend it never happened; but until then, I'm going to have to carry the thing on my person at all times and defend it with my life. Well, that or I can set Operational Oversight on him—but my life doesn't need the excitement of being the subject of two simultaneous boards of enquiry.

"Jesus, Brains," I murmur. "Is it something in the water?" I poke at the Options set up in OFCUT admiringly. He's done a thorough job of porting it—this is almost as tightly integrated as the old version I used to have on my Treo, before they pulled it because it violated our RoHS waste disposal statement.

HALF AN HOUR LATER, MY OLD AND UNWANTED MOTOROLA rings. I pick it up and see WITHHELD on the display. Which means one of two things: a telemarketer, or work, because I've put my unclassified desk phone on call divert.

"Yes?"

"Bob?" It's Andy, my onetime manager. Nice guy, when he's not stabbing you in the back.

"What's up? You know I'm on—"

"Yes, Bob. Er, it's about Mo." I sit down hard. "She's flying into London City from Amsterdam on KL 1557"—my heart starts up again—"and I think it would be a really good idea if you were to meet her in.

She's due to land around nine, you can just get there if you leave in the next ten minutes—"

"What's happened to her?" I realize I'm gripping the phone too hard and force myself to open my fist. It wouldn't do to break the bloody thing before I've ported my number across—

"Nothing," he says, too quickly. "Look, will you just—"

"I'm going! I'm going! I'm dragging myself from my sickbed groaning and limping in my nightgown to the airport, okay?" I look round, trying to locate my shoes: I dumped them in the hall the night before—"Are you *sure* she's okay?"

"Not entirely," he says quietly, and hangs up.

I'm dressed and out of the house like a greased whippet, round the corner to the tube station and the train to Bank and then the DLR line to London City Airport, out in the east end near Canary Wharf. I remember to grab the JesusPhone at the last minute, shoveling it into an inside zippered pocket in my fishing vest. I'm at the DLR platform waiting for a train before I realize I've forgotten to shave. If Andy is yanking my chain . . .

All doubts fade when I get to Arrivals at ten to eleven and see KL 1557 on the board, on schedule for fifteen minutes hence. *If she's hurt—*

But she won't be. At least, not physically. In her line of work, if something goes wrong, it's probably fatal; at best she'd be clogging up a hospital high dependency unit, and I'd be on my way out to see her with many hand-wringing apologetics and a complimentary budget-price ticket from Human Resources.

Hanging around in an airport Arrivals hall is not a good thing to do if you're nervous. I can feel the cops' eyes on the back of my neck, wondering what the unshaven agitated guy who can't keep his feet still is doing. The minutes and seconds trickle by with glacial, infuriating slowness. Then the Arrivals board changes the flight status to *arrived*, and—

There she is. Coming out of the door from baggage claim in the middle of a clot of suits, violin case slung over her shoulder. Freckled skin stretched over high cheekbones, long red hair tied back out of her face, uncharac-teristically dressed in office drag: that's unusual, must be urban camouflage for whatever she's been sent to do. Something about her gait, or the set of her shoulders, tells me she's bone-deep weary. I wave: she sees me and changes course and I move towards her and we collide in a deep embrace that ends in a kiss.

She pulls back after a couple of seconds. "Get me home. Please." She sounds—low.

"Andy said—"

"Andy is a wee bawbag and we're going home. Taxi. Right now." She's leaning on me, swaying slightly.

"Mo? What's wrong?"

"Later." She draws a deep, shuddering breath. "Right now, let's go home."

"Can you walk?" She nods. "Okay, we'll get a taxi." It'll be about twenty quid: I can't afford to make a habit of it. But scratch worrying about money for the time being. If she feels too crap to face the tube . . .

We ride home in silence, wincing in synchrony as we bump over speed pillows and sway through chicanes and suffer all the other traffic-annoying measures that slow down ambulances and cost lives and triple the price of a simple taxi ride. I pay the driver and hold the door open for her and then we're inside our front hall again, the door shut behind us, and she slumps against the wall as if she's just run a marathon. "Coffee, tea, or something stronger?" I ask.

"Coffee." She pauses. "With something stronger." After a moment she levers herself up and shuffles into the living room, then collapses on the overstuffed sofa we inherited from her sister Liz when she emigrated.

I hurry back into the kitchen and refill the caff, then add a generous shot of cooking whisky to her mug. When I get back to the living room she's still on the sofa, her violin case sitting on the pile of magazines on the coffee table. She seems to be shaking at first, in silent laughter: then I realize she's crying.

I put the coffee mugs on the table and sit down next to her. After a moment she shuffles round and I pull her against my shoulder, so that her tears trickle down the base of my neck.

Mo cries helplessly, almost silently, pausing every few seconds to take a little hiccuping gasp of air. She's so quiet—almost as if she's afraid to make a sound. I hold her gently, and murmur inanities over the top of her head, stroking her shoulders. I'm angry at my own helplessness: I've seen her upset before, but never anything like this—

"What happened?" I ask, eventually, after the shudders give way to an occasional twitch.

"You don't need to know." She sniffles. "God, I'm a mess. Fetch the tissues?" We disentangle and I go in search of something for her to wipe her nose on. When I get back she's sitting up, clutching her coffee mug and staring at the brick-surround fireplace we've been meaning to get rid of ever since we moved in, with eyes like wrecking balls.

I put the tissues in front of her on the table. She ignores them. "Was it wet?" I ask.

"You have no need to—" She shudders slightly, puts the mug down, and grabs a tissue. I notice her hands are a mess, reddish-brown grime ingrained around her nail beds: Jonathan Hoag territory. Holding the kleenex to her face she blows her nose once, twice: a peal of bloody trumpets. "It was ghastly. They made me—I think I can say this—Bob, remember the Plumbers?"

I nod. Deep in the pit of my stomach, I feel dread. "The job in Amsterdam. They shut you up with a geas afterwards, didn't they? Was it that bad? No, don't try to tell me. You just stay right there."

She nods convulsively. "I can't talk about it." Emphasis on the *can't*.

I stand up. "I'm going to make a call." I go through to the kitchen and speed-dial Andy.

"Hello?" Andy sounds distracted.

I take a deep breath. "Pay attention now, I will ask this only once: Who should I blame for this? You? Or that motherfucker Tom in Conflict Resolution? Or someone else? Because I've got a situation here."

"What—" Andy pauses. "Bob? Is that you?"

"Mo is home from Amsterdam," I say carefully. "She's in a state, and she can't unload on me because some cretin in Plumbing has drawn the magic circle too tight. I don't know what happened out there, but she's about two millimeters away from a nervous breakdown. I can't help her if she's blocked from talking to me, so let me explain the situation in words of one syllable: you are going to get the geas relaxed so she can vent about whatever happened yesterday, or the Laundry is going to have to replace a valued employee. No, make that two—no, three new employees they'll be needing, by the time I'm through with whoever's responsible. *Capisce?*"

"It wasn't me!" Andy sounds shocked. "Stay on the line. Where are you, exactly?"

"I'm in the kitchen at home, that's on file as safe house Lima Three Six. Mo was in the living room, last time I looked. Is that *exact* enough for you?"

"Probably . . ." I hear keys clicking hastily, a keyboard on a desk near his phone. "Listen, you aren't cleared for this, and I can't do it over the phone. Normally you *would* be cleared but that enquiry that's pending has screwed up your—look, I'm tied up right now, but I'll send someone round immediately, as soon as I can find a warm body. Can you hold the fort for an hour?"

"Who are you going to send, exactly?"

"The office bloody intern if I have to, as long as they've got an Oyster card and can carry a Letter of Release, will that do you?"

I sigh. "It'll have to. Better hurry, though, or you're going to be short-staffed next week."

I go back to the living room. Mo is sitting on the sofa, immobile, in exactly the position she was in when I left. I shove the coffee table aside and kneel in front of her. "Mo? Talk to me?"

She's staring right through me at the fireplace, vague and unfocused. "Can't," she says.

"I called Andy. The reason it won't let you talk to me is the pending enquiry on my record." *It* being the simpleminded geas someone in Plumbing dropped on everyone who witnessed the scene in Amsterdam. "I threatened to kick his arse and he's sending a courier with a Letter of Release just for you." A physical token that will release her from the geas. "He said it'll take about an hour, maybe a bit longer. Can you wait that long?"

Abruptly, she makes eye contact. "Oh thank God," she says. Then she slowly slumps forward, like a puppet whose strings have just been cut.

THIRTY MINUTES LATER, THE DOORBELL RINGS.

I'm upstairs in the bedroom, sitting up with Mo, when I hear the chimes. It took a while to get her up there and into bed, propped up on pillows with the duvet pulled up to her chin—still wearing most of her street clothes—and a mug of coffee to hand. She's shivery and a bit shocky but the color has begun to return to her cheeks, and ten minutes ago she asked me to bring her violin. She doesn't like to leave it unattended, and she's right—fuck knows what would happen if one of the local lowlifes put a brick through the window and snatched it, the thing's about as safe as a loaded machine gun with no safety catch. So it's sitting on the bed, and she's got one hand on it, just to maintain contact.

We're talking inconsequentialities, waiting for the letter to arrive. "A weekend would be good," she agrees.

"If I can find a bed and breakfast—"

"In Harrogate? It won't be cheap but it'll be quiet and there are places to walk, and it's not far off the East Coast Main Line."

"Maybe York, instead?"

"York, in summer? It'll be sunny, but the river *smells*—"

Ding-dong.

"That'll be the letter," I say, rising. "Back in a minute." I'm through the door and taking the stairs two at a time. *That was fast,* I think, eagerly reaching for the door handle.

My head hurts. Then the next thing I think is, *That's funny. Why am I on the floor?*

I'm looking up and my vision is blurred, like a migraine. Uncle Fester leans over me, pointing a gun with a fat barrel at my face.

"Где же она?" he says.

"Uh?"

Actually, my face feels like it's split open. The bastard shoved the door in my face, hard.

Uncle Fester pokes my forehead with the gun, provoking a bright metallic flash of pain. "Скажи мне сейчас, или я буду убивать вас."

He looks like Niko Bellic's mad uncle, the bad one with the child abuse convictions and the questionable personal hygiene, not to mention a bright red-glowing zit in the middle of his forehead. And I am utterly fucked, because I don't understand a word he's saying: but I'll swear I saw him or his twin brother at the bus stop yesterday—

He's pulling back the gun. I can see its barrel looking huge and dark, and if I knew where my hands were there's this neat trick you can do when some idiot points an automatic at you at short range, you grab the slide by laying your hand on top of the barrel and pushing back to stop the breech closing, which is a great secret agent stunt if you're not lying on the floor of your own front hall with one arm trapped under you and blood trickling down your face.

"Do you speak English?" I ask.

Uncle Fester looks annoyed. "Waar is ze?"

I look him in the eyes and feel my guts freeze. I've been here before, staring at the luminous green worms swirling behind the glazed surface of his eyes, writhing in the muddy waters of a mind that's been sucked into a place where human consciousness melts like grease on a hot frying pan—

There is a noise behind me like a cat the size of a bus yowling rage and defiance at a rival who has dared to enter his territory.

Uncle Fester (or whatever it is that wears the mortal skin of a dead man walking) raises his gun to bear on the staircase. My left arm twists almost without me willing it and I push at his right leg just above the ankle, shoving as hard as I can at his trousers *don't think about what happens if you touch his flesh* because that would be as bad as not forcing him off balance while he's aiming at Mo—

And he topples across me.

These things are never terribly good at coordinating a tensegrity structure like a mammalian musculoskeletal system: even when they're in the driving seat they're trying to work a manual transmission with automatic-only training. His gun bangs, a curiously muffled thudding sound as the feedback howl from the top of the staircase rises to a pitch that makes my teeth ache and overflows into an ear-numbingly harsh chord, music to snap necks to.

Uncle Fester goes abruptly limp as he falls on my legs. There's a horrid sigh and a smell I don't want to think about as unlife and animation departs.

"Bob?" Her voice is small and terrified.

"I'm okay!" I call. "Are you?"

Pause. "Check." She advances down the stairs, instrument raised and bow poised, wearing an intent, emotionless expression utterly at odds with her voice. As she comes closer I see a trickle of blood emerging from her fingertips where she grips the neck of the bone-colored violin. There's always a cost to being entrusted with such instruments, and she's half-past overdrawn at the bank of life, her hands spidering twitchily as she stalks the house room by room, confirming that Uncle Fester was alone.

My forehead's damp and I feel sick. I reach out to push myself up so I can shut the front door in case a curious neighbor sees something that might damage their house valuation, and my vision blurs again. I try to wipe my face and my hand comes away red and sticky. *That's odd,* I tell myself, *I've never been shot before.* Then everything gets very hazy and far away for a while.

4.

PROMPT CRITICAL

HOSPITALS ARE BORING PLACES: MY ADVICE IS TO AVOID THEM wherever possible, unless you happen to work there. Unfortunately I'm not always good at taking my own advice, which is why I spend three hours in the A&E unit, having my head bolted back together.

Actually, that's a bit of an exaggeration. It's just a bash and a scrape to my scalp: but head wounds bleed like crazy and they wanted to make sure I wasn't concussed and didn't have a fractured skull or a subdural hematoma or something. Then it was time for about a million butterfly sutures and I'm told I may never be able to take the paper bag off in public again, but that's okay because they let me go home with Mo and the nice folks from Plumbing who look like extras from *The Matrix*.

Being attacked by a demonically possessed Russian with a silenced pistol is unusual but not exceptional in my line of work; sloppy of me not to have replaced my ward, though, or to have checked the spy lens in the door before opening up. Inexcusable not to have noticed that Andy's messenger was at least half an hour early, too . . . but in my defense, I wasn't exactly *expecting* to be attacked by a demonically possessed Russian with a silenced pistol. (At least, I *assume* he was Russian. He was speaking

Russian, wasn't he? I have some broken schoolboy French: therefore I'm from Quebec. Such are the perils of inductive logic. It was certainly demonic possession: probably class two, one of the minor feeders in the night. Otherwise I'd be worse than dead.)

Anyway. The point is, that sort of thing is *just not done*, at least not without some degree of warning, especially to someone who's signed off sick for the rest of the week—I'm feeling distinctly peeved. It's *unprofessional*. I'm just lucky Mo realized something was wrong and grabbed her violin in time to switch him off. She may be pale and shaking in the aftermath of—something very bad, I guess—but she's a trouper, or trooper, or something, and her reflexes are everything that mine are not.

When we get home, our house has been invaded by spooks. An entire team of Plumbers are at work, rewiring the perimeter defenses and daubing exclusion sigils on the window frames. Andy is sitting at the kitchen table, tapping his fingers, briefcase open, which makes it official: it's serious enough to drag management off-site. "Bob, Mo, good to see you!" He sounds relieved, which is worrying.

"Letter of Release." I cross my arms.

"You don't need it." Andy glances at Mo. "Whether we like it or not, Bob is now involved in CLUB ZERO. At least, I'm assuming that's what followed you home . . ."

"Oh dear," she says heavily, and pulls out a chair. "Bob, I really didn't want—"

"Too late, whatever it is." I grimace. I still feel a little sick, but it's mostly overspill from the music—not concussion, just a little *totenlied*—and I'm heartsick for her, too. "Andy, what's going on?"

"Angleton's missing," he says, with a curious little half smile, as if he's just cracked a really filthy joke and is wondering if you've even heard of the perversion he's alluding to.

"Angleton's *what*?" says Mo, just as I open my mouth to say exactly the same thing.

"He's missing. Do you have any information . . . no, I guess not." His cheek twitches.

Mo reaches across the table and takes my hand. I barely notice.

Angleton is just about the bedrock of the department. Yes, his position is shrouded in rumor and misinformation—to some, he's simply a DSS, a Detached Special Secretary doing boring and esoteric work in Arcana Analysis; to others he's involved in the occult equivalent of counter-espionage: but the truth is a lot weirder. Angleton actually gets to talk to *the Board*, who nobody has actually seen in the flesh in forty years. He's the whetstone that sharpens the cutting edge of the blade our political masters fancy they wield when they tell us what to do: the dog's bollocks, in other words. He's not the heart of the Laundry—no one person is ever indispensable to any well-run agency—but he's probably important enough that if he is indeed missing, things are going to get unpleasantly exciting.

"What happened?" Mo asks.

"He missed a meeting this morning. I went to look in on him—he wasn't in his office. A couple of hours later I ran into Sally Alvarez from Accounting, and she said he'd missed a meeting, too. So I began asking around, and it transpires that he didn't check in this morning. Nobody's seen him since he went home yesterday evening." Andy's bright and brittle tone reminds me of a thin layer of paint applied to cover the ominous cracks in the plaster that widen and shift over time . . .

"Why didn't you phone him at home?" asks Mo.

"Because there's no home phone number on file for him!" Andy grins manically. "No address, for that matter, would you believe it? HR don't have any contact details at all! Just a bank account and a PO Box for correspondence."

"But that's—"

"Ridiculous?" Andy's smile slips. "Yes, I'd have said so, but remember this is *Angleton* we're talking about. Did either of you see him yesterday?"

The phrase "Yes, I did" escapes before I can press my lips together. Mo gives me a withering look. "I'm not concealing anything," I tell her: "Nothing to hide!"

Andy goes for the jugular. "Tell me. Everything."

"Not much *to* tell." I slump back on my chair. "I was on my way home, but I figured I'd drop in on him on the way." I frown, then wince as the butterfly stitches on my forehead tell me not to be an idiot. "Thing is, the other day—he sent me to Cosford to see something in a hangar—"

"The exorcism that went wrong," Andy interrupts.

"No, *not* the exorcism—something else, something in the museum. It's his usual showing-not-telling thing: he wanted me to see it before he explained. So I dropped in to talk to him because I didn't manage to get to Hangar 12B in the end. He spun me some kind of line about an RAF squadron that was decommissioned in 1964, some photoreconnaissance unit or other, and gave me some file references to follow up next week. Squadron 666, he said. Yes, it was tangentially connected, but there's no bloody way of knowing what he's got in mind until you follow the trail of bread crumbs he lays out for you—you know how he is, mind as twisty as a derivatives trader. Then he said something about wanting me to deputize for him on a codeword committee, something like BLOODY BARON."

"Damn. What time was this?"

"About twelve, twelve fifteen, I think. It was right after my session with Iris and Jo Sullivan. Why?"

"Because he was in the Ways and Means monthly breakout session on pandemic suppression systems that ran from two to four, according to at least six eyewitnesses." Andy looks gloomy. "Whatever happened, it wasn't you." He glances at Mo. "What time did Boris call you?"

She jerks upright and pulls her hand away from me. "Around noon. Why?"

"Hmm. Doesn't fit." The pall hanging over him is threatening to throw a miniature thunderstorm. "You didn't run into"—he jerks his chin sharply over his shoulder: in the hall, one of the Plumbers is reinscribing a Dho-Nha curve on the wall with a protractor and a Rotring pen full of colloidal silver ink—"until after, so it's not *that* . . ."

"What's not that?" I ask.

Andy takes a deep breath.

"Angleton's missing, work is following people home, and the Russians are trying to put the dead back into 'dead letter drop.' You know the old saying, twice is coincidence but three times is enemy action? Well, right now I think it applies . . ."

"*Was* our visitor Russian?" Mo leans forward.

"Don't know." Andy looks mulish. "Did you get any indication of what he wanted?"

"He kept asking something," I volunteer. "In at least two different languages, neither of which I speak."

"Oh great," he mutters. Stretching, he shakes his head. "Been a bad day so far, going to be a long one as well. Don't suppose there's any chance of a cup of tea?"

"Certainly—for you I can recommend the special herbal teas, monk's hood and spurge laurel, although if you insist I can make a pot of Tetley's . . ."

"That'd be fine." Mo's sarcasm flies right past him, which is the final warning I need that Andy is about ready to drop. Time to ease up on him a little, maybe, if he grovels for it.

"I'll get it," I say, standing up. "So let me see . . . Boris is running some kind of operation code named BLOODY BARON which involves something going down in Amsterdam which required Mo's offices, and—"

They're both shaking their heads at me. "No, no," says Andy, and: "Amsterdam was CLUB ZERO," says Mo. "It's a sideshow, and . . . did you bring that letter?" Andy produces an envelope. She pockets it: "Thanks."

"Actually, it all boils down to CASE NIGHTMARE GREEN," Andy says heavily. "The other operations are side projects; CASE NIGHTMARE GREEN is where it all starts."

"Oh yes?" I ask casually, although those words send a chill up my spine.

"Yes." He laughs halfheartedly. "It appears we may have been working under some false operating assumptions," he adds. "The situation seems to be deteriorating . . ."

CASE NIGHTMARE GREEN IS THE CODE NAME FOR THE END OF the world.

You might have noticed that Mo and I have no children. We don't even have a pet cat, the consolation prize of the overworked urban middle classes. There's a reason for this. Would you want to have children, if you knew for a fact that in a couple of years you might have to cut their throats for their own good?

We human beings live at the bottom of a thin puddle of oxygen-nitrogen vapor adhering to the surface of a medium-sized rocky planet that orbits a not terribly remarkable star in a cosmos which is one of many. We are not alone. There are other beings in other universes, other cosmologies, that think, and travel, and explore. And there are aliens in the abyssal depths of the oceans, and dwellers in the red-hot blackness and pressure of the upper mantle, that are stranger than your most florid hallucinations. They're terrifyingly powerful, the inheritors of millennia of technological civilization; they were building starships and opening timegates back when your ancestors and mine were clubbing each other over the head with rocks to settle the eternal primate disagreement over who had the bigger dick.

But the Deep Ones and the Chthonians are dust beneath the feet of the elder races, just as much so as are we bumptious bonobo cousins. The elder races are ancient. Supposedly they colonized our planet back in the pre-Cambrian age. Don't bother looking for their relics, though—continents have risen and sunk since then, the very atmosphere has changed density and composition, the moon orbits three times farther out, and to cut a long story short, they went away.

But the elder races are as dust beneath the many-angled appendages of the dead gods, who—

You stopped reading about a paragraph back, didn't you? Admit it: you're bored. So I'll just skip to the point: we have a major problem. The dimensions of the problem are defined by computational density and geometry. Magic is a branch of applied mathematics, after all, and when you process information, you set up waves in the platonic ultrastructure of reality that can amplify and reinforce—

To put it bluntly, there are too many humans on this planet. Six-billion-plus primates. And *we think too loudly*. Our brains are neurocomputers, incredibly complex. The more observers there are, the more quantum weirdness is observed, and the more inconsistencies creep into our reality. The weirdness is already going macroscopic—has been, for decades, as any disciple of Forteana could tell you. Sometime really soon, we're going to cross a critical threshold which, in combination with our solar system's ongoing drift through a stellar neighborhood where space itself is stretched thin, is going to make it likely that certain sleeping agencies will stir in their aeons-long slumber, and notice us.

No, we can't make CASE NIGHTMARE GREEN go away by smashing all our computers and going back to pencils and paper—if we did that, our amazingly efficient just-in-time food delivery logistics would go down the pan and we'd all starve. No, we can't make CASE NIGHTMARE GREEN go away by holding a brisk nuclear war and frying the guys with the biggest dicks—induced megadeaths have consequences that can be exploited for much the same ends, as the Ahnenerbe-SS discovered to their cost.

CASE NIGHTMARE GREEN is the demonological equivalent of an atomic chain reaction. Human minds equal plutonium nuclei. Put too many of them together in too small a place, and they begin to get a wee bit hot. Cross the threshold suddenly and emphatically and they get a *lot* hot. And the elder gods wake up, smell the buffet, and prepare to tuck in.

Our organization was formed as the British Empire's occult countermeasures organization during the struggle against Nazism, but it has continued to this day, serving a similar purpose: to protect the nation from an entire litany of lethal metanatural threats, culminating in the goal of surviving CASE NIGHTMARE GREEN. The UK's in a good position: a developed country, overwhelmingly urban (meaning its inhabitants are located in compact, defensible cities) with nearly neutral population size (no hot spots), and the world's most sophisticated surveillance systems. If you think the UK's been sliding into an Orwellian nightmare for the past decade, policed by cameras on every doorstep, you're right—but there is a reason for it: the MAGINOT BLUE STARS defense network and its SCORPION STARE basilisk cameras are fully deployed, ready to track and zap the first outbreaks. There are other, less obvious defensive measures. Our budget's been rising lately; ever wondered why there are so many police vans with cameras on the streets?

CASE NIGHTMARE GREEN is coming, and it's going to be perilous in the extreme. It's a bigger threat than global warming, peak oil, and the cold war rolled into one. We may not live to see the light at the other end of the tunnel, as we finally drift out from the fatal conjunction and the baleful stars close their eyes and reality returns to normal. Survival is far from assured—it may not even be likely. But one thing's for sure: we're going to give it our best shot.

THAT EVENING, AFTER THE PLUMBERS HAVE UPGRADED OUR defenses and Andy has finished picking our brains and left, I order in a curry—paying strict attention to the spy-hole this time when answering the doorbell—then retreat upstairs with Mo, a bottle of single malt, and a box of very expensive chocolates I've been hoarding against an evening like this. I'm dead tired, my face throbs around the butterfly sutures, and I feel unspeakably old. Mo . . . is better than she was earlier, for what it's worth.

"Here." I pass her the Booja-Booja box as I sit on the edge of the bed and unroll my socks.

"Oh, you shouldn't—did you set the alarm?"

"Yeah."

"You're sure?"

The rest of my clothes are piling up atop the socks: "Trust me, any burglar who tries their luck tonight is going to get the biggest shock of their life." Biggest, because afterwards they're going to run out of life in which to cap it. "Remember you need to deactivate it before you set foot on the stairs. Or open any windows."

"And if the house burns down . . ."

"And if the house burns down, yes." I shove the pillows up against the headboard. "We're safe here, as safe as can be." Which isn't saying much if the bombshell Andy dropped turns out to be true, but I'm not about to remind her of that. I lean back. "A wee dram?"

"Don't mind if I do. How about death by chocolate?"

"Sounds good to me."

For a minute we're silent; me filling two glasses, Mo working her way into the box of cocoa-dusted delights. Presently we exchange gifts. Outside, it's raining: the rattle and slap of water on glass merges with the distant noise of wheels on wet road surfaces, but inside our insulated, centrally heated bubble of suburbia we're isolated from the world.

"By the way, I haven't said thank you, have I?" she asks.

"What for?"

"Picking up the pieces, bollocking Andy for me, being a dear, that sort of thing. Just existing, when you get down to it."

"Um." I put my glass down. "Thank *you*. For saving my life this afternoon—"

"—but if you hadn't punched his legs out from under him he'd have shot me—"

"—he was going to shoot me first! Did you see where—"

We stop, looking at each other in mutual disbelief and incomprehension.

"How did we get here?" I ask her.

"I don't know." She frowns, then offers me the box of chocolates. "Pick one."

I pick something that looks like it came out of the wrong end of a hedgehog, except that it smells better. "Why?"

"Let's see . . . that one's unique in this collection, right? Let's consider life as a box of chocolates. All of them are unique. Let each chocolate be a, a significant event. All we can say of any chocolate before we eat it is that it was selected from the slowly diminishing set of chocolates we have not already encountered. But one thing they've all got in common is—"

"*Theobroma cacao*," I say, shoving it in my mouth and chewing. "Mmph."

"Yes. Now, let *Theobroma cacao* stand for the defining characteristics of our reality. We don't know precisely what the next chocolate will be, but we expect it to be brown and taste heavenly. But the previous chocolates we've eaten have narrowed the field of choice, and if, say, we've been picking the crunchy pralines selectively, we may find ourselves experiencing an unexpected run of soft centers—"

"I thought we were taking them at random?"

"No; we're picking them—without a menu card—but we can choose them on the basis of their appearance, are you with me? We can choose our inputs but not the outputs that result from them. And we have a diminishing array of options—"

"What kind of chocolate did you pick in Amsterdam?" I ask.

She pulls a face. "Wormwood. Or maybe *Amanita phalloides*." (The death cap mushroom, so called because the folks who name poisonous toadstools have no sense of humor: it's shaped like a cap, and you die if you eat it.)

"Are you ready to talk about it?"

She takes a sip of Lagavulin. "Not yet." Her lips twitch in the faintest ghostly echo of a smile—"But just knowing I can unload when I need to—" She shudders, then abruptly knocks back the contents of her glass in one.

"Do you believe Andy?" she asks, presently.

"I wish I didn't have to." I pause. "You mean, about the, the—"

"The acceleration."

"Yeah, that." I fall silent for a moment. "I'm not sure. I mean, he says it came out of Dr. Ford's work in Research and Development, using analytical methods to observe bias in stochastic sequential observations at widely separated sites, and Mike Ford's not the kind of man to make a mistake." Sly and subtle, with a warped sense of humor—and a mind sharp enough to cut diamond, that's our avuncular Dr. Ford. "I'd love to hear what Cantor's deep-duration research team at St. Hilda's made of it, but I suspect you'd have to go all the way to Mahogany Row to get permission to talk to them about current work—they're sandboxed for a reason." Mostly to protect everybody else's sanity: it's a team of no less than *four* DSS-grade sorcerers working on a single research project for more than thirty years. They've grown more than slightly weird along the way. Just talking to them, then thinking too hard about their answers can put you at risk of developing Krantzberg syndrome, the horrible encephalopathy that tends to afflict people who spend too much time thinking about symbolic magic. (The map is one with the territory; think too hard about the wrong theorems and you shouldn't be surprised if extradimensional entities start chewing microscopic chunks out of your gray matter.)

"I want to see Ford's raw data," Mo says thoughtfully. "Someone ought to give it a good working-over, looking for artifacts."

"Yeah."

She puts her glass down and plants the box of chocolates on top of it. "If the acceleration is real, we've only got a few months left."

And there's the rub. What Ford has detected—so Andy told us—is an accelerating rip in the probabilistic ultrastructure of spacetime.

If it exists (if Dr. Ford is right) the first sign is that it will amplify the efficacy of all our thaumaturgic tools. But it'll gather pace rapidly from there. He's predicting a phase-change, like a pile of plutonium that's decided to lurch from ordinary criticality—the state of a controlled nuclear reactor—to prompt criticality—a sudden unwanted outburst of power, halfway between a normal nuclear reaction and a nuclear explosion. Nobody predicted this before: we all expected CASE NIGHTMARE GREEN to switch on with a bang, not a weeks-long transition, an explosion rather than a meltdown. For a few days, we'll be gods—before it tears the walls of the world apart, and lets the nightmares in.

"Ought to make the best use of what time we've got left," she thinks aloud.

I put my glass down and roll on my side, to face her. "Yes."

"Come here," she says, stretching her free arm towards me.

Outside the window, the wild darkness claws at our frail bubble of light and warmth, ignored and temporarily forgotten in our primate frenzy. But its time will come.

THE NEXT MORNING WE OVERSLEEP, BY MUTUAL CONSENT, then slouch about the kitchen for a scandalously prolonged breakfast. Mo looks at me, sleepy-eyed with satisfaction, over a bare plate. "I needed that." A guilty glance across at the empty egg carton by the frying pan on the hob: "My waistline disagrees, but my stomach says 'fuck it.'"

"Enjoy it while you can." I've got plans for the weekend that include blowing a week's salary on stuff we might not need: brown rice, lentils, canned beans, camping gas cylinders. I can make room for it in our abbreviated joke of a cellar if I toss the rusting bicycle and a bunch of other crap that's taking up space . . . "I was thinking about going into the office this afternoon."

"But you're signed off sick," Mo points out.

"Yeah, that's the trouble." I refill my coffee mug from the cafetière. "After what Andy said, I figure I ought to at least poke around Angleton's office. See if I can spot something that everyone else has missed, before the trail goes cold. And there are some files I want to pull so I've got something to read over the weekend."

"You are not bringing work home." She crosses her arms, abruptly mulish.

"The thought never crossed my mind." I play the innocent expression card and she raises me one sullen glare. I fold. "I'm sorry, but there's also some reading matter I want to pick up."

"You're not bringing work home! We're not certified, anyway."

"Yes we are—as of yesterday, this is a level two secure site," I point out. "I'm not bringing anything secret home, just archive stuff from the stacks. It's tagged 'confidential' but it's so old it's nearly ready to claim its pension. Strictly historical interest only."

"Um." She raises an eyebrow. "Why?"

"Angleton"—I swallow—"when he sent me to Cosford he forgot to give me the backgrounder first. But he gave me a reading list."

"Oh fucking hell." She looks annoyed, which is a good sign. But then her eyes track sideways and I realize I'm not off the hook yet. "What's *that*?"

"That?" I ask brightly, suppressing the impulse to squawk *oh shit*. "It appears to be a cardboard box."

"A cardboard box with a picture of an iPhone on it," she says slowly.

"It's empty," I hurry to reassure her.

"Right." She picks up her coffee and takes a mouthful. "Would I be right in thinking it's empty because it *used* to contain an iPhone? Which is now, oh, I dunno, in your pocket?"

"Um. Yes."

"Oh, Bob. Don't you know any better?"

"It was *at least* a class four glamour," I say defensively, resisting the urge to hunch my shoulders and hiss *preciousss*. "And I needed a new phone anyway."

She sighs. "Why, Bob? Has your old phone started to smell or something?"

"I left my PDA in Hangar Six at Cosford," I point out. "It's slightly scorched around the edges and I don't have room for half my contacts on my mobile."

"So you bought an iPhone, rather than bugging Iris to sign off on a replacement PDA."

"If you *must* put it that way . . . yes."

Mo rolls her eyes. "Bob loses saving throw vs. *shiny* with a penalty of –5. Bob takes 2d8 damage to the credit card—just how much did it cost? Will you take it back if I guilt-trip you hard enough? Do pigs fly?"

"I was considering it," I admit. "But then Brains came round and installed something."

"Brains *installed*—"

"He's working on a port of OFCUT to the iPhone platform at work. I think he thought mine was an official phone . . . I've got to take it into the office and get it scrubbed before I even *think* about trading it in, or the Auditors will string us both up by the giblets." I shudder faintly, but Mo is visibly distracted.

"Hang on. They've ported OFCUT to the iPhone? What does it look like?"

"I'll show you . . ."

Fifteen minutes later I am on my way to the office, sans shiny. Mo is still sitting at the kitchen table with a cold mug of coffee, in thrall to the JesusPhone's reality distortion field, prodding at the jelly-bean icons with an expression of hapless fascination on her face. I've got a horrible feeling that the only way I'm going to earn forgiveness is to buy her one for her birthday. Such is life, in a geek household.

ACTUALLY, I HAVE A MOTIVE FOR GOING IN TO WORK THAT I don't feel like telling Mo about.

So as soon as I've stopped in my office and filled out a requisition for the file numbers Angleton scribbled on that scrap of paper for me—we can't get at the stacks directly right now, they're fifty meters down under the building site that is Service House, but there's a twice-daily collection and delivery run—I head down the corridor and across the walkway and up the stairs to the Security Office.

"Is Harry in?" I ask the guy in the blue suit behind the counter. He's reading the afternoon *Metro* and looking bored.

"Harry? Who wants to know?" He sits up.

I pull my warrant card. "Bob Howard, on active. I want to talk to Harry—or failing that, whoever the issuing officer is—about personal defense options."

"Personal def—" He peers at my warrant card: then his eyes uncross and he undergoes a sudden attitude adjustment. "Oh, you're one of *them*. Right. You wait here, sir, we'll get you sorted out."

Contrary to popular fiction, there is no such thing as a "license to kill." Nor do secret agents routinely carry firearms for self-defense. Me, I don't even *like* guns—I mean, they're great fun if all you want to do is make holes in paper targets at a firing range, but for their real design purpose, saving your ass in a life-or-death emergency, no: that's not on my list of fun things. I've been trained not to shoot my own foot off (and I've been practicing regularly, ever since the business on Saint Martin), but I feel a lot safer when I'm *not* carrying a gun.

However, two days ago my primary defensive ward got smoked in a civilian FATACC, yesterday I got doorstepped by a killer zombie from Dzerzhinsky Square, and I now have a dull ache in the life insurance policy telling me that it's time to tool up. Which in my case means, basically, dropping in on Harry, which means—

"Bob, my son! And how's it going with you? Girlfriend glassed your head up?"

Harry the Horse is our departmental armorer. He looks like an extra from *The Long Good Friday*: belt-straining paunch that's constantly trying to escape, thinning white hair, and a piratical black eye-patch. Last time I saw him he was explaining the finer details of the care and feeding of a Glock 17 (which we've standardized on, damn it, because of an ill-thought requirement for ammunition and parts commonality with the Sweeney); I responded by showing him how to take down a medusa (something which I have unfortunately too much experience at).

I recover from the back-slapping and straighten up: "It's going well, Harry. Well, kinda-sorta. My ward got smoked a couple of days ago and I'm on heightened alert—there's been an incident—"

"—As I can see from your head, my son, so you're thinking you need to armor up. Come right this way, let's see what we can kit you out with." He yanks the inner door open and pulls me into his little shop of—

You know that scene in *The Matrix*? When Neo says: "We need guns," and the white backdrop turns into a cross between Heathrow Airport and the back room at a rifle range? Harry's temporary office in the New Annexe Third Floor Extension Security Area is a bit like that, only cramped and lit by a bare sixty-watt incandescent bulb supervised by a small and very sleepy spider.

Harry pulls something that looks like an M16 on steroids off the wall and picks up a drum magazine the size of a small car tire. "Can I interest you in an Atchisson AA-12 assault shotgun? Burst-selectable for single shot or full auto? Takes a twenty-round drum full of twelve-gauge magnum rounds, and I've got a special load-out just for taking down paranormal manifestations—alternate FRAG-12 fin-stabilized grenades, white phosphorus rounds, and solid silver triple-ought buck, each ball micro-engraved with the Litany of Khar-Nesh—right up your street, my son." He racks the slide on the AA-12 with a clattering clash like the latch on the gates of hell.

"Er, I was thinking of something a little smaller, perhaps? Something I could carry concealed without looking like I was smuggling antitank guns on the bus?"

"Wimp." Harry puts the AA-12 back on the rack and carefully stows the drum magazine in a drawer. I can tell he's proud of his new toy, which from the sound of it would certainly blast any unwanted visitor right off my doorstep—and the front path, and the pavement, and the neighbors opposite at number 27, and their back garden too. "So tell me, what is it you *really* want?"

That's the cue for business: "First, I need to indent for a new class four–certified defensive ward, personal, safe to wear 24x7." I pause. "I also want to draw a HOG, cat three with silvered base and a suitable carrier. And—" I steel myself: "I'll take your advice on the next, but I was thinking about drawing a personal protective firearm—I'm certificated on the Glock—and a box of ammunition. I won't be routinely carrying it, but it'll be kept at home to repel boarders."

"You don't need a Glock to get rid of lodgers, my son." He spots my expression. "Had a problem?"

"Yeah, attempted physical intrusion."

"Hmm. Who else will have access to the weapon?"

I choose my next words carefully: "The house is a level two secure site. The only other resident is my wife. Dr. O'Brien isn't certificated for firearms, but she has other competencies and knows not to play with other kids' toys."

Harry considers *his* next words carefully: "I don't want to lean on you, Bob, but I need more than your word for that. Seeing as how it's for you and the delectable Dominique—give her my regards—I think we can bend the rules far enough to fit, but I shall need to put a ward on the trigger guard."

"A— How?" That's new to me.

"It's a new technique the eggheads in Q-Projects have come up with: they take a drop of your blood and key the trigger guard so that the only finger that'll fit through it is yours. Of course," his voice drops confidingly, "that doesn't stop the bad guys from chopping your finger off and using it to work the trigger; but they've got to take the gun *and* the finger off you before they can shoot you with it. Let's just say, it's more about stopping pistols from going walkies in public than about stopping your lady wife from offing you in a fit of jealous passion."

I roll my eyes. "Okay, I can live with that."

He brightens: "Also, we can make it invisible, and silent."

"Wha—hey! You mean you've got *real* concealed carry?"

He winks at me.

"Okay, I *would* like that, too. Um. As long as it's not invisible to me, also. And, um, the holster. An invisible gun in a visible holster would be kind of inconvenient . . ."

"It'll be invisible to anyone who doesn't have a warrant card, my son, or your money back."

"Will you match my life insurance, if it isn't and some bright spark sets an SO19 team on me?" (One of the reasons I am reluctant to carry a handgun in public is that the London Metropolitan Police have a zero-tolerance approach to anyone else carrying guns, and while their specialist firearms teams don't officially have a shoot-to-kill policy, *you* try finding a Brazilian plumber who does call-out work during a bomb scare these days.)

"I think we can back that, yes." Harry sounds amused. "Is that your lot?"

"It'll do." A new ward for myself, a Hand of Glory if I need to make a quick strategic withdrawal, and a gun to keep at home that I can carry in public if I absolutely have to: What more could an extremely worried spook ask for? *Ah, I know.* "Do you have any alarms?" I ask.

"I thought you was dead-set on home defense the DIY way." Harry looks momentarily scornful, then thoughtful: "Things ain't that bad yet, are they?"

"Could be." I shove my hands deep in my pockets and do my best to look gloomy. "Could be."

"Whoa." Harry's forehead wrinkles further. "Listen. There could be a problem: you drawing a HOG and a gun, and your good lady wife's violin, that makes you a regular arsenal, dunnit? Now, if I was signing out an alarm to, oh, that nice Mrs. Thompson in Human Resources"—I shudder— "there'd be no problem, on account of how she and her hubby and that no-good son of theirs ain't certificated for combat and wouldn't know a receiver from a slide if they trapped their fingers between them. Right? But let me just put it to you: suppose I sign an alarm out to you, put you and your missus on the watch list, and a bad guy comes calling at your front door. You and Dr. O'Brien go to the mattresses, and you activate the alarm, and being you and the missus you give as good as you get. Thirty seconds later the Watch Team are on your case and zoom in. Heat of battle, heat of battle: How do the Watch Team know that the people shooting from inside your house are you and your wife? What if you've gotten out through the back window? That's how blue-on-blue happens, my son. I figure you ought to think this one through some more."

"Okay." I look around the compact armory. "Guess you're right."

We've got a panic button, it's part of the kit the Plumbers fitted us out with; but an alarm of the kind I'm talking about is portable, personal, you carry it on your body and there's a limited list of folks who carry them— that kind of cover is computationally expensive—and if you're on the watch list and you trigger the alarm, SCORPION STARE wakes up and starts looking for you. And for everyone who might be threatening you. You don't want to press that button by accident, believe me.

"One ward, one HOG, and a +2 magic pistol of invisible smiting. Anything else I need to know?"

"Yeah. Come back in an hour and I'll have all the paperwork waiting for you to sign. The HOG and the ward I can give you once I get your chop; the pistol will take a little longer." Harry shrugs. "Best I can do, awright?"

"You're a champ." I make my good-byes, then head off. I've got other things to do before I go home.

I'M ON MY WAY TO ANDY'S OFFICE WHEN IRIS RUNS ME down.

"Bob! What are you doing here? I thought I told you to take the week off?" She sounds mildly irritated, and a little out of breath, as if she's been running around looking for me. "Hey, what happened to your head?"

I shrug. "Stuff came up."

She looks concerned. "In my office."

I demur: her office is her territory. "Look, Mo came back from . . . a job . . . in pieces, really rattled. Then the job followed her home, and *that's* a full-dress panic—"

Her eyes narrow: "How bad?"

"This bad." I point to the row of butterfly closures on my head and she winces. "Have you heard anything about—about upswings in non-affiliated agency activity in London this week?"

"*My* office," she says, very firmly, and this time she means it.

"Okay."

Once inside her office, she locks the door, switches on the red DND lamp, then lowers the blinds on the glass window that lets her view the corridor. Then she turns to me. "What codewords do you know?"

"I've been approved for CLUB ZERO"—she gives a sharp intake of breath—"and CASE NIGHTMARE GREEN. Not to mention MAGINOT BLUE STARS, but Harry the Horse wouldn't give me an alarm buzzer without your chop on the order form. And Angleton just told me to deputize for him on BLOODY BARON, although I haven't been briefed on that yet."

"Wow. That's a bundle." She eyes me warily. "Angleton dumps a lot on your shoulders." *For someone so junior,* she leaves unsaid.

"Yes." I focus on her more closely: wavy chestnut hair that is currently unkempt and beginning to show silvery roots, crow's-foot worry lines at the edges of her eyes, a restlessness to her stance that suggests she's far busier than she wants me to see. "Your turn."

"Wait, first—what happened yesterday?"

"Andy was with the Plumbers on cleanup; it should be on today's overnight events briefing sheet."

"That was"—her eyes widen—"you? Active incursion and assault by a class three, repelled by agents? Those stitches, it was *that*?"

"Yeah." I flop down on her visitor's chair without a by-your-leave. "They tried to rearrange my features: it was a close call. I came in today to draw a personal defense item, but also to ask what the hell is going on? And this business about Angleton—"

"You saw him the day before yesterday."

"Yes." I pause. "He's still missing. Right?"

She nods.

"Do you want me to look round his office? In case he left anything?"

Iris sniffs. "No." I think she's a poor liar. "But if you know any-thing . . . ?"

"I don't like being kept in the dark." Coming over all snippy on the person who is my nominal manager isn't clever, I know, but at this point I'm running low on self-restraint. "It seems to me that a whole bunch of rather bad things are happening right now, and that smells to me like enemy action." I'm echoing Andy. "Whoever the enemy is, in this context. Right, fine, you keep on playing games, that's all right by me—except that it isn't, really, because one of the games in question just followed my wife home and tried to kill her. Us." I point to the row of butterfly sutures on my forehead, and to her credit, she winces. "Remember, it *costs*."

"You've made your point," she says quietly, sitting down behind her desk. "Bob, if it was just up to me, I'd tell you—but it isn't. There's a committee meeting tomorrow, though, and I'll raise your concerns. Ask me again on Monday and I should be able to pull you in on the BLOODY BARON committee, and at least add you to the briefing list for CLUB ZERO. In the meantime, if you don't mind me asking—what items did Harry sign out to you?"

"He's processing them now." I enumerate. "We've also had our household security upgraded, in case there's a repeat visit, although I think that's unlikely. We're alerted now, so I'd expect any follow-ups to happen out in public: it's riskier for them than it was, but right now the house is a kill zone so if they want Mo badly enough they'll have to do it in the street."

"Ouch." She leans back in her chair and rests one hand on her computer keyboard. "Listen. If you're really sure you want an alarm, I'll sign for one. But . . . what Harry said? Listen to him. It's not necessarily what you need. The gun—well, you're certified. Certificated." She gives a moue of annoyance at the mangled language we have to use: "Whatever. Just keep it out of sight of the public and don't lose track of it. As for the rest—"

She exhales: "There has been an uptick in meetings in public places conducted by three junior attachés at the Russian embassy who our esteemed colleagues in the Dustbin"—she means the Security Service, popularly but incorrectly known as MI5—"have been keeping track of for some time. It's hard to be sure just which organization any given diplomat with covert connections is working for, but they initially thought these guys were FSB controllers. However, we've had recent indications that they're actually working for someone else—the Thirteenth Directorate, probably. We don't know exactly what's going on, but they seem to be looking for something, or someone."

"And then there was the Amsterdam business," I prod.

Another sharp look: "You weren't cleared for that."

"Andy procured a Letter of Release for Mo." I stare right back at her, bluffing. The *I'll tell you my secrets if you tell me yours* tap dance is a tedious occupational hazard in this line of work.

"Well, yes, then." The bluff works—that, and her ward told her I'm telling the truth about the Letter of Release. "Amsterdam, CLUB ZERO, was indirectly connected."

"So we've got an upswing of activity in the Netherlands and the UK—elsewhere in Europe, too?" I speculate: "Remember I've sat in on my share of joint liaison meetings?"

"I can't comment further until after the steering group meeting tomorrow." And my bluff falls apart: "I've told you everything I can tell you without official sanction, Bob. Get your kit sorted out, clear down your chores, and go home for the weekend. That's an order! I'll talk to you on Monday. Hopefully the news will be better by then . . ."

5.

LOST IN COMMITTEE

I GO BACK TO HARRY'S PLACE AND COLLECT MY KIT. THEN I catch the bus home, shoulders itching every time it passes a police car. Yes, I'm legally allowed to carry the Glock and its accessories, which are sleeping in my day sac in a combination-locked case. The gun and its charmed holster are supposed to be invisible to anyone who doesn't carry a Laundry warrant card; but I'll believe it when I see it. Luckily the bus is not stormed by an armed SO19 unit performing a random check for implausible weapons. I arrive home uneventfully, unpack the gun and place it on the bedroom mantelpiece (which is just to the left of my side of the bed), and go downstairs to sort out supper with Mo.

Friday happens, and then the weekend. I register the JesusPhone: it wants a name, and Mo suggests christening it (if that's the right word) the NecronomiPod. Her attitude has turned to one of proprietorial interest, if not outright lust: damn it, I *am* going to have to buy her one.

We do not discuss work at all. We are not doorstepped by zombies, shot at, blown up, or otherwise disturbed, although our next-door neighbor's teenage son spends a goodly chunk of Saturday evening playing "I Kissed a Girl" so loudly that Mo and I nearly come to blows over the pressing question of how best to respond. I'm arguing for Einstürzende Neubauten delivered over the Speakers of Doom; she's a proponent of Schoenberg delivered via the Violin that Kills Monsters. In the end we agree on the polite voice of reason delivered via the ears of his parents. I guess we must be growing old.

On Saturday morning, it turns out that we are running low on groceries. "Why not go online and book a delivery from Tesco?" asks Mo. I spend a futile hour struggling with their web server before admitting to myself that my abstruse combination of Firefox plug-ins, security filters, and firewalls (not to mention running on an operating system that the big box retailer's programmers wouldn't recognize if it stuck a fork in them) makes this somewhat impractical—by which time we've missed the last delivery, so it looks as if we're going to have to go forth and brave the world on foot. So I cautiously hook the invisi-Glock to my belt for the first time, pull my baggiest jacket down to cover it, and Mo and I hit the road.

Anticlimax. As we trudge home from the supermarket, laden down with carrier bags, I begin to relax slightly: even when my jacket got caught up on the front of a suicide grannie's shopping trolley, nobody noticed the hardware and started screaming. (This is twenty-first-century England, home of handgun hysteria: they're not being polite.) "By the way," Mo comments edgily as we wait to cross a main road, "don't you think you should be keeping your right hand free?"

I scan the surroundings for feral supernatural wildlife: "If I need my hand the shopping can take its chances."

"Then don't you think it'd be better to be carrying the bag with the bread and cheese in that hand, rather than the milk and the jar of pickled cucumbers?"

I swear quietly, try to switch hands, and get the bags inextricably entangled, just as the green man illuminates. We are a cover-free couple for the entire duration of our panicky scurry across the street crossing: "I should have held out for an attack alarm," I grumble.

"We'll sort one out on Monday," Mo says absentmindedly. "Watch the vegetables, dear."

On Sunday, we're due to have lunch with my parents, which means catching the tube halfway across London and then rattling way the hell out into suburbia on a commuter line run by a bus company distinguished for their hatred and contempt for rail travelers. I wear the holster, this time keeping my right hand free, and Mo carts her violin case along. Our trains are not ambushed by dragons, suicide bombers, or chthonian tentacle monsters. Frankly, given the quality of the postprandial conversation, this is not a net positive. Mo's face acquires much the same impassive expressiveness as an irritated Komodo dragon when Mum makes the usual fatuous (and thoughtless) comment about wishing for the patter of tiny feet. We are not, perforce, allowed to discuss our work in the presence of civilians, so we are short of conversational munitions with which to retaliate—they still think I work in computer support, and Mo's some sort of statistician. By the time we make our excuses and leave I'm thinking that maybe I'd better leave the gun behind on future parental visits.

"Did you enjoy the vegetables?" I ask the steaming vortex of silence beside me as we walk back up the street towards the railway station.

"I thought you were going to roast them at one point."

"Sorry, I'm chicken."

She sighs. "You don't need to apologize for your parents, Bob. They'll get over it eventually."

"They're not to know." I glance back over my shoulder. "We could, you know. There's still time. If you want."

"Time to fit in all the heartbreak and pain of raising wee ones so they're just old enough to appreciate the horror of it all? No thanks."

We've had this conversation before, a few times: revisited the situation for an update. No, the world we work in isn't a suitable one to inflict on a child you love.

"Besides, you're not the one who'd have to go through a first pregnancy in your late thirties."

"Certainly not just to please them."

We walk back to the station in morose silence, a thirty-something couple out for a Sunday afternoon stroll; nobody watching us needs to know that we're pissed off, armed, and on the lookout for trouble.

It's probably a very good thing indeed for the local muggers that they're still sleeping off their Saturday night hangovers.

MONDAY DAWNS BRIGHT AND HOT AND EARLY. AND I FIND MY-self waking to the happy knowledge that I can *go back to work*, and nobody will order me home. I roll over, feel the cooling depression across the mattress—continue my roll and sit up, relieved, on the wrong side of the bed.

Mo's clearly been up for a while: when I catch up with her in the kitchen she's listlessly spooning up a bowl of yogurt and gerbil food. I attend to the cafetière. She's wearing what I think of as her job-interview suit. "What's up?" I ask.

"Need to look the part for an off-site." She frowns. "Do you think this looks businesslike?"

"Very." She looks like she's about to foreclose on my mortgage. I spill coffee grounds all over the worktop, finish spooning the brown stuff into the jug, and add boiling water. "What kind of meeting?"

"Got to see a man about a violin. Conservation."

"Conservation . . . ?"

"They don't grow on trees, you know." The frown relaxes: "It's not something common like a Stradivarius. We've got three on inventory, but only twelve were ever made and they're all unavailable for one reason or another. A couple got bombed during the war, three are unaccounted for—presumed lost during extra-dimensional excursions—and the rest belong to other agencies or collectors we can't touch. Operational Assets are looking for a supplier who can make more of them, but it's turning out to be really difficult. Nobody is quite sure of the order in which Zahn applied his bindings; and as for what it's made of, just owning the necessary supplies probably puts you in breach of the Human Tissues Act of 2004, not to mention a raft of other legislation."

"Ow." I look at the battered violin case, propped up in the corner next to the recyclables bin. That's the trouble with a defense policy based on occult weapons: the sort of folks who make magic swords can rarely be bothered with the BS 5750 quality certification required by government procurement committees. "So what are you doing?"

"Carting my violin across town so an expert can examine it." She finishes her cereal bowl. "A restorer, very expensive, very exclusive. The cover story is I'm working for one of the big auction houses and we've been commissioned to get an estimate of its worth—don't look at me like that, they do this all the time, for stuff they don't have any in-house expertise with. I've got to go along because our other two violins are booked solid, and I'm not letting this one out of my sight . . ." She eyes the coffeepot. "What are you planning?"

"Got to go see Iris after her morning meeting, then we'll see." My cheek twitches as I pour two mugs of coffee. "Got some files to read. Angleton told me to deputize for him on a committee. Then there's the structured cabling in D Block to worry about. The glamorous life of the secret agent, when he's not actually out there saving the world . . . I was thinking, that story Andy came up with—do you want to look into it? Sanity-check Dr. Ford's analysis?" I finish the question slowly, trying not to think too hard about the implications.

"You read my mind." She adds milk to her coffee, stirring. "Not that everybody else in Research and Development with CASE NIGHTMARE GREEN won't be doing exactly the same thing, but you never know. I think I'll go pay Mike a little visit this afternoon, if he's got time." She looks at me, eyes wide. They're blue-green, I notice; it's funny, that: I don't usually pay attention to her eyes. "Are you all right?"

I nod. "Just a little unfocused today."

"You and me both." She manages a little laugh by way of conversational punctuation. "Well, I need to be off." She takes a too-big mouthful of coffee and winces. "Sorry I'm leaving you with the washing up again."

"That's okay, I've got an extra hour." No point showing up before Iris's steering group meeting, is there? "Take care."

"I will." She picks up her handbag and the violin case and heads for the door, heels clicking: "Bye," and she's away, looking more like an accountant than a combat epistemologist.

I putter around for a while, then get dressed (jeans, tee shirt, gun belt, and linen blazer—mine is not a customer-facing job at present, and I hate ties) and prepare to head out. At the last minute I remember the Necronomi-Pod, sleeping (but not dead) beside the laptop. I grab it along with my usual phone and head for the bus stop.

"WELCOME TO BLOODY BARON." SAYS IRIS. OFFERING ME A recycled cardboard folder with MOST SECRET stamped on the cover: "You have two hours to familiarize yourself with the contents before the Monday afternoon team meeting."

She smiles brightly as she drops it on my desk, right on top of the archive box full of dusty paperwork that I've just signed for, care of the wee man with the handcart who does the twice-daily run to the stacks: "There *will* be an exam. On the upside, I've given your structured cabling files to Peter-Fred and the departmental email security awareness committee meeting for Wednesday is canceled due to illness—Jackie and Vic are spouting from both ends, apparently, and aren't expected in until next week—so you've got some breathing space."

"Thanks." I try not to groan. "I'll try not to obsess about Peter-Fred fucking up the wiring loom too much."

"Don't worry." She waves a hand vaguely: "The cabling's all going to be outsourced from next year anyhow."

That gets my attention. "Outsourced?" I realize that shouting might deliver entirely the wrong message about my suitability for return to work and moderate my voice: "There are four, no, five, no—several, very good reasons why we do our own cabling, starting with security and ending with security. I really don't think outsourcing it is a very good idea at all, unless it's the kind of outsourcing which is actually insourcing to F Division via a subcontractor arrangement to satisfy our PPP quota requirements . . ."

And that's another ten minutes wasted, bringing Iris up to speed on one of the minutiae of my job. It's not her fault she doesn't know where the dividing line between IT support scut-work and OPSEC protocol lies, although she catches on fast when I explain the predilection of class G3 abominations for traveling down Cat 5e cables and eating clerical staff, not to say anything about the ease with which a bad guy could stick a network sniffer on our backbone and do a man-in-the-middle attack on our authentication server if we let random cable installers loose under the floor tiles in the new building.

Finally she leaves me alone, and I open the cover on BLOODY BARON and start reading.

AN HOUR AND A HALF LATER I'M THOROUGHLY SPOOKED BY MY reading—so much so that I've had to put the file down a couple of times when I caught myself scanning the same sentence over and over again with increasing disbelief. It comes as something of a relief when Iris knocks on my door again. "Showtime," she says. "You coming?"

I shake the folder at her. "This is nuts!"

"Welcome to the monkey house, and have a banana." She taps her wristwatch. "Room 206 in four minutes."

I lock up carefully—the files I requisitioned from the stacks aren't secret or above, but it'd still be professionally embarrassing if anyone walked in on them—and sketch a brief ward over the door. It flickers violet, then fades, plugging into the departmental security parasphere. I hurry towards the stairs.

Room 206 is up a level, with real windows and an actual view of the high street if you open the dusty Venetian blinds. There's a conference table and a bunch of not-so-comfortable chairs (the better to keep people from falling asleep in meetings), and various extras: an ancient overhead slide projector, a lectern with a broken microphone boom, and a couple of tattered security awareness posters from the 1950s: "Is your co-worker a KGB mole, a nameless horror from beyond spacetime, or a suspected homosexual? If so, dial 4-SECURITY!" (I suspect Pinky has been exercising his curious sense of humor again.)

"Have a chair." Iris winks at me. I take her up on the invitation as the door opens and three more attendees show up. Shona I recognize from previous encounters in ops working groups—she's in-your-face Scottish, on the plump side, and has a brusque way of dealing with bureaucratic obstacles that doesn't exactly encourage me to insert myself in her line of fire. I think she's something to do with the Eastern Europe desk. "This is Shona MacDonald," says Iris. "And Vikram Choudhury, and Franz Gustaffson, our liaison from the AIVD—Unit G6." Franz nods affably enough, and I try to conceal my surprise. It's an unusual name for the Netherlands, but I happen to know that his father was Danish. The last time I saw him, he was on what I was sure was a one-way trip to a pad-ded cell for the rest of his life after sitting through one PowerPoint slide too many at a certain meeting in Darmstadt. The fine hair on the back of my neck stands on end.

"We've met," I say, guardedly.

"Have we?" Franz looks at me with interest. "That's interesting! You'll have to tell me all about it later."

Oh. So they only managed to save part of him.

"Allow me to introduce Bob, Bob Howard," Iris tells them, and I nod and force a bland smile to cover up the horror.

"Mr. Howard is an SSO 3 and double-hats as our departmental IT se-curity specialist and also as personal assistant to Dr. Angleton. A decision was taken to add him to this working group." I notice the descent into passive voice; also some disturbing double takes from around the table, from Shona and Gustaffson. "He also—this is one of those coincidences I was talking about earlier—happens to be married to Agent CANDID."

At which name Gustaffson drops all pretense at impassivity and stares at me as if I've just grown a second head. I nod at him. *What the hell? Mo has a codeword all of her own?* Presumably for overseas assignments like the Amsterdam job, but still . . .

"Bob. Would you be so good as to summarize your understanding of the background to BLOODY BARON for us?"

Oh Jeez. I clear my throat. "I've only had an hour and a half with the case files, so I may be misreading this stuff," I admit. *Shit, stop making excuses. It just makes you look lame.* "BLOODY BARON appears to be a monitoring committee tasked with—well. The cold war never entirely ended, did it? There are too many vested interests on all sides who want to keep it simmering. And the upshot is that Russian espionage directed against the West has been rising since 2001. We kind of forgot that you don't need communism to set up an east/west squabble between the Russian Empire and Western Europe—in fact, communism was a distraction. Hence the current gas wars and economic blackmail."

Iris winces. (I'm wincing inside: if you had our heating bills last winter, you'd be wincing too.) "Enough of the macro picture, if you don't mind. What's the micro?"

"FSB activity in London has been rising steadily since 2001." I shrug. "The Litvinenko assassination, that embarrassing business with the wifi-enabled rock in Moscow in '05, diplomatic expulsions; the old confrontation is still bubbling under. But BLOODY BARON is new to me, I will admit."

I glance at the file on the table in front of me. "Anyway, there's an organization. We don't know their real designation because nobody who knows anything about them has ever defected and they don't talk to strangers, but folks call them the Thirteenth Directorate—not to be confused with the original Thirteenth Directorate, which was redesignated the Fifth Directorate back in the 1960s. Nasty folks—they were the ones responsible for wet work, *Mokryye Dela.*

"The current bearers of the name seem to have been forked off the KGB back in 1991, when the KGB was restructured as the FSB. They're an independent wing, much like us."

The Laundry was originally part of SOE, back during the Second

World War; we're the part that kept on going when SOE was officially wound up at the end of hostilities.

"They're the Russian OCCINTEL agency, handling demonology and occult intelligence operations. Mostly they stay at home, and their activities are presumably focused on domestic security issues. But there's been a huge upsurge—unprecedented—in overseas activity lately. Thirteenth Directorate staff have been identified visiting public archives, combing libraries, attending auctions of historic memorabilia, and contacting individuals suspected of having contact with the former parent agency back before the end of the real cold war. They've been focusing on London, but also visible in Tallinn, Amsterdam, Paris, Gdańsk, Ulan Bator . . . the list doesn't make any obvious sense."

I swallow. "That's all I've got, but there's more, isn't there?"

Everyone's looking at me, except for Gustaffson, who's watching Iris. She nods. "That's the basic picture. Vikram?"

Choudhury looks at me curiously. "Is Mr. Howard replacing Dr. Angleton on this committee?"

I nearly swallow my tongue. Iris looks disconcerted. "Dr. Angleton isn't currently available," she tells him, sparing me a warning glance. "There are Human Resources issues. Mr. Howard is deputizing for him."

Oh Jesus. Wheels within wheels—committee members who haven't been briefed, Russian secret demonologists, cold war 2.0. *What have I got myself into?*

"Oh dear." Choudhury nods, mollified. "Allow me to express my sympathies." He has a fat conference file in front of him: he taps the contents into line with tiny, fussy movements. His suit is black and shiny, like an EDS consultant's in the old days.

"Well then. We have been tracking a number of interesting financial aspects of the KGB activity. They appear to be spending money like water—we have requested information on IBAN transactions and credit card activity by the mobile agents we have identified, and while they're not throwing it away on silly luxury items they have certainly been working on their frequent flier miles. One of them, Agent Kurchatov, managed to fly half a million kilometers in the last nine months alone—we believe he's a high-bandwidth courier—as an example. And they've been bidding in estate auctions. The overall pattern of their activity focuses on memorabilia from the Russian Civil War, specifically papers and personal effects from the heirs of White Russian leaders, but they've also been looking into documents and items relating to the *Argenteum Astrum*, which is on our watch list—BONE SILVER STAR—along with documents relating to Western occultist groups of the pre-war period. Aleister Crowley crops up like a bad penny, naturally, but also Professor Mudd, who tripped an amber alert. Norman Mudd."

Civil war memorabilia . . . ? A nasty thought strikes me, but Vikram looks as if he's about to continue. "What's special about Mudd?" I ask.

Choudhury looks irritated. "He was a mathematics professor and an occultist," he says, "and he knew *F*." The legendary *F*—the Laundry's first Director of Intelligence, reporting to Sir Charles Hambro at 64 Baker Street—headquarters of the Special Operations Executive. *Whoops.* He cocks his head to one side: "If you don't mind . . . ?"

I shake my head. "Sorry. I'm new to this." *Touchy, isn't he?* "Please continue."

"Certainly. It looks as if the Thirteenth Directorate are taking an unusual interest in the owners of memorabilia associated with the late Baron Roman Von Ungern Sternberg, conqueror of Mongolia, Buddhist mystic, and White Russian leader. In particular, they seem to be trying to trace an item or items that Agent S76 retrieved from Reval in Estonia on behalf of our old friend *F*." Choudhury looks smugly self-satisfied, as if this diversion into what is effectively arcane gibberish to me is supposed to be enlightening. "Any questions?" he asks.

For once I keep my gob shut, waiting to see if anyone else is feeling as out-of-the-loop as I am. I don't have to wait long. Shona bulls ahead, bless her: "Yeah, you bet I've got questions. Who is this Baron Roman Von Stauffenberg or whoever? *When* was he—did he die recently?"

"Ungern Sternberg died in September 1921, executed by a Bolshevik firing squad after Trotsky's soldiers captured him." Choudhury taps his folio again, looking severe: "He was a *very bad man*, you know! He had a habit of burning paperwork. And he had a man nicknamed Teapot who followed him around and strangled people the Baron was displeased with. I suppose we could all do with that, ha-ha." He doesn't notice—or doesn't care about—Iris's fish-eyed glare. "But, aha, yes, he was one of *those* Russian occultists. He converted to Buddhism—Mongolian Buddhism, of a rather bloody sect—but stayed in touch with members of a certain Theosophical splinter group he had fallen in with when he was posted to St. Petersburg. Obviously they didn't stay there after the revolution, but Ungern Sternberg would have known of his fellows in General Denikin's staff, and possibly known of *F*, due to his occult connections. And the, ah, anti-Semitism."

He looks pained. All intelligence agencies have skeletons in their closets: ours is our first Director of Intelligence, whose fascist sympathies were famous, and only barely outweighed by his patriotism.

"What can that possibly have to do with current affairs?" Shona's evident bafflement mirrors my own. "What are they looking for?"

"That's an interesting question," says Choudhury, looking perturbed. He glances at me, his expression unreadable. "Mr. Howard might be able to tell us—"

"Um. What?"

My confusion must be as obvious as Shona's, because Iris chips in: "Bob has only just come in on the case—Dr. Angleton didn't see fit to brief him earlier."

"Oh my goodness." Choudhury looks as if he's swallowed a toad. Live. "But in that case, we really must talk to the doctor—"

"You can't." Iris shakes her head, then looks at me again. "Bob, we—the committee—asked Angleton to investigate the link between Ungern Sternberg, *F*, and the current spike in KGB activity." She looks back at Choudhury. "Unfortunately, he was last seen on Wednesday evening. He's now officially AWOL and a search is under way. This happened the same night as Agent CANDID closed out CLUB ZERO. The next morning, CANDID and Mr. Howard were assaulted by a class three manifestation, and I don't believe it's any kind of coincidence that Agent Kurchatov was seen visiting the Russian embassy in Kensington Palace Gardens that morning—and left on an early evening flight back to Moscow.

"Let me be straightforward: all the signs suggest that the Thirteenth Directorate are suddenly playing very dangerous games on our turf. If the cultists who CLUB ZERO shut down turn out to be a front for the Thirteenth Directorate, then we have to assume that CLUB ZERO is connected with BLOODY BARON—and that turns it from a low-key adversarial tactical analysis into a much higher priority for us. They're not usually reckless, and they're not pushing the old ideological agenda anymore— they wouldn't be acting this openly for short-term advantage—so we need to find out what they're doing and put a stop to it, before anyone else gets hurt. Yes, Bob? What is it?"

I put my hand down. "This might sound stupid," I hear myself saying, "but has anyone thought about, you know, *asking* them?"

I'M NOT BIG ON HISTORY.

When I was at school, I dropped the topic as soon as I could, right after I took my GCSEs. It seemed like it was all about one damn king after another, or one war after another, or a bunch of social history stuff about what it was like to live as an eighteenth-century weaver whose son had run off with a spinster called Jenny, or a sixteenth-century religious bigot with a weird name and a witch-burning fetish. Tedious shite, in other words, of zero relevance to modern life—especially if you were planning on studying and working in a field that was more or less invented out of whole cloth in 1933.

The trouble is, you can ignore history—but history won't necessarily ignore you.

History, it turns out, is all around us. Service House—where I used to have my cubicle—is where the Laundry moved in 1953. Before that, it used to belong to the Foreign Office. Before *that*, we worked out of an attic above a Chinese laundry in Soho, hence the name. Before *that* . . .

There was no Laundry, officially.

The Laundry was a wartime work of expedience, magicked into existence by a five-line memo headlined ACTION THIS DAY and signed *Winston Churchill*. It was directed at a variety of people, including a retired major general and sometime MI6 informer, whose dubious status was probably the deciding factor in keeping his ass out of an internment camp along with the rest of the Nazi-sympathizing Directorate of the British Union of Fascists—that, and his shadowy connections to occultists and mathematicians, his undoubted genius as a tactician and theorist of the arts of war, and the nuanced reports of his political officer, who figured his patriotism had a higher operator precedence than his politics. That man was *F*: Major-General J. F. C. "Boney" Fuller. He's been in his grave for nearly half a century, and would doubtless be spinning in it fast enough to qualify for carbon credits as an environmentally friendly power source if he could see us today in all our multi-ethnic anti-discriminatory splendor.

But who cares?

That is, indeed, the big-ticket question.

Before the Laundry, things were a bit confused. You can do magic by hand, without computers, but magic performed by ritual without finite state automata in the loop—calculating machines, in other words—tends to be haphazard, unreliable, uncontrollable, prone to undesirable side effects, and difficult to repeat. It also tends to fuck with causality, the logical sequence of events, in a most alarming way.

We've unintentionally rewritten our history over the centuries, would-be sorcerers unwinding chaos and pinning down events with the dead hand of consistency—always tending towards a more stable ground state because chaos is unstable; entropy is magic's great enemy. When the ancients wrote of gods and demons, they might well have been recording their real-life experiences—or they may have drunk too much mushroom tea: we have no way of knowing.

Let's just say that you can't always trust the historical record and move swiftly on.

On the other hand, unreliability never stopped anyone from using a given technology—just look at Microsoft if you don't believe me.

During the nineteenth and early twentieth centuries, the scholars of night systematized and studied the occult with all the zeal Victorian taxonomists could bring to bear. There was a lot of rubbish written; Helena Blavatsky, bless her little cotton socks, muddied the waters in an immensely useful way, as did Annie Besant, and Krishnamurti, and a host of others.

And then there were those who came too damned close to the truth: if H. P. Lovecraft hadn't died of intestinal cancer in 1937 something would have had to have been done about him, if you'll pardon my subjunctive. (And it would have been messy, very messy—if old HPL was around today he'd be the kind of blogging and email junkie who's in everybody's RSS feed like some kind of giant mutant gossip squid.)

Then there were those who were sitting on top of the truth, if they'd had but the wits to see it—Dennis Wheatley, for example, worked down the hall in Deception Planning at SOE and regularly did lunch with a couple of staff officers who worked with Alan Turing—the man himself, not the anonymous code-named genius currently doing whatever it is they do in the secure wing at the Funny Farm. Luckily Wheatley wouldn't have known a real paranormal excursion if it bit him on the arse. (In fact, looking back to the dusty manila files, I'm not entirely sure that Dennis Wheatley's publisher wasn't on the Deception Planning payroll *after* the war, if you follow my drift.)

But I digress.

It was to our great advantage during the cold war that the commies were always terrible at dealing with the supernatural.

For starters, having an ideology that explicitly denies the existence of an invisible sky daddy is a bit of a handicap when it comes to assimilating the idea of nightmarish immortal aliens from elsewhere in the multiverse, given that the NIAs in question have historically been identified as gods (subtype: elder). For seconds, blame Trofim Lysenko for corrupting their science faculty's ability to cope with new findings that contradicted received political doctrine. For thirds, blame the Politburo, which, in the 1950s, looked at the embryonic IT industry, thought "tools of capitalist profit-mongers," and denounced computer science as un-Communist.

Proximate results: they got into orbit using hand calculators, but completely dropped the ball on anything that required complexity theory, automated theorem proving, or sacrificial goats.

But that was then, and this is now, and we're not dealing with the Union of Soviet Socialist Republics, we're dickering with the Russian Federation. (When we're not trying to save ourselves from the end of the world, that is.)

The Russians are no longer dragged backwards by the invisible hand of Lenin. Their populace have taken with gusto to god-bothering and hacking, their official government ideology is "hail to the chief," and Moscow is the number one place on the planet to go if you want to rent a botnet.

There's a pragmatic and pugnacious attitude to their overseas operations these days. Their ruling network, the *siloviki*, aren't playing the Great Game for ideological reasons anymore, even though they came up through the KGB prior to the years of chaos: they're out to make Russia great again, and grab a tidy bank balance in the process, and they're playing hardball because they're pissed off at the way they were shoved off the board during the 1990s—consigned to the dustbin of history, asset-stripped by oligarchs and bamboozled by foreign bankers.

And so, to the present. The whole of Western Europe—and a bunch of far-flung outposts beyond—are currently crawling with KGB foot soldiers. No longer the stolid gray-suited trustees of Soviet-era spy mythology, they come in a variety of shapes and sizes, but they have two things in common: snow on their boots and blood in their eyes. And if they're looking for something connected with our founder, and deploying supernatural weapons on our territory—

We need to know why.

6.

RED ORCHESTRA

LET US TEMPORARILY LOOK ASIDE FROM YR. HMBL. CRSPNDNT'S
work diary to contemplate a very different matter: a vignette of street life
in central London. I am not, myself, a witness: so this is, to some extent,
a work of imaginative reconstruction.

Visualize the scene: a side street not far from Piccadilly Circus in London, an outrageously busy shopping district crammed on both sides with
fashion chains and department stores. Even the alleys are lined with bis-
tros and boutiques, tidied up to appeal to the passing trade. Pedestrians
throng the pavements and overflow into the street, but vehicle traffic is
light—thanks to the congestion charge—and slow—thanks to the speed
bumps.

Here comes a red-haired woman, smartly dressed in a black skirt,
houndstooth-check jacket, medium heels. She's holding a violin case in
one hand, her face set in an expression of patient irritation beneath her
makeup: a musician heading to a recital, perhaps. She looks slightly un-
comfortable, out-of-sorts as she weaves between a pair of braying office
workers, yummy mummies pushing baby buggies the size of lunar rovers,
a skate punk in dreads, and a beggar woman in hijab. She cuts across the

pavement on Glasshouse Street, crosses the road between an overheating BMW X5 and a black cab, and turns into Shaftesbury.

Somewhere in the teeming alleys behind Charing Cross Road there is a narrow-fronted music shop, its window display empty but for a rack of yellowing scores and a collection of lightly tarnished brass instruments. The woman pauses in front of the glass, apparently examining the sheet music. In fact, she's using the window as a mirror, checking the street behind her before she places one hand on the doorknob and pushes. Her close-trimmed nails are smoothly sheathed in enamel the color of overripe grapes: there are calluses on the tips of her fingers.

A bell jingles somewhere out of sight as she enters the shop.

"Good afternoon?"

One side of the shop is occupied by a counter, glass bound in old oak, running back towards a bead-curtained alcove at the rear of the premises. A cadaverous and prematurely aged fellow with watery eyes, dressed as conservatively as an undertaker, shuffles between the hanging strings of beads and blinks at her disapprovingly.

"Mr. Dower? George Dower?" The woman smiles at him tightly, her lips pursed to conceal her teeth.

"I have that honor, yes." He looks at her as if he wishes she'd go away. "Do you have an appointment?"

"As a matter of fact"—the woman slides a hand into her black leather handbag and produces a wallet, which falls open to display a card—"I do. Cassie May, from Sotheby's. I called yesterday?" The card glistens with a strange iridescent sheen in the dim artificial light.

"Oh yes!" His expression brightens considerably. "Yes indeed! A restoration project, I am to understand . . . ?"

"Possibly." The woman swings her violin case up above the glass counter then gently lowers it. "Our client has asked us to obtain a preliminary valuation, and also to inquire about the cost of certain necessary restoration work for an instrument of similar manufacture that is currently in storage in a degraded condition—it's too fragile to move." She reaches into her handbag again and when she takes her hand out, she's holding an envelope. "Before examining the instrument, I would like you to sign this non-disclosure agreement." She removes a thin document from the envelope.

Mr. Dower is surprised. "But it's just a violin! Even if it's a rarity—" He does a double take. "Isn't it?"

The woman shakes her head silently, then hands him the papers.

Mr. Dower scans the first page briefly then glances up at her. "This isn't from Sotheby's—"

"If anybody asks you who I am and why I'm here, you will tell them I'm Cassie May, from Sotheby's auction house, inquiring about a valuation." She doesn't smile. "You will now read the document and sign it."

Almost as if he can't help himself, Mr. Dower's eyes return to the document. He scans it rapidly, mumbling under his breath as he turns the three pages. Wordlessly, he produces a pen from his inside jacket pocket.

"Not like that." The woman offers him a disposable sterile needle: "First, you must draw blood. Then sign using this pen." She waits patiently while he presses a digit against the needle, winces, and rubs the nib of the pen across the ball of his thumb. He makes no complaint about the unusual request, and doesn't seem to notice the way she produces a small sharps container for the office supplies and carefully folds the document back into its envelope. "Good. By the authority vested in me I bind you to silence, under pain of the penalties specified in this document. Do you understand?"

Mr. Dower stares at the violin case as if stunned. "Yes," he mutters.

The woman who calls herself Cassie May unclips the lid of the violin case and lays it open before him.

Mr. Dower stares into the case for ten long seconds, barely breathing. Then he shudders. "Excuse me," he says, hastily covering his mouth. He turns and stumbles through the bead curtain. A few seconds later she hears the sound of retching.

The woman waits patiently until Mr. Dower reappears, looking pale. "You can shut that," he tells her.

"If you want." She shrugs. "I take it you've seen one before."

"Yes." He shudders again, his gaze unfocused. He seems to be staring down inner demons. "What do I have to do to get you to take it away?"

"You give me a written evaluation." She has another piece of paper, this one containing a short list of bullet points. "As I said, a preliminary estimate of the cost of repairing such a . . . relic. A half-gram sample excised from the corpse of another identical instrument. All necessary materials to be provided by the customer. If you can assess the nature of the bindings that hold it together, my employers would like to be able to replicate them."

He stares at her. "Who are you from? Who sent you here?"

"I'm from the government department responsible for keeping instruments like this out of your shop. Unfortunately there is a time for business as usual, and then . . . well. Can you do it?"

Mr. Dower stares at the wall behind her. "If I must."

"Good. If you attach your invoice to the report I will see that it is processed promptly."

"When do you need the report?" he asks, shaking himself as if awakening from a dream.

"Right now." She walks over to the door and flips the sign to CLOSED.

"But I—" He swallows.

"I'm required to stay within arm's reach of the instrument at all times. And to remove it from your premises when you are not working on it." The woman doesn't smile; in fact, her expression is faintly nauseated.

"Why? To prevent me stealing it?"

"No, Mr. Dower: to prevent it from killing you."

I'M BACK IN MY OFFICE AFTER THE BLOODY BARON MEETING. The committee have minuted that I am to try and think myself into Angleton's shoes (ha bloody ha); the coffee mug is cooling on the mouse mat beside my cranky old HP desktop as I sit here, head in hands, groaning silently and wishing I'd paid more attention in history classes rather than staring at the back of Zoe McCutcheon's head and thinking about—let's not go there. (Sixteen-year-old male: fill in the blanks.) All this Russian stuff is confusing the hell out of me—why can't we go back to worrying about Al Qaida or pedophiles on the internet or whatever it is that intelligence services traditionally obsess about?

There's a pile of dusty manila folders sitting on my desk. Angleton said they were interesting, right before he went missing, and if that wasn't a deliberate clue I'll eat my pants. He's a slithy old tove and I wouldn't put it past him to have meant something significant, damn him. But all I've got is a list of hastily scrawled file reference numbers, pointers into the shelf positions documents are stored at in the stacks—nothing as simple as filenames, of course, *that* would be giving valuable information to the enemy. How like Angleton.

I pick up the first folder and open it. It contains a creased, dog-eared, and much folded letter, handwritten on paper that's a weird size. I peer at the faded scrawl, trying to make head or tail of it. "Jesus, boss, what the *hell* . . . ?" Luckily I have a scanner with an automatic document feeder. I carefully feed the brittle pages to the computer, one at a time, twitching the software to maximum resolution. On the first page I pick up a reasonable high-contrast scan—there's some ghosting, what looks like pale scribble showing through, as if the author tried to scrub something out—and zoom in. I puzzle out the date, first: *October 11th, 1921*. Then I turn the handwriting recognition software loose and sit back. After a while, it's cooked and ready to read.

CLASSIFIED: S76/45

Dear John,

First of all, greetings from Reval! I sincerely hope this letter finds you experiencing a more clement climate than the Estonian autumn, which has clamped down in earnest this past week. Please give my best regards to Sonia.

I assume you have already received word through the wires about the execution of the Beast of Dauria last month. By all accounts he was given as fair a trial as the Reds could manage, and if even a tenth of the allegations leveled against him are true then I can't see that they had any alternative but to shoot him. I have been paying special attention to the reports filtering out of Siberia about Semenov's bandits, and Ungern Sternberg was by far the worst of a bad bunch. It was a beastly affair, and a bad end to a thoroughly bad fellow, and perhaps we should thank the Reds for ridding us of this monster.

However, his death leaves certain questions unanswered. I decided to visit his parents—not his father, but his mother and her husband, Sophie Charlotte and Baron Oskar Von Hoyningen-Huene. They live in Jerwakant, and although the weather is dismal—the snow is already lying four feet thick on the ground—I was able to arrange a weekend visit.

As you probably know, madness stalks the Ungern Sternberg line; the Baron's father Theodor—once a keen amateur geologist, noted for his interest in unusual fossils—is in a sanatorium to this day. In my estimate Sophie Charlotte suffered considerably by proximity, for he deteriorated while they were still married; it is a difficult topic to raise in conversation, especially in light of the unfortunate fate of her son, and so I did not seek to disturb her, but made my observations indirectly.

The Hoyningen-Huene estate is a stately home that would grace any family of means, in any country. By winter it presents a fairy-tale face to the world, its steeply pitched roofs and turrets peaceful beneath a blanket of snow, an island of tranquility in the middle of the gloomy pine forest. But it is a fairy tale out of the Brothers Grimm, rather than the bloodless and bowdlerized fare that our parents' generation sought to raise us on! This is a castle of the German aristocracy, descendants of the Teutonic Knights and servants of the Russian Empire until the late upheaval deprived them of the object of their loyalty. And it is an estate that has been cut down to size, thanks to the decrees of the Riigikogu relating to land reform and the rights of the peasants to the fruits of their labor.

Evgenia and I visited with the Hoyningen-Huenes last weekend, ostensibly to write a tub-thumper for the *Guardian* about the equitable settlement in Rapla County, which has not seen so much turbulence and persecution of the former rulers as other areas: I put it about that we would also like to see the countryside thereabouts, and talk to some of the local landlords about the recent changes. The *Guardian*'s status as an English newspaper outweighs its political reputation in the backwoods: I had no shortage of correspondents, mostly of the Indignant of Colchester variety so familiar to us from the letter columns.

On Sunday afternoon, after the obligatory morning visit to the chapel—which was very Lutheran in that manner that is peculiar to the Baltic territories, with gloomy *danse macabre* and carved skull heraldry above the bare wood pews, and do I need to add, unheated even in winter?—I had a chance to chat with the Baron, and by way of two or three glasses of schnapps the subject of the Prodigal rose to the surface.

"He has always been a disappointment to me, and a tribulation to his mother," quoth Oskar Hoyningen-Huene. "This latest shame is but the final straw—luckily the final one—on the pyre of his depravity." He sighed deeply at this point. "I tried to beat sense into him when he was young, you know. But he was always a wild one. Took after his father, and then there was the obsession with Shamanism, like the nonsensical garbage Theodor plagued my wife with before she divorced him."

"Garbage?" I asked, digging. I intimated, indirectly, that I had been asked to prepare a column about his adoptive son, but had declined to do so out of respect for the recently bereaved.

Oskar snorted. "No son of mine," he said, with cold deliberation, "would have done what that *beast* did. He wrote us letters, you know, boasting of it! Executing prisoners by quartering—tying their limbs to springy saplings. Mass hangings, stabbings, shootings. Said he was going to line the road to Moscow with Commissars and Jews, impaled every couple of yards—heaven knows I've got no time for yids myself, but he pledged to kill them all, to purify Russia and reinstate serfdom.

Can you believe it? And there was other stuff, dark stuff. Absolutely disgusting."

I asked what he did with the letters.

"I burned them!" he said indignantly. "All but a couple that Sophie refused to let me have. I hadn't the heart to deprive her of . . . well. Memories." He subsided into a sulky silence for a few minutes, but bestirred himself with the assistance of a fresh glass. "There were his father's fossils, you know. I think that's where the rot set in."

"Fossils?" I asked.

"Rum things, never seen anything like them. I think Sophie left them in the boy's room. He used to play with them when he was a tot, you know. I'd find him staring at the things. Thought he was going to grow up to be a geologist like his pa, which would have been no bad thing compared to how he turned out."

Knowing of your interests, and learning that his mother had actually preserved the Prodigal's bedroom—untouched! As if she expected her son to return!—I availed myself of an opportunity to look inside, in hope of getting some insight into his character.

(ENCLOSED: 8 faded black and white photographs of irregular pieces of rock, cleaved along fracture planes. Most of the pieces appear to be slate, although it is hard to be certain. The fossils resemble certain other samples referenced by codeword: ANNING BLUE SKULL.)

I think we've seen the like of these pieces before, haven't we? "In those days, giants walked the Earth . . ."

I shall make indirect enquiries to see if it is possible to acquire Roman Von Ungern Sternberg's boyhood fossil collection for the nation, and (if possible) his mother's collection of letters. I shall also attempt to arrange a follow-up visit, although it is now unlikely to be practical until the spring thaw. (Chateau Hoyningen-Huene is somewhat isolated, and polite society does not travel much in winter: a premature visit would invite unwelcome scrutiny.) Meanwhile, I shall be wintering in Reval and will make use of my free time to investigate

further the matter of the Bloody White Baron and the mystery he discovered in the Bogd Khan's palace.

Your obedient friend,
Arthur Ransome

THE WOMAN WHO CALLS HERSELF CASSIE MAY WAITS PATIENTLY,
sitting on a backless stool behind the antique cash register in George
Dower's shop while keeping an eye on the proprietor, who is busy in the
workshop behind the bead curtain (which she has tied back, to afford her
a clear view).

The back of the shop is not what she had expected. She's been in instrument makers' workshops before, smelled the glue and fresh-planed
wood, the wax and varnish. She's familiar with other musical special-
ties as well, with signal generators and plugboards, amps and filters, the
hum and hot metallic smell of overdriven amplifiers. Dower's shop is not
like any of these. It has some of the characteristics of a jeweler's workshop, or a watch repairer's—but it is not entirely like either of those. It's
summer but the air is uncharacteristically chill, and not from air conditioning: it's stuffy, and there's a faint charnel-house scent, as if something
has died under the floorboards.

Dower has donned a pair of white cotton conservator's gloves and
hung a dictaphone around his neck. He keeps the bone-white violin at
arm's length, as if he doesn't want to hold it too close, muttering into his
microphone: "C-rib thickness varies between 3.2 and 5.5 millimeters; as
with the right lower curve, this material appears to be ductile and rigid,
although examination at 6X magnification reveals the characteristic
spongiform structure of endochondral ossification . . ." He swallows, as
if nauseous—as well he might be. (The instrument is indeed made of
bone, preserved and treated to give it a rigidity and resonance similar to
mountain maple. The treatments that modify the material in this way are
applied while its donor is still alive, and in excruciating pain.) Peering
into a fiber-optic probe, the end of which is inserted through one of the

violin's f-holes: "The upper block appears to be carved from the body and lesser cornu of *os hyoideum*; the greater cornu is avulsed in a manner usually indicative of death by strangulation . . ."

Dower may suspect, but the woman knows, that the materials used to construct this instrument were harvested from the bodies of no less than twelve innocents, whose premature deaths were believed to be an essential part of the process. Before he became a highly specialized instrument maker, Dower trained as a surgeon. He's a sensitive, trained to see what lies before his eyes: most people wouldn't recognize the true horror of the instrument, seeing merely a white violin. Which is why the woman came here, after checking the files for a list of suitable examiners.

After almost three hours, Dower is flagging, but his work is nearly done. The woman is checking her watch now, with increasing concern. Eventually, finally, he replaces the bow in its recess and folds the lid of the case shut, snapping the latches closed. He steps back and fastidiously peels off his gloves, then drops them in a rubbish bin, being careful not to touch their contaminated outer surface with his bare skin. Finally he clicks off the dictaphone. "I'm done," he says flatly.

The woman stands, smooths the wrinkles out of her skirt, and nods. "Your written report," she says.

"I'll write it up after I've had some lunch. You can collect it after four, this afternoon . . ."

She shakes her head. "I won't be back." Reaching into her bag she pulls out another envelope. "Print out one copy of your report—and no more—and place it in this envelope. Then seal it and post it." There is no address on the envelope. "After you have done that, you should destroy your records. Erase your word processor files, burn the tapes, whatever it takes. You will be held responsible if your report leaks."

"But there's no—" He takes the envelope. "You're sure?"

"If you post that envelope I will have the contents on my desk by morning," she tells him, staring at him with pale green eyes as unquiet as a storm surge.

"I don't want to see that thing ever again," he tells her.

"You won't."

"But you want to know how to make *more*—"

"No." Her face is as smooth as plaster, as if any hint of human emotion might crack the surface of her glaze: "I want to prove to my superiors that the cost is too high."

"Isn't that obvious?"

"Not given the magnitude of the threat we face. Desperate measures are called for; I merely believe this one to be *too* desperate. Good-bye, Mr. Dower. I trust we shall never meet again."

BACK IN THE OFFICE:

Photograph One:

A large slate, resting on a table beside a wooden measuring rod. According to the rod it is twenty inches high and (inferred using a ruler) eighteen inches wide. Cleaved along a plane, it reveals a well-preserved fossil of what appears to be a starfish of class Asteroidea.

On closer inspection, there is something wrong with the fossil. Although it possesses the characteristic five-fold symmetry, each tentacle tip appears to be blunt, as if truncated. Moreover, the body doesn't show signs of radial segmentation—it's an integral whole, giving an effect more like a cross section through an okra fruiting body, or perhaps an oversized echinoderm—a sea cucumber.

Photograph Two:

Is another large slab of broken rock, this time revealing the partially dissected and fossilized arm of a juvenile BLUE HADES . . .

Photograph Three:

Is in the pile Bob has just dumped on the floor.

I rub my eyes and quietly snarl: "Fuck this shit!" The temptation to start jumping up and down and shouting is well-nigh irresistible, but my office shares a plasterboard partition with that of an easily distracted computer-phobic project manager, and the last time I punched the wall he made me come round and put all of his GANT chart stickies back in the right order on pain of being forced to attend a training course on critical path analysis. Which is deeply unfair, in my book—if the lines on one of Roskill's charts don't join up, all that happens is a project goes over budget: nobody gets eaten or goes insane (unless the Auditors decide to get involved)—but there's no arguing with him: ex-RAF type, thinks he runs the country.

It's almost too late for lunch, and all I've succeeded in figuring out so far is that *F* had a lot of interesting correspondents in the Baltic states, not to mention a huge and not entirely rational hard-on for the Bolsheviks. (Mind you, he was a bit unhinged in more ways than that.) On the other hand, this Ransome chap seems to have had his head screwed on. A journalist, obviously, but corresponding with a colonel in the War Office? And his correspondence ended up filed in the Laundry archives? That's pretty suggestive. And those photographs . . . ! Roman Von Ungern Sternberg clearly had a disturbed childhood if his idea of fossil-collecting involved elder race relics. No wonder Daddy ended up in the loony bin and Mummy shacked up with a boringly conventional country squire with no questionable hobbies.

I look at the stack of files: nine of the bloody things, brown manila envelopes with dates and security classifications scribbled on their front, beneath the familiar Dho-Nha geometry curve of the Internal Security Sigil ("read this without authorization and your eyeballs will melt," or words to that effect in one of the simpler Enochian metalanguages).

They're identified by number, using a system we call the Codex Mathe-magica—four three-digit quads, just like IP addresses (and isn't *that* a significant coincidence, given that the Laundry archives predate the inter-net by thirty years? Although the Laundry stacks use decimal as a native format, not two hex digits, now that I think about it: Does that mean their original numeric routines were written to manage BCD primitives?)—with no overall meaning except that they're unique in the index . . .

Nine folders.

I rummage around on my desk for the original paper Angleton gave me. Weren't there ten files there? Ten sets of numbers? I can't find the note, damn it, but I know where I entered the document retrieval re-quest. I wake my computer and call up the transaction log. Yup, ten files requested.

I look under my desk. Then I look behind my desk. Then I look in the circular filing cabinet, just in case. I recount the folders, double-checking inside them just in case the missing file has been interleaved.

Nine folders. Shit.

Have you ever found yourself in a cold sweat, your palms clammy and your clothes sticking to the small of your back? Heart hammering, even though you're sitting down? Mouth dry as a mummy's tomb?

I am a rough, tough, hardened field agent (yeah, right). I have been in the Laundry for nearly a decade. I've met gibbering horrors from other universes, been psychically entangled with a serial killer fish goddess, stalked by zombies, imprisoned by a megalomaniac billionaire, and I've even survived the attention of the Auditors (when I was young, foolish, and didn't know any better). But I've never lost a classified file before, and I don't *ever* want there to be a first time.

I force myself to sit down and close my eyes for what feels like an hour, but is actually just under two minutes according to the clock on my computer's screen. When I open my eyes, the problem is still there, but the sweat is beginning to dry and the panicked feeling has receded . . . for now. So I get down on my knees and start picking up the photographs, working through them until I am certain I've got them all in sequence, and then I put them in the correct envelope and very carefully stack it on my chair.

I pick up a Post-it pad and copy the number on the front of the envelope. Then I repeat, eight times, for the remaining envelopes. Then I hunt across my desk until—aha!—I find Angleton's original spidery scrawl, numbers swimming before my eyes like exotic fish.

Ten numbers. I go through them checking off the files I've got, until I identify the number that's missing. 10.0.792.560. *Right.*

I call up the requisition and look for 10.0.792.560. Sure enough, it's there. So I ordered it, but it isn't in my office. *Double shit.* I dumpster-dive the transaction file, looking for my request: Did they fill it? *Oh. Oh my.* DOCUMENT NOT FOUND ON DESIGNATED SHELF.

I just about faint with relief, but manage to force myself to pick up the phone and dial the front desk number. "Hello? Archives?" The voice at the far end is female, distracted, a little squawky, and all human—for which I am grateful: not all the archive staff are warm-blooded.

"Hi, this is Bob Howard in Ops? Back on Thursday I requested an archival document retrieval, ten dead files. I'm going through them now, and one of them is missing. I've got a file number, and an annotation saying DOCUMENT NOT FOUND ON DESIGNATED SHELF. Can you tell me what that means?"

"It means"—she sounds irritated—"the librarian couldn't find your file. They looked where it was supposed to be and it wasn't there."

"Oh. Is there a direct mapping between the document reference number and a given shelf?"

"Yes, there is. You should really use code names and the index in case the file's been assigned a new number, you know. It happens sometimes. Do you have a codeword for me? I could look it up for you . . ."

"I'm sorry, my colleague just gave me a list of document reference numbers," I explain. "And he's, uh, off sick. So I'm trying to figure out what's missing. I was worried that the file had been sent over and got misplaced, but if it's missing in the stacks I suppose that just means it's been renumbered. Or he wrote down the wrong reference. Or something." I don't believe that last one for a split second—no way would Angleton get a file number wrong—but I don't want some nosy librarian poking her nose into my investigation. "Bye." I put the phone down and lean back, thinking.

Let's see: Angleton was working on BLOODY BARON. When I came back to the office he gave me a list of ten files to read, then he went missing. This coincides with an upswing in Russian activity, including a marked willingness to use extreme measures. Nine files came from the stacks, and they turn out to be tedious backgrounders relating indirectly to the historical investigation side of BLOODY BARON. The tenth file isn't on its shelf. All I've got is a number, not a name.

I think it's time to do some unofficial digging . . .

MEANWHILE, BACK TO THE HISTORICAL RECONSTRUCTION:

It is nearly six o'clock when Mr. Dower finishes typing his report.

He's lost track of the time, his head locked inside the scope of his post-mortem on the instrument. He's read about its like before. Their design is attributed to a deaf-mute German violinist in Paris in the early 1920s, but nobody actually built one until the ghastly Dr. Mabuse commissioned an entire string section from a certain Berlin instrument maker in 1931. (It should be no surprise that the instrument maker prospered under the subsequent regime, but was executed after a summary trial by SMERSH investigators in 1946.) This particular instrument made its way to the West in the luggage of a returning GI, was retrofitted with electric pick-ups during the 1950s, and after a spectacular run of accidents was acquired by a reclusive collector in 1962—believed by some to be a front for a British government department who, as a matter of state policy, did not like to see such instruments in the wrong hands.

He dreads to think what its reappearance portends. On the other hand, the young woman who brought it to him—Mr. Dower thinks of everyone aged under fifty as "young"—seemed to have a sober appreciation of its lethality.

He shudders fastidiously as the last of five pages of single-spaced description hisses out of the ink-jet printer. It joins the half dozen contact pages of photographs, including his fiber-optic examination of the interior of the instrument, and an invoice for just over two thousand pounds. He shakes the bundle of pages together, and binds them neatly with a paper clip from a desk drawer. Then they go inside the envelope the woman who called herself Cassie May gave him. He licks the flap and seals it, then, in a moment of curiosity, he switches on the anti-counterfeit lamp he keeps by the cash register and examines it under ultraviolet light. Nothing shows up: it bears none of the UV-fluorescent dots the Post Office prints on envelopes to control their routing.

If "Cassie May" thinks she can retrieve an unmarked envelope from the postal system she's welcome to it, in Mr. Dower's books. He turns back to the computer and deletes his work, then sighs and glances at the clock. Five minutes to closing time: no point keeping the shop open any longer. He stands and stretches, switches the computer off, and goes through an abbreviated version of his regular closing routine; no point banking the cash register contents (his takings before the woman's visit barely amounted to petty cash). He pulls on his coat, turns his coffee mug upside down on the draining board, switches off the lights, and opens the front door.

The woman is waiting for him. She smiles. "Have you finished your report?" she asks.

Mr. Dower nods, confused. "I was going to post it, as you requested." He pats his coat pocket.

"I'm in a hurry. There's a rush on. If you don't mind . . . ?" She looks at him impatiently.

"Of course." He pulls out the envelope and hands it to her. "My invoice is enclosed."

"You don't need to worry about that side of things." She slides the envelope into her black patent leather handbag and smiles.

"I suppose not. You people always pay your debts eventually."

"Yes, you can be absolutely certain of that."

He turns back to the door and fumbles with his key ring. Which is why he doesn't see her withdraw a silenced pistol from her bag, raise it to the back of his head, and discharge a single round into his cerebellum. The gun makes little sound—just the racking click of its action—but as she fires, the suppressor fitted to its muzzle frosts over with clear fluid, air in contact with it liquefying as it chills to just above absolute zero. Mr. Dower slumps forward against the door. The woman's arm follows him down with absolute precision and discharges a second round into the top of his skull, but it is unnecessary: he is already dead.

She looks around with green eyes as deep as sacrificial cenotes, eyes in which a sensitive witness might see luminous worms writhing. But there are no sensitive witnesses to see through the glamour: just the ordinary post-work crowd hurrying about their business on the London streets. For a moment her face shimmers, the facade sliding—her attention is strained, flying in too many directions to maintain the illusion effectively— but then she notices and pulls herself together. She returns the chilly pistol to her bag. Then, turning on one spiked heel, she strides away from the corpse: just another professional woman on her way home from the office. Nobody has witnessed the killing, and it will be twenty minutes before a passing policeman realizes that the drunk sleeping in the doorway is never going to rise again.

7.

BEER AND TEA

YOU CAN FOCUS ON THINKING YOURSELF INTO THE OTHER
guy's shoes until the cows come home, but it's not going to do you a
whole lot of good if he's actually wearing sandals. More to the point,
what if he's got an entire shoe rack to choose from, and the pair you need
is the one that's missing? There is a chicken-and-egg problem here, or
more accurately a sole-and-bootstrap one, and I'm not going to solve it
by sitting in my office. Nor am I going to fix matters by hollering down
the speaking tube at the gnomes buried in the stacks, not with just two
delivery runs a day.

On the other hand, if you go and actually look at the other guy's foot-
prints you might just find something new. And so, in a spirit of enquiry, I
set out to burgle Angleton's office.

Now, it just so happens that Angleton has officially been declared
missing. And I am his assistant trainee tea-boy. In a more paranoid working environment I might just be under suspicion of having disappeared
him myself: perish the thought and pass the ammunition. But Angleton is
reckoned to be sufficiently formidable that . . . well, let's say it's unlikely.
Besides, we don't generally play politics with the kid gloves off. (There

are exceptions, such as the late and unlamented Bridget; but they're exactly that: exceptions. The hard fact is that all the real players can turn the game board into a smoking hole in the map. Which generally forces them to tread lightly.)

Skulking past Iris's office window, I tiptoe around the coffee station and duck down the back staircase, through the fire doors, round the bend, down the fire escape stairs, and then pause outside the unmarked green metal door. I do not encounter anyone in the process, but you can never be sure—there are cameras, and there is Internal Security, and if you're really unlucky there are the caretakers from the night shift. This is a security agency after all. However slipshod and dustily eccentric it might appear at times, you should never take things for granted if you are perpetrating monkey business.

I pull out the NecronomiPod and fire it up. Happy fun icons glow at me: Safari, YouTube, Horned Skull, Settings, Bloody Runes, Messaging, Elder Sign, you know the interface. Bloody Runes gets me into the ward detector, which is showing the usual options. I point the camera at the door and peer into the shiny screen. Sure enough, in addition to Angleton's trademark Screaming Mind someone has ploddingly inscribed a Langford Death Parrot, with a sympathetic link to a web stats counter so they can monitor how many intruders it's headcrashed from the comfort of their laptop. *Tch*, what are standards coming to? I pause as a nasty thought strikes me and I triple-check the door frame, then the ceiling above the entrance, then the other side of the corridor, just in case—but no, nothing. This is strictly amateur hour stuff, so rather than zapping the LDP I pull out my conductive pencil and sketch in a breakpoint and then an exception list with a single item: the signature of my new ward. The Screaming Mind already knows me well. Three minutes later I put the phone away, place my hand on the doorknob, twist and push.

Angleton's office: here be monsters. Silent and cold, it is home to the ghosts of a war colder by far than the one the ignorant public thought we won in 1989—a room walled in floor-to-ceiling file drawers, a gunmetal desk with organ-pedals and teletype keyboard, dominated by a hooded microfiche reader—the silent heart of an intelligence stilled, no longer beating out the number station signals across the Iron Curtain. I half-expect to see cobwebs in the corners, to smell the stale cigarette ash of a thousand tense nights beneath the arctic skies, waiting for the bombers.

I shake myself. History lies thick as winter snow in this room: I could drown beneath its avalanche weight if I don't pull myself together. And in any case, Angleton was here—in his office I mean, not in this actual spot—*before* the cold war. I've seen a photograph from 1942, the man himself smiling at the camera, visibly no older (or younger) than he is today. It's an open question, the extent to which he was involved in the occult affairs of government before the Second World War. Just how far back does he go? Human Resources don't have a home address on file, which is itself suggestive. I wonder . . .

Before I sit down behind his desk, I scan the walls, floor, and ceiling up and down with the NecronomiPod. Sure enough, certain of the file drawers are booby-trapped with lethal-looking webworks of magic—not drawn in the plodding journeyman hand of the outer door's vandal, but sketched in Angleton's spidery scrawl, complex arcs and symbols linking arcane declarations and gruesome probability matrices. I could reverse engineer them in time and maybe worm my way inside, but knowing the boss there's probably nothing there but nitrogen triiodide on the drawer rails and a jack-in-the-box loaded with tear gas: he was a firm believer in keeping the crown jewels in his head—or its annex, the thing in the green metal desk.

The Memex . . .

You've got to understand that although I've read about the things, I've never actually *used* one. It's an important piece of the history of computing, leaked to the public as a think-piece commissioned by the *Atlantic Weekly* in 1945; most of the readers thought it was a gosh-wow-by-damn good idea, but were unlikely to realize that a number of the things had actually been built, using a slush fund earmarked for the Manhattan Project. The product of electromechanical engineering at its finest, not to mention its most horrendously complex, each Memex cost as much as a B-29 bomber—and contained six times as many moving parts, most of them assembled by watchmakers. It wasn't until HyperCard showed up on the Apple Mac in 1987 that anything like it reached the general public.

I believe Angleton's Memex is the only one that is still working, much less in day-to-day use, and to say it takes black magic to keep it running would be no exaggeration. I approach the seat with considerable caution, and not just because I'm absolutely certain he will have taken steps to ensure that anyone who sits in it without his approval and pushes the big red on button will never push another button in their (admittedly short) life; *he* knows how to use the thing, but if I crash it or break the cylinder head gasket or something *and he comes back,* the only shoes I'd be safe in would be a pair of NASA-issue moon boots (and maybe not even then).

I drag the wooden chair back from the Memex—the tiny casters squeak like agonized rodents across the worn linoleum floor—and lower myself gingerly into the cracked leather seat. The oak arms are worn smooth beneath my hands, where his palms have pressed upon them over the decades. I grab the solid sides of the desk and ease myself forward until my feet rest lightly on the pedals. There's an angled glass strip facing me from the far end of the desk, and a light in the leg-well that comes on as my heels touch the kick-plate: it's a periscope, giving me a view of my toes and the letters at the back of each pedal. I turn the gunmetal turret of the microfiche reader towards me, place the NecronomiPod on the desktop, and push the power button.

There's a clunk of relays closing, and then a thrumming vibration runs through the machine. It's easy to forget that though it weighs more than a ton, its average component weighs less than two grams: the gears alone took two months' entire output from the largest watch factory in America. I stare into the hooded circular screen in something like awe. Machined to submicron precision, yet less powerful than the ancient 68EC000 in my washing machine, these devices were the backbone of the Laundry's Intelligence Analysis section in the late 1940s. It's like a steam locomotive or a stone axe: just because it's obsolete doesn't make it any less of an achievement, or any less fit for purpose.

The screen lights up—not like an LCD monitor, or even an old cathode ray tube, but more like an antique film projector.

WRITE USERNAME.

The moment of truth: I cautiously kick-type BOB, then spend a fruitless minute hunting for the return key before I realize there's a paddle-shaped lever protruding level with my left knee—like the handle on a manual typewriter. I nudge it.

There's a *clunk* from inside the desk and the injunction vanishes, to be replaced by a picture of the organization coat of arms. Then more words appear, scrolling in from the bottom of the screen, wobbling slightly:

WRITE CLEARANCE.

What the hell? I laboriously type BLOODY BARON, and knee the return paddle. (There's something weird about the foot-keyboard: then I twig to the fact that its abbreviated supply of characters means it's probably a Baudot Code system. Which figures. Older than ASCII . . .)

The screen fades to white after a couple of seconds, then a bloody sigil flashes into view. It doesn't kill me to look at it, but the disquieting sense that the void is inspecting the inside of the back of my skull makes me squirm on my seat. There is an eye-warping loop to one side of it that feels familiar, as if it's tied to my soul somehow.

WRITE: STILL ALIVE? Y/N:

Knees knocking, I type Y (RETURN).

WELCOME BOB, YOU ARE AUTHENTICATED.

If you are reading this message, I am absent. Welcome to the dead man's boots: hope you don't find them too tight. You are one of only four people who have access to this machine (and at least two of them are dead or dying of K Syndrome).

You may: read all files not flagged with a Z-prefix, search all files not flagged with a Z-prefix, and print any files flagged with a prefix from A to Q.

You may not: read or search Z-prefix files. Print files flagged with a prefix from S to Z. Dismantle or reverse-engineer this instrument.

WARNING: LETHAL ENFORCEMENT PROTOCOLS ARE EN-
FORCED.

WRITE: GOTO MAIN MENU? Y/N:

This is Angleton. He doesn't bluff. I make a note of those clearances
on my phone, then, hesitantly, I type Y.

I have, in fact, seen worse-designed user interfaces. There are abominations out there that claim to be personal media players that—but I digress. The Memex is a miracle of simplicity and good design, as long as
you bear in mind that it's operated by foot pedals (except for the paper
tape punch), the display is a microfilm reader, and it can't display more
than ten menu choices on screen at any time. Unlike early digital computers such as the Manchester Mark One, you don't need to be Alan Turing
and debug raw machine code on the fly by flashing a torch at the naked
phosphor memory screen; you just need to be able to type on a Baudot
keyboard using both feet (with no delete key and lethal retaliation promised if you make certain typos). There's nothing here that's remotely as
hostile as VM/CMS to a UNIX hacker. I've just got an edgy feeling that
the Memex is reading *me*, and sitting in quietly humming judgment. So I
spend half an hour reading the quick start guide, and then . . .

WRITE: DOCUMENT TO RETRIEVE:

I find the shift pedal, kick the Memex into numerical entry mode, and
type:

FETCH 10.0.792.560

NOT FOUND.

WRITE: DOCUMENT TO RETRIEVE:

Shit. I try again.

FETCH INDEX.

There is a whirring and a chunking sound from within the desk. *Aha!*
After several sluggish seconds a new menu appears.

WRITE: ENTER DOCUMENT CODE NUMBER:

FETCH 10.0.792.560

More whirring and a brief pause. Then the screen clears, to display
everything the Memex knows about the missing file:

DOCUMENT INDEX ENTRY:
NUMBER: 10.0.792.560
TITLE: THE FULLER MEMORANDUM
DEPOSIT DATE: 6-DECEMBER-1941
STORAGE LOCATION: STACK VAULT 10.0.792.560
COPY STATUS: FORBIDDEN
CLASSIFICATION: BEYOND TOP SECRET, Z-CLEARANCE
EXPIRATION: DOES NOT EXPIRE
CODEWORDS: TEAPOT, WHITE BARON, CASE NIGHTMARE
GREEN
SEE ALSO: Z-ANGLETON, Z-EXECUTION PROTOCOLS, Z-
FINAL EXIT
END OF INDEX ENTRY

CLASSIFIED: S76/47

Dear John,

Once again, greetings from Reval. I hope you can forgive my lack of enthusiasm; it's godforsaken cold here in January. I thought I knew what winter was (Moscow in winter is enough to teach anyone a grudging respect for Jack Frost) but this is absolutely unspeakable. There are few railways in Estonia, and those which remain after the armistice are under military control, to deter any passing fancy that might occur to Comrade Trotsky in his spare time. (I am sure we shall not be invaded again, at least before he has finished pacifying Siberia, but one can hardly blame Mr. Piip for his caution.)

I have a most unexpected cause to write to you—a gift horse just presented its head at my transom window! Such a gift horse was this that it would be insane not to look it in the mouth, but I have inspected its back teeth and I assure you that the mare is, although middle-aged, by no means anything other than that which it appears to be: namely, the bereaved mother of the Prodigal we were discussing in our earlier correspondence.

It seems that my sympathetic questioning made more of an impression on Madame Hoyningen-Huene than I imagined. There was a brief thaw in the bitter cold we have lately been experiencing, and being of a mind to visit the capital for a few weeks she took advantage of it. She is even now ensconced in our parlor, where Evgenia is entertaining her.

And the Prodigal son's fossil collection?

"Take them!" she cried. "Oskar told me how they caught your fancy; perhaps you know of a curator in London who will put them to some better use? Vile things, I don't want to remember my son by them!" Her man, who was burdened with the heavy box all the way from Rapla to Reval, can only have wholeheartedly agreed. And so they are even now in a shipping trunk, awaiting more clement weather before I dispatch them to you by sea.

Madame Hoyningen-Huene is a sensitive soul, and her life has been blighted by domestic tragedy, from her first husband's breakdown and incarceration to the deaths of two baby daughters, and now to the fate that has overtaken her son (however much he might have deserved it). She takes little interest in politics, and is transparently what she is: the daughter of Baron Von Wimpffen of Hesse, wife of Baron Oskar Von Hoyningen-Huene, a devoted family lady. Quite why her life has circled this vortex of unspeakable tragedy eludes her entirely, as does the nature of her privileged upbringing and the precarious status of the Prussian aristocracy in the Baltic states—but she is near to sixty, a child of the previous century, and simply unable to adapt to the chill winds of change sweeping the globe.

"He wrote to me often of his fears and uncertainties," she said, showing me a sheaf of letters. I think she needed to share her pain, that of a mother for her son, the last love and succor of any man, however much of a brute he may be. "You see, he was by inclination deeply religious, but unfortunately it brought him much pain. I hold the shamanic eastern mystics responsible—vile orientals! And the Jews." Her aristocratic nostrils flared. "If they hadn't fomented this disgraceful revolution he would not have thought to rise up against the government." (Such sentiments are common among the aristocracy here; they have an unhealthy identification with the late Tsar.)

"What *did* he believe?" I asked. "As a matter of curiosity . . ."

"Ohh—he took it into his head to convert to a vile farrago of oriental superstitions! Nothing as honest and Aryan as Theosophy. He picked these filthy beliefs up in Mongolia, nearly ten years ago, when visiting. He met a witch doctor by all accounts, a man called the Bogd Khan—" She rattled on at some length about this.

"Would you mind if I read his letters on religion?" I asked her, and to cut a long story short, she acceded. I now have not only Ungern Sternberg's fossil collection, inherited from his father, but his surviving letters—those he sent to his mother. And they are very interesting indeed.

I attach my (admittedly imperfect) translation of selected extracts of his letters from 1920; I will forward the originals by separate cover from the fossils. Meanwhile, I strongly recommend that you should motivate your fellows in the Order to start searching for the missing Teapot.

Your obedient friend,
Arthur Ransome

THERE COMES A TIME IN EVERY COUNTERESPIONAGE INVESTI-gation when you have to grit your teeth, admit that you're at your wits' end, admit defeat, and bugger off home for a Chinese takeaway and a night in front of the telly. Then you get a good night's sleep (except for the nocturnal eructations induced by too much black bean sauce) and awaken, refreshed and revived and in a mood to do battle once more with—

Bollocks.

I *have* gotten somewhere: I now know that the missing file is called the Fuller Memorandum (which by a huge leap of inductive logic—I hope I'm not getting ahead of myself here—I deduce is a memorandum, by or about *F*). It was filed in 1941, was absolutely mega-top-secret burn-before-reading stuff sixty-five years ago, and has some bearing on CASE NIGHTMARE GREEN. It's also missing. Those last three facts would be enough to give me industrial-grade stomach ulcers if it was my fault. Luckily, it's not my fault. All I have to do is find Angleton and I'm sure he can explain it all, and also explain what the flaming fuck it has got to do with BLOODY BARON.

This much is not time-critical. Getting that Chinese takeaway, with or without black bean sauce, is time-critical, lest I starve to death on the case. Going home and doing sweet, sappy, quality time things with Mo is time-critical too, lest she files for divorce on grounds of neglect. And so is not having a nervous breakdown while waiting for the board of enquiry findings, lest I find myself without a career, in which case they'll put me in charge of pushing that handcart full of dusty files around the department. So I stand up, stretch, push the off button on the Memex, and leave Angleton's lair.

I pause briefly in my own rabbit hutch of an office, scan my email, respond to a couple of trivial pestiferations (no, I am no longer in charge of the structured cabling specifications for D Block; yes, I am still attached to the international common insourcing and acquisition standards committee, for my sins in a previous life; no, I do not have a desktop license for Microsoft Office, because my desktop PC is a Microsoft-free zone for security reasons—and would you like fries with that?). The scanner has finished digesting all those dusty letters from Arthur to John; I squirt the PDFs across to the NecronomiPod and then I grab my backpack and umbrella and head for home. Iris isn't in her office as I pass the window, and Rita on the front desk has pissed off early—then I check my watch and do a double take. It's six forty. Shit. *Mo will kill me,* I think as I head down the main staircase at a fast clip and barrel through the staff exit.

This is London. South Bank, south of the center, north of Tooting, and west of Wandsworth (come on, you can alliterate too)—suburban high street UK. It is early evening and the streets are still crowded, but most of the shops are closed. Meanwhile, the pubs are half-full with the sort of hardcore post-work crowd that go drinking on a Monday evening. I turn left, walking towards the nearest tube station: it's fifteen minutes away but once it gets this late there's no point waiting for a bus.

This is London. The worst thing that can happen to you is usually a mugging at knifepoint, and I do my best not to look like a promising victim, which is why it takes me a couple of minutes to realize that I'm being tailed. In fact, it takes until the three of them move to box me in: at that point, disbelief is futile. I've done the mandatory Escape and Evasion training, not to mention Streetwise 101; I just wasn't expecting to need it here.

Two of them are strong, silent types in black leather biker jackets worn over white tees and jeans. They've got short stubbly blond hair and the sort of muscles you get when you go through a Spetsnaz training course—not bodybuilders: more like triathletes. They come up behind me and march along either side, too damn close. The third of them, who I guess is their boss, is a middle-aged man in a baggy Italian suit, his open shirt collar stating that he's off the office clock and on his own time. He slides in just ahead and to the left of Thug #1 as I glance sideways. He winks at me. "Please to follow this way," he says.

I glance to my right. Thug #2 matches my stride, step for step. He stares at me like a police dog that's had its vocal cords severed. I glimpse his eyes and look away hastily. Shit.

"Who are you?" I ask, my tongue dry and stumbling, as Mr. Baggy Suit pauses in the doorway of the Frog and Tourettes.

"You may wish to call me Panin." He smiles faintly. "Nikolai Panin. It's not my real name, but it will serve." He gestures at the door. "Please allow me to buy you a drink. I assure you, my intentions are honorable."

My ward is itching; nevertheless I am disinclined to bet my life on it. Panin, whoever he is, is a player: his definition of "honorable" might not encompass allowing me to escape with my life, but he's unlikely to start something in the middle of a pub with an after-work crowd. "Would you mind leaving the muscle outside?" I ask. "I assume they're not drinking."

"*Nyet.*" He snaps his fingers and says something to the two revenants. They split, taking up positions to either side of the street front of the pub. "After you," he says, waving me into the entrance.

If I was James Bond, this is the point at which I would draw my concealed pistol, plug both heavies between the eyes, get Panin in an armlock, and pistol-whip some answers out of him. But I am not James Bond, and I don't want to precipitate a diplomatic incident by assaulting the Second Naval Attaché and a couple of embassy guards or footballers or whatever (not to mention sparking a murder investigation which would result in the Plumbers having to conduct a gigantic and expensive cover-up operation, all of which would come out of my departmental operating budget and drive Iris to distraction). And anyway, everyone knows that you don't get useful answers by torturing people, you get useful answers by making them trust you.

(*Why don't you talk to them?* I'd asked the committee.

(*Because we might unintentionally tell them something they don't already know,* said Choudhury, after staring at me for a minute as if I'd grown a second head.

(Fuck that shit, like I said.)

So I let Panin buy me a pint. "By the way, do you mind if I text my wife to tell her I'm going to be late?" I ask.

"If you think it necessary, but I promise I will keep you only half an hour."

"Thanks." I smile gratefully and whip out the NecronomiPod and tap out a text: HAVING A BEER WITH UNCLE FESTER'S BOSS, HOME LATE. Panin holds up a purple drinking voucher and it has the desired effect: money and a pair of pint glasses change hands. He carries them over to a small table in the back of the pub and I follow him. Panin's assistants gave me a nasty turn, but it seems this is to be a friendly chat, albeit for extremely unusual values of friendly. I keep both my hands on the table. Wouldn't do to give the Spetsnaz goons the wrong idea—I have a feeling it would take more than Harry's AA-12 shotgun to stop them in their tracks.

"To health, home, and happiness," he proposes, raising his glass.

"I'll drink to that." My ward doesn't nudge me as I bring the drink to my lips. "So. I guess you wanted to talk?"

"Mm, yes." Panin, having taken a mouthful, puts his glass down. "Do you have any clues to its whereabouts?"

"Have what?" I ask cautiously.

"The teapot."

"Tea—" I take another mouthful of ESB. "Pot?" There was something about a teapot in those letters, wasn't there? Something Choudhury said in the meeting, maybe?

"It's missing." Panin sounds impatient. "Your people have lost it, yes?"

I decide to play dumb. "If any teapots have gone missing, I suppose Facilities would be the people who'd deal with that . . . Why do you ask?"

"You English!" For a moment, Panin looks exasperated, then he quickly pulls a lid over it. "The teapot is missing," he repeats, as if to a very slow pupil. "It has been missing since last week. Everyone is looking for it, us, you, the opposition . . . ! You were its last keepers. Please, I implore you, find it? For all our sakes, find it before the wrong people get their hands on it and *make tea*."

Committed to paper, this dialogue might sound comical: but coming from Panin's mouth, in his soft, clipped diction, it is anything but.

I shiver. "Ungern Sternberg's teapot didn't get misplaced by accident," I hazard.

Panin's response takes me by surprise: "Idiot!" He leans back in disgust, raises his glass, and takes a deep and disrespectful swig. "You are fishing, now."

Bother, I've been rumbled. "'Fraid so. Let me level with you? I know it's missing, but that's all I know. But I'll tell you what, if you can tell me what happened in Amsterdam last Wednesday and why it followed my wife home on Thursday I would be very grateful."

"Amster—" Panin shuts his mouth with a click. "Your wife is unhurt, I hope?" he asks, all nervous solicitude.

"Shaken." But not stirred. "The—intruder—was attributed to your people, did you know that?"

"Not unexpected." Panin makes a gesture of dismissal with one hand. "They do that, you know. To muddy the waters."

"Who? The opposition?"

Panin gives me that look again, the look you might give to the friendly but stupid puppy that's just widdled on the carpet for the third time that day. "Tell me, Mr. Howard, what do *you* know?"

I sigh. "Not much, it seems. I have been seconded to a committee that's trying to work out why you folks are currently running up an eBay reputation score like there's no tomorrow. I am trying to deal with an unpleasant domestic situation, namely work following my wife home. My boss is out of the office, and I'm trying to pick up the pieces. If you thought you could shake me down for useful information, I'm afraid you picked the wrong spy. I could tell you more than you could possibly want to know about the structured cabling requirements for our new headquarter building's fourth subbasement, but when it comes to missing teapots, nobody put me on the flash priority classified briefing list."

"I see." Panin looks gloomy. "Well, Mr. Howard, many would not believe you—but I do. So, here is my card." He passes me a plain white business card—unprinted on either side, but pressed from a very high grade of linen weave. It makes my fingertips tingle. "Should you have anything to discuss, call me."

I slide it into my breast pocket. "Thanks."

"As for the teapot, it was never the same after Ungern Sternberg retrieved it from the Bogd Khan's altar."

He's studying my face. I do my best not to twitch. I've heard those names before. "I'll keep my eyes open for it," I reassure him.

"I'm sure you will," he says gravely. "After all, it would be in everyone's best interests for the teapot to return to its rightful office." He drains his beer glass. "I will see you around, I am sure," he says, rising.

"Bye." I raise my glass to his back as he turns towards the door, shoulders hunched.

CLASSIFIED: S76/47 ANNEX A

Dear Mother,

Salutations from Urga! I greet you as Khan Sternberg, Outstanding Prosperous-State Hero of Mongolia, first warlord and general of the Living Buddha and Emperor of Mongolia, His Holiness Bogd Djebtsung Damba Hutuktu! Great events, bloody battle, heroic struggle, and glorious victory have contrived to elevate me to the threshold of my destiny, as inheritor of the empire of Genghis Khan. It is spring in Mongolia, and already I have purged this land of Bolsheviks, terrorists, and subhumans; soon my armies will commence their march on St. Petersburg, to restore the blessed Prince Michael to his rightful throne and to cleanse Mother Russia of the depravity of revolution and the filthy degenerates who have turned their back on the holy Tsar.

(Once I have restored the Tsar I consider it my duty to retake those lands that have been stolen from the Empire, including our homeland. I trust you will think kindly of me for raising the yoke of anarchist tyranny from the necks of the true aristocracy of Estonia when I come to purify the Baltic lands and restore the just weight of monarchy to the upstart Poles.)

The conquest of Urga presented me with a considerable challenge, and I shall describe it for you. Urga lies in a valley between hills, along the banks of the Tula river. When I laid siege to it, the river was frozen; but the degenerate Chinese occupiers had constructed trenches, barricades and barbed wire defenses around Upper Maimaichen . . .

[*Lengthy description of the siege of Ulan Bator, 1920.*]

Now *here* is a curiosity:

When we stormed the palace of the Bogd Khan to take the Living Buddha from his Chinese captors, the fighting was fierce: after liberating His Holiness my men executed a tactical withdrawal. But once his excellency was safe, when I ordered the main attack on the Chinese host occupying the city, I detailed a reliable man—my ensign Evgenie Burdokovskii, who the men call Teapot—to secure the treasury against looters. It is a sad fact that Reds and wreckers are everywhere and in these degenerate times the swine I have to work with—rejects and deserters of the once-great army—are as likely to turn to banditry and crime as to bend the neck before my righteous authority. Burdokovskii is a stout fellow, a cossack: powerful and broad-chested, with a little curly blond head and a narrow forehead. He always does what I ask of him, which is a blessing, and if there is one man I would trust to stand guard on a treasure-house for me, it is he.

During the occupation, Teapot set his sixteen men to stand guard with bayonets fixed outside the great hall where the treasures and gifts of five hundred lamaseries are kept. It is a remarkable place, a museum of wonders unknown in all of Europe. There is a library with shelves devoted to manuscripts in a myriad of languages, and there are chests full of amber from the shores of the Northern Sea, carved walrus and ivory tusks, rings with sapphires and rubies from China and India, rough diamonds the size of your fingertip, bags of golden thread filled with pearls, and side-rooms filled with cases containing statues of the Living Buddha made from every precious material under the sun.

Now Teapot is among the most obedient of my officers, but in the course of restoring order to the city and chasing the remaining enemy rabble out into the wilderness it was some days before I could return with the Bogd Khan to inspect his treasures. In that time I am afraid to say that he disgraced himself. Teapot did not steal the Buddha's treasures, else I would have hanged him as high as any other wretch; but he idly looked through the library, and I fear what he did may turn out for the worse in the long run.

There are, as you can imagine, scrolls and books unnumbered in there, and they include the most remarkable works of sorcery and prophecy imaginable. All the numerous punishments of hell that are reserved for souls who indulge in the sins of the flesh are documented and indeed illustrated in the finest, one might almost say pornographic, detail. It was to these works that Teapot allowed his salacious imagination to draw him.

It is not clear exactly when Teapot found the scroll, but two days after the fall of the palace his sergeant was dismayed to come upon him lying on the floor of the library, crying inarticulately and clutching a crumpled fragment of scripture in his chubby hands. According to the other witnesses, who I have questioned diligently, Teapot showed other signs of distress: bleeding from the eyes, moaning, and clutching his belly.

They put him to bed in the hospital supervised by Dr. Klingenberg, who was minded to euthanize Teapot to spare him from this misery, but wiser counsel prevailed and my cossacks continued to care for him until he began to recover the following day, babbling in tongues and occasionally ululating: "Ieyah! Ieyah!"

On the third day, just as I was on my way back to the palace, Teapot is said to have sat up in bed, whereupon he asked, "What year is it?" Upon being told it was 1920, he collapsed in a dead faint. And although he is now back at his duties, he is *not the same*. There is a cold intellect in him that was hitherto absent. Before, he was a loyal brute, but limited: he gave no thought to the morrow. Now he anticipates my orders with eerie efficiency, organizes the men under his command to meet any contingency, shows an unerring ability to sniff out spies—indeed, he has begun to unnerve me, the more so since I discovered he has other qualities. It is commonplace for war to degrade a good man to the level of a brute, but unique in my experience for it to elevate one such as Ensign Burdokovskii.

Consequently, I would like to ask a favor of you, dear mother.

Enclosed with this letter I send a copy of the Buddhist scripture that so turned Teapot's mind. It is written in an archaic dialect of Barghu-Buryat. I have heard that Professor Sartorius of the Schule des Toten Sprachen in Berlin has some expertise in material of this nature, and I would deeply appreciate it if you could forward the document to him and commission a translation, at my expense! This is a matter that I am extremely reluctant to entrust to any of my political associates, for they scheme and plot incessantly, and I am sure there are many who believe that I dabble in the blackest sorcery; I would not like to place such incendiary ammunition in their hands. I implore you not to soil your precious eyes with the contents of this scroll, for it is illustrated with such vile and obscene diagrams that I would be tempted to burn it, were it not for the effect it seems to have on those who read it! But it is for that very reason that I urgently need to obtain the advice of a savant who might tell me what those who read the fragment become. And so, I commit it to your gentle hands.

Your loving son,
General Baron Ungern Von Sternberg

8.

CLUB ZERO

I GET HOME AN HOUR AND A HALF LATE, BONE-TIRED, BAMBOO-zled, and bothered. I haven't had a good day at the office, all things considered: a confusing briefing on Russian OCCINT activities in Western Europe, an old acquaintance who doesn't recognize me anymore, the discovery that the Fuller Memorandum is missing, and now Panin's evident patronizing contempt for my lack of insight. I've got a feeling that all the pieces of the jigsaw are within my grasp, if only I could figure out where they lie—probably dragged under the sofa by an invisible cat, knowing my luck.

It's after eight as I turn my key in the lock, pass my left hand over the ward, and slope into the front hall. The lights are on in the kitchen, and there's a pleasant smell—Mo is roasting a chicken, I think. "Hello?" I call.

"Up here!" She's upstairs and she doesn't sound pissed off, which is a relief.

I dump my jacket and take the stairs two at a time. The bathroom door's open and she's stewing herself in the tub in an inordinate amount of green foam and some kind of mud mask, so that she looks a little like the creature from the black lagoon. "Did you get my text?" I ask.

"Yes. Who was the Addams Family reference about?"

I do a double take: "What— Oh shit." I shake my head. "Never mind." Obviously she can't read my mind, otherwise there'd have been an Artist Rifles' brick staking out the pub before I'd taken my first mouthful of beer. *I'm losing my touch.* "I'm screwing up," I admit.

"You're . . . ? Huh. Bet you I've had a more boring day."

"*Boring*, maybe; unproductive, hardly."

She snorts and blows a handful of bubbles my way. "I spent most of the morning and afternoon sitting on a wooden stool, watching a burned-out sixty-something expert mumble into a dictaphone. Then I had to run for a meeting. After that I looked in on the office but Mike wasn't there, so I came home. Picked up a free-range bird at Waitrose; it's in the oven now. I was hoping you might want to fix some side helpings?"

"I can do that." I glance at the bath. "You going to be long?"

"Half an hour at least. I put the chicken in before I came up here; you want to look in on it in fifteen minutes or so."

I'd rather spend my time here with her, but I can tell the difference between an order and a request: I sketch a salute. "By the way," I say, trying to sound casual about it, "I've been stuck with Angleton's work on BLOODY BARON, and I'm finding it a bit confusing. And nobody's sent me the briefing papers on the other job yet, the one—you know. Last week."

She's silent for almost a minute. Then she sighs. "There's a bottle of Bordeaux at the back of the cupboard under the plates and crockery. Open it and give it a while to breathe."

"Okay. Um, sorry." I back out of the bathroom, leaving her to try and rebuild the warm, scented bubble that I just burst.

I scrub and boil potatoes, then shove them in a roasting pan, check the chicken, chop some carrots, and have the vegetables just about ready when Mo comes downstairs in her bathrobe, hair in a towel. "Smells good," she remarks, then looks skeptically at my potatoes. "Hmm." She takes over; I get the plates out and pour two generous glasses of wine. It's later than I expected and I'm really rather hungry.

Food and wine settle stomach and soul; neither of us is a very sophisticated cook (although Mo is much more experimentally minded than I am), but we can eat what we prepare for ourselves, which is a good start, and after half an hour we've methodically demolished half a small roast chicken and a pan of roast vegetables, not to mention most of a bottle of wine. Mo looks content as I shove the plates in the dishwasher and sort out the recyclable bits. "You wanted to know what Thursday was about," she says, staring at what's left in her wineglass.

"I keep running into people who expect me to know." I go in search of another bottle to open. "It's not something I can ignore."

"How much of CLUB ZERO are you familiar with?"

"I'm not." I get the waiter's friend out and go to work on a pinot noir.

"Oh." She pauses. "I'm sorry, but—are you *sure* you don't know?"

"Don't know *what*?" I ask irritably as I scrape away the plastic seal on the bottle. "Are we in known unknowns territory, or unknown unknowns?"

"They're *known* okay." She shakes her head. "Fucking cultists."

"Cul—" I do a double take. "*That's* CLUB ZERO?"

She nods. "None other."

Cultists. They're like cockroaches. We humans are incredibly fine-tuned by evolution for the task of spotting coincidences and causal connections. It's a very useful talent that dates back to the bad old days on the savannah (when noticing that there were lion prints by the watering hole and then cousin Ugg went missing, and today there are *more* lion prints and nobody had gone missing yet, was the kind of thing that could save your skin). But once we developed advanced lion countermeasures like stone axes and language, it turned into our secret curse. Because, you see, when we spot coincidences we assume there's an intentional actor behind them—and that's how we create religions. Nature does weird stuff, so it must be governed by supernature. There's lightning in the clouds: Zeus must be throwing his thunderbolts again. Everyone's dying of plague except those weird folks with the strange god who wash every day: it must be evil sorcery. And so on.

Being predisposed to religion has its uses, but it's a real Achilles' heel if your civilization is under threat by vastly powerful alien horrors. We have a rich repertoire of primate behavior which includes the urge to suck up to the big bad alpha male, and a tendency to assume that any intelligence smarter or nastier than we are is the top of the pack hierarchy. Finally, we've got any number of dark religions out there. The followers of Kali or Mictecacihuatl or the various other faces of the lady of death. Certain splinter sects of millennialist Christianity who believe that the Revelation of St. John is black propaganda and that Satan will triumph. Strange heresies, by-blows of the Albigensians who trace their heritage back to secret cells who worshiped Ahriman in the palace basements of the Persian Empire. Other groups who are less familiar: syncretistic heresies spawned by bizarre collisions between seekers of hidden knowledge and followers of Tibetan demon princes. And, of course, bat-winged squid gods, although I find it hard to believe that anyone takes *that* seriously these days.

None of their specific beliefs matter. What matters is that if a cell or coven or parish or whatever get their hands on a genuine summoning ritual, the things at the other end of the occult courtesy phone aren't fussy about what they're called as long as the message is "chow time."

I take a deep breath. "What variety of cult was it this time?"

"The rich American expat kind." She takes a deep breath.

"American? But didn't the Black Chamber—"

"*They* didn't lift a finger." Her voice rises. "Instead, the Dustbin got a reluctant tip-off from the FBI that a bunch of nutty Jeezmoids from the every-sperm-is-sacred crowd were planning on making a big splash at the UN Population Fund summit in Den Haag last week. It's not terrorism in America this decade if they shoot doctors or firebomb family planning clinics, you know?"

I let her simmer for a minute while I pull the cork on the wine bottle and pour the last of the first bottle into her glass. "How did it get punted our way?"

"Chatter and crosstalk." She drains her glass and shoves it towards me. "These aren't your regular god-botherers, they've got form." (A history of criminal activity, in other words.) "The Dustbin and the Donut are both keeping tabs on them. They tipped off the Dutch AIVD, which is good, but then they forgot to include us in the loop, which was anything *but* good. What finally pulled us in was when the AIVD Watch Team who were keeping an eye on the hundred kilograms of sodium chlorate and the primer cords they'd stockpiled noticed the church supplies catalog and the white goats. The Free Church of the Universal Kingdom—"

"The Free Church of the *what*?"

Mo takes a big mouthful of wine. "The Free Church of the Universal Kingdom. Officially they're pre-millennial dispensationalists with a couple of extra twists, subtype: utterly barking and conflicted; oh hell. According to their party line Jesus was just there to set a good example, and we all have the ability to save ourselves. *Who* will be saved is predestined from the beginning of time, it's their job to bring the Church militant to everybody on the planet by fire and the sword, and, er, it gets complicated real fast, in ever diminishing epicycles of crazy. I swear, the doctrinal differences between some of these schismatic churches are fractal . . . Anyway, the key insight you need to bear in mind is, they're anti–birth control. *Very* anti–birth control, with overtones of accelerating the Second Coming by bringing more souls to Earth until Jesus can't ignore their suffering anymore—is this ringing any bells yet?"

"You're telling me they're CASE NIGHTMARE GREEN groupies?"

Mo nods vigorously. "They're mesmerized. What they believe *doesn't make sense* in terms of traditional Christian theology, never mind real-world logic. That's because the outer church is just a cover for something even weirder. The members we were monitoring were laboring under a really horrid glamour, level four or higher—I'm not sure."

I shudder. I knew someone with a level three glamour about her once. Men would die for a chance to bed her if she crooked her little finger at them—often literally. The theological equivalent . . . I don't want to think about it. "So. Amsterdam, then . . . ?" I prompt her.

"Four of them were already there. Another three flew in the week before; that's why the full-dress incident watch was started. AIVD thought it was preparation for an abortion clinic bombing campaign at first. But then the pastor bought a couple of white goats and the penny dropped and they threw it at Franz and his friends, who asked us to chip in."

"Goats—"

"Goats, sacrificial, summoning, for the purpose of. The Watch Team were so busy keeping an eye on the explosives stockpile that nobody noticed the metalworking tools and the crucifixes, or the fact that they'd rented a deconsecrated Lutheran chapel three months earlier and invited their bishop over for a flying visit. It was only last Tuesday that they put two and two together and realized what was really going on. That's when they called me in."

She looks bleak and alone, clutching her wineglass as if it's the sole source of warmth in the world.

"The bomb was a decoy. Turns out there were two cells working, one of whom—outer church—didn't know they were set up as a cover story. The other cell, the ones with the goat and the summoning grid in the crypt of the chapel, they were the *real* operators, initiates of the true faith. They were all set to open a gate to a, a—" She swallows. I sit down next to her and take her free hand in mine. "I *hate* those things," she says plaintively.

"It wasn't just goats, was it?" I probe. "The goats were the setup for something else."

"The chapel was right next to a nursery school," she says, and falls silent.

Ick is about all I can say to that, so I keep my mouth shut and squeeze her hand gently until she feels like continuing.

"We'd picked up a squad of UIM specialists and a police anti-terrorism group who prepared to seal off the area. Trouble is, it was mid-afternoon and the neighborhood was busy; the last thing you want to do is to run an anti-terrorism exercise next door to a nursery school when the parents are coming to pick their kids up. It's a target-rich zone and it draws journalists like flies to a sewage farm. So we were going to hold off until evening. But then the OCCULUS command truck monitors lost the sound from the bugs, and I began to pick up probability disturbances in the vicinity of the chapel, and it looked too risky to hold off. The troops went in, and I followed them. It was unpleasant."

"What did they . . . ?"

"They'd built a summoning grid in the altar. And they'd set up a greater circuit, with a geodesic pointing straight at the . . . the nursery school over the road." She dry swallows again. "They started with the goats as a warm-up exercise. But there was a homeless woman, and they'd used her as, as—" Mo gulps, then wipes her lips. "Intestines. Ropes and hanks and skeins of—a greater circuit made of human guts, still joined to the sacrifice." She's not swallowing: she's trying not to throw up.

"Stop." I try to let go of her hand. "You don't need to go on."

"I *need* to." She clenches her fist around my fingers and stares at me. "They'd crucified her, you know? The microphones picked up their prayers earlier: *I am the way and the truth and the life. No one comes to the Father except through me*—they meant it *literally*. I don't know why we didn't hear the screams, I think they might have sedated her first. I hope they, they did that." That's a forlorn hope; pain is a power source in its own right. But I don't remind her of this. She's shaking now: "The gate was *open*, Bob. I had to go through."

My Joan of Arc. I rescued Mo, once, years ago; it's ironic, a real giggle, that she turns out to be stronger and tougher than I am. Would you dive through a steaming intestinal gate into a soul-sucking void, armed only with a violin flensed from the bones of screaming sacrifices? *She* did. And she kept a lid on it afterwards, a stiff upper lip, while I was shuddering and stressed over what was basically an industrial accident. It's a good thing to put your problems in perspective from time to time, but right now I'd rather not, because I'm doing the comparison right now and I find I'm coming up so short I'm ashamed of myself.

"The things in the cultists' bodies had already eaten the blonde teacher's face and most of her left leg," Mo tells me earnestly, "but the Somali boy-child was still screaming, so I had to go after him."

I feel my gorge rising: "Too much." I splash wine into my empty glass and take a too-hasty swig. "Jesus, Mo—"

Jesus was evidently the wrong word; she stands and manages to make it as far as the doorway, en route to the bathroom, before she doubles over and sprays the wine-soaked remains of her dinner on the floor.

I make it to the sink and pull the plastic bowl and the cleaning supplies out, then fetch her a glass of tap water. "Rinse and spit," I say, holding the bowl under her mouth.

"Fucking gods, Bob—"

"Bed. *Now.*"

"We killed the bad things, but, but the little girl with the pigtails, I managed to carry her head back but it was too late—"

She's crying now, and it's all coming out, all the ugly details in a torrent like a vomiting storm sewer unloading a decade of pain and bloody shit and piss, and I carry her up the stairs as best I can and tuck her under the duvet. And she's still crying, although the racking sobs are coming further apart. "Sleep and remember," I tell her, touching her forehead: "Remember *it's all over.*" I pull my ward over my head and hang it round her neck. "Repeat command light paramnesia level two, eight hours REM, master override, endit." Then I touch her forehead again. "It's *over*, Mo, you can let go of it now."

As I go downstairs to clean up, I hear her beginning to snore.

MOPPING UP VOMIT AND CONSIGNING THE WRECKAGE OF DINNER to the recycling bin and the dishwasher keeps me distracted for ten minutes, but unfortunately not distracted enough to avoid looping through everything Mo said in my mind's eye. I can't help it. I've been through some bad shit myself, similar stuff. I've been through situations where you just keep going, keep pushing through, because if you stop you'll never start again: but for all that, this one was particularly horrifying.

I think it's the civilian involvement that does it; I'm more or less able to look after myself, and so is Mo, but a primary school . . . I don't want to think about that, but I can't stop, because this is where we're *all* going, when the walls of reality come tumbling down and the dead gods begin to stir in their crypts. It's put me in a theological frame of mind, and I *hate* that.

Let me try to explain . . .

I generally try to avoid funerals: they make me angry. I know the purpose of a funeral is to provide comfort and a sense of closure for the bereaved; and I agree, in principle, that this is generally a good thing. But the default package usually comes with a priest, and when they start driveling on about how Uncle Fred (who died aged sixty-two of a hideous brain tumor) is safe in the ever-loving arms of Jesus, the effect it has on me is not to make me love my creator: it's to wish I could punch him in the face repeatedly.

I'm a child of the enlightenment; I was raised thinking that moral and ethical standards are universals that apply equally to everyone. And these values aren't easily compatible with the kind of religion that posits a Creator. To my way of thinking, an omnipotent being who sets up a universe in which thinking beings proliferate, grow old, and die (usually in agony, alone, and in fear) is a cosmic sadist. Consequently, I'd much rather dismiss theology and religious belief as superstitious rubbish. My idea of a comforting belief system is your default English atheism . . . except that I know too much.

See, we *did* evolve more or less randomly. And the little corner of the universe we live in is 13.73 billion years old, not 5,000 years old. And there's no omnipotent, omniscient, invisible sky daddy in the frame for the problem of pain. So far so good: I live free in an uncaring cosmos, rather than trapped in a clockwork orrery constructed by a cosmic sadist.

Unfortunately, the truth doesn't end there. The things we sometimes refer to as elder gods are alien intelligences, which evolved on their own terms, unimaginably far away and long ago, in zones of spacetime which aren't normally connected to our own, where the rules are different. But that doesn't mean they can't reach out and touch us. As the man put it: Any sufficiently advanced technology is indistinguishable from magic. Any sufficiently advanced alien intelligence is indistinguishable from God— the angry monotheistic sadist subtype. And the elder ones . . . aren't friendly.

(See? I *told* you I'd rather be an atheist!)

I push the button on the dishwasher, straighten up, and glance at the kitchen clock. It's pushing ten thirty, but I'm wide awake and full of bleak existential rage. I don't want to go to bed; I might disturb Mo, and she really needs her sleep right now. So I tiptoe upstairs to check on her, use the bathroom, then retreat downstairs again. But that leaves me with a choice between sitting in a kitchen that smells of bleach and a living room that smells of sour fear-memories. I can't face the inanities of television or the solace of a book. I feel restless. So I clip on my holster, pull on my jacket, and go outside for a walk.

It may be summer but it's already dark and the streetlights are on. I walk down the leafy pavement, between the neatly trimmed front hedges and the sleeping cars parked nose to tail. The lichen-stained walls and battered wheelie bins are stained by the stale orange twilight reflected from the clouds. Traffic rumbles in the distance, pulsing with the freight of the unsleeping city. Here and there I see front windows illuminated from within by the shadow puppet play of televisual hallucinations. I turn a corner, walk downhill under the old railway bridge, then left past a closed back street garage. Cats slink through the moonless twilight with nervous stealth; the smell of night-blooming pollen meshes with the gritty taste of diesel particulates at the back of my throat. I walk through the night, wrapped in my anger, and as I walk I think:

Angleton is missing. Why? And where? He doesn't live anywhere, according to Human Resources; doesn't have a life. Well, that's not much of a surprise. Angleton's grasp on mundane humanity has always struck me as tenuous—the idea that there's a four-hundred-year-old stone cottage in a village in the countryside, and a Mrs. Angleton puttering around hanging out the laundry on a line in the back garden, simply doesn't work for me. He goes beyond the usual monasticism of the man who married his job; he never takes holidays, he's *always* in the office, and then there's the photograph. (Maybe he inherited it from Dorian Gray?) So, let this be Clue #1 that something is wrong. Angleton never does anything by accident, so either something is rotten in the state of Denmark, or he's embarked on a caper he didn't see fit to tell anyone about.

I turn right, across a main road—quiet at this time of night—then along and left down an alleyway that leads between rows of high back-garden fences. Grass grows beneath the crumbling, silvery woodwork and around the wheelie bins; here's a concrete yard where someone has parked a decaying caravan, its windows frosted dark in the urban twilight.

The Fuller Memorandum is missing. Whatever is in it is still a hot potato after seventy-odd years. Angleton was interested in it, and in BLOODY BARON, and in this new business about CASE NIGHTMARE GREEN coming into effect sooner rather than later.

Item: Why are the Russians sniffing around? And what did Panin mean about finding the Teapot? He can't be talking about Ungern Sternberg's psychotic batman, can he? I did some checking. Teapot was fragged by Ungern Sternberg's own rebellious troops in 1921, right before they handed the Baron over to Trotsky's commissars. At least, the mutineers *said* they shot him. If he'd run away into the Siberian forest, alone, might they have concocted some cock-and-bull cover story . . . ?

I make a right turn into a narrow path. It leads to a tranquil bicycle track, walled in beech and chestnut trees growing from the steep embankments to either side and sporadically illuminated by isolated lampposts. It used to be a railway line, decades ago, one of the many suburban services closed during the Beeching cuts—but it wasn't a commuter line. (I stumbled across it not long after we moved to this part of town, and it caught my attention enough to warrant some digging.)

The Necropolis Service ran from behind Waterloo station to the huge Brookwood cemetery in Surrey; tickets were sold in two classes, one-way and return. This is one of its tributaries, a tranquil creek feeding the great river of the dead. Today, cyclists use it to bypass the busy main roads on their way into the center. It is, however, unaccountably unpopular with the after-work exercise set, and I have the left lane to myself as I walk, still chewing over what I know and what I don't know.

CLUB ZERO and Mo. Who sent Uncle Fester? I see three alternatives: Panin and his friends, the cultists she was sent to shut down, or some third party. Taking it from the top: Panin is a professional, and can be expected to usually play by the rules. Sending a zombie to doorstep an officer in a foreign nation's service at home just *isn't done*; it's not businesslike, and besides, once you start sending assassins to bump off the oppo, you've got no guarantee that *their* assassins aren't going to outperform *yours*. The reason great powers don't usually engage in wars of assassination is that it levels the playing field. On the other hand, cultists like the perps behind CLUB ZERO are far more likely to do that sort of thing. Assassination and terrorism are Siamese twins: tools for outsiders and pressure groups. So my money is on Uncle Fester being an emissary from the cultists the AIVD called Mo in to neutralize . . . unless there's a third faction in play, a prospect I find far too scary to contemplate.

The cycle path narrows, and descends deeper into its cutting. The lights are more widely spaced here, and a number of them are out. Hearing a rustling scampering sound behind me, I glance round as something flickers in the bushes between lights—dog-like, with a great bush of a tail. An urban fox? Maybe: I didn't see the ears or muzzle, though. Urban foxes aren't a problem (unless you're a cat), but feral dogs might be another matter. I keep walking in the twilight. London is warm and humid in summer, but down here it's almost clammy-cold, and there's a faint whiff of something like a sewer, sweet and slightly rotten. I break into a slow jog, aiming to outrun the stench.

I have a growing, edgy feeling that I've missed something critically important. I've been plowing along, in harness and under stress, assuming that the crises I'm trying to deal with are all independent. *But what if they aren't?* I ask myself. *What if Angleton's disappearance is connected to Panin's search for the Teapot, what if the Fuller Memorandum holds an explanation, what if the cultists know that we stand closer to the thresh-*

old of the End Times than we realize and are trying to topple the balance, or perhaps to steal—

There's a crack of dead branches under the trees behind me. Panting inhuman breath punctuates the thudding of a four-footed pursuit. The orange sodium glare leaches away around me, giving way to a different shade of darkness. Trees loom overhead, clutching at each other with wizened arms as bony as concentration camp victims'. A thin mist at foot level obscures the tarmac path and my stomach lurches. I'm not running through suburban London anymore; I'm running along the ghostly track bed of the Necropolitan line, and the hounds of hell are on my trail, and I left my protective ward with Mo, and I am a fucking imbecile. *Shit, shit, shit.*

Whatever the thing behind me is, it's only seconds away. My heart's already thudding uncomfortably from jogging an hour after dinner—fucking stupid of me—but while I'm ninety percent sure that I'm being tracked by something that's about as bad as the proverbial hellhound, in which case I really ought to simply plug it with my pistol and ask questions later, I've got an even nastier feeling that it's tracking me *for* someone, or worse, herding me along.

I have: a gun, a Hand of Glory, and a JesusPhone. So of course I draw my phone and flip the case open, thumb-swipe to unlock, and spin round, raising the camera to focus as I tap the grinning skull icon.

There's method in my madness and my pursuer isn't mindless—I get a glimpse of flying haunches and bushy tail as it leaps off the path and into the trees with a startled *"yip!"*

The screen flashes a red-rimmed maw gaping at me and my hair stands on end as the phone and my fingertips are engulfed in pale blue fire. *Balefire*, it used to be called. I hastily go back to the main screen and stab another app: a diagnostic. Seeing what it says, I swear quietly and pull up another one that sets a spinning wireframe projection of a 5D Tesseract on the screen as it does its valiant best to set up a ward around me. The dog-thing is hiding and the tendrils of mist draw away from my feet, so I shove the phone in my pocket—still running—and draw my pistol. Then I turn back to the way I was going.

The emulator running on the phone's a poor substitute for a real ward, and it's only going to keep it up for as long as its battery can keep its tiny electronic brain running at full power, but armed and warded is the first step to survival and now I see the peril I'm in with an icy clarity. The second app I looked at was the thaumometer, and I should have kept an eye on it earlier, as I walked—it's almost off the chart. And all because I'm walking the Necropolitan line. If you wanted to set up a ley line, what better source of power could you hope for than the accumulated grief and sorrow of millions of mourners, to say nothing of the decaying lives of the corpses that traveled it? I should have seen it coming—but I usually only use this cycle path as a shortcut to and from the tube station, in daylight.

I'm pretty sure I'm being trailed by cultists. When I left home I was angry in the abstract but now I am *really* fucked off. These are the bastards who murdered a bunch of nursery school tots and their teachers, put Mo through the horrors—and they're trying for me now. The only question is, are they chasing me or herding me?

I keep going, slowing my jog to a brisk walk, scanning ahead as I move. I hold my gun at the ready with both hands, close to my chest, relying on the invisibility ward to make it look as if I'm just clutching my right wrist with my left hand. The mist at ground level coils and curdles around a pair of translucent parallel rails the color of old bones, resting on a bed of ethereal track sleepers. The trees writhe and knot overhead, clutching at each other, imploring and beseeching. In the distance I hear odd noises— the ghost of sobbing, deep voices intoning something, words I can't quite make out.

I'm sure it's all very eerie, but when reality starts to imitate a second-rate computer game you know the bad guys have over-egged the pudding. Some fuckhead is hitting me with a glamour in hope of spooking me. It's the sort of tactic that might stand a chance of working if I was a little less cynical, or if they had enough imagination to make it, oh, you know, *horrifying*, or something. Luckily for me they don't seem to have grasped the difference between a Sam Raimi movie and standing by your dad's hospital bed trying to work up the nerve to switch off the ventilator. So I find the fact that they're sending me woo-woo noises and mist perversely encouraging.

(I'm having second thoughts about the cultist thing, though. The probability of running into two different cells of the fuckers in the same month is vanishingly slim; and if this nonsense is a message from the same group that tried to landscape downtown Amsterdam last week, they've definitely sent the B-Team.)

I up my pace again, and just then I hear a scraping noise from the embankment to my left and every hair on my neck stands on end simultaneously.

I swing round, extending my arms in front of my face and sliding my index finger through the trigger guard as this *thing* clatters and scrambles down the side of the cutting in a mad dash towards me, a growl of hatred and hunger sounding an organ note deep in its chest, and I have time to think, *I hate fucking dogs*, just as it launches itself towards me.

I squeeze the trigger twice, aiming below where my eyes are focused on it—I can't look away; I get a flash of bared fangs and slavering tongue, eyeless and horrid and taller than any dog I've ever imagined—and there's a sound like a palm slapping a lump of wet meat as the gun kicks silently in my hand. I jump sideways as it slams into the track sleepers where I was standing a moment ago, howling a scream of agony and snapping those huge jaws at its own shoulder.

It's not a dog. Dogs aren't as black as a hole in space, and their musculature and articulation follow mammalian norms—this thing bends wrong as it bites and flails around, and I have an inkling of a memory that tells me I should be very afraid right now. But I'm not. I started out pissed off and I am now toweringly angry. Which is why I walk behind the flailing body, lower my aim towards the back of its skull, and call: "Show yourself *right now*, or the doggie gets it!"

There's a low chuckle. "Give us the Teapot and we will let you live, mortal."

Mortal? Yes, it's the B-Team all right; probably in robes with upside-down crucifixes or something. They're the occult equivalent of the kind of suicide bombers who post their confession videos on YouTube two weeks before they learn the hard way that trying to blow themselves up with chapatti flour isn't going to do anything except give the police an excuse to pat themselves on the back and reassure the public that Everything Is Under Control. "Come out where I can see you," I demand.

The hound-thing on the ground whines in agony. It's getting on my nerves, cutting through the barricade of my determination—then I notice out of the corner of one eye that the shoulder I blew a fist-sized chunk out of is writhing and foaming, dark tubules questing inwards from the ripped and shredded edges. *Shit*. If this is what I think it is, then by summoning it the B-Team have bitten off more than they can chew—and so have I. "You've got five seconds," I add. "It won't die, but it's going to be *real* pissed off. And I reckon it's fifty-fifty whether it blames me or blames you."

"Do you truly believe you can shoot one of the Hounds with impunity, mortal?"

I've got a bearing on Windbag now. Your typical B-Team idiot is either a religious fanatic who's grown up listening to preacher-men ranting and foaming in seventeenth-century English, or they're a wannabe who's seen too many horror flicks. I'm betting on the second kind here. I take a step back—accidental contact with this particular species of doggie is about as safe as licking the third rail on the Underground—then quickly slip my left hand into my pocket and mutter the command word to ignite the Hand of Glory as I pull it out of my pocket.

Of course the HOG lights off promptly, but its little pinky is tangled in my pocket lining and comes free with a foul gust of scorched linen—something else to hold against the gloating ratfucker. I take a long step sideways, then another, holding the wrinkled hand at arm's length out to one side. The Glock is a numbing drag on my opposite arm: nothing like as bad as a Browning, but I can't keep this up forever.

A second voice chirps up from behind the thrashing Hound, about where I was standing five seconds ago: "Hey, where'd he go?"

(He sounds . . . dim. Let's call him Minion #1.)

"Fuck!" That's Windbag. He sounds pissed off. "We're going to lose him! All-Highest will be displeased!"

"I've got the path." A *third* voice, female and coldly controlled. Maybe she's an A-Team player assigned to ride herd on the clown car. (She can be Minion #2 until proven competent.) "You walk the—"

No plan survives contact with the enemy—especially when the enemy is invisible, within earshot and taking notes—but even more importantly, no cultist survives physical contact with one of the Hounds. The doggie of doom flails one paw against the ground and its back arches as it goes into the seizure I've been expecting ever since I plugged it with a banishment round. Which is bad luck for Minion #1, who is in the path of one viciously barbed paw. He gives a brief gurgling scream, but is already dead by the time the sound reaches me: it's just air venting from the corpse's lungs and reverberating through its larynx on the way out. Every muscle in his body contracts simultaneously with a strange popping sound as his joints dislocate and ligaments tear, in a spasmodic breakdance that ends in a pile beside the Hound.

I don't wait to see what they do next—I scramble up the dry soil embankment, moving diagonally between tree trunks.

"We're going to lose him!" Minion #2 calls in a high, bell-ringing voice. "Fallback plan!" *Okay, she's promoted to Mistress.* I think for a moment that she's telling Windbag to withdraw, but then I hear the second truly spine-chilling noise of the evening, the unmistakable sound of someone racking the slide on a pump-action shotgun.

I throw myself flat against the side of the embankment and roll over on my back, still clutching the Hand of Glory and my pistol as the two robed figures on the path raise their weapons and pour fire past each other, sweeping up and down the bike path. They set up a reverberating roar that jars the teeth in my head: they're not aiming, they're simply spraying clouds of buckshot at waist level. I'm about two meters up the embankment above them, and twenty meters away. Holding my breath, I glance at the HOG in my left hand. The fingertips are burning steadily—I have perhaps three or four minutes of invisibility. Odds of two to one, shotguns against silenced pistol, at twenty meters? *Not good.* I could probably take them—probably, but I'd have to put the Hand of Glory down, and if I didn't get them both with my first two shots I'd be giving the survivor a muzzle flash to aim for. With a shotgun, let's not forget.

Fucking B-Team cultists. If this was the A-Team, they'd summon something exotic and deadly to set on my ass—something I'd have a chance of banishing. But the B-Team were at the back of the queue the day All-Highest was handing out death spells, so they just blaze away with shotguns.

Ten rounds later—it feels like having my head slammed in a doorway ten times in a row—they lower their guns. "He's legged it," says Windbag.

"Right. We're leaving." Mistress's voice is so chilly you could rent it out as an air conditioner. "Philip is dead. This will not be received well by All-Highest. Let me do the talking, if you value your life."

"But can't we—" Windbag whines.

I don't hear what he says next, though, because Mistress says something in a voice that distorts weirdly as she speaks: and then a hole in the air opens and closes, and they're not there anymore. Neither is the Hound. It's gone, taking the corpse of Minion #1 back to wherever it is that the Hounds come from. The glamour is gone, too: below me, the cycle path is restored—just another rustic suburban alleyway, lit by the streetlight glare from the nighttime clouds overhead.

I shudder uncontrollably for a minute. Then I carefully extinguish the fingers of the HOG, holster my pistol, stumble back down the embankment to the footpath, and dust myself off.

They weren't after Mo: they were after *me*. They knew how to find me and they wanted to know about the Teapot. Once is happenstance, but twice is enemy action, which means it's time to go to work.

9.

NIGHT SHIFT

WALKING TO THE OFFICE ISN'T SOMETHING I'D NORMALLY DO, because it takes about three hours, but I am feeling inconveniently surveilled and I don't like the idea of the MAGINOT BLUE STARS network being able to track me. So I follow the footpath for another half kilometer before reigniting the Hand of Glory and dashing back almost all the way I've come, then exiting onto a side street. I take two corners and jump a fence into somebody's backyard before I extinguish the HOG again, then walk out casually with my shoulders back and my chin up.

A bus ride in an irrelevant direction takes me ten minutes farther away from the office—then it's into a back alley and time to reignite the HOG for a brisk kilometer. Finally I snuff it out and catch a different bus that passes close enough to the New Annexe that I can walk from the stop.

I march up to the darkened C&A staff entrance and key my number, then swipe my pass card. The door clicks, and I step inside. It's totally black, and in the gloom I can hear the restless shuffling of one of the night staff. I pull out my warrant card hastily, lest I be eaten by a grue: arguing with the night watchmen is singularly futile unless you do it with a chain saw or a baseball bat.

"Brrrrr—"

"Get me a torch," I snap. The warrant card is all very well—it sheds a faint, nacreous glow—but the backlight invocation has unpleasant side effects if you crank up the lumens too high. (Why is it that all the movies make it look as if wizards find invoking light *easy*? Tenuous glows and balefire are all very well, but there's a reason we use fluorescent tubes around here.)

"—rains?" he asks plaintively.

A torch flicks on and I see the wizened face of its holder. "Here, give me that." I take the torch, being careful to hold the warrant card between me and the doorman. I think he might be Fred from Accounting, but if so, he's definitely a bit the worse for wear these days; it's several years since he died, and not everyone around here gets the deluxe Jeremy Bentham treatment. Mostly HR just arrange for one of us to stick them in a summoning grid and bind one of the eaters in the night to service (weak, minimally sentient efflorescences of alien will, that can animate a corpse and control it just about enough to push a broom, or scare the living daylights out of unwanted nighttime visitors). I gather it saves on funeral expenses. "Stay here and forget I came this way. That's an order."

I climb the stairs, leaving the residual human resource behind to eat any unwitting B-Team cultists who were stupid enough to tail me. It's past midnight and they make regular inspection rounds, so I keep my card out and hope like hell the battery in this plastic piece of shit lasts until I make it to my office. I keep a proper torch there, a Maglite that'll work properly when it's time to go visit Angleton's lair and turf those files from top to bottom. Luckily the plastic piece of shit holds out and I let myself in, flick on the light, shut the door, and flop down behind my desk with a sigh of relief.

"Took your time getting here, didn't you, boy?"

In the time it takes me to peel myself off the ceiling and return my pistol to its holster, Angleton takes up residence in my visitor's chair, folding his ungainly limbs around himself like a spindly black spider. The skeletal, humorless grin tells me I'm in trouble even before I open my mouth.

"I've waited here for three consecutive nights. What delayed you?"

I close my mouth. Then I open it and close it again a couple of times, just for practice. Finally, when I trust myself to speak, I say one word: "Cultists."

"*Three days*, boy. Suppose you tell me what you've learned?"

"One moment." My paranoia is growing. I take out my phone and peer at him through its camera. TRUESEER tells me that I am, indeed, looking at my boss, who is looking increasingly irritated. I make the shiny vanish. "Okay. From the top: the Fuller Memorandum is missing, the Russians have gotten all upset, cultists are throwing their toys out of the pram, and everyone wants to know about the Teapot. Oh, and someone in Research and Development says that CASE NIGHTMARE GREEN isn't going to wait a couple of years, but is due to kick off in a few weeks or months at the most. What am I missing?"

Angleton stares at me coldly. "You're missing the *spy*, boy."

"The"—I nearly swallow my tongue—"spy?"

"Yes: Helen Langhorn. Aged seventy-four, widow of Flight Lieutenant Adrian Langhorn, long-term resident of Cosford, working part-time at the museum as a volunteer. Met her husband while she was in the WRAAF back in 1963. Which is a pretty interesting occupation for her to have been in, considering that she was also a captain in the Russian Army and a GRU Illegal who was inserted into the UK in 1959, when she was barely out of her teens."

I make an inarticulate gurgling noise. "But she—the *hangar*—she wasn't—she can't have—"

Angleton waits for me to wind down. "The many-angled ones are not the only enemy this country has ever faced, boy. Some of us remember." (It's okay for *him* to say that—I was about ten when the cold war ended!)

"Helen Langhorn's primary assignment did not come to an end just because the Soviet Union collapsed. To outward appearances her utility had been in decline for many years, after her husband failed to achieve advancement, costing her access to people and bases; once she hit sixty with no long-term prospects they wrote her off. That is one of the risks one runs with long-term Illegals—their entire life may be marginalized by one or two unfortunate and unpredictable errors. There are probably fifty others like her in the UK—retired bank managers and failed politicians' wives pruning their privet hedges and daydreaming of the revolution that failed them. Or perhaps they accept it gladly, happy to no longer be a pawn on the chessboard. But in any case, Helen's career appears to have undergone a brief second flowering in the last few years."

"But she"—I flap my jaws inarticulately—"she was halfway to dementia!"

"Was she?" Angleton raises a skeptical eyebrow. "She was on the front desk of a museum gallery barely two hundred meters from Hangar 12B, where Airframe 004 is being cannibalized for spare parts to keep the other three white elephants airworthy. You may think *that* no more than a coincidence, but I don't."

"You never told me what that stuff about the white elephants was about—"

"I expected you to *find out for yourself,* boy." Then Angleton does something I absolutely never expected to see: he sighs unhappily.

"Boss?"

Angleton leans back in his chair. "Tell me about Chevaline," he asks.

"Chevaline?" I frown. "Wasn't that some sort of nuclear missile program from the sixties or seventies, something like that?"

"Chevaline." He pauses. "Back in the 1960s, when Harold Wilson cut a deal with Richard Nixon to buy Polaris missiles for the Royal Navy, the tacit assumption was that a British nuclear deterrent need merely be sufficient to pound on Moscow until the rubble bounced. During the 1970s, the Soviets began to construct an anti-ballistic-missile shield around Moscow. It was crude by modern standards: anti-missile rockets with nuclear warheads—but it would have rendered the British Polaris force obsolete. So during the 1970s, a succession of Conservative and Labour governments pushed through a warhead upgrade scheme that replaced the original MRV warheads with far more sophisticated MIRV buses, equipped with decoys and able to engage two targets rather than one. The project was called Chevaline; it cost a billion pounds back in the day—when a billion pounds was *real* money—and they didn't even tell the Cabinet."

"A billion pounds? With no oversight?" I blink rapidly. *We're* subject to spot audits on office stationery, all the way down to paper clips.

"Yes." Angleton smiles sepulchrally. "We helped ensure security, so that it was relatively easy for them to spend an extra two hundred million pounds in 1977 to keep the Concorde production lines at Filton and Bristol open for long enough to produce four extra airframes for the RAF," Angleton says blandly. "The Plumbers ensured that nobody remembered a thing afterwards."

"RAF 666 Squadron fly *Concordes*?"

"Flew them," Angleton corrects me. "The long-range occult reconnaissance model, not the nuclear-armed model the RAF originally asked for in 1968. You may not be aware of this, but Prototype 002 was built with attachment points for a bomb bay before the project was abandoned; Bomber Command wanted to replace V-force with a fleet of supersonic bombers that could carry Blue Steel nuclear stand-off bombs to Moscow, but the Navy won the toss. Instead, the RAF got the recon version, with supercargo space for the six demonologists and the optics bench to open the gate they needed to fly through."

My jaw is beginning to ache from all the speechless opening-and-closing cycles. "You're shitting me."

Angleton shakes his head. "The Squadron was based in Filton and Heathrow, flying in British Airways livery—the aircraft movements were described as charter flights, and they wore the hull numbers of BA airframes that were currently undergoing maintenance. They flew one mission a week, departing west over the Atlantic. They refueled from a VC-10 tanker, then the supercargo would open a gate and they'd make a high-speed run across the dead plateau before reopening the gate home and landing at Filton for decontamination and exorcism. It's all in CODICIL BLACK SKULL. Which you are cleared to read, incidentally."

I shake myself and take a deep breath. "Let me get this straight. You're telling me that the RAF has a squadron of black Concordes which they currently keep in a hangar at RAF Cosford? Helen Langhorn was a former Soviet spy who, by a happy accident—for her employers—was in a position to poke around them? Which she did, with results that . . ." I shudder, remembering again: a purple flash, face shrinking and crumpling in on itself around the harsh lines of her skull. "And now the Thirteenth Directorate are sniffing round?"

"Very good! We'll make a professional paranoid out of you one of these days." Angleton nods, grudging approval.

"*Concorde*." I do a double take. "But they've been retired, right?"

"That put a crimp on the cover story, certainly. These days they fly only at night, described as American B-1Bs if anyone asks. A big bomber with four engines and afterburners is a much flimsier cover, and the plane spotters and conspiracy theorists keep the Plumbers busy, but we cannot neglect the watch on the dead plateau. If the thing in the pyramid should stir—" He makes an abrupt cutting gesture with the edge of one hand.

"Dead plateau? Thing in the pyramid?" I've got no idea what he's referring to, but it sounds ominous.

"You've been through a gate to *elsewhere*." I remember a world in the grip of *fimbulwinter*, where the rivers of liquid air ran down through valleys of ice beneath a moon carved with the likeness of Hitler's face. "There are other, more permanent, *elsewheres*. Some of them we must monitor continuously. *That* world . . . pray you never see it, boy, and pray that the sleeping god in the pyramid never awakens."

I tilt my head from side to side, trying to spill the invisible goop that's clogging up my mind. Thinking in here is difficult, as if the air, hazy with the congealed fumes of state secrets, is impeding my ability to reason—

"Boss. Why are you *here*? Everyone thinks you've gone missing, AWOL with no forwarding address."

Angleton grins skeletally. "*Good*. Let's keep it that way."

My eyes are feeling hot and gritty from too much stress and too little sleep, but I manage to roll them anyway. "Big problem: you just tipped me off. Can you give me a reason not to out you to the BLOODY BARON team—other than 'because I said so'?"

"Of course." He looks increasingly, alarmingly, amused. *What have I gotten myself into this time?* "You'll keep it to yourself because while the cat's away the mice may play, and one of this particular bunch of mice appears to be a security leak, and I'm setting a trap for them. You're the bait, by the way."

"I'm the—"

"And to sex you up so they come after you, I've got a little job for you to do."

"Right, that's *it*, I'm through with—"

"Assuming you want to nail the scum responsible for the CLUB ZERO incident in Amsterdam."

"—fucking cultists—*really?*"

"Yes, Bob." He has the good grace not to look too smug. "Now shut up and *listen*, there's a good boy."

He deposits a slim memo on my desk, then places a small plastic baggie on top of it. I squint at it: it's empty except for a paper clip.

"Here's what I want you to do . . ."

CLASSIFIED: TEAPOT BARON TYBURN
FROM: Fuller, Laundry
TO: 17F, Naval Intelligence Division

Dear Ian,

Hope all's well (and my best regards to your mother, long may she keep her nose out of operational matters).

You enquired about Teapot.

Subsequent to the death of Burdokovskii in 1921, Q Division determined that the *preta* referenced in the Sternberg Fragment had returned to the six paths, and if it could be recalled and bound into a suitable host it might be compelled to the service of the state. Given the magnitude of the powers possessed by this particular entity, this was considered a desirable objective; however, its reincarnation required that we provide the hungry ghost with a new host. Obviously, this presented them with a headache; so some bright spark finally came up with the idea of asking the Home Office. A request was accordingly submitted in 1923.

Due to the 1924 election and subsequent upheavals and crises, the request was not actually considered at ministerial level until 1928, in which year the Prime Minister and Home Secretary agreed, not without considerable argument, to sanction the use of the ritual as an alternative method of capital punishment on one occasion only. I am not at liberty to disclose the identity of the murderer in question—he has in any case paid the ultimate price—but after his hanging was announced, he was relocated to a secret location. No less a surgeon than Mr. Gillies, working under an oath of strict secrecy, was employed to remodel the features of the sacrificial vessel lest any former acquaintance recognize him. Then the Hungry Ghost Ritual was performed, in a ceremony so harrowing that I would not relish being called upon to perform it again.

I shall not burden you with the tiresome sequence of obstacles that fate threw before us after we summoned the Teapot. Teaching it to speak, and to walk, and to make use of a human body once more was tedious in the extreme; for example we had to straitjacket and gag it for the first six months, lest it eat its fingers and lips. For almost a year it seemed likely that we had made a horrible mistake, and had merely driven a condemned murderer into the arms of insanity. However, in early 1930 Teapot began to communicate, and then to retrieve portions of the deceased memories—speaking in Russian as well as English, a language with which the vessel was unfamiliar. Shortly thereafter, it began also to evince a marked skill in the more esoteric areas of mathematics, and to show signs of the monstrous, cold intellect that so disturbed Baron Von Ungern Sternberg.

When the Teapot committee received permission to reincarnate the *preta* it was immediately realized that we would need to bind it to our service. Ungern Sternberg was able to placate it with a steady supply of victims, but His Majesty's Government in time of peace was not so well placed. (If we had received the go-ahead to deal with the Socialists, things would have been different; but it's no use crying over spilt milk.) Consequently, from 1928 to 1930 we worked tirelessly on a new model *geas* or binding—one that can restrain not only a human soul, but an eater of same. I shall spare you the grisly details, but in April 1930 we performed the binding rite for the first time, and Teapot was demonstrated to be under our full authority. It did not submit willingly, and I regret to inform you that the death of Dr. Somerfeld in that year—attributed to an apoplectic fit in his obituary in the *Times*— was only one part of the heavy price we paid.

Having bound the *Angra Mainyu* it was now necessary to indoctrinate it and train it to pass for a true Englishman. To this end, we obtained a place for it as Maths tutor at Sherborne, where it was enrolled in Lyon House as a master. Every public school in England is crawling with masters who are not entirely right in the head as a result of their experiences on the Front, and it was our consensus opinion that Teapot's more minor eccentricities would not attract excessive notice, while the major ones (such as the regrettable tendency to eat souls) could be kept under control by our *geas*.

I retired from the Teapot committee with my official retirement from service in 1933. I did not encounter Teapot again until 1940 and my reactivation in this highly irregular role.

Today, Teapot is almost unrecognizable. When we set out to turn the monster into an Englishman we succeeded too well. He is urbane, witty, possessed of a wicked but well-concealed sense of humor, and utterly lacking in the conscienceless brutality of the hungry ghost that possessed Ensign Evgenie Burdokovskii in Ulan Bator all those years ago. Sherborne did its usual job—that of turning savages into servants of empire—and did it to our carefully constructed house master just as thoroughly as to any Hottentot from the home counties.

I am afraid that our initial objective—to chain a hungry ghost to the service of the state—has only been a qualified success: qualified because we succeeded *too well*. Teapot sincerely believes in *playing the game*, in honor and service and all the other ideals we cynically dismiss at our peril. Unfortunately this renders him less than useful for the task in hand. We have (I hesitate to say this) reformed a demon in our own image, or rather, in the image we were trained to revere. We would be fools to undo this work now: this *preta* knows us too well. We captured it once, but next time we might not be so lucky.

Despite being useless to us as an Eater of Souls, Teapot is not without worth. I have drafted it into this new organization, where I believe we can put it to good use while maintaining a discreet watch. We can always use a hungry ghost, possessed of a disturbing brilliance in the dark arts, hidden within the urbane skin of an Englishman. It understands what makes us tick, shares—thanks to years of compulsion and indoctrination—our goals, and it has an eerie judgement of character, too—I believe it may be of significant use to the Doublecross committee in rooting out enemy spies. But if you're thinking of using it as a weapon, I would advise you to think again: I'm not sure the *geas*, or Teapot's indoctrination, would hold together if it is allowed to unleash its full power. Teapot is the sort of gun you fire only once—then it explodes in your hand.

Signed: J. F. C. Fuller

I'M NOT GOING TO EXPLAIN HOW I GOT *HERE* FROM *THERE*: JUST take it as given that it is now ten o'clock in the morning, I am still in the office (but called Mo half an hour ago to see she's okay), I haven't shaved or slept, and there's a BLOODY BARON meeting in five minutes. I've got Amarok running on my desktop (playing "Drowning in Berlin" on endless repeat, because I need a pounding beat to keep me awake) and I've plowed through the CODICIL BLACK SKULL file that Angleton left me, and then on into a bunch of tedious legwork for this morning's session.

I'm suffering from severe cognitive dissonance; every so often you think you've got a handle on this job, on the paper clip audits and interminable bureaucracy and committee meetings, and then something insane crawls out of the woodwork and gibbers at you, something crazy enough to give James Bond nightmares that just happen to be true.

I close the CBS file and I'm just sticking it back in my secure document safe when Iris pops her head round the door. "Bob? Are you ready to do battle with BLOODY BARON yet?"

I groan quietly. "I think I need a coffee, but yeah, I'll be along just as soon as I've locked this . . ." I poke at the keypad and it tweedles happily. Not that an electronic lock is the only security we rely on; anyone who tries to crack this particular safe is going to wake up in hospital with a hangover the size of a whale.

"White, no sugar, right?"

"You're a star. I'll be right with you." Did I remember to say good management cures the King's Evil and makes coffee, too? Because if not, it's all true.

Ten minutes later I'm sitting in Room 206 again, with a mug of passable paint stripper in front of me and a printout of the minutes. It's a very cut-down rump session today. Franz is absent, Iris is tapping her fingers and Shona is looking as if she'd like to be away with the fairies while Choudhury drones on: "No observed deviations from traffic intercept patterns established over the past week, and no notified agent movements yesterday—"

What the hell, I'm *bored*. I clear my throat.

Choudhury glances at me, irritated: "What is it, Howard?"

"These non-existent agent movements wouldn't happen to include Panin, would they? Because I'm sure if Panin so much as farted in F-flat minor our boys would be up his arse with a gas spectrograph, wouldn't they?"

I am pleased to see that both Shona and Iris are paying attention: Shona's nostrils flare unconsciously and Iris raises an eyebrow at me.

Choudhury, however, is a harder nut. He frowns. "Don't be silly. Of course they'd spot him if he was in the UK."

"Really?" I lean back, cross my arms, and bare my teeth at him. Maybe he'll mistake it for a grin. "Explain last night, then."

"Last n—" He stops dead. "What happened last night?"

I glance at the Sitrep folder. "Panin isn't in the UK, according to that folder. So how exactly is it that he picked me up as I was leaving work and bought me a pint of ESB in the Frog and Tourettes?"

"Preposterous." Choudhury glares. Neither Shona nor Iris is smiling.

"You'd better explain," Iris tells me.

"What I said. Here is a hint: Panin *knew*. He tried to pump me about Teapot, so I played dumb. He knows the rules; left me a calling card. It's downstairs in the Security Office safe. For reasons of operational security I didn't report the contact immediately, but I'm reporting it *now*. The Plumbers should be able to confirm it from the pub CCTV." I sit up. "Personally, I find the implications highly suggestive."

"Why did you not tell Security—" Shona stops, her eyes widening.

"We're not as secure as we'd like to be. I'd rather not spread it around beyond this committee for the time being."

Iris's brows furrow. "You're taking rather a lot on your shoulders, aren't you?"

"I'm only doing what Angleton would advise."

Choudhury has spent the past thirty seconds or so looking hurt and offended. Now he collects his dignity: "This can't possibly be right—Oversight don't get their movement reports wrong. Perhaps you were taken in by an impostor? I assure you, you didn't see Panin last night—he was in Madrid."

I am getting tired of this shit. "According to your Sitrep he was sighted in Madrid at four p.m.," I point out. "That's plenty of time to catch a flight into London City and accost me outside the front door at a quarter past eight. If you had bothered to check the duty rota behind that sighting"—*gosh, I didn't know he could turn that shade of pink!*—"you'd know that the Madrid office files their report at five, local time, which is sixteen hundred hours on British Summer Time, and they go home at six. And if you got out from behind your desk once in a while you'd know that the Madrid office consists of two cotton tops and their pet chihuahua, whose job is to take whatever the Guardia Civil feeds them and barf it over the wire on demand, rather than actually running surveillance boxes on visiting opposition controllers. Like I said: the pub CCTV—not to mention the MAGINOT BLUE STARS network and Panin's mobile phone company's logfiles—will back me up on this. I'm right, you're wrong, and I would appreciate it if you'd stop acting like a complete prat and *pay attention.*"

I find that during my little rant I must have stood up: I'm leaning over the table, balanced on my fists, and Choudhury is leaning over backwards in his chair, not balanced in the slightest. "This is harassment!" he splutters. "Intimidation!"

"No." I sit down hastily, before Iris can get a word in: "*Intimidation* is when you're boxed by a Thirteenth Directorate officer and two Spetsnaz thugs he borrowed from the embassy. I'd recommend it sometime: it'll be good practice for when the Auditors decide to rake you over the coals."

Shona has been bottling it up for some time, and now she lets rip: "Bob, what *exactly* did Panin want? I think you'd better make a full statement *right now.*" That's right, she's with Oscar-Oscar, same as Jo, isn't she?

"Panin tried to pump me; I don't pump easily. His specific concern is Teapot. *The Teapot is missing,* he told me: *You'd better find it before the wrong people get their hands on it and use it to make tea.* There was a lot of tap-dancing, but that's the basic substance of it." I carefully avoid thinking about our inconclusive exchange on the topic of Amsterdam, which is now looking even murkier in context: *They do that, you know. To muddy the waters.* (Fucking cultists.) "He offered to trade, if we have anything to offer."

"Wonderful." Shona is making notes. "So that's it?"

"Substantially, yes." Because all I know for sure about the cultist con-

nection is inference—and Angleton's instructions. (Thus do we damn ourselves, by the treachery of our own words.)

"Okay, I'll compile this and add it to the minutes, so at least we've got
it on paper somewhere. That should cover you. Then we can decide how
and when to send it up the chain." She stares at me blackly. "I assume
that's why you brought it up here?"

"Yes. I want to keep it confidential to the BLOODY BARON committee for now. I'm worried about how Panin knew who to talk to and where
to find him. Not to mention *when*."

Iris speaks up: "Yes, that's very disturbing." She looks appropriately
disturbed for a split second, then flexes her management muscle. "Vikram,
would you be a dear and make sure to accidentally lose the minutes of
this session between your desk and your email program? I think it wouldn't
hurt for distribution to be delayed for a few days, until the situation settles one way or the other."

Despite the aging biker chick style that she affects, the temperament
and training of a steely home-counties matron lurk not too far under the
skin; put her in twinset and pearls and you can see her biting the heads
off hunt saboteurs. When she turns the big guns on Choudhury he runs
up the white flag at once. "Ah, certainly, madam." He spares me a poisonous glance, which I ignore. "SSO 3 Howard's unfortunate encounter will
be thoroughly misfiled until I hear otherwise."

"Do you expect Panin to make contact again?" Shona demands. "In
your personal judgment."

"Um." Now *that's* a question and a half. "He left me a card in case *I*
want to contact *him*, but I wouldn't rule it out. I got the impression he
was worried about timing. If the Thirteenth Directorate are running to
some kind of schedule we need to know, don't we?"

Iris looks grimly pleased. "Minute that."

"Schedules." Shona stares at Vikram. "What does the calendar have
for us?"

"The calendar? It's August bank holiday in a couple of weeks—"

"I believe she was asking about significant intersections," Iris interrupts, sparing me a quelling glance. "Summit conferences, international treaties, Mayan great cycle endings, general elections, prophesied apocalypses, that sort of thing. It'll be in Outlook under *events*. You're the one with the laptop, why don't you look it up?"

Choudhury manages to look long-suffering. "What exactly am I supposed to be looking for?"

"Anything!" Shona makes a curse of the word. "Whatever might interest Panin."

I blink. Suddenly a rather unpalatable thought occurs to me. Forget dates that interest Panin: What about dates relevant to the Teapot? Assuming the Teapot in question is the one I'm thinking of.

Trying not to be too obvious about it, I pull out my phone and start hunting. There's an ebook reader, and a Wikipedia client, and a bunch of other stuff. *What was Ungern Sternberg's adjutant called again . . . ?*

"Bob, what are you doing?" It's Iris.

I grin apologetically. "Checking a different calendar." *19 August 1921.* That's when the mutineers murdered Teapot. At least, that's when they *said* they did the deed. And the ninetieth anniversary is coming up in the next week: *How interesting.* I quickly scan for other significant anniversaries on that date: *Salem witch trial executions, Hungerford massacre, twentieth anniversary of the collapse of the USSR* . . . "No, sorry, nothing there," I say, putting my phone away. *Liar, liar, pants on fire.*

It's like this: If you were going to try and break the geas that restrains an extra-dimensional horror called the Eater of Souls, wouldn't you pick the anniversary of its last taste of freedom? Dates have resonance, after all, and this particular horror has been living quietly among human beings, the lion lying down with the lamb, for so long that our patterns of thought have imprinted upon it.

Isn't that just the sort of nutso thing that the cultists might be up to? Trying to free a vastly powerful occult force from its Laundry-imposed chains? And isn't this exactly the sort of thing that Panin might anticipate? Well maybe. There's a slight motivational gap: Just what makes cultists tick, anyway? Besides the obvious—having your head turned by a hugely powerful glamour, being bound by a geas, that sort of thing—what's in it for them? Fucked if I know: I mean, what makes your average high school shooter tick, for that matter?

Suddenly, not knowing is making me itch—but the only person who can answer for sure is the one person I don't dare to ask: Angleton.

"Maybe we could wire Bob?" Shona suggests.

What? I shake my head. "What do you mean?"

"If Panin makes contact again, it would really help if you had a re-cording angel," she points out.

"There was a word in that sentence: *if*." I look at Iris for support but she's nodding thoughtfully along with Shona. "Panin's not going to make contact on working hours, and if it's all right by you, I'd rather not wear a wire during all my off-duty life. Now, if you want me to use that busi-ness card and wear a recorder while we're talking, that's another matter. But I think we ought to have something to trade with him before we go there, otherwise he's not going to give us anything for free."

"Point," says Iris.

Vikram looks at me through slitted eyes. "We should wire him any-way," he suggests maliciously, "just in case."

I sink back in my chair, racking my brain for plausible defenses. We've only been in this meeting for half an hour and already it feels like a de-cade: what a morning! But it could be worse: I've got to run Angleton's little errand at two o'clock . . .

10.

THE NIGHTMARE STACKS

THERE IS A RAILWAY UNDER LONDON, BUT IT'S PROBABLY NOT the one you're thinking of.

Scratch that. There are *many* railways under London. There are the tube lines that everyone knows about, hundreds of kilometers, dozens of lines, carrying millions of people every day. And there are the London commuter rail lines, many of which run underground for part or all of their length. There are the other major railway links such as CrossRail and the Eurostar tunnel into St. Pancras. There's even the Docklands Light Railway, if you squint.

But these are just the currently operational lines that are open to the public. There are other lines you probably don't know about. There are the deep tube tunnels that were never opened to the public, built to serve the needs of wartime government. Some of them have been abandoned; others turned into archives and secure stores. There are the special platforms off the public tube stations, the systems built during the 1940s and 1950s to rush MPs and royalty away from the capital at an hour's notice in time of war. These are the trains of government, buried deep and half-forgotten.

And then there are the weird ones. The Necropolis railway that ran from behind Waterloo to Brookwood cemetery in Surrey, along the converted track bed of which I ran last night. The coal tunnels that distributed fuel to the power stations of South London and the buried generator halls that powered the tube network. And the MailRail narrow-gauge tunnels that for over a century hauled sacks of letters and parcels between Paddington and Whitechapel, until it was officially closed in 2003.

Closed?

Not so fast.

The stacks, where the Laundry keeps its dead files, occupy two hundred-meter stretches of disused deep-dug tube tunnel not far from Whitehall. They're thirty meters down, beneath the hole in the ground where Service House is currently being rebuilt by a private finance initiative (just in time for CASE NIGHTMARE GREEN). How do you think we get files in and out? Or librarians in and out, for that matter?

Angleton has a job for me to do, down in the stacks. And so it is that at one thirty I'm sitting in my office, nursing a lukewarm mug of coffee and waiting for the little man with the handcart to call, when the Necronomi-Pod begins to vibrate and make a noise like a distressed U-boat.

"'Lo?"

It's Mo. "Bob?" She doesn't sound too happy.

"Yeah? You at home?"

"Right now, yes . . . not feeling too well."

I hunch over instinctively. "Is there anything I can do?"

"Yes." *Oh, right.* "Listen, about last night—thanks. And thanks for letting me lie in. I'm just wrung-out today, so I've begged off my weekly and I was thinking about taking the afternoon to do what we talked about earlier, to go visit Research and Development. But there's a little job I needed to do in the office and I was wondering if you could . . ."

I glance at the clock on my desktop. "Maybe; depends what, I'm off to the stacks in half an hour."

"The stacks? In person?" She cheers up audibly. "That's great! I was hoping you could pull a file for me, and if you're going there—"

"Not so fast." I pause. "What kind of file?"

"A new one, a report I asked for. I can give you a reference code; it should be fresh in today."

"Oh, right." Well, that shouldn't be a problem—I can probably fit it in with my primary mission. "What's the number?"

"Let me . . ." She reads out a string of digits and I read it back to her. "Yes, that's it. If you could just bring it home with you this evening?"

"Remind me again, who was it who didn't want work brought home?"

"That's *different*. This is me being lazy, not you overdoing it!"

I smile. "If you say so."

"Love you."

"You too. Bye."

AT SEVEN MINUTES PAST TWO, I HEAR FOOTSTEPS AND A squeak of wheels that stops outside my door. I pick up a pair of brown manila files I'm through with and stand. "Archive service?" I ask.

The man with the handcart is old and worn before his time. He wears a blue-gray boiler suit and a cloth cap that has seen better days; his skin is as parched as time-stained newsprint. He looks at me with the dumb, vacant eyes of a residual human resource. "Archive service," he mumbles.

"These are going back." I hand over the files, and he painstakingly inscribes their numbers on a battered plywood clipboard using a stub of pencil sellotaped to a length of string. "And I'm going with them."

He stares at me, unblinking. "Document number," he says.

I roll my eyes. "Give me that." Taking the clipboard I make up a shelf reference number and write it down in the next space, then copy it onto my left wrist with a pen. "See? I am a document. Take me."

"Document . . . number . . ." His eyes cross for a moment: "Come." He puts his hands to the handcart and begins to push it along, then glances back at me anxiously. "Come?"

For an RHR he's remarkably communicative. I tag along behind him as he finishes his round, collecting and distributing brown manila envelopes that smell of dust and long-forgotten secrets. We leave the department behind, heading for the service lifts at the back; Rita doesn't even raise her head to nod as I walk past.

The heavy freight lift takes forever to descend into the subbasement, creaking and clanking. The lights flicker with the harsh edge of fluorescent tubes on the verge of burnout, and the ventilation fans provide a background white buzz of noise that sets my teeth on edge. There's nobody and nothing down here except for storerooms and supply lockers: people visit, but only the dead stay.

Handcart man shuffles down a narrow passage lined with fire doors. Pausing before one, he produces an antiquated-looking key and unlocks a padlock-and-chain from around the crash bar. Then he pushes his cart through into a dimly lit space beyond.

"How do you re-lock that?" I ask him.

"Lock . . . at night," he mumbles, throwing a big switch like a circuit breaker that's mounted on the wall just inside the door.

We're in a narrow, long room with a couple of handcarts parked along one wall. The other side of the room is strange. There's a depression in the floor, and a hole in each of the narrow ends: rails run along the depression between the holes. Such is the wildly unusual scale of it all that it takes me several seconds to blink it back into the correct perspective and see that I'm standing on the platform of an underground railway station—a narrow-gauge system with tracks about sixty centimeters apart, and an electrified third rail. I hear a sullen rumbling from one of the tunnel mouths, and feel a warm breath of wind on my face, like the belch of a very small dragon. The original MailRail track only ran east to west, but extensions were planned back in the 1920s; I suppose I shouldn't be surprised to find one here, for what else would commend this extremely boring sixties office block to the Laundry as a temporary headquarters?

I look at handcart man. "Can I ride this?" I ask.

Instead of answering, he pulls a second lever. I shrug. You'd think I'd have learned better than to ask zombies complex questions by now, wouldn't you?

The rumbling builds to a loud roar, and a remarkable object rolls out of the tunnel and screeches to a halt in the middle of the room.

It's a train, of course—three carriages, all motorized. But it's *tiny*. You could park it in my front hall. The roofs of the carriages barely rise waist-high, and they sport external handles. Handcart man shambles to the front carriage and hinges the roof right up. Not even breaking a sweat, he begins to load the files from his cart into a storage bin.

"Hey, what about"—I focus on the second carriage. It's got wire mesh sides, and what looks like a bench—"me?"

Handcart man lifts a box of files out of the front carriage, deposits it in his cart, and lowers the lid. Then he walks to the second carriage, lifts the roof, and looks at me expectantly.

"I was afraid you were going to say that," I mutter, and climb in. The wooden bench seat is about five centimeters above the track bed, and I have to lean backward as he drops the lid with a clang. The carriage is only big enough for a single passenger. It smells musty and dry, as if something died in here a long time ago.

Turning my head sideways, I watch as handcart man walks over to the big circuit breaker and yanks it down and up, down and up. It must be some kind of trackside signal, because a moment later I feel a motor vibrate under me, and the train starts to roll forward. I make myself lie down: it'd be a really great start to the mission to scrape my face off on the tunnel roof. And a moment later I'm off, rattling feetfirst into the darkness under London, on a false-flag mission . . .

AT ABOUT THE SAME TIME I'M FALLING FEETFIRST INTO A PIECE of railway history, another part of the plot is unfolding. Let me try to reconstruct it for you:

A red-haired woman holding a violin case is making her way along a busy high street in London. Wearing understated trousers and a slightly dated Issey Miyake top, sensible shoes, and a leather bag that's showing its age, she could be a college lecturer or a musician on her way to practice: without the interview suit, nobody's going to mistake her for an auction house employee or a civil servant. Which shows how deceptive appearances can be.

Kids and shoppers and office workers in suits and shop staff in uniforms move around her; she threads her way between them, not looking in shop windows or diverting her attention from the destination in hand. Here's a side street, and she turns the corner wide—avoiding a baby buggy, its owner nattering on her mobile—and strides along it before turning into another, wider street at a corner where a bland seventies office rises six stories above the pavement.

The office has glass doors and a reception desk fronting an austere atrium; a bank of lifts behind it promises a rapid ascent into crowded beige cubicle heaven. The woman approaches reception, and holds up an ID card of some sort. The guard nods, signs her in, then waves her on to the lift bank on the right. She could be a session musician turning up at one of the TV production companies listed on the wall panel beside the reception desk, or a member of staff on her way back from a lunchtime lesson.

But she's not.

The lift control panel shows five numbered floors. As the door slides closed, the woman pushes the third-floor button, then first floor (twice), then the fourth floor. The lift begins to move. The illuminated floor display tracks it up from ground to first, second, third—and it goes out. Then, safely stranded between indicated floors, the doors open.

There are no cubicles here: only rooms with frosted glass doors that lock shut, and red security lights to warn against intrusion. Some of the rooms are offices, and some of them are laboratories, although the experiments that are conducted in them require little equipment more exotic than desktop computers and hand-wired electronic circuitry.

The red-haired woman makes her way through the building with ease born of familiarity, until she finds room 505. She knocks on the door. "Come in," the occupant calls, his voice muffled somewhat by the wood.

Mo opens the door wide. "Dr. Mike," she says, smiling.

"Mo?" He has a large head for his average-sized torso: brown hair fighting a hard-bitten retreat, bound in a ponytail; his eyebrows, owlishly peaked, rise quizzically at her approach. "Good to see you!"

"It's been too long." She walks in and they embrace briefly. "Are you busy?"

"Not immediately, no." His desk tells a different story, piled high in untidy snowdrifts of paper—there's a laser printer on a table in one corner, and a heavy-duty shredder right below it—with a coffee mug balanced atop one particularly steep pile. The mug reads: *DURING OFF HOURS TRAINS STOP HERE.* There's a bookcase beside the desk, crammed full of phrase books and travel guides, except for one shelf, which is occupied by a tiny Z-gauge model railway layout. "Were you passing through or can I be of service in some way?"

"I was hoping to talk to you," she confesses. "About . . ." She shrugs. "Mind if I sit down?"

"It's the cross-section growth coefficient, isn't it?" he asks, and one of his eyebrows tries to climb even farther. "Yes, yes, make yourself comfortable. *Everyone* has been asking about it this week." He sighs, then backs towards his own chair, bearish on his short legs.

"I got an edited, probably garbled, version of it from Andy last week," she explains. "The original paper isn't on the intranet so I thought I'd ask you about it." She nods at the door. "In person."

"Yes . . . very wise." His expression relaxes moment by moment.

"The scholars of night have been busy."

"Word leaked." Saturnine, he rests one hand on a graph-ruled notepad. "Or so I gather from Angleton."

"That's interesting." Mo rests her violin against the side of her chair and crosses her legs. "He's missing too, you know."

"That's *very* interesting!" Now Ford's expression lightens. "The time has come, the Walrus said, to talk of many things."

Mo nods. "Footwear and naval architecture I know, but I never could get my head around why you'd put wax in the ceiling. Some kind of late-Victorian loft-space insulation?"

"No, it's—" Ford stops. "Okay, you won that round. Is this about the paper, or the leak?"

"The paper." She leans forward expectantly.

"The first rule of paper is, there is no paper—well no, not exactly, but it's not the kind of result I could punt at *Nature*, is it?"

"Right. So who reviewed it?"

Ford nods. "That's the *right* question. Whose hat are you wearing?"

Mo's eyes go very cold. "There's a little girl in Amsterdam whose parents don't have much time for hair-splitting right now. Not that I'm accusing you of playing games, but I need to *know*. See, I'm conducting some research in applied epistemology. It would be rather unfortunate if you made a mistake in your logic and the Brotherhood of the Black Pharaoh have gotten themselves worked up over nothing."

"The Brotherhood? I say, are they still going?" He meets her cold stare with one of his own. "That is simply not on. I rather thought we'd put a stop to their antics in Afghanistan a few years ago."

"They're a broad franchise: they've got any number of fronts." She makes a gesture of dismissal. "*Whoever*. I'm looking into this on my own initiative. Do you have a draft I can see?"

"I think I could manage that." He begins to hunt through the papers on his desk. "Ah, here." He passes her three pages, held together by a paper clip.

Mo peers at the top page. "Wait, I can't read—"

"Ah. Just a moment." Ford waves his left hand across the paper and mutters something unintelligible under his breath.

Mo blinks. "Was that entirely safe?"

He grins. "No."

"I, uh, see." She peers at the abstract. "That's interesting. Let me paraphrase. You've tried to quantify memetic transmission effects among a population exposed to class three abominations and find . . . belief in them spreads? And it's a power function?"

He nods. "You must understand, previous models all seem to have looked at how possession spreads through a sparse network, like classical epidemiological studies of smallpox transmission, for example. But that's flawed: if you posit an uncontrolled outbreak, then people can see their neighbors, random strangers, being possessed. And that *in turn* weakens the observer-mediated grid ultrastructure, making it easier for the *preta* to tunnel into our reality. It's a feedback loop: the more people succumb, the weaker everyone else's resistance becomes. I modeled it using linear programming and the results are, well, they speak for themselves."

"And the closer we come to the Transient Weak Anomaly the more outbreaks we're going to see, and the—it contributes to the strength of the TWA?" She looks at him sharply.

"Substantially, yes." Dr. Mike shuffles uncomfortably in his chair.

"Well, *shit*." She folds the paper neatly and slides it into her handbag. "And here I was hoping Andy had gotten the wrong end of the stick."

"Second-order effects are always gonna getcha." He shrugs apologetically. "I don't know why nobody looked into it from this angle before."

"Not your problem, not *my* problem."

"Says Wernher von Braun, yes, and who says satire is dead?"

"Tom Lehrer. Or maybe Buddy Holly."

"*Right*. But you said something that interests me strangely. How did the Black Brotherhood—or whoever wants us to think they're the BBs—get the news?"

"That's what a lot of people are asking themselves right now." She gives him a peculiar look. "It made quite a stir, unfortunately. Lots of wagging tongues. Unfortunately Oscar-Oscar are drawing blanks and they can't Audit the entire organization—at least not yet. We'll have to examine the second-order consequences if the cultists learn they've got a turbocharger, though. If you can come up with anything . . ."

"Angleton would be the one to talk to about that," he says slyly. "After all, he's the head of the Counter-Possession Unit."

"Angleton's missing—" Mo freezes.

For a moment they sit in silence. Then Dr. Mike raises one preposterous eyebrow. "Are you certain of that?"

* * *

I'M GLAD I'M NOT CLAUSTROPHOBIC.

Well, I'm not *very* claustrophobic. Lying on my back in a coffin-sized railway carriage, rattling down a steep incline in a tunnel less than a meter in diameter that was built in the 1920s is not my idea of a nice relaxing way to spend an afternoon. Especially knowing that the station staff are zombies and I'm barreling headfirst into the depths of a high security government installation with only my warrant card to speak for me, on a mission of somewhat questionable legality.

Pull yourself together, Bob. You've been in darker holes.

Yes, but back then Angleton at least had the good grace to tell me what the fuck I was supposed to be doing! This time around it's just *I want you to be my tethered goat.* That and the 440 volt DC rail fifteen centimeters below my spine give me a tingling sensation like my balls want to climb right up my throat and hide. I suppose I shouldn't be surprised that there's a back door into the stacks, or that it's a hinky little narrow-gauge tube system constructed by a Quango and forgotten by everyone except train spotters, but to find myself actually *riding* it . . . that's something else.

Angleton had the decency to scribble me a written order, and a good thing too, otherwise I would have thrown a strop. The librarians don't appreciate unannounced visitors, much less informal withdrawals, and like so many of our more eccentric outposts they have their own inimitable and unspeakable ways of dealing with vandals and intruders. If they catch me, a signed order from a DSS ought to make them pause long enough to give me a fair hearing before they rip my lungs out; but, really and truly, it *is* usually best to just put in a request and wait for the little man with the cart.

I try not to think too hard about everything that can go wrong with Angleton's plan. Instead, I lie back and think of libraries.

The Laundry keeps its archive stacks in a former tube tunnel. It was originally going to be a station, but during World War Two it was converted into an emergency bunker and in the end they never got around to connecting it up to the underground network. There are six levels rather than the usual three, two levels built into each half of a cylindrical tunnel eight meters in diameter and nearly a third of a kilometer long. That makes for a *lot* of shelves—not quite in the same league as the British Library, but close. And it's not just books that occupy the stacks. We store microfiche cards in binders, row after row of them, and there are rooms full of filing cabinets full of CD-ROMs. There's a lot of stuff down here, a lot of moldering secrets and fatal lies: a complete transcript of every numbers channel transmitted since 1932, the last words of every spy hanged during the Second World War, every sermon preached by a minister in the Church of Night—*our* minister—before his followers found out and tore him toe from nail . . .

The train tilts so that my feet are raised, and the clattering rush begins to slow. I've only been here for three or four minutes but it feels like hours in the roaring dark. I cross my arms around my body, hugging myself, and try not to think about premature burials. Instead I try to remember more secrets and lies: such as the recordings of every spy and defector executed by Abu Nidal. (Famously paranoid, if he suspected a recruit of spying he had them buried in a coffin, fed through a tube while being interrogated: after which they would be executed by a bullet fired down the same pipe. I gather he killed more of his own followers than any hostile power.) The last confessions of every member of the Green Hand Sect arrested and interrogated by the Kripo in Saxony in the late 1930s. (Which led to secret and unsanctioned executions—which the Occupying Powers declined to investigate, after a brief, horrified review of the Nazi-era records.) There is even a sealed box of DVDs containing high-resolution scans of the mechanical blueprints from the Atrocity Archives. (That one was my own contribution to the stacks, I'm afraid.)

The carriage squeals to a halt. A few seconds later, I hear the clatter of lids being raised. I take this as my cue and, bracing myself, I push against the roof.

I sit up to find myself in another room, this time with a rounded tunnel-like roof and raw brick walls. It's dimly lit by red lights set deep in shielded sockets; it smells of corruption and memories. A pair of residual human resources are lethargically unloading the wagon in front of me. I lever myself off the bench seat and clamber over the side of the carriage, trying not to bash my head on the low, curving ceiling. There are human-sized doors at either end of the platform, but I don't dare try them at random—I'm pushing my luck just by being here. Instead, I approach one of the shambling human figures, and thrust my ink-stained forearm under what's left of its rotting nose. *"Document,"* I say, stabbing my opposing index finger at the numbers: "File me!"

Leathery fingers close lightly around my wrist and tug me towards a half-loaded handcart. I grab onto the edge of it and the hand drops away; I suppress a shudder. (One of the office unions is currently taking HR to court over the use of residuals, claiming it's a violation of their human rights; HR's argument is that once you're dead you have no rights to violate, but the union's lawyers have said that if they lose the case they'll bring a counter-suit for interfering with corpses—either that, or they'll demand equal pay for the undead.)

After a couple of minutes, one of the working stiffs shuffles over to a control board on one wall and starts pulling handles. With a grumbling buzz of motors and the screech of steel wheels on rails, the mail train rolls forward into the next tunnel mouth, on its way back to the realm of worms and darkness. Then they take their handcarts and shamble slowly towards the farthest door.

I walk alongside, resting one hand on the file cart at all times. Doors open and close. Using my free hand, I produce my warrant card and orders, then hold them clenched before me. We walk down whitewashed brick-lined passages like the catacombs beneath a recondite order's monastery, dimly lit by yellowing bulbs. A cool breeze blows endlessly towards my face, into the depths of the MailRail tunnels.

A twist in the passage brings us to another pair of riveted iron doors, painted battleship gray. It's probably their original wartime livery. I'm close to lost by this point, for I've never been in the lower depths of the stacks before: all my dealings have been with the front desk staff on the upper levels. The lead zombie places a claw-fingered hand on the door and pushes, seemingly effortlessly. The door swings open onto a different shade of darkness, a nocturnal gloom that raises gooseflesh on my neck. I tighten my grip on the cart and swear at myself silently. *I left my ward with Mo, didn't I?* I hastily raise my warrant card and orders and grip them with my teeth, then fumble for the NecronomiPod with my free hand. *Should have replaced it . . .*

As my bearer walks forward I thumb-tap the all-seeing eye into view and bring the phone's camera to bear. What I see does not fill me with joy: the dark on the other side of the portal isn't just due to an absence of light, it's the result of a very powerful ward. Being of a nasty and suspicious disposition it strikes me as likely that it's part of a security cordon— after all, this is a secret document repository I'm trying to break into, isn't it? And I know what I'd plant just inside the back door if I was in charge of security: Shelob, or a good emulation thereof, the better to trap intruders in my sticky web.

It's time to break from my assigned shelf space so, not entirely regretfully, I let go of the document cart. Before the dead man walking can take me in hand again, I remove the papers from my mouth, then lick the ink on my wrist and frantically rub it on my jacket. "Not a document!" I crow, showing my smeary skin to the walking corpse. "No need to push, file, stamp, index, brief, debrief, or number me!"

It stands still for a moment, rocking gently on the balls of its feet, and I can almost see the exception handler triggering in the buggy necrosymbolic script that animates and guides its behavior. A sudden thought strikes me and I raise my warrant card. "Command override!" I bark. "Command override!"

The zombie freezes again, its claws centimeters from my throat. *"Overrr-ride,"* it creaks. "Identify authorization." The other zombie, standing behind it, hisses like a truck's air brake.

"In the name of the Counter-Possession Unit, on the official business of Her Majesty's Occult Service, I override you," I say, very slowly. A harsh blue light from my warrant card shows me more of its death mask than I have any desire to remember. The next bit is hard: my Enochian is rusty, and I'm told I have an abominable accent, but I manage to pull together the ritual phrases I need. These residual human resources are minimally scriptable, as long as you've got the access permissions and know what you're doing. The consequences of getting it wrong are admittedly drastic, but I find that the prospect of a syntax error getting your brains gnawed out through a hole in your skull concentrates the mind wonderfully. (If only we could convince Microsoft to port Windows to run on zombies—although knowing how government IT sector outsourcing is run, that's probably redundant.) "Accept new program parameters. Subroutine start . . ." Or words to that effect, in questionable medieval cod-Latin gibberspeak.

After fifteen minutes of chanting I'm cold with sweat and shaking with tension. My audience are displaying no signs of acquiring a taste for *pâté de foie programmer*, which is good, but if security is paranoid enough they'll be flagged as overdue any minute now. "End subroutine, amen," I intone. The zombies stand where they are. *Oops, have I crashed them?* I pull out my phone and fire up its poxy excuse for a personal ward, then stick it in my jacket's breast pocket. *There's only one way to find out if this is going to work, isn't there?* I snap my fingers. "What are you waiting for?" I ask, reaching into one of my pockets again. "Let's go to work."

The Hand of Glory has seen better days—the thumb is worn right down to the base of the big joint, and only two of the fingers still have unburned knuckles—but it'll have to do. "Do we have ignition, do we have *fucking ignition*," I snarl under my breath, and a faint blue glow like a guttering candle rises from each of the stumps. I climb into one of the document carts, carefully holding on to the waxy abomination, and the residual human resource gives me a tentative shove towards the dark.

There's a tunnel out of nightmares in the library in the underside of the world. I'm not sure I can quite describe what happens in there: cold air, moist, the dankness and silence of the crypt broken only by the squeaking of the overloaded wheels of my cart. A sense of being watched, of a mindless and terrible focus sweeping across me, averted by the skin of the Hand of Glory's burning fingertips. A rigor fit to still the heart of heroes, and only the faint pulsing ward-heart of my phone to bring me through it with QRS complex intact. There is a reason they use residual human resources to run the files to and from the MailRail system: you don't need to be dead to work here, but it *really* helps.

I'm in the darkness for only ten or fifteen seconds, but when I come out I am in soul-deep pain, my heart pounding and my skin clammy, as if on the edge of a heart attack. Everything is gray and grainy and there is a buzzing in my ears, as of a monstrous swarm of flies. It disperses slowly as the light returns.

I blink, trying to get a grip, and I realize that the handcart has stopped moving. Shivering, I sit up and somehow slither over the edge of the cart without tipping the thing over. There's carpet on the floor, thin, beige, institutional—I'm back in the land of the living. I look round. There's a wooden table, three doors, a bunch of battered filing cabinets, and another door through which the mailmen are disappearing—black painted wood, with a motto engraved above the lintel: ABANDON HOPE. Trying to remember what I actually saw in there sends my mind skittering around the inside of my skull like a frightened mouse, so I give up. I'm still clutching the Hand of Glory. I hold it up to look at the flames. They've burned down deep, and there's little left but calcined bones. Regretfully, I blow them out one by one, then dispose of the relic in the recycling bin at one side of the table.

No mailmen, but no librarians either. It's all very Back Office, just as Angleton described it. I head for the nearest door, just as it opens in front of me.

"Hey—"

I blink. "Hello?" I ask.

"You're not supposed to be here," he says, annoyed if not outright cross. "Visitors are restricted to levels five and six only. You could do yourself a mischief, wandering around the subbasement!" In his shirt and tie and M&S suit he's like an intrusion from another, more banal, universe. I could kiss him just for existing, but I'm not out of the woods yet.

"Sorry," I say contritely. "I was sent to ask for a new document that's supposed to have come in this morning . . . ?"

"Well, you'd better come with me, then. Let me see your ID, please."

I show him my warrant card and he nods. "All right. What is it you're after?"

"A file." I show him the slip of paper on which I've written down Mo's document reference. "It's new, it should have come in this morning."

"Follow me." He leads me through a door, to a lift, up four levels and along a corridor to a waiting room with a desk and half a dozen cheap powder-blue chairs: I vaguely recognize it from a previous visit. "Give me that and wait here."

I sit down and wait. Ten minutes later he's back, frowning. "Are you sure this is right?" he asks.

Annoyed, I think back. "Yes," I say. I read the number back to Mo, didn't I? "It's a new file, deposited last night."

"Well, it's not here yet." He shrugs. "It may still be waiting to be allocated a shelf, you know. That happens sometimes, if adding a new file triggers a shelf overflow."

"Oh." Mo won't be happy, I guess, but it establishes my cover. "Well, can you flag it for me when it comes in?"

"Certainly. If you can show me your card again?" I do so, and he takes a note of my name and departmental assignment. "Okay, Mr. Howard, I'll send you an email when the file comes into stock. Is that everything?"

"Yes, thanks, you've been very helpful." I smile. He turns to go. "Er, can you remind me the way out . . . ?"

He waves a hand at one of the doors. "Go down there, second door on the left, you can't miss it." Then he leaves.

THE SECOND DOOR ON THE LEFT OPENS ONTO A SMOOTH- floored tunnel lined in white glazed tiles and illuminated by overhead fluorescent tubes of a kind that are sufficiently familiar that, when I reach the end of the tunnel and step through the gray metal door (which locks behind me with a muffled *click*) I am unsurprised to find myself in a passage between two tube platforms.

Half an hour and a change of line later, I swipe my Oyster card and surface, blinking at the afternoon sun. I pat the inside pocket where I secreted the sheaf of papers that Angleton gave me. And then I head back to my office in the New Annexe, where I very pointedly dial open my secure document safe and install those papers, then lock it and go home, secure in the knowledge of the first half of a job well done.

(Like I said: fatal accidents never happen because of just *one* mistake.)

11.

CRIME SCENES

I DON'T FUNCTION WELL IN THE SMALL HOURS OF THE MORNING.
I sleep like a log, and I have difficulty pulling my wits about me if something wakes me in the pre-dawn dark.

So it takes me a few seconds to sit up and grab the bedside phone when it begins to snarl for attention. I fumble the handset close to my face: "Whuuu—" I manage to drone, thinking, *If this is a telesales call, I'll plead justifiable homicide*, as Mo spasms violently in a twist of the duvet and rolls over, pulling the bedding off me.

"Bob." *I know that voice. It's—*"Jo here. Code Blue. How soon can you be ready for a pickup?"

I am abruptly awake in an icy-cold drench of sweat. "Five minutes," I croak. "What's up?"

"I want you in here stat, and I'm sending a car. Be ready in five minutes." She sounds uncertain . . . *afraid?* "This line isn't secure, so save your questions."

"Okay." The phrase *this had better be good* doesn't even reach my larynx: declaring Code Blue is the sort of thing that attracts the Auditors' attention. "Bye." I put the phone down.

"What was that?" says Mo.

"That was a Code Blue." I swing my feet over the edge of the bed and fish for yesterday's discarded socks. "There's a car calling for me in five minutes."

"*Shit* . . ." Mo rolls over the other way and buries her face in a pillow. "Am I wanted?" Her voice, muffled, trails away.

"Just me." I paw through an open drawer for pants. "It's Jo Sullivan. At four in the morning."

"She's with Oscar-Oscar, isn't she?"

"Yup." Pants: on. Tee shirt: on. Trousers: next in queue.

"You'd better go." She sounds serious. "Phone me the instant you hear something."

I glance at the alarm. "It's twenty to five."

"I don't mind." She pulls the bedding into shape. "Take care."

"And you," I say, as I head downstairs, carrying my holstered pistol.

I'm standing in the front hall when blue and red strobes light up the window glass above the door. I open it in the face of a cop. "Mr. Howard?" she asks.

"That's me." I hold up my warrant card and her eyes age a little.

"Come with me, please," she says, and opens the rear door for me. I strap myself in and we're off for another strobe-lit taxi ride through the wilds of South London, speeding alarmingly down narrow shuttered streets and careening around roundabouts in the gray pre-dawn light until, after a surprisingly short time, we pull up outside the staff entrance to a certain store.

The door is open. Jo is waiting for me. One look at her face tells me it's bad. Angleton warned me: *This is where it starts.* I tense. "What's happened?" I ask.

"Come this way." Jo leads me up the stairwell. The lights are on, which is abnormal, and I hear footsteps—not the steady shuffle of the night staff, but boots and raised voices. Something in the air makes me think of a kicked anthill.

We head past reception where a couple of blue-suited security men are standing guard over a stapler and six paper clips, then back along the corridor past Iris's corner office, then round the bend to—

"*Fuck,*" I say, unable to contain myself. My office door is closed. But I can see the interior, because there's a gigantic hole in the door, as if someone hit it with a wrecking ball. (Except a wrecking ball would leave rough jagged edges of splintered wood, while the rim of this particular hole looks oddly melted.) The interior isn't much better; an avalanche of paper and scraps of broken metal are strewn across half an overturned desk. A thin blue glow clings patchily to some of the wreckage, fading slowly even as I watch. "What happened?"

"Am hoping you tell us." It's Boris, bags under his eyes and an expression as dark as midnight on the winter solstice. *When did he get back? Wasn't he doing something overseas connected with BLOODY BARON . . . ?*

"What have you *done,* Bob?" Jo grabs my left elbow. "First a civilian FATACC, now this. What are you into?"

I blink stupidly at the destruction. "My secure document safe, is it . . . ?"

She shakes her head. "We won't know until we go inside. It's still active." I feel a thin prickling on the back of my neck. Demonic intruders have been at work, summoned to retrieve something. *Angleton was right,* I realize.

"What did you have in your safe?"

"I'm not sure you're cleared—"

Boris clears his throat. "Is cleared, Bob. *I* will clear her. What was in safe? What attracted attention of burglars in night?"

I squint through the hole in the door. "I had documents relating to several codeword projects in there," I say. "The stacks can probably reconstruct my withdrawal record, and once it's safe to go in there we can work out what is missing."

"Bob, you went to the archives in person yesterday." Jo tightens her grip on my elbow, painfully tight. "What did you withdraw most recently? Tell us!"

Truth and consequences time. "I asked for a copy of the Fuller Memorandum," I tell her, which is entirely true and correct: "I was following up something Angleton told me to do a while ago." Which is also entirely correct, and the most misleading thing I've said in front of witnesses all year.

"Fuller Memo—" I see a flicker of recognition on Boris's face. "Tell me, when you go home last night, is Fuller Memorandum in safe?"

I nod. I don't trust my tongue at this point because, as the man who used to be president said, it all depends on what you mean by the word "is."

Jo stares at Boris. "What classification level are we talking about?" she asks.

Boris doesn't answer at once. He's staring at me, and if looks could kill, I'd be a tiny pile of ash right now. "Does Angleton say you are to the memorandum read?" he asks.

"Yup. Took me a while to track it down," I extemporize. "So I left it in the safe overnight; I was going to look at it today." All of which is truthful enough that I will happily repeat it in front of an Audit Panel, knowing that if I tell a lie in front of them the blood will boil in my veins and I *won't die*—

Boris looks at Jo and nods, minutely. "Am thanking you for calling me. This is *mess*."

"What was in the memo that's so red-hot?" I ask, pushing my luck, because somewhere in all the fuss of expediting Angleton's little scheme— taking the forgery he'd prepared and inserting it into the archives, then withdrawing it and planting the bait in my office safe—I hadn't gotten round to asking him just what the original was about.

"Memorandum is control binding scripture for asset called Eater of Souls," Boris says, and strangely he refuses to meet my eyes. "Codeword is TEAPOT. Consequences of loss—unspeakable."

"Oh, *shit*." I swear with feeling, because I'm not *totally* stupid: I worked out who Teapot was some time ago. I didn't realize the Fuller Memorandum was his *control document*, though. The control document is the source code and activation signature for the geas that binds the entity called Teapot—the thing that over an eighty-year span became

Angleton. It doesn't even matter that our safe-breakers have stolen a ringer—at least, I *assume* Angleton gave me a ringer—the fact that they knew what to look for in the first place is *really bad news.*

"You'd better come with me," says Jo, and I suddenly notice that she's shifted her grip to my forearm and she's got fingers like handcuffs. "Form R60 time, Bob. And this time it's not just a FATACC enquiry. As soon as my people have gone over the incident scene with a fine-toothed comb this will be going before the Auditors. I'm sorry."

I DO NOT PASS GO. DO NOT COLLECT £200. AND DO NOT BUY Piccadilly Circus. I don't go to jail, either—not yet—but by the middle of the morning a thirty-year stretch in Wormwood Scrubs would come as a blessed relief.

"Committee of enquiry will come to order."

I've been here before, and I didn't like it the first time. The panel has requisitioned a small conference room, furnished in nineties government brutalist-lite: Aeron chairs and bleached pine table, health and safety posters on one wall, security notices on the other. The tribunal sits at the far end of the table, like a pin-striped hanging judge and his assistants. And they've rolled out that fucking carpet again, the one with the gold thread design woven into it, and the Enochian inscription, and the live summoning grid powerful enough to twist tendons and snap bones.

There is no peanut gallery at this trial. Jo is waiting outside with a couple of blue-suiters and the other designated witnesses, but the Auditors want no inconvenient onlookers who might have to be bound to silence or memory-wiped, should I accidentally disclose material above their level of classification.

"Please state your name and job title." There's a recorder on the desk, as usual: its light is glowing red.

"Bob Howard. Senior Specialist Officer grade 3. Personal assistant to Tea—er, DSS Angleton."

That causes a minor stir. One of the Auditors—female, blonde, late-forties—turns sideways and says something to the others that I ought to be able to hear, but can't. The other two nod. She turns back and addresses me directly. "Mr. Howard. You are aware of the terms of this investigation. You are aware of the geas it is conducted under. You have our special dispensation to respond to any question, the first time it is posed—and only the first time—by warning us if in your judgment the reply would require you to disclose codeword-classified information. Please state your understanding of this variance, in your own words."

I clear my throat. "If you ask me about sensitive projects I'm allowed to stonewall—once. If you ask me again, I have to tell you, period. Uh, I assume that's because you'd prefer to keep the enquiry from accidentally covering so many highly classified subjects that nobody is allowed to read its findings . . . ?"

She smiles drily. "Something like that." It feels like the Angel of Death has just perched on my shoulder, paused from sharpening its blade, and quietly squawked: *Who's a* pretty *Polly?* Then the sense of immanent ridiculous demise passes. *Ha ha, I slay myself . . .*

The Chief Auditor nods, then looks at the legal pad before him. "Yesterday you visited the library front desk. What was your objective?"

Lie back and think of England—and nothing else. "Angleton gave me a reading list," I said. "He told me to bring back a particular document." *Pause.* "Oh, and Mo wanted me to pick up a copy of a report she'd asked for, but it wasn't in yet."

There is no prickling of high tension current in my legs to warn me that my partial truth is unacceptable.

"Who is 'Mo'?" asks Auditor #3.

"Dr. Dominique O'Brien. Epistemological Warfare Specialist grade 4."

Auditor #3 leans forward hungrily. "Why did this person ask you to collect a document on their behalf?" he demands.

I blink, nonplussed. "Because I told her I was going to the library, and she was busy. She's my wife."

Auditor #3 looks baffled for a few seconds, his bloodhound trail evaporating in a haze of aniseed fumes. "You're *married?*"

"Yes." This would be hilarious if I wasn't scared silly by the sleeping horror I am standing on that will sense any attempt at deception and—

"Oh." He makes a note on his pad and subsides.

The blonde Auditor gives him a very old-fashioned look, then turns to me: "Are you cleared for the content of her work?" she asks.

Huh? "I have no idea," I say sincerely. "We only discuss projects we're working on after comparing codeword access and if necessary asking for clearance." Then the glyph on the goddamn rug forces me to add, "But this time it doesn't matter, the document hadn't arrived anyway."

She scribbles something on her own notepad. "Did Dr. O'Brien tell you anything about this particular note?" she asks.

I blink. "I have no idea. She simply gave me the file reference number— no codeword."

More notes, more significant looks. The senior Auditor stares at me over the gold half-moon rims of his spectacles. "Mr. Howard. Please indicate if you are familiar with any of these individuals. Matthias Hoechst, Jessica Morgenstern, George Dower, Nikolai Panin—" He nods at my hand signal. "Describe what you know about Nikolai Panin."

"I had a pint with him in the Frog and Tourettes the day before yesterday."

The effect is astonishing: the Auditors jerk to attention like a row of frogs with cattle prods up their backsides. I meet their appalled gaze with a sense of sublime lightness. *They want the truth? Okay, they can fucking have the truth.*

"I reported it as a contact to the BLOODY BARON committee at the first opportunity, and it was agreed to keep it quiet for the time being. Panin seems to have wanted to pass on a warning about Teapot. He was concerned that it was missing, and that as its last custodians we ought to ensure it was found before the wrong persons got their hands on it and, uh, 'made tea.'" I smile blandly. "Angleton authorized me to read the WHITE BARON files and I have inferred the identity of Teapot."

The Chief Auditor shakes his head. "Bloody hell," he grumbles, then, to me: "Do you know where Angleton is?"

I open my mouth—then pause. *Now* I can feel the electric flare of the geas tickling the fine hairs on my legs.

The blonde Auditor narrows her eyes. "Speak," she commands.

I can't *not* speak, but I still have some control. "I don't believe Angleton has assigned it a codeword yet," I hear myself saying, "but his disappearance is connected with an ongoing investigation and I don't think he wants me to tell anyone about it . . ."

My legs feel as if they're immersed in cold fire up to the knees. I gasp for breath, just as the Chief Auditor hastily holds up his hand: "Stay of execution! The subject has invoked the security variance." He peers at me. "Can you confirm that you are cognizant of Angleton's whereabouts?"

I nod, jerkily. The chilly, searing fingers recede down my calves.

"*In your judgment*, is Angleton working in the best interests of this institution?"

I nod like a parcel shelf ornament.

"Also in your judgment, would it impair his work on behalf of this institution if we continue to explore this line of enquiry?"

I think for a moment. Then I nod, emphatically.

"Very well." Light glints on his spectacles as he looks at me for a few seconds. "On your recommendation, we will not enquire further—unless you have something you would like to tell us?"

Careful, Bob! This is an Audit board you're up against. They're at their most dangerous when they're being reasonable, and they can turn all the fires of hell—imaginary or otherwise—on you if you don't cooperate.

I take a deep breath. "I'm confused," I finally say. "I thought this was an enquiry about the break-in and theft from my office safe, but you've been asking questions about Angleton and Mo instead. What's going on?"

Wrong question: Auditor #3 smiles sharkishly and the blonde Auditor shakes her head. "It is not in the remit of this committee to *answer* questions," says the Chief Auditor, a trifle archly. "Now, back to the matter in hand. I have some questions about office supplies. When did you last order stationery fasteners from office stores, and how many and what type did you request . . . ?"

WHILE I'M BEING HAULED OVER THE COALS. MO RISES AT HER usual hour, makes coffee, eats a cereal bar, reads my text message. It's along the lines of HELD UP AT WORK IN COMMITTEE. She frowns, worried but not unduly alarmed. (My texts range from verbose and eloquent—when I'm bored—to monosyllabic, when the entire cesspit is about to be ingested by a jet engine. This intermediate level is indicative of stress, but not of mortal danger.)

She leaves the dregs of the coffee in the pot, and the cereal bar wrapper on top of the other waste in the kitchen bin. She goes upstairs, dresses, collects violin and coat, and leaves.

Sometimes Mo works in the New Annexe; and sometimes she doesn't. There's an office in the Royal College of Music where her name is one of three listed on the door. There's a course in philosophy of mathematics at King's College where she sometimes lectures—and forwards reports on her pupils to Human Resources. And she's a regular visitor at the Village, across the fens and up the coast by boat, where the Laundry keeps certain assets that don't belong in a crowded city. Today, she sets out by tube, heading for the city center. She is on her way to ask Mr. Dower whether he did in fact mail his report. And she is in for a surprise.

Watch the red-haired woman in a black suit, violin case in hand, walking up the pavement towards the shuttered shopfront with the blue-and-white police incident tape stretched across the doorway. Traffic cones with more tape stand to either side of the shop front, fluttering in the light breeze. She pauses, nonplussed, then looks around. There is a police officer standing discreetly by, hands clasped behind his back. She glances back at the taped-off doorway. There is no dark stain on the lintel—the SOC officers and the cleanup crew did their job well—but the ward she wears under her blouse buzzes a warning. Her expression hardens, and she walks towards the constable, reaching into her handbag to produce an identity card.

"What happened here, officer?" she asks quietly, holding the card where he can't help but see it.

He doesn't stand a chance. "Who, uh, oh dear . . ." He shakes his head. "Ma'am. Murder scene. You can't go, I mean, you shouldn't . . ."

"Who's in charge here?" she enquires. "Where can I find them?"

"That'd be DI Wolfe, from MIT 4. He's set up shop round the back—that way, that alley there—who should I say—"

"In the name of national security, I command and require you to forget me," she says, slipping the card away and turning towards the alley that runs around to the back of the row of four shops. The constable's eyes close momentarily; by the time he opens them again, the woman with the violin case is gone.

Ten minutes later, the back door to George Dower's shop clicks open. Two figures step inside: a uniformed detective sergeant and the woman. Both of them wear disposable polythene slippers over their shoes; she still holds her violin case. "Don't touch anything—tell me what you want to look at," he says, pulling on a pair of disposable gloves. "What exactly are you after?"

"First of all, what state is his PC in?"

"It wasn't stolen, so we bagged it." The sergeant sounds sure of himself. "If you're wanting to scrape the hard drive, we can have an image of it available in an hour or so."

Mo cools slightly. If the killer left the PC behind, then there's almost certainly nothing left on it but random garbage, an entropic mess that not even CESG will be able to unerase. "Any memory sticks? Small stuff? CD-Rs?"

"We bagged them, too." The sergeant picks his way into Dower's workshop, which still reeks of rosin and varnish. A row of disemboweled instruments hang from a rail overhead, like corpses in the dissectionist's cold parlor. Those tools that are not in their places on the pegboard that covers one wall are laid out on the bench in parallel rows, neatly sorted by size. The metal parts gleam like surgical steel, polished and unnaturally bright.

"Any papers?"

The sergeant pauses beside a rolltop desk, itself an antique, Victorian or Edwardian. "Yes," he says reluctantly. "They're scheduled for pickup tomorrow so we can continue working on the contact list. Receipts, suppliers' brochures, estimates, that sort of thing."

"I'm looking for an appraisal of a customer's instrument," she tells him. "It will be dated yesterday or the day before, and it relates to a violin. It may be in an unmarked envelope, like this one." She produces an envelope from her bag.

"Like that—" The officer's eyes widen and his back straightens. "Would you happen to have any information about the killer?" he asks. "Because if so—"

Mo shakes her head. "I do not know who the killer is." The sergeant stares at her, seeking eye contact. "The victim was commissioned to prepare a report for my department. He was due to post it on the evening when the incident occurred. It has not been delivered."

"What was he meant to report on?"

Mo makes eye contact at last, and the detective sergeant recoils slightly from whatever he sees in her expression. "You have no need to know. *If it appears that there is a connection between the report and the killing,* my department will notify Inspector Wolfe immediately. Similarly, if the identity of the killer comes to our attention." She doesn't add, *in such a way that we can disclose it without violating security protocol*: that much is always understood to be a minor chord in the uneasy duet of spook and cop. "The report, however, is a classified document and should be treated as such." And she raises her warrant card again.

The detective sergeant is clearly torn between the urgent desire to get her into an interview room and the equally urgent desire to get her the hell out of this shop, and away from what was until a few minutes ago a straightforward—if rather unusual—murder investigation; but being on the receiving end of a Laundry warrant card is an *oh-shit* moment. It begins with the phrase *Her Britannic Majesty's government commands and compels you to provide the bearer of this pass with all aid and assistance*, written atop a design of such subtle and mind-numbing power that it makes the reader's breath catch in his throat as suddenly as if trapped by a hangman's noose. He can no more ignore it—and no more ignore her instructions—than he can ignore a gun pointed at his head.

"What do you want?" he finally asks.

"I want the contents of that report." She lowers her card. "I suspect the killer doesn't want me to have it. So if you find it, call me." She produces a business card and he takes it. Then her roving gaze settles on the desk. "Oh, and one other thing. Are there any paper clips or staples in there? Because if so, I want them all."

"Paper clips?"

"Yes, I want all the paper clips and staples in that desk." Her cheek quirks. "Mr. Dower was the type to fasten a report together before folding it and putting it in an envelope. And where there's a link, there's a chain of evidence."

THE AUDIT BOARD CHEWS ME UP AND SPITS ME OUT IN LESS than an hour. Light as thistledown and dry as a dead man's tongue I walk through the door, past the seated witnesses—the blue-suiters are collecting Choudhury now, ushering him into the Presence—and drift on stumbling feet towards my office. Except I don't get very far: instead I bump up against a blue translucent bubble that seems to have swallowed the corridor, and everything in it, just before Iris's office door. The bubble is warm and rubbery and I have a feeling that it would be a very bad idea indeed to try and bull my way through it, so I turn round and go back the other way, towards the coffee station.

I'm just scooping brown powder into a filter cone (the jug was empty right when I most needed it, as usual) when Iris clears her throat behind me.

"I've been Audited," I say, in answer to her silent question. "I don't think it went badly, but I gather I'm not allowed back in my office just yet."

"No one is," she says, surprisingly calmly. "Are you making a fresh pot?"

"Sure." I slide the basket back into the coffee maker and hit the brew button. Iris watches me silently.

"Um, as a matter of fact, you won't be going back to work for a bit," she says.

"I—what?" The coffee machine clears its throat behind me as I stare at her.

"The civilian FATACC incident when you were out at Cosford has been upgraded." Her expression is apologetic. "Sorry doesn't begin to cut it, I know, but the Incident Committee has escalated it to Internal Affairs and they actioned me to notify you that you're being suspended on full pay pending a full hearing."

"They're *what*?" I hear my voice rise uncontrollably, cracked. *But what about Angleton's plan?* "But it's not a FATACC anymore—"

"Bob! Bob? Calm *down*. This isn't the end of the world. I'm sure the hearing will exonerate you; they don't want you in the office until it's over. It's just a routine precaution—Bob?"

She's talking to my back—I'm halfway down the corridor by the time she says my name, then round the bend and halfway down the twist that takes me to the stairwell to Angleton's office. Because (*fuck* Helen Langhorn *and her KGB sleeper medals*, part of me is swearing furiously) I know damn well that I'm going to be exonerated, because the victim wasn't a victim: she was a hostile agent who poked her nose into an off-limits area at the wrong time. So the question is: *Why now?* And there's only one species of answer that fits—

I take the stairs two at a time, thudding down them hard enough to raise dust from the elderly carpet, bouncing off the bannister rail and caroming up against the door. I raise my phone and squint through its magic-mirror eye, seeing that the wards are merely the usual ones, and then I twist the doorknob and push.

"Boss?" I glance around the empty room. The Memex sits in its corner, hulking like a sleeping baby elephant; the filing cabinets are all neatly shut and sealed. *"Boss?"*

He's not here. My spine crawls. *Need to leave him a message.* I head for the Memex and slide into the operator's seat.

WRITE CLEARANCE.

I foot-type TEAPOT and wait for the soul-mangling symbol to disappear.

WRITE.

The menu prompt is empty. MESSAGE, I type. The prompt changes, and I keep going.

BOSS, THEY TOOK THE BAIT. PROBLEM: IA ARE SUSPENDING ME OVER COSFORD. AUDITORS MORE INTERESTED IN PAPER CLIPS. MY MOBILE NUMBER IS: . . .

Angleton isn't a total technophobe. As long as he has my phone number he can get in touch. But now I've got another problem: I'm not supposed to be here. So I switch off the Memex carefully and stand up, and I'm just on the point of tiptoeing out of the room when two blue-suiters appear out of nowhere and grab my wrists.

"Careful now, sir. We wouldn't want to make a fuss, would we?"

I look past his shoulder at Iris. She looks concerned. "Bob, what are you *doing*? Didn't I tell you you were being suspended?"

I pant for breath. My heart's hammering and my palms are slippery. "I was hoping—Angleton—"

She shakes her head sympathetically, then tuts to herself. "I think you're overwrought. He's been having a bad time lately," she explains to the blue-suiters. "You need to go home and relax badly, *don't you*, Bob?"

I can take a hint. I nod.

Blue-suit #2 clears his throat apologetically. "If he's not cleared for this room, ma'am—" he begins.

"No, that's all right," Iris says, casting me a quelling look. "He's—he was—personal secretary to DSS Angleton. He's cleared for this room, and he's not required to be off the premises until noon, and he obviously hasn't touched anything"—I blink at that, but keep my mouth shut—"so you *may* feel free to report it, but he hasn't actually violated the security articles. Yet." She taps her wristwatch. "Not for another nine minutes. So I suggest you might want to take a deep breath and let these gentlemen escort you to the front door, Bob?"

She's right. I really *don't want to still be in the building when my permission is suspended*—the consequences would be drastic and painful, I imagine. "I'll go quietly," I hear myself saying. "If you'd like to lead the way . . ."

AT TWELVE THIRTY EXACTLY I FIND MYSELF STANDING ALONE in the middle of a concrete emptiness, the blurred ghosts of shoppers darting around me like shadows beneath a pitiless sun. I can't remember how I came to this place. My hands are shaking and I can't see the future. All I can see is gray. The sun is beating down but I'm cold inside. I keep seeing a purple flash, the old woman's face rotting and flaking and shrinking around her skull before me; the thing on the bike path, growling deep in its throat.

(They took my pistol. "Don't want you to go carrying that around when you're all depressed, sir," the blue-suiter told me.) I'd phone Mo and ask her to pick up another ward if I wasn't feeling so frustrated and ineffectual.

Everything's fallen apart at the very worst time, and it's *all my fault*.

Item: There is a security breach. The Free Church of the Universal Kingdom—hereafter and forevermore to be known as the Goatfuckers, because that's the least of what they get up to and I don't want to think about them *eating the blonde teacher's face*—have got an informer inside the Laundry.

I walk past a bus stop and an overflowing litter bin, the ashtray on its lid smoking and fulminating. There's a disgusting stench of cheap tobacco and smoldering filter wadding. A convoy of buses rumbles past slowly, like a troupe of implausibly red elephants walking trunk-to-tail.

Item: They followed Mo home and they're following me, and unless I'm very much mistaken they want the key that binds the Eater of Souls, which is probably one of our most powerful weapons. (Disguised as a public school master indeed!)

There's a rundown concrete suburban shopping mall here, a brutalist plaza surrounded by walkways overlooking cheap supermarkets, an off-license, and a shuttered chemist's. Abandoned disposable carrier bags clog the gutters. I walk beneath a bridge between two piers, and up an arcade walled by the display windows of empty shop units, as grimy as my sense of self-worth.

Item: The Goatfuckers aren't the only people who are into the Laundry; Panin and the Thirteenth Directorate clearly know a lot more than *I* do about the CODICIL BLACK SKULL flights, Triple-six Squadron, and the Eater of Souls (who keeps cropping up in this mess like a bad penny). And anything that worries the KGB ought to worry the hell out of me, too.

I come out of the arcade in a wide alley lined with loading bays, rusting metal shutters drawn down across concrete slabs. Overflowing dumpsters redolent with the sweet fetor of dead rats lean between scraped and battered steel bollards, huddling together like school kids sharing a fag behind the bike shed. The sky is clouding over, the merciless sun shrouded by dirty clouds of doubtful provenance. I keep walking.

Item: The Auditors wanted to know about Mo, and about paper clips. I know about paper clips and why they're a security risk. (The laws of contagion and sympathy are fundamental to all systems of magic: quantum entanglement and spooky action-at-a-distance for the witch doctor set. More prosaically, if you've got a paper clip from the same box as a sibling that's clipped to a top secret file . . . you figure it out. Okay?) But why did they want to know about Mo? What *was* the document she wanted me to retrieve? Am I missing something? What if it's not all about me, or Angleton? The business in Saint Martin a few years ago should have been a wake-up call. Just because I'm under investigation, it doesn't mean she—

—*The hell I'm under investigation. No. I'm under* suspicion. *But suspicion of* what?

My feet carry me past the end of the delivery alley and across a road where a cast-iron railway bridge shadows the terraced houses, their fronts smeared with smuts from the diesel locomotives that rumble overhead, freighting coal to the power stations that keep the lights burning and the hard drives turning. There is a cycle path here, and my feet seem to know which way they're going. I turn left and find myself on an incline, ascending a tree-flanked slope. The faint tinkle of a bell prompts me to stand aside as an urban cyclist in luminous lycra zips past, coasting in the opposite direction.

Item: Angleton wants to use me as a tethered goat, but I'm not much use to him if I'm not in the right place when the Goatfuckers come calling. *Damn, I hope he gets my message via the Memex.* Where are we leaking? Is it via the BLOODY BARON committee? That seems to be the logical place, but . . .

A chill creeps over me and I glance up at a turbid cloudscape that wasn't there five minutes ago, swirling masses of dirty cumulonimbus crammed with a promise of rain to come. *Uh-oh.* Here's me, out and about in a lightweight summer jacket. I really ought to head for home. I keep walking, because it seems like the thing to do, although the shadows are lengthening among the dark green trees to either side. The cycle path is empty; I ought to start looking for an exit from it that'll take me back down to street level and a bus stop or tube station. I glance behind me, but I can't see the ramp I came up anymore.

Item: Doctor Mike's research finding about the early onset of CASE NIGHTMARE GREEN. Let's hypothesize that the Goatfuckers heard about it by way of our security breach. We know the Goatfuckers want CASE NIGHTMARE GREEN to come about—they're fans of the old, dead nightmares that will stalk the planet once more. (They *worship* the things. How twisted is that?) Ford's new finding suggests that the onset conditions for tearing a hole in the structure of reality are a bit more flexible than we previously thought. Which suggests that there are things the Goatfuckers can do to accelerate the onset of apocalypse, the *stars coming right* as the pulp writer put it. They're showing an interest in the Eater of Souls. Why? Do they think that if they get their hands on the Fuller Memorandum they can control him, make him do something unspeakable that will shiver the stars in their tracks and split the sky apart like—

—I look up. "Oh *fuck.*" Then I shut my mouth and save my breath for more important activities. Like, for example, *running away.*

While I have been wandering aimlessly, locked in my head, my feet have guided me onto a dismal path. There are no cyclists or pedestrians in sight, just an endless dark strip of tarmac that curves out of sight ahead and behind me, surrounded by impenetrable walls of spiny evergreen shrubs that lean inwards above my head. I can't see through the hedge, but there are pallid mushroom-like structures bursting from the soil around their roots. The cloudscape overhead is turbulent and dappled, side-lit by sunlight slanting under its floor—even though there are hours yet to go until sunset—and the ever-shifting whirlpools and knots of darkness roll and dance, lit from within by the snapshots of cosmic paparazzi.

I have no idea how I got here and I'm not amused with myself for succumbing to what was, at a guess, a very low-key glamour, but the urge to get out and find a safe refuge is overwhelming. Every instinct is screaming that I'm in immediate danger. And so I begin to jog, just as the U-boat klaxon starts to honk urgently from my breast pocket.

"Bob?" It's Mo.

"I'm kind of busy right now," I pant. "What's up?"

"The memo I was after, are you *sure* it wasn't in?"

Huh? "I'm dead sure. Listen, what was it about?"

"That external appraisal of my violin, I told you about that, remember?"

"Oh, that—"

"The examiner was murdered! About thirty-six hours ago. Bob, if they think you've got the violin report—"

"Listen, let me give you an update. I've been suspended on pay. I need you to pick up a ward for me, as soon as you can. I'm heading home now, but I'm in a spot of bother and they took my pistol. Angleton isn't AWOL: Can you find him and tell him he was right, the Goatfuckers are after the bait and I need backup *right now*—"

The NecronomiPod beeps at me three times and drops the call.

"Fuck." I thumb-tap the software ward back to life, then shove the JesusPhone back in my pocket and keep jogging, breathing heavily now. There's a breeze in my face, shoving me back and slowing me down, and the surface of the footpath feels greasy and turgid, almost *sticky*. The sense of wrongness is overwhelming. I have a sense of déjà vu, harking back to my midnight run, although that path was miles away and didn't look anything like . . .

Oh. *Am I on a siding?* I ask myself, as the headwind builds and the shadows deepen. I hear distant thunder and the first heavy slap of raindrops on the path ahead: *Did the Necropolitan line have branches that were edited out of the public record decades ago, by any chance?*

The hoarse scream of a ghostly steam whistle echoes in my ears. It's behind me. And it's gaining ground.

It's funny how you lose track of a situation while it spins out of control: in the space of about fifteen minutes I've let myself be led by the nose—or rather, the feet—from a busy suburban high street in London, right into an occult trap. There are places where the walls of reality are thin; the service corridors of hotels, subway footpaths at night, hedge-mazes and cycle paths. You can get lost in such places, led astray by a lure and a snare and a subliminal suggestion. These routes blend into one another. Of all the myriad ways that link the human realm to the other places, these are the ones we know very little about—because those of us who stumble into them seldom return with their minds intact.

I can feel my heart hammering as I run. The hedges to either side brandish spikes edged with a nacreous rind of blight. There are pale white shapes embedded in the wall of leaves, the flensed bones of intruders trapped in the interstices of the vegetative barrier. Overhead, the clouds are black as smoke from the funnel of a racing steam locomotive, boiling and raging at the ground. I don't dare look back, even though I'm sure I'm being herded towards an ambush: the phone in my pocket is buzzing and vibrating in urgent Morse, signaling the presence of hostile intent.

I need to get off the path. The trouble is, there's nowhere to go— *Hang on,* I think. *Am I seeing true?*

There is this about the interstitial paths: it takes a fair bit of power to open a gate, and I didn't notice any pentacles and altars draped in eviscerated goats during my walk through the decaying shopping center. On the other hand, it takes relatively little power to fake up a glamour to provide the illusion of a dark path. Wheezing, I reach for my phone, thumb it on, and slow my stride just enough that I can see the display. Bloody Runes, ward detector, turn the camera on the footpath—

A silver thread, disappearing around the bend ahead of me. I pan sideways, and the camera blurs then clears, showing me ordinary English nettles and a thinly spaced row of trees pruned well back from the path. It's bright, too, the ground dappled with summer daylight filtered through the branches overhead. *Gotcha.* I jink sideways, towards the menacing hedgerow on my right, slowing, eyes focused on the face of my phone as the shadows of the thorny wall loom over me—

And I crash through a stand of waist-high nettles and narrowly miss a young beech tree as the hedge and the thunderstorm sky vanish like the illusion they are.

"Ow!" I swear under my breath, the hot-bright pinprick sting of nettles rising on the back of my phone hand. I examine the side of the cutting the path runs through. Yes, it's familiar. I've been here before, or somewhere very like it. Except for the lack of pedestrians walking the dog, or cyclists en route from one side of town to the other, it could be a normal bike track. But this one's been warded off; anyone starting down it who isn't wanted is going to feel a mild sense of dread, rising after a while to an urgent conviction that they need to be anywhere else.

I thumb my phone back to the start screen, and look for a signal. There's nothing showing. That shouldn't be possible, not on a major network in the middle of a city, but there are zero bars. Do the bad guys have a jammer? It wouldn't be unheard of. And they knew enough to lay a snare right outside the New Annexe, one tailored for me . . . that is not good news. I sit down behind a tree, careful to check that I'm concealed from the path by that stand of stinging nettles, and then I do something that's overdue: I compose an email to the two people I know I can trust— Angleton and Mo. The JesusPhone is smart enough to keep looking for a connection, and to send the mail as soon as it snags a signal. Then I compose a slightly different email to a whole bunch of people I don't entirely trust, remembering to include Angleton and Mo on the recipient list, and send it. Now *that* should set the cat among the pigeons. My heartbeat is just about back to normal by the time I finish, and my lungs aren't burning anymore, so I slide my phone into an inside jacket pocket and stand up.

Click-clack. "Don't move."

12.

COUNTERMEASURES

MEANWHILE, OVER ON THE OTHER SIDE OF THE LOOKING GLASS: "Listen, let me give you an update. I've been suspended on pay. I need you to pick up a ward for me, as soon as you can. I'm heading home now, but I'm *inaudible* and they *inaudible* can you find him and tell him *inaudible*—"

Mo sighs, exasperated, as her phone beeps three times and hangs up on Bob. She waits five seconds, then hits redial. It connects immediately.

"Hello, you have reached the voice mail of—"

She puts her phone away, leaving it for later. Bob's obviously in a poor reception zone, but if he's heading home they can compare notes in a couple of hours. Being suspended is bad news for Bob, but she's been half-expecting it. They've both been under too much pressure lately: the business with the cultists, the suspected leak, all the other minutiae of being part of the operational front end of an organization under increasing strain. *Everyone* is under strain these days; even the people who aren't cleared to know about Dr. Mike's bombshell.

Mo heads towards an anonymous industrial estate in the suburbs out near Croydon, where some of the more technical departments have relocated while Service House is being rebuilt. She travels by tube and then commuter train, and finally by bus, keeping one hand on her violin case at all times. It takes her an hour and a half to make the journey: strap-hanging in grim silence, alone with her worries about the evidence she removed from Mr. Dower's workshop. She travels under the gaze of cameras; cameras on the tube platforms, cameras in the railway station concourses, cameras on the buses. Many of them are linked to the SCORPION STARE network, part of the huge surveillance web the government is spinning to keep the nation safe in the final days. But the final days may be about to arrive with a bang, two or three years earlier than anticipated . . .

She walks the hundred meters to the car park entrance, then enters an anonymous-looking office reception area in an otherwise windowless building. A plain signboard on the high razor-wire-topped fence outside proclaims it the property of Invicta Security Ltd., and the portrait of a slavering German shepherd beneath the sign promises a warm welcome to would-be burglars. Both signs are, of course, lying: the building currently houses most of the Occult Forensics Department, and there's no easy way to visually depict the protean, gelatinous horrors that ooze around the premises by night.

"Hello, Invicta—" The blue-suiter behind the counter pauses. "Dr. O'Brien. Can I see your pass, please?"

Mo presents her warrant card. "Hi, Dave. Is Dr. Williams in?"

"I think so." Dave pokes at his computer terminal. "Yes, he's booked in. Do you need to see him?"

"I've got a job on. Can you page him?"

"I'll do that." Dave points a webcam on a stalk at her, then prints off a temporary badge. "Here, wear this. It's valid for zones one and two, you know the drill."

"Yes." Mo doesn't smile. Whereas the New Annexe mostly deals with paper (apart from the armory), the OFD handles physically—and in some cases spiritually—hazardous materials. Access to the inner zones is restricted for good reason.

While Dave pages Dr. Williams, Mo plants herself on one of the powder-blue waiting area seat-things, and idly pages through some of the magazines on the occasional table: *Forensic Sciences Digest, Gunshot Wounds Monthly, Which? PCR.* Her attention is a million kilometers away from the articles, but they serve as a distraction for her eyes. She has one of the magazines open at a color spread of spent bullets retrieved from victims of crime when a shadow falls across her. "Mo! What brings you out here?"

She looks up, forcing a smile. "Nick? Are you busy? Can we discuss this in your office?"

Five minutes later, another windowless office with overflowing bookshelves and too many filing cabinets. "What have you got for me?" he asks. Balding, in his late forties, Nick is the research lead in this particular lab.

"A special job." Mo pauses. "Sub rosa."

"Sub— Oh *shit*. Tell me it isn't so."

She shakes her head. "I think it's probably a leak rather than an inside job, but even so, this is for you, not the office junior. Eyes only." She pulls out the tub of paper clips from Mr. Dower's workroom, and the small stapler from beside his cash register, and places them on the worktable opposite Dr. Williams's desk. "The owner of these items was murdered about forty-eight hours ago. He'd just prepared a special report for me. I'm pretty certain the killer took the report, and knowing George—the victim—he would have paper-clipped or stapled it. So I want a full read on the top copy—and a locator."

Dr. Williams whistles between his front teeth. "You don't want much, do you?" He pauses. "When do you need it by?"

"Right now." Mo positions her violin case on the visitor's chair, then lets go of it. "It's very urgent."

"Oh. I can have it with you by eight tonight, if I—"

"No." She smiles, letting him see her teeth. "When I said *now*, I meant *right now*."

"What's so urgent?" Williams, unwilling to be rushed, crosses his arms and stares at her.

"Are you on the distribution for CLUB ZERO?"

Williams's face turns ashen. "That was the business in Amsterdam, wasn't it?"

"They're over here, too. The document in question is a detailed report on *that*." She points at the violin case. "Whoever has got the report is almost certainly a live hostile, and may I remind you that the item they're after is in your office?" Her smile evaporates. "You really want to get me out of here . . ."

THERE IS A PHILOSOPHY BY WHICH MANY PEOPLE LIVE THEIR lives, and it is this: life is a shit sandwich, but the more bread you've got, the less shit you have to eat.

These people are often selfish brats as kids, and they don't get better with age: think of the shifty-eyed smarmy asshole from the sixth form who grew up to be a merchant banker, or an estate agent, or one of the Conservative Party funny-handshake mine's-a-Rolex brigade.

(This isn't to say that all estate agents, or merchant bankers, or conservatives, are selfish, but that these are ways of life that provide opportunities for people of a certain disposition to enrich themselves at the expense of others. Bear with me.)

There is another philosophy by which people live their lives, and it goes thus: *you will do as I say or I will hurt you.*

It's petty authoritarianism, and it frequently runs in families. Dad's a dictator, Mum's henpecked, and the kids keep quiet if they know what's good for them—all the while soaking up the lesson that mindless obedience is the only safe course of action. These kids often rescue themselves, but some of them don't. They grow up to be thugs, insecure and terrified of uncertainty, intolerant and unable to handle back-chat, willing to use violence to get what they want.

Let me draw you a Venn diagram with two circles on it, denoting sets of individuals. They overlap: the greedy ones and the authoritarian ones. Let's shade in the intersecting area in a different color, and label it: *dan-*

gerous. Greed isn't automatically dangerous on its own, and petty authoritarians aren't usually dangerous outside their immediate vicinity—but when you combine the two, you get gangsters and dictators and hate-spewing preachers.

There is a third philosophy by which—thankfully—only a tiny minority of people live their lives. It's a bit harder to sum up, but it begins like this: *in the beginning was the endless void, and the void spawned the Elder things, and we were created to be their slaves, and they're going to return to Earth in the near future, and it is only by willingly subordinating ourselves to their merest whim that we can hope to survive—*

Now let me drop another circle on the diagram, and scribble in the tiny patch where it intersects with the other two circles, and label it in deepest fuliginous black: *here be monsters*.

Greedy: *check*. Authoritarian: *check*. Worshipers of the most bizarre, anti-human monsters you can imagine: *check*. That's the Brotherhood of the Black Pharaoh (and their masks like the Free Church of the Universal Kingdom) and all of their ilk. Hateful, dangerous, unpleasant, greedy, and all-around bad people who you don't want to have anything to do with if you can help it.

There's just one problem with this picture . . .

That bit about *in the beginning was the endless void*?

They're right.

(Oops.)

Here's the problem:

We live in a hideously reticulated multiverse, where most of the dimensionality of spacetime is hidden from our view—curved in on themselves in closed loops, tucked away in imaginary spaces—but the stuff we can observe is a tiny fraction of the entirety of what we live in. Magic, the stuff I deal with in the office on a day-to-day basis, involves the indirect manipulation of information flow through these unseen dimensions, and communication with the extra-dimensional entities that live elsewhere. I'm an applied computational demonologist—how can I *not* believe this stuff?

Not the bit about original creation, oh no. Beings like N'yar lath-

Hotep didn't mold us out of the black clay of the Nile delta: I've got no beef with modern cosmology. But those of them who take an interest in our kind find it useful for humans to believe such myths, and so they encourage the cultist numpties through their pursuit of forbidden lore.

We aren't alone in this cosmos; we aren't even alone on this planet, as anyone who's met a BLUE HADES can attest (there's a reason all those domed undersea cities of the future never got built in the 1950s) . . . and don't get me started on DEEP SEVEN, the lurkers in the red-hot depths. But our neighbors, the Deep Ones and the Chthonians, are adapted for wildly different biospheres. There is no colonial overlap to bring us to the point of conflict—which is a very good thing, because the result would be a very rapid *Game Over: Humans Lose.*

The things that keep me awake in the small hours aren't anything like as approachable as a Deep One. (Hell, I've *worked* with a Deep One. Left a part of my soul behind with her. No matter.) The things that terrify me are blue-green worms, twisting and coiling luminous intrusions glimpsed in the abruptly emptied eyes of a former colleague; minds patient and incomprehensibly old that find amusement in our tortured writhing; Boltzmann Brains from the chaotic, necrotic depths of the distant future, reaching back through the thinning ultrastructure of spacetime to idly toy with our reality. Things that go "bump" in the night eternal. Things that eat us—

There is a fourth and final philosophy by which some of us live our lives, and it boils down to this: *do not go quietly into that dark night.* Draw a fourth circle on that now-crowded Venn diagram and you'll see that while it intersects the greedy and authoritarian circles, and even has a tiny overlap with the greedy authoritarian bit, it doesn't *quite* intersect with the third circle, the worshipers. It holds up a mirror to their self-destruction. Call it the circle of the necromantic apostates. That's where I stand, whether I'm greedy or authoritarian or both. (I don't think I'm either, but how can I be sure?)

I may *believe* in mind-eating horrors from beyond spacetime, but they'll have to break my neck before I bend it to their yoke.

Keep telling yourself that, Bob.

* * *

MO CARRIES HER VIOLIN AND FOLLOWS DR. WILLIAMS AS HE
picks up a chipped plywood tea tray and backs through a swinging door,
carrying the jar of paper clips and the stapler. The glass window in the
door is hazed by a fine wire mesh, and the edges of the door are lined with
copper fingers that close against a metal strip inside the frame. Williams
places the tray on one end of an optical workbench, then bolts the door
and flips a switch connected to a red lamp outside his office.

"You've worked with one of these before?" he asks.

"Of course." Mo shrugs out of her jacket and hangs it on a hook. "It's
the entanglement-retrieval bit I'm unfamiliar with. That, and I may need
a lab report. I know my limits."

"Good." Williams's smile is humorless. "Then if I tell you to stay in the
isolation grid over there you know what the consequences are for getting
things wrong."

"Indeed." She opens the violin case and removes her bone-white instrument and its bow. Williams stares at it for a moment.

"Do you really need that?"

"When I said they're targeting me, I wasn't exaggerating. Besides, the
document they stole was a report on this very instrument. If they're trying
to backtrack from it to find the original, then when you bring up the
Adams-Todt resonance it might lead them here."

Dr. Williams snorts. "I'm sure the front desk will be very happy to see
them." He turns to the bench and unclamps a swinging arm, uses it to
position a glass diffraction grating in a path defined by a set of curious
pentagonal prisms positioned at the ten vertices of an irregular pentacle.
"Would you pass me the data logger? It's the second one along on the top
shelf . . ."

It takes Dr. Williams a quarter of an hour to set up the forensic magician's workbench. Apart from the odd geometric layout it doesn't resemble
the popular imagination's picture of a sorcerer's laboratory. Colored chalk

lines and eye of newt are gone, replaced by solid-state lasers and signal generators: pointy hats and robes have given way to polarized goggles and lab coats. The samples, stripped of their containers, are transferred to windowed containers using perspex tongs. Williams slots them into place in the observation rig. "Okay, stations," he says conversationally. "I haven't modified the beam line so there should be no overspill, but I'll run a low power test first just in case."

Mo and the forensic demonologist move to stand inside complex designs inlaid in the floor in pure copper. "How's your personal ward?" he asks.

Mo reaches for the fine silver chain around her neck. "Mine's fine," she says slowly. "Damn, I should have drawn a spare for Bob. It's a bit late now, do you have any kicking around?"

"I'll see what I can do afterwards. Okay, goggles on, lights going out. Testing in ten, nine, eight . . ." He pushes a switch. The red laser beam is only visible where it passes through the prisms. "You getting any overspill?"

"None." The room is dark, the only light source the faint trickle through the thickly frosted glass of the window in the door.

"Good." Williams cuts the power, then reaches across the bench by touch and rotates the sample tubes a quarter turn, lining them up with the beam path. Then he adjusts a mirror, flipping it to face a different and bulkier laser. "Okay, I'm switching to the high power source. Going live in ten, nine, eight . . . ."

An image shimmers faintly in the darkness, stitched out in violet speckles across the translucent face of the screen on the optical bench. A pallid rectangle, violet with black runes.

"That might be it," Mo says quietly.

"I expect so. I'm upping the power." The rectangle fills in, glowing brighter and brighter. "Okay, I'm exposing the photographic paper now."

"What kind of camera . . . ?"

"Pinhole, with two holes. Yes, it's a double-split interferometer. Quiet, now . . ." There's a soft click. Ten seconds later there's another click.

"Okay, I got the exposure done. Shame we can't use CCDs for this job, but you wouldn't want to feed some of the things we look at to a computing device . . . Right. You want to look at the bearer?"

"Yes." Mo leans forward, careful to stay within her ward (which glows pale blue, the nacreous glimmer washing over her feet). "It might retrieve Mr. Dower; I can identify him. If it's anyone else, I'd like a portrait, please."

"I'll just reload the interferometer. Wait one . . . Okay, I'm ready. Now comes the fun bit. Do you know Zimbardo's Second Rite?"

Mo pauses for a while. "I think so."

"Good, because we're going there. Don't worry, your part isn't hard. Let's get started."

After five minutes of minute adjustments, Williams runs a certain specialized script on his workstation, which starts up a sound track of chants in an esoteric language and sends a sequence of commands to the microcontrollers in the workbench. As the baritone voices intone meaningless syllables with the mindless precision of a speech synthesizer, he whispers to her: "Some visitors say it spoils the fun, but I rather think it's better than taking the risk of a slip of the tongue . . ."

A new image begins to fuzz into being in the screen, the drawn face of a male, fifty-something, wearing an expression of intent concentration. "That's Dower," Mo confirms. "He wrote the report. Who do you get next?"

"Let's see. It'll cycle through the bearers soon enough . . ."

Dower's face is melting, morphing into a likeness. Mo's breath catches in her throat. "Shit."

"You get around, do you?" Williams sounds amused.

"No, I told you they're targeting me directly—" She stops, her voice rising. "It would be the best way to get the report out of Dower—send an agent who looks like me—"

"I believe you." The amusement drops from his voice. "Thousands wouldn't."

"Let them." She takes a deep breath. "Is there anyone else?"

"Wait." The face is fading, slowly. As it dims, Mo sees a faint shimmer about the eyes: the only sign that it may be a false sending. Whoever is behind the glamour is very good. "Come on, come on . . ." Dr. Williams murmurs under his breath.

Mo shifts her weight uneasily from one foot to the other, as she does when her feet are complaining about too many hours in smart shoes. She glances sidelong into the darkness, where the shadows are swirling and thickening. A faint spectral scatter of spillage from the violet laser shimmers across the wall. "Any res—"

She is in the process of turning her head back towards Dr. Williams and the workbench as the imago shudders and distorts, twisting into another's face.

Williams is meticulous, and doesn't cut corners. This is why he and Mo survive.

There's a crack like a gunshot, and two near-simultaneous bangs from the power supplies that feed the workbench: high-speed krytron switches short the output to earth. A rattle of broken glass follows, as shards from the diffraction screen and some of the pentaprisms follow. The synthesized voices stop. Seconds later, a thin wisp of smoke begins to curl from the top of the laptop.

"Sitrep," snaps Williams.

"Contained and uninjured. Yourself?" Mo raises a hand to her cheek. One finger comes away damp with blood: *not uninjured*. The pain hasn't reached her yet.

"Keep your goggles on and stay in the grid until I say you're clear." The smoke is nauseatingly thick. Williams reaches out with the perspex tongs and flips the light switch. "Thaumometer says we're grounded. Clear to step out of the grid." He demonstrates. "Damn, what a mess."

Mo swallows. "Is there a CCTV track?"

"What did I tell you earlier about images and computers . . . ? No, but we ought to be able to confirm whether it's your document." He sounds unhappy. "Did you get a glimpse of, of whatever that was?"

She nods. "Been there, done that."

"*Countermeasures.*" Williams makes an obscenity of the word. "Does that tell you anything useful?"

"Yes." Mo picks up her handbag from the workbench on the opposite wall, hunting for a tissue. "Whoever's got the report knows what it is—and they're willing to fight to keep it." She draws a deep, shuddering breath. "Do you have a secure voice line? I need to make a call."

CLICH-CLACH. "DON'T MOVE."

I stand very still. The sound of a shotgun slide being racked at a range of less than three meters is a fairly good indication that your luck has run out—especially if you can't see where the shooter's positioned.

"Very good, Mr. Howard." The speaker is male, standing somewhere behind me. He's on the embankment, of course. Even the B-Team learn eventually. (Maybe I *should* have tried to shoot them the other night. And maybe I should cultivate my inner psychopath some more. Oh well.) "Do what I say and I won't shoot you. If you understand, nod."

I nod like a Churchill dog, thinking furiously. His accent is odd. *Welsh?* I can't place it.

"When I stop speaking I want you to slowly remove your pistol and place it on the ground in front of you. Then I want you to turn around. Do you understand?"

"But I'm not—"

"Did I *ask* you to speak?" His voice is icy. I shut up fast.

"If you understand, nod," he repeats. I nod. It's not my job to disillusion him about my imaginary invisible handgun. Like I said: the B-Team are more dangerous than the A-Team, just like sweating dynamite is more dangerous than Semtex. "Do it," he says. "Do it *very slowly* or I'll shoot you."

I *very slowly* lift the right side of my jacket, and mime unhooking a non-existent pistol from a non-existent belt clip. Then I lean over sideways until I nearly topple, and lower my hand towards the roots of a tree. Finally I straighten up—still moving slowly—and turn round, raising my hands.

My first reaction is, *A man without a face is pointing a shotgun at me.* Then I realize that he's glammed up, his head masked by a shimmer of random snapshots of other people, like something out of a Philip K. Dick novel. Other than that, he's wearing jeans and a gray hoodie—just like a million other men in and around this great capital city; the only deviant part of the ensemble is the tactical shotgun.

"Take two steps downhill, until you're on the path," he tells me. "Then kneel with your hands on top of your head."

My heart, barely under control a minute ago, is pounding, but I do what he tells me to do. Arguing with a shotgun isn't clever. I manage to kneel with my hands on my head—which is harder than you might think, when the ground's uneven, you're amped up on adrenaline, and you're over thirty—and wait.

"Don't move," he says. The sun beats down on us as we wait in a frozen diorama for almost a minute. Then I hear footsteps, and a jingling sound, from behind. "Don't move," repeats Mr. Faceless, as someone takes hold of my left wrist and clips one ring of a pair of handcuffs around it. "Got him, boss," says another male voice.

Shit, I think, tensing and ready to make a move if the opportunity presents—but they're not total idiots and they've already got my other wrist.

"Now lie down," says Mr. Faceless.

What can I do? I take a dive, making a controlled sprawl forward on the dusty cycle path. Thinking: *They wouldn't be doing this if they were going to kill*—Mr. Faceless's companion plants one knee on the small of my back and thrusts a sickly sweet-smelling wad of cotton under my nose—*me . . .*

The lights go out.

FROM THE VOICE TRANSCRIPT CALL LOG, NEW ANNEXE:
(Click.) "Angleton."
"Angleton? O'Brien here." (Pause.) "What have you done with him?"

(Pause.) "What?"

"Have you checked your email?"

"I don't believe—excuse me."

(Pause.) "Well?"

(Dry chuckle.) "He's a clever boy."

"And that's an interesting distribution list on the second message, *isn't it*. What have you set him up for this time?"

(Pause.) "A task I would perform myself, were I allowed to, my dear."

"Bullshit."

"No, you misunderstand. I am no more permitted to read the Fuller Memorandum than you are permitted to read and revise your own articles of service."

"But you sent Bob out with a, a fake . . ."

"Yes. He's the hare to lure the greyhound—or more accurately the mole—after him. I expect their identity will become clear tomorrow morning, in the course of the BLOODY BARON brown bag session. Which I for one can heartily recommend to you as the cheapest entertainment you'll see all week—"

"Angleton. Shut up."

"What?"

"You've forgotten something."

"Hm, yes?"

"Bob's been suspended on pay."

(Impatiently.) "Yes?"

"I called Boris."

"And what has that to do with the price of cheese . . . ?"

"Boris says his firearm was recalled. And he doesn't have a ward. He left it with me this morning. He's on the outside and he's naked. Have you heard from him?"

"No . . ."

"I tried to phone him a couple of minutes ago. His number is ringing straight through to voice mail."

(Pause.) "Oh."

"I think you'd better make sure that your greyhound hasn't actually *caught* your hare. Otherwise the Auditors are going to be handling a couple more enquiries."

(Icily.) "Are you threatening me?"

"You know better than that. I merely note that if Bob doesn't make it home tonight we can assume that CLUB ZERO have him. Which would rather blow the wheels off your little game with the BLOODY BARON committee, wouldn't it? Not to mention the collateral damage."

(Pause.) "Yes."

"So." (Pause.) "What are you going to do?"

"I'm going to tell Major Barnes to put his merry men on notice—those of them who aren't playing cowboys and indians in the hills above Kandahar. Then I'm going to locate Bob. Alan can take it from there."

"I want to come along."

"I wouldn't dream of telling you to stay away, my dear, not with your specialist expertise. The problem is—"

"What problem?"

"I was building a waterproof case to hand over to Internal Affairs for prosecution before the Black Assizes. Trying to map the mole's contacts. Cultists are fragile: if they commit suicide we may never find their accomplices."

"Angleton. Would you rather lose Bob?"

"Hmm. If you *must* put it that way, no. But remember, in the endgame, we are *all* expendable."

"I'm so glad to hear it."

"As for you, would you like to make yourself useful?"

"How?"

"This little interruption has, as you reminded me, disrupted certain plans. But not, I hope, irretrievably. On your way to hook up with Alan's boys and girls, I'd like you to go and have a glass of wine with a friend of mine, and convey a proposition to him. It'll put me in his debt if he takes it, I'm afraid, but I think it's necessary. I'll email you the details."

"Who are you talking about?"

"Nikolai Panin."

(End of call log.)

I'M DREAMING.

I'm looking out across a wasteland of rolling ground, gray and crumbly as lunar regolith, beneath a starry sky. There's no vegetation, not even stunted cacti or lichen crawling across the rocks that dot the ground. In the distance I see a low wall, writhing across the landscape like a dead snake: it's as gray as the ground, too. The stars—

I can see at a glance that this is not Earth's sky.

A lurid band of orange and green swirls across half the void, bisecting it with a smoky knife a million times brighter than the Milky Way. The stars sprinkled across it are eye-stabbingly visible, several of them as bright and red as Mars. They cast a harsh and pale radiance across the sloping desert floor. This is not the skyscape of a planet quietly orbiting a star in the suburban spiral arms of a regular galaxy—I'm looking at the view from a world much closer to the active core of a galaxy or globular cluster. And it's an ugly, elderly galactic core, deep in the throes of senescence, a blaze of dust and gas spewing across the heavens from the dying exhalations of supernovae.

I try to turn my head, but my neck doesn't want to work. It's very strange—I can't feel my body. I don't seem to be breathing, or blinking, and I can't feel my heartbeat—but I'm not afraid. Maybe I'm dead?

In the distance, so far away that I can barely see it, low down and close to the horizon, the landscape takes a rectilinear turn. A shallow pyramid or volcanic mound as symmetrical as Mount Fuji reaches for the sky. I've got no way of telling how high it is, but instinct tells me it's vast, rising kilometers from the center of the flatlands. Something about it creeps me out, almost as much as the murdered sky. I've got a feeling about it, a sense of dreadful immanence. There's something inside the pyramid, something that has no right to exist in this or any other universe. *I shouldn't be here,* but the thing in the pyramid is even more out of its place and time. It's contained, that I know, but why it might *need* to be contained—

"—*Told* you not to overdo the ether! Can't you get anything right? If he's *dead*—"

The words buzz around my ears like meaningless insects, distracting me from the watch on the sleeper. The sleeper needs watching, demands witnesses who will collapse its quantum states and render it inert, incarnate in bosonic mass. I'm here because I'm part of the watch. They're scattered to either side of me, the White Baron's victims, impaled on stainless steel spikes, dead and yet undead, watching the sleeper. A massive sacrifice planned by the architect of terror to keep—

"—Got the smelling salts? Good—"

I can feel the pain gnawing at my abdomen, a deep and terrible burning pressure, and I'm on the edge of understanding that something awful has been done to me just as a horrible stench of cat piss steals up my nostrils and I feel a twitching in my eyelids.

"Is he responding?"

I understood that.

Abruptly, the dead plateau and the nightmare watchers and the sleeper in the pyramid are a million lightyears away from the headache that's stabbing at the back of my eyes, and the stench of ammoniacal smelling salts tickles my nose harshly, evoking a sneeze.

"Ah, that looks promising. Hello, Mr. Howard? Can you hear me?"

Fuck.

Suddenly wisps of memory slot into place. I find myself wishing I was back on the plateau, just another mummified corpse, another upright fencepost in the necromantic wall that hems in the pyramid. "Yuuuuh . . ." My mouth isn't working right; I'm slobbering like an out-of-control drunk, drooling incontinently. I blink, and the buzzing I've only just noticed recedes as I sense light and movement and chaos and an outside world that is acquiring color again.

"He's awake." The woman's voice is heavy with satisfaction. "All-Highest will be most pleased." As words to wake to, those leave something to be desired; but beggars can't be choosers. A boot nudges me in the vicinity of my right kidney. "You. Say something."

"S-s-something."

It's not as classy as *you'll never get away with this* or *if it wasn't for you interfering kids* . . . but I have an idea that I wouldn't enjoy Ms. Boot renewing her acquaintance with Mr. Kidney, and if there's one thing extreme god-botherers of every stripe have in common, it's that they don't have any sense of humor at all where their beliefs are concerned.

"Ow." That's for my head, which is now telling me in no uncertain terms that I'm nursing a ten-vodka hangover. Oh, and my wrists are handcuffed in front of me. I blink again, trying to see where I am.

I'm lying on my side on a thin foam mattress that's seen better days, in a small room with walls painted in that peculiar rotted cream color that landlords like to call Magnolia. They've removed my jacket while I was out for the count. There's a cheap IKEA chest of drawers and wardrobe, and a sash window half-masked by thin cotton curtains. Apart from the lack of a bed it could be just about any anonymous rented room in a shared flat—that and the two B-Team goons. Mr. Headless-Shotgun—who has left his trench broom somewhere else—nudges me in the back; another guy (young, blond, probably the friend with the handcuffs) is watching from the far side of the room, while the woman from the cycle path the other night squats in front of me, peering at my face. She's a twenty-something rosy-cheeked embryonic Sloane Ranger—the anti-goth incarnate—with bouncy ponytail and plumped-up lips quirking with humor beneath eyes utterly devoid of anything resembling pity. She probably shops in Harvey Nicks and dotes on her pony.

"It speaks," she declares, in a home-counties accent so sharp you could cut glass with it. "Pharaoh be praised."

Pharaoh? Bollocks. She's an initiate. Inner circle, then, which means I am potentially in a tanker-load of trouble. I try to clear my throat, but my head's throbbing and I still don't have full muscle control back. (Ether is vile stuff, as Hunter Thompson noted.) "W-w-water."

"Do you want some water?" Her face is instantly concerned. I try to nod. She gets the message. "Julian, fetch Mr. Howard some water." She doesn't look at Mr. Headless-Shotgun as she issues the order: she's focusing on me, with a strangely concerned look. "We wouldn't want him to get dehydrated."

"Yah. Er, Jonquil, should I fetch . . . ?"

His hesitant question brings a smile to her face. "Yes, a little aperitif would be good. Bring it."

Aperitif? I clear my throat as Julian Headless-Shotgun leaves through a door I can't see. "Drinking before you take me to the All-Highest? Isn't that a bit unwise?" It's a calculated risk, but her pink court shoes are a bit less likely to do Mr. Kidney an injury than Julian's size-twelve DMs.

"Oh, *I'm* not going to get drunk." She gives a little giggle.

Mr. Blond clears his throat: "*You're* the one who's going to be drunk."

"Oh do shut up, Gareth," Jonquil says tiredly.

"I'm just trying to explain—"

"Yes, you're very trying." Her world-weary tone suggests to me that Mr. Blond is definitely from the B-Team—unlike Jonquil, who has proven frighteningly competent, so far. "Why don't you go through Mr. Howard's jacket pockets instead, in case he's carrying any nasty surprises for us?"

"Yes, Dark Mistress. I live only to obey."

I must be slow today because it takes several seconds for the coin to drop. "You're not vampires, are you?" I ask, trying to stay calm; the prospect of falling into the clutches of the Brotherhood of the Black Pharaoh is quite bad enough without accidentally crossing the streams with a bunch of live-action *Vampire: The Masquerade* fans—and you can never be too sure. (Cultists aren't usually noted for their tight grip on reality.)

"No!" She giggles again. "Vampires don't exist! We're just going to drink your blood and eat a teeny-tiny bit of your flesh, silly."

I can't help myself: I try and wriggle away from her. Which is fine as far as it goes, but as there's a wall about half a meter behind my back I don't get very far. "Why?" I manage to ask as Julian the Blood-Drinking Shotgun-Toting Cultist reappears with a bottle of Perrier, a scalpel, and a pair of unpleasantly fat syringes.

"Transubstantiation: it's not just for Christians anymore!" She sits on my back to stop me squirming away from Julian, then takes the scalpel and lays my left sleeve open from cuff to elbow. "Be a good boy and I'll let you have the water afterwards. This won't hurt much, if you don't struggle."

She sticks me on the inside of the elbow with the first needle, and pokes around for a vein with expertise that is clearly born of much practice. I grit my teeth. "Won't your All-Highest take exception to you sampling the buffet?"

"Mummy won't mind," she announces airily. "Next tube, Julian darling." She stabs me again, and this time there's a brief spark of searing pain as she nails a nerve. "It was her idea, actually," she says confidingly. "If your active service units find us and try to set up a geas to immobilize everyone but you, the law of contagion will keep us moving."

"Yeah," echoes Gareth from the other side of the room, doing his dimwitted best to keep up with the program.

I boggle slightly. "Would it change your mind if I said I was HIV-positive?"

She pauses for a moment, then points her nose in the air. "No," she says dismissively. "Mummy's seen your medical records, she'd have said. Don't tell lies, Mr. Howard, it will only get you into trouble." She passes the second syringe—turgid with purplish-red blood—up to Julian, then raises the scalpel. "Now this *will* hurt!" she announces as she bends over me with a curiously intent expression.

I swear for a few seconds. Then I give in and scream.

13.

THINGS THAT EAT US

AT SIX O'CLOCK, ANGLETON EMERGES FROM HIS OFFICE——
where he has been inexplicably overlooked by the searchers for the entire
duration of his "disappearance"—and stalks the darkening corridors
of the New Annexe like the shade of vengeance incarnate. A humming
cloud of dread follows him as he passes the empty offices and the taped-
over doorway in the vaguely titled Ways and Means Department. My
office is, of course, empty: Angleton has rearranged meeting schedules in
the departmental Exchange database to ensure that certain players will
be elsewhere when he makes his way to Room 366.

There's a red light shining over the door, and a ward inscribed on the
wood veneer beneath it glows gently green in defiance of the mundane
rules of physics. Angleton ignores the DND light and the ward and enters.
Faces turn. "James." Boris's face is ashen. "What are happen?"

(Boris isn't Russian and the accent isn't a fake; it's a parting kiss from
Krantzberg syndrome, brain damage incurred by performing occult operations on Mark One Plains Ape computing hardware—the human ce-
rebral cortex. Magicians use computers because chips are easier to repair
than brains which have had chunks scooped out by the Dee-space entities

they accidentally let in when they began to think too hard about those symbols they were manipulating.)

"The baited trap has been sprung," Angleton says lightly. He pulls out a chair and collapses into it like a loose bag of bones held together by his dusty suit. "Trouble is, our boy was holding the bait when they grabbed it."

"Oh bugger." Andy, tall and dandelion-haired as the famous graphic artist whose name he uses as an alias, looks distinctly displeased. "Do we know who they are yet?"

"Not yet." Angleton plays a scale on the invisible ivories of the table-top, his fingertips clattering like drumsticks. "I was expecting to reel them in at tomorrow's BLOODY BARON meeting, but that might be too late."

"Where's Agent CANDID?"

Angleton grimaces. "I sent her on a little errand, en route to hook up with Alan Barnes and the OCCULUS unit. They're on station in Black-heath, ready to hit the road as soon as we give them a target. I've gone to the Board: they authorized an escalation to Rung Three. I have accord-ingly put CO15 on notice to provide escort and routing." CO15 is the Traffic Operational Command Unit of the London Metropolitan Police. "MAGINOT BLUE STARS are in the loop and ready to provide covering fire if we need to go above Rung Five." The notional ladder of escalation's rungs are denominated in steps looted from Herman Kahn's infamous theory of strategic conflict: in a good old-fashioned war, Rung Five would mark the first exchange of tactical nuclear weapons.

"Is it that bad?" Boris asks, needy for reassurance. Even old war horses sometimes balk in the face of a wall of pikes.

"Potentially." Angleton stops finger-tapping. "CLUB ZERO is defi-nitely getting ready to perform in London. The new research 'findings'"— Andy flushes—"are out in the wild and widely believed, and with any luck they've swallowed them whole and are going for broke this time. They successfully stole a report on Agent CANDID's weapon, which I admit I did *not* anticipate, and they *think* they've stolen the Fuller Memorandum."

There's a sharp intake of breath from Choudhury, whose previous stuffed-shirt demeanor has evaporated. "That's what the break-in was about?"

Angleton nods. "As I said, the baited trap has been sprung. They're going to try and steal the Eater of Souls, bind him to service and use him as a Reaper. I cannot be certain of this, but I believe their logical goal would be to break down the Wall of Pain that surrounds the Sleeper in the Pyramid. With the Squadron grounded we've had perilously little recon info on the state of the Sleeper for the past two years—the drone overflights had to be suspended due to erratic flight control software glitches—and during CASE NIGHTMARE GREEN, awakening the Sleeper will be an obvious goal for the cultists. Of course, the logical flaws in Dr. Ford's report will take somewhat longer to come to light, and I am confident that even if they mounted such an attack it would fail, but the collateral civilian damage would be unacceptable to our political masters." His smile is as ghastly as any nuclear war planner's.

"Why has nobody nuked the pyramid?"

Angleton inclines his head as he considers Choudhury's question. "There is a contingency plan for the Squadron to fly such an operation," he admits. "But it probably won't work, and it might disrupt the Wall of Pain. Can we take this up later? I believe we have an operation to mount—tonight."

"Tell us what to do." Andy lays his hands on the table. They're white with tension. "Are we going to be able to recover Bob?"

"I hope so." Angleton reaches into his pocket and produces a small cardboard box. "Here is a standard paper clip. Until yesterday, it spent nearly five years at the back of a drawer, in close proximity to another paper clip, which is currently attached to the false Fuller Memorandum. The clips were stored in close proximity inside a Casimir amplification grid designed to boost the contagion field. It should be quite receptive right now." He places it on the conference table and produces a conductive pencil from his breast pocket. "If you will excuse me?"

Angleton places a sheet of plain paper on the tabletop, then rapidly sketches an oddly warped pentacle, with curves leading off from its major vertices. Next, he shakes the paper clip from its box into the middle of the grid. Then he produces a sterile needle and expresses a drop of blood from his left little finger's tip, allowing it to fall on the paper clip. Finally he closes his eyes.

"Somewhere on Norroy . . . Road," he says slowly. "Off Putney High Street." Then he opens his eyes. The glow from his retinas spills sickly green across the paper, but fades rapidly.

"Wouldn't it be simpler to use a GPS tracker?" carps Andy.

MEANWHILE: A WOMAN WITH A VIOLIN WALKS INTO A PUB.

An hour and a half has passed since Mo spoke to Angleton. She's been home to get changed and collect her go-bag, but still makes the meeting in a popular wine bar off New Oxford Street with time to spare, thanks to her warrant card and a slightly confused police traffic patrol. (External Liaison will raise hell about it tomorrow, but tomorrow can fend for itself.)

The middle-aged man in the loose-cut Italian suit is already there and waiting for her, sitting in the middle of a silent ring of empty tables while his dead-eyed bodyguards track the access routes.

"Mrs. O'Brien," says Panin. "Welcome."

She pulls out a chair and releases her bulky messenger bag, dropping it between her feet as she sits. She has her violin case slung across her chest, like a soldier's rifle.

"Добрый вечер, как ты?"

Panin's lips quirk. "Quite well, thank you. If you would prefer to continue in English . . ."

"My Russian is very limited," Mo admits. "My employers are more interested in Arabic—not to mention Enochian—these days."

"Well, let us consider drinking to the bad old days, may they never return." He raises an eyebrow. "What's your poison?"

His English is very good. Mo shakes her head. "A lemonade. I don't use alcohol before an operation."

Panin glances over his shoulder. "A lemonade for the lady. And a glass of the house red for me."

"I didn't know they had table service here."

"They don't. Rank has its privileges."

They wait for a surprisingly short time. The minder delivers the drinks, as ordered, and retreats to his stool in the corner. "Angleton told you he was sending me," she says, tentatively laying out the terms of discussion.

"He did." Panin nods. "We share a common interest. Other agencies of our two great nations continue to bicker like bad-tempered children, but we must rise above, perforce. Alas, all is not always clear-cut." He reaches into his inside pocket and brings out a wallet, then produces a small portrait photo. "Do you recognize this man?"

Mo stares at the frozen face for several seconds, then raises her eyes to meet Panin's gaze.

"I'm not going to start by lying to you," she says.

Panin relaxes minutely—it is not evident in his face, but the tension in his shoulders slackens slightly. "He left a widow and two young children behind," he says quietly. "But he was dead before you met him."

"Before . . . ?"

"He was one of ours. I emphasize, *was*. Abducted two weeks ago, not thereafter seen until he appeared on your doorstep, possessed and controlled—we would say превратилась, turned—a tool of the enemy."

"Whose enemy?"

Panin gives her a look. "Yours. And mine. James advised me to tell you that I have been involved in CLUB ZERO from another angle. The Black Brotherhood do not only fish in British waters."

"That's not news. Nevertheless, I hope you will excuse me for saying that if your illegals are taken while working overseas, blaming the local authorities is not—"

"He disappeared in St. Petersburg."

"Oh. Oh, my sympathies."

"I take it you can see the problem?"

"Yes." Mo takes a sip of lemonade, looks apprehensive. "I'd be very grateful if you could tell me everything you know about this particular incident. Did Ang—James—explain why it's of particular interest to us right now?"

"One of your mid-level controllers has been taken, no?"

"Not definitely, yet." Her fingers tense on the glass. "But he's out of contact, and there are indications that something has gone badly wrong, very recently. We've got searchers looking for him right now. Anything you can tell me before I brief the extraction team . . ."

"You are briefing—" Panin's eyes unconsciously flicker towards her violin case. "Oh, I see." He eyes her warily. "What do you know of the Brotherhood of the Black Pharaoh?"

"As much as anybody on the outside—not enough. Let's see: the current group first surfaced in the Kingdom of Yugoslavia after the establishment of the monarchy there, but their roots diverge: White Russian émigré radicals, freemasons from Trieste, Austrian banking families with secrets buried in their family chapels. All extreme conservatives, reactionaries even, with a basket of odd beliefs. They're the ones who reorganized the Brotherhood and got it back in operation after the hammering it took in the late nineteenth century. They're not based in Serbia anymore, of course, but many of them fled to the United States immediately before the outbreak of war; that's the trouble with these cults, they fragment and grow back when you hit them."

"Let me jog your memory. In America, they infiltrated—some say, founded—the Free Church of the Universal Kingdom as a local cover organization. They do that everywhere, taking over a splinter of a larger, more respectable organization; in Egypt they use some of the more extreme mosques of the Muslim Brotherhood. In America . . . the Free Church is a small, exclusionary brethren who are so far out of the mainstream that even the Assembly of Quiverful Providentialist Ministries, from whom they originally sprang, have denounced them for heretical practices. Some of the Church elders are in fact initiates of the first order of the Black Brotherhood; the followers are a mixture of Christian believers, who they see as dupes, and dependents and postulants of the Brotherhood. The Church is mostly based in the United States—it is very hard to move against a church over there, even if it is suspected of fronting for another organization, they take their religious freedom too seriously—but it has missions in many countries. Not Russia, I hasten to add. The nature of the Church doctrine makes the personal cost of membership very high—they tend to be poor, with large families—and discourages defection from the ranks; additionally, the Brotherhood may use low-level glamours to keep the sheep centered in the flock. We hear little more than rumors about the Brotherhood itself; despite fifty years of attempted insertions, we've been unable to penetrate them. Their discipline is terrifying. We have heard stories about ritual murder, incest, and cannibalism. I would normally discount these—the blood libel is very old and very ugly—but complicity in war crimes has been repeatedly used to bind child soldiers into armies in the Congo, and I have some evidence that *those* practices were originally suggested by a Brotherhood missionary . . ."

Mo shudders. "Whether they eat their own children or not, they have no problem eating somebody else's."

"You have evidence of this?" Panin leans towards her eagerly.

"I've *seen* it." Panin flinches at the vehemence of her response. "Although they may not have been strictly human anymore, by that point—they had been thoroughly possessed—"

"That was the Amsterdam business, was it not?"

Mo freezes for several seconds. Then she takes another deep breath, and a hasty mouthful of lemonade, then wipes her mouth. "Yes."

"Cannibalism is a very powerful tool, you know. The transgression of any strong taboo—it can be used for a variety of purposes, bindings, and geases. The greatest taboo, murder, provides two kinds of power, of course, both the life of the victim and the murderer's own will to violate—"

Mo shakes her head, raises a hand. "I don't need that lecture right now."

"All right." Panin sips at his wine. "Excuse me, but—there is a personal connection?"

"What?"

"You appear unduly upset . . ."

"Yes." She looks at her hands. "The missing officer is my husband."

Panin puts his glass down and leans back, very slowly, with the extreme self-control of a man who has just realized he is sharing a table with a large, ticking bomb. "Is there anything I can do to help?"

"Yes." She raises her glass and drains it, then puts it back on the table with a hard *clack*. "You can tell me anything you're at liberty to say, about why the Free Church attracted your attention. And what you think they're doing." She glances round. "Now might be a good time to check your wards." The bar is filling up, but the other after-hours drinkers are all crowding away from the table Mo and Panin share, as if a glass sphere encloses them.

Panin nods. "The ward is adequate," he assures her. "As for the Church, I need to tell you a story of the Revolution.

"During our civil war—the war that split families and slew the spirit of a nation, ending with Lenin's victory in 1922—many factions fought against the Reds; and as the traditional White leadership collapsed, strange opportunists sprang to prominence. In Siberia, there was a very strange, very wicked man, a Baron by birth, of German ancestry: Roman Von Ungern Sternberg, or Ungern Von Sternberg as he styled himself. Sternberg was a monster. An early obsession with Eastern mysticism warped his mind permanently, and then he found something . . . He was a personal friend of the Bogd Khan, a mass poisoner and coincidentally the Mongolian equivalent of the Dalai Lama. During the civil war, Sternberg ran an extermination camp near Dauria, east of Lake Baikal. The Whites used to send the death trains to Sternberg, and he used their cargo for his own horrible ends. It's said that there was a hillside in the woods above Dauria where his men used to kill their Red prisoners by tying them to saplings and quartering them alive. In summer, Sternberg used to go to that hill and camp there under the stars, surrounded by the bones and dismembered bloody pieces of his enemies. It was said by his soldiers that it was the only time he was at peace. He was a *terrible* man, even by the standards of a time of terror."

Mo is nodding. "Was he a member of the Brotherhood?"

Panin licks his lips. "Sternberg was not a worshiper of Iath-Hotep; whenever he found such he slew them, usually by flogging until the living flesh fell from their bones. As a matter of fact, we don't really know *what* he was. We know what he did, though. It was one of the great works of pre-computational necromancy, and it took the priests of the Black Buddha to achieve it, fed by the blood and gore of Sternberg's victims.

"There are places where the wall between the worlds is thin. Many of these are to be found in central Asia. The Bogd Khan's gruesome midnight rituals—the ones he drank to forget, so heavily that he went blind—there was true seeing there, visions of the ancient plateau on an alien world where the Sleeper in the Pyramid lies sightless and undead. The Bogd was *terrified*. When his friend Ungern Sternberg offered him the sole currency that would buy relief from these visions—the lives of tens of thousands of victims—the Holy Shining One, eighth incarnation of the Bogd Gegen and Khan of Mongolia, fell upon his shoulder and wept bloody tears as he promised eternal friendship.

"The priests of the Bogd's court worked with Ungern Sternberg's torturers to build a wall around the pyramid, sent death squads shambling into the chilly, thin air on the Sleeper's Plateau to erect a fence of impaled sacrificial victims. No countermeasure to the Sleeper was created on such a scale for many years, not until your Air Force began their occult surveillance program in the 1970s. As for Sternberg"—Panin shrugs—"he went on to back the wrong side in a civil war. But that does not concern us."

"What an interesting story."

"Is it?" Panin looks at her sharply.

She shrugs. "I suppose if I say 'not really' you'll tell me why I'm wrong."

"If you insist." He snaps his fingers. "Another round, please." To Mo: "It *is* important. You see"—he waits for his minder to depart in the direction of the bar—"one of the tools used by the monks was a *preta*, a hungry ghost; a body in its custody could function on the Sleeper's Plateau far more effectively than any of Sternberg's men, who had a tendency to die or go mad after only a few hours. The hungry ghost needed bodies to occupy, though its kind is far more intelligent and powerful than the run-of-the-mill possession case. This particular hungry ghost knows the transitive order in which the Death Fence around the Sleeper's Pyramid was constructed—by implication, the order in which it must be *de*-constructed if the Sleeper is ever to be released. It was summoned by a ritual that Sternberg documented and sent west, for translation by the only woman he ever trusted: a trust that was misplaced, as it happens, because the document vanished into your organization's archives and has never been seen since. If the Black Brotherhood could get their hands on the document—I believe you call it the Fuller Memorandum—they might well imagine they could bind the hungry ghost into a new body, compel it to service, and order it to begin dismantling the Death Fence."

Mo nods jerkily. "Yes, that's very interesting," she says distractedly.

"If someone had convinced them that the time was right *now*, not in a couple more years, they might be induced to premature action. And if that someone allowed them to obtain a falsified, corrupted version of the Fuller Memorandum, they might well try to use it to release their master—"

Mo focuses. "The Sleeper. You're not saying it's N'yar lath-Hotep itself?"

"No, nothing that powerful: there is a hierarchy of horrors here, a ladder that must be climbed. But the thing in the pyramid can set the process in motion, starting a chain of events that will ultimately open the doors of uncreation and release the Black Pharaoh. To do so, they would best wait for the conjunction of chance; but it is in the nature of mortal cultists that they are impatient. And James is of the opinion that they should be encouraged to indulge their fatal impatience."

"I see."

"No, I don't believe you do. The Black Brotherhood are at their most dangerous when they work *within* an organization that is unaware it has been infiltrated. Your—husband. Has be been missing long?" She shakes her head. "Exactly. Something alerted you?" She nods. "James sent him on an errand, yes?" She nods again. "Imagine you are an initiate of the Brotherhood. You see an agent of a hostile organization, and you have acquired the Sternberg Fragment and are prepared to carry out the ritual of summoning and binding the hungry ghost. Would it not be to your advantage to pick, as a carrier, that hostile agent? So that you can send him back in among them, ridden by your own demon . . ."

Mo's pupils dilate. Her face is pale. "You think they're going to try to possess Bob."

Panin spreads his hands palm-down on the table. "It is a logical supposition, nothing more." He meets her gaze. "He is tapped for rapid advancement, is he not? James's personal secretary, I gather. Years ago, he established a reputation as a casual layabout, a bit of a bumbler. It served him well in his field days. We see reports, you know. A very talented man, with a very beautiful, very talented wife. He will go far, if he is not eaten by a hungry ghost. Or worse."

"What could be *worse*?" Mo says bitterly.

Panin shrugs. "Firstly, they have a corrupted copy of the Sternberg Fragment. Whatever James saw fit to concoct, I suppose, not expecting them to perform it on his personal secretary. Secondly—the *preta* they wish to summon has already been summoned: it is, in fact, already walking around in flesh. Who knows what the ritual might dredge up, given a dangling pointer into the demon-haunted void? And thirdly . . ."

"Thirdly?" Her voice begins to rise dangerously.

"We have merely been assuming that the copy of the Fuller Memorandum that James gave your husband contains a corrupted copy of the Sternberg Fragment. But James did not intend the situation to spin this far from his control. The *worst* possible case is that they have the real thing, the Sternberg Fragment *and* the document describing the binding of the Eater of Souls, and that they know what to do with it."

* * *

JONQUIL THE PSYCHOPATHIC SLOANE RANGER HACKS AWAY AT my arm for what feels like a year and is probably a bit less than a minute. Then she gets annoyed. "Julian, do something about the screaming, will you? It's giving me a headache."

Julian Headless-Shotgun pulls a leather glove out of one of his pockets and tries to stuff it in my mouth. I clamp my jaw shut, shivering and hyperventilating, but he responds by squeezing my nostrils painfully. After a few seconds I surrender to the inevitable. The glove fingers taste of sweat and sour, dead leather. Chewing on them helps.

Did I mention I've got a low pain threshold?

Jonquil goes back to hacking on my arm. The pain is excruciating. If you've ever been bitten by a dog—this is worse. The scalpel makes a clean incision, but I can still feel blood welling up and dripping along my arm. The pain isn't sharp—it's a widespread violent ache. After a while it feels as if my arm has been clubbed repeatedly with a meat tenderizer. She hacks and saws and tugs—the tugging is the worst, it's so bad my vision blurs and I feel light-headed—and then it stops.

But not the pain.

"He's bleeding. Gareth, fetch a sock and a bandage at once. And a plate."

I can't see very well: my eyes are blurring. I can't seem to get enough air through my nose, even when I blow out around the saliva-sticky glove. My heart is hammering and I feel sick with pain. There's a hole in my arm and it feels like it's about half a meter long and goes right down to the bone. *I'm dying,* I think dizzily, even though I know better. Jonquil and her muscle wouldn't want to risk their precious All-Highest's ire. I lie there moaning quietly for a while, then Gareth returns. "You, lie still," Jonquil says, and shoves what feels like a cast-iron cannonball into the hole in my arm. I try not to scream as she roughly winds a gauze bandage around the wadded-up sock, then stands up to inspect her work.

Julian bends over and holds a plate under my nose. Two red and blubbery lumps of raw meat about as long as my index finger sit in the middle of a thin pool of blood. "Anyone for sashimi?" he asks. Jonquil giggles; Gareth makes lip-smacking noises.

"Jolly good, that man." Julian's accent is plummy, camped-up; he peels one of the strips of meat off the plate and stuffs it in his mouth.

Jonquil follows suit, passing the plate to Gareth. "Nom nom nom," she says around her mouthful. "Chewy!"

Goatfuckers, I think fuzzily, then everything goes blank.

The next thing I know, Jonquil's hand is hovering in front of my nose. She's holding a couple of white cylindrical tablets. "Here, swallow these—oh." Her other hand tugs at the glove. I let go of it. She drops the tablets into my mouth, careful not to let her fingers close enough for me to bite. As if I would; all she'd need to do is breathe on that fucking hole in my arm. It's kind of hard to bite someone's fingers off when you're screaming in mortal agony. I try to spit the tablets out but she pinches my nostrils shut. "Naughty naughty!" I hold out until my lungs are burning, but there's only one way this contest of wills can end. "They're only pain-killers," she chides. "By the way, if you don't swallow them toot sweet I'll grind them up and inject them into you, there's a good boy."

Fucking Goatfuckers. She's entirely capable of making good on the threat; I swallow. "What do I taste like?" I ask, trying to distract myself.

"Like raw pork, only not as smoky. Want some? Oh, sorry: the boys have eaten it all." She giggles again. "Don't worry, give the Coproxamol time to work and you'll feel fine for your interview with Mummy."

My heart's still hammering, and I feel a little dizzy. My arm is cold and damp all the way down to my wrist. I don't want to think about how much blood I must have lost. Half a liter? More? *Fucking bastard goat-fucking cultists*. I flash on a momentary fantasy, digging my thumbs into her eye sockets—but only momentary. I have a bad feeling about my right arm. It's throbbing like an overheated diesel engine, sending waves of pain radiating up to my shoulder and down to my elbow. I don't know whether I can bend it. Hell, I probably need surgery to repair what these fine young cannibals have just done. Anything that takes two arms—forget it.

"What are you going to do with me?" I ask.

"Patience, patience! You're going on a magical mystery tour! It'll be fun!" She turns to Gareth. "What's he got in his pocketses?"

"This." Gareth produces my wallet and opens it in her direction. She jumps back with a hiss as my warrant card falls out. "Ooh, nasty! You naughty boy!" She grabs the wallet and turns it round. "Credit card, debit card, driving license, library card, Tesco clubcard. Huh." She pulls out a solitary twenty-pound note. "Civil servant. *Right.*"

Gareth and Julian seem to think it's funny. Civil servants shop at Tesco, don't have platinum credit cards, and suffer being eaten alive by cannibals in the course of their duty—and they think it's *funny*? A vast sense of indignation threatens to overwhelm me. *Fucking bastard over-privileged snooty upper-class goatfucking cultists.*

"Ooh, look! Shiny!" Gareth has found my NecronomiPod.

"What's that—ooh!" Julian leans over, and they nearly bang their heads together, cooing over the glamour-shedding curves of the JesusPhone. "Wow! Here, let me feel that—"

"Mine! Preciouss! Is it an iPod Touch?"

"No I think it's a—" Julian straightens up suddenly. "It's an iPhone, isn't it? How do you turn it off?"

I lie on the foam pad, a puddle of dizzy throbbing misery.

"Why would you want to switch it off?" Gareth demands.

"Because it's a phone. They can trace them, can't they?"

"Let's see . . ." I hear a familiar sound effect as his finger finds the home key. "How does this work—ooh! Wow. What are all these icons?"

"I thought you knew—"

"Yes, but he's been messing with the home screen." Gareth finds the earbuds, untangles the white wires trailing from the jacket pocket. "Let's see what we've got here."

"Guys." Jonquil sounds tense. "We don't have time for this—"

I lie there, trying to be invisible, hoping Gareth is as stupid as he seems.

"It must have an off button somewhere," Julian mumbles. "Shiny . . ."

"Mine!" Gareth clutches it possessively. The earbuds are wrapped around his hand, convolvulus climbing.

Jonquil clears her throat: "If you can't switch it off, leave it behind. It's time to go. Now."

"Bah." Julian shakes himself and steps back. *Bastard,* I think. "Put it down, Gareth—"

"Mine!" Gareth squeaks, and plugs the earbuds into his head as his thumb is inexorably dragged to the NecronomiPod's home button.

"*Stop him—*" Jonquil is too late, and she and Julian are clearly *not* B-Team members in my eyes because she steps behind Julian as he grabs up his shotgun and brings it to bear on Gareth—

Who is limned in black, dancing to a different beat as the writhing white wires drill deep into his consciousness through the shortest possible path, drilling and eating and consuming the unauthorized intruder who has had the temerity to plug himself into a device running a Laundry countermeasure suite—

And he's jitterbugging across the floor, a shadowy silhouette of his former self twitching as if he's plugged into a live wire. It only lasts for a couple of seconds, then the 'Pod finishes discharging its lethal load through his brain and Gareth's body drops to the floor, crashing across my legs like a dead weight.

The white earbuds roll away from his corpse, satiated and somehow *fat*.

"You *bastard*—" Julian is across the room and the shotgun muzzle is a subway tunnel filling my right eye.

"*Stop!*"

Julian takes a deep, shuddering breath. The gun doesn't waver.

"Gareth fucked up," Jonquil says shakily.

"Don't care. He's got to die." I can see a snarl building in Julian's chest, sense the tension in the set of his jaw. I've stopped breathing: if I move—

"Gareth *failed the All-Highest*." Jonquil is standing behind Julian now. "He was weak. He surrendered to a naff little glamour. Are *you* going to surrender to a stupid impulse, Julian? Are *you* weak? Do you want to hear what All-Highest will say if you damage the vessel?"

For a moment Julian does nothing—then he breathes out. "No." He squints at me along the barrel of his gun. "You're going to die, *meat*. And I'm going to watch you go." The shotgun swings away suddenly, pointing at the floor.

"What are we going to do with that?" he asks Jonquil, gesturing sideways at Gareth's body.

"Drag it downstairs and stack it with the others." She shrugs dismissively.

"The vessel's phone—"

"*This* for his phone." She kicks the NecronomiPod; it caroms off the wall and skids beneath the chest of drawers. "Gareth's safe to touch now. Get him downstairs."

"How are you going to move the prisoner?"

"I'm sure he can walk." Jonquil rests a hand on my right shoulder. I shudder. "You *can* walk, can't you, Mr. Howard? Please say you can walk? Because if you can't—" She moves her hand a couple of centimeters down my arm and squeezes.

"I can walk!" I yelp, gasping for breath. "Let me . . . up . . ."

Julian grabs me under the left armpit—the undamaged one—and heaves me to my knees. I try to get my feet under me, and everything goes gray for a few seconds, but I don't faint. I'm just gasping for breath and dizzy, and a bit nauseous, and my right arm feels awful.

"That's good," says Jonquil, taking my right elbow as Julian lets go and bends down to pick up their phone-fiddling former friend. "Now you're just going to step this way, Mr. Howard, and then you're going to follow Julian downstairs and get in the back of the car and sit quietly, aren't you?"

I nod. *Bastard Goatfuckers.* If they think a blood-soaked man with his arms handcuffed behind his back won't draw attention in the average London suburban street—

Shit, I think despairingly as I reach the bottom of the staircase and

Julian opens a side door onto a garage, *for B-Team cultists these two have really got their shit together*. Jonquil opens the rear door of the silver Mercedes saloon and Julian grunts as he slides Gareth's body onto the passenger seat and positions the corpse so that it looks like it's sleeping. Then he opens the boot of the silver Mercedes saloon and pushes me into it headfirst, so that I land on my right arm in a blaze of agony. And that's the last clear thought I think for a while.

14.

THE MUMMY'S TOMB

PUTNEY HIGH STREET, ABOUT FIFTEEN KILOMETERS SOUTHWEST of the center of the capital, is a bustling shopping and retail area, humming with shops and pubs and other civic amenities: the rail and tube stations, the local magistrate's court, fire stations. Leafy tree-lined roads curl away behind the high street, host to uncountable thousands of houses and maisonettes, every curb crammed with the parked cars of commuterland.

Right now it's early evening. A fire-control truck—bulky and red, its load bed occupied by a boxy control room—is drawn up on the drive-through parking area of the court, its nearside wheels on the pavement, blue lights strobing. A couple of police cars wait nearby, ready to clear the way if the truck starts to roll.

Despite appearances, it isn't really a fire-control truck: it's owned by OCCULUS—Occult Control Coordination Unit Liaison, Unconventional Situations—that branch of the military that my employers call in when a situation, to use Angleton's ladder of apocalypse, escalates above Rung One. And right now, its occupants are doing what soldiers frequently do best: waiting for a call.

A short, wiry fellow with horn-rimmed glasses, wearing a tweed jacket with patched elbows over a green wool sweater, lounges in an office seat in front of a desk with a laptop and a bunch of communications gear bolted to it. He's prematurely balding—he isn't forty yet—and his skin is slightly translucent, as if aged beyond his years. There's an olive-green telephone handset jammed between his shoulder and his right ear, and he's twiddling his fingers impatiently as he waits on the line.

"Yes? Yes?" he demands busily.

"Connecting you now, sir . . ." More static. The handset doesn't lead to a phone, mobile or otherwise, but to a TETRA terminal dedicated to OCCULUS's use: an early nineties digital radio technology, horribly obsolete, but one that the government has been locked into by a thirty-year contract. "Dr. Angleton is on the line."

"Ah, James! Are you there?"

"Major Barnes?"

"Yes, it's me! Any word on our boy?"

"We can find him." Angleton's voice is clear. Barnes sits up unconsciously expectant.

Farther back in the OCCULUS truck, a man wearing a bright yellow HAZMAT suit glances up from the H&K MP5 he's checking for the third time. Another HAZMAT-suited soldier, shorter and stockier, knuckles him in the back. "Hey, Scary, nobody ever tell you it's rude to eavesdrop?"

"Sorry, sir."

Major Barnes ignores them: Angleton is talking. "I have a preliminary fix and I'm on my way over right now. I should be with you in about five minutes. Once I'm on location I can guide you to the target in person."

"Are you sure that's advisable?"

"No, but I'll leave tactical command up to you; the problem is, I don't have an exact fix to within less than a hundred meters. I need to be on the spot."

Major Barnes swears silently. "All right, we'll have to work with that. What *exactly* do you think we're facing?"

"No idea," Angleton says cheerfully, "but whatever we're looking at, it's been set up by a cell of the Black Brethren. If we're lucky it'll prove to be a safe house with just a couple of residents. If not . . . remember the Scouts' motto?"

"Be prepared," Barnes echoes, wearing an expression of pained martyrdom. "Dib dib dib and all that. I hope this isn't going to go pear-shaped . . ."

"The good news is, I've raised a SCORPION STARE control order. So once we know what we're looking at, you should have no trouble containing the outbreak."

"How wonderful," Barnes says sourly. "Are you anticipating mass civilian casualties?"

"Hopefully not." Angleton pauses. "What I'm hoping for is low-hanging fruit. Ah, with you in a moment—"

Another police car pulls up, lights flickering; as Major Barnes glances out of the truck's side window, he sees the rear door open and Angleton unfolding himself. He looks back at the HAZMAT-wearers behind him. "Showtime coming up. Sitrep, Jim?"

Warrant Officer Howe puts his carbine down and glances back at the seven other members of his half-size troop: "We're ready, sir." His unspoken question—*ready for what?*—hangs in the air, but he's been working with Barnes for long enough that he doesn't need to say it aloud.

"Angleton's coming up," says the major. "So look sharp."

The door opens and Angleton steps inside the truck. He smiles, cadaverous. "Ah, gentlemen. I wish I could say it was good to see you again; we really need to stop meeting like this." That gets a chuckle from Sergeant Spice. Angleton walks forward towards Major Barnes's area, his head bowed to avoid the overhead equipment racks. "We're very close," he says quietly. "I can smell it."

Barnes knows better than to roll his eyes. Dealing with the spooks often involves playing nursemaid—to a particularly paranoid witchfinder-general, in this case. "If you could just tell the driver where to go, sir?"

"Certainly." Angleton squeezes past the back of Barnes's chair, and slides into the front passenger seat.

The driver glances at him sidelong. "Sir?"

"Kill the blues, then pull out. I want you to drive up the high street slowly. I'll tell you when to pull over."

The truck lurches heavily off the curb, bouncing on its suspension as the driver pulls it through a U-turn—just missing being T-boned by an oblivious minivan driver, her mobile glued to her ear. It rumbles back towards the Richmond Road intersection.

Angleton's nostrils flare. "Keep going." He peers through the windscreen, searching. The driver tries to ignore his hands—he's fiddling with something small that seems to bend the light around it. "Slow down, it's just ahead. On our right. There—no, keep going. That was it. That building . . . it's in the library." He swears under his breath, words of painful power that make the driver wince.

"You want us to raid a *public library?*" Major Barnes is incredulous. "What are we looking for, an overdue book?"

"In a manner of speaking." Angleton sounds weary. "Gentlemen, I believe we may have been led on a wild-goose chase. I am tracking a missing classified document. I was expecting it to lead us to a nest of cultists, but it seems they've learned how to use a photocopier and *this*"—his over-the-shoulder wave conveys world-weary regret—"is their idea of a joke. Unfortunately the document in question is classified, and we can't ignore it. We can't ignore the possibility of an ambush, either, but at least it ought to be easy enough to evacuate. Alan, would you mind contacting the local fire control? I think a snap inspection of the library sprinkler system ought to get our feet under the table."

Barnes nods, wordlessly, and starts to call the fire-control room on one of the other handsets. In the back, Warrant Officer Howe nods at his men: "Strip." The HAZMAT suits come off, to reveal regular Fire Brigade overalls underneath. "Okay, as soon as we get the go-ahead . . ."

Angleton waits tensely in the front passenger seat, fidgeting with something small and dark. Nobody is watching him. But an observer might think, from his behavior, that he's worried they're too late.

* * *

WHILE ANGLETON AND THE OCCULUS TEAM ARE GETTING READY
to raid a public library in search of a missing document, Mo is midway
through her second glass of lemonade in a wine bar with the man who
would be Panin, and I am phasing in and out of consciousness, in airless
darkness and pain, in the boot of a speeding car.

Regrets: I have them.

For instance, I never wrote to my MP to express my displeasure at
the widespread deployment of sleeping policemen around the capital. It
never occurred to me to do so: Mo and I don't own a car, and speed
bumps are a rarely sighted problem in our world. But right now I am
learning to hate the things with a livid passion usually reserved for broken software installers and lying politicians. My abductors appear to be
incapable of slowing for obstructions, and every time we bounce over a
speed cushion or crunch down off a raised speed table or swerve through
a chicane I take the full force of it on my right arm. That goatfucking
cannibal cultist arsehole Julian packed me in the boot damaged side
down; I don't have the strength, the room, or the leverage to turn myself
over. I swear, when I get out of this thing I'm going to run for mayor, and
the first item on my manifesto will be to order the transport planners to
scrape the fucking things off every road in London with their tongues.
Second item on the agenda: making it legal to shoot any cultists seen in
the city after sundown with a bow and arrow. Sort of like that bylaw
York has, the one about Welshmen. Or was it Scotsmen? *Where was I—*

Oh. I blacked out again. This is bad. My wrist feels damp . . . think
I'm bleeding again.

They got my phone. I don't have a ward. If I'm lucky Mo or Angleton
got my messages and they know I'm in trouble. (If Angleton finds my
phone I'll be in trouble. How much trouble? How much do *you* think—
running classified software on an unauthorized system?) How long will
it take them to figure out I'm missing? What time is it, anyway? How long
have the Goatfuckers had me? Hey, why am I scrunching up—

Fuck. I *hate* roundabouts.

When I'm mayor of London I'm going to require all cars to have transparent boot lids, on pain of—on pain of pain. So what if you can't leave your shopping in the car while it's parked? Fuck 'em, why won't they think of the kidnap victims? *Oof.* That was a bad one.

Where are they . . . where are they taking me?

To see the mummy. Dust from the mummy's tomb, ha-ha. A line of bandage-wrapped can-can dancers high-kick in the gallery of dreams. Brotherhood of the Black Pharaoh: how strange . . .

Whoa. We've stopped. Engine running—traffic lights, damn it. Maybe that means we're on a main road? *Pull yourself together, Bob: Observe, Orient, Decide, Act, rinse, spin, repeat . . .*

I'm facing forward, arms handcuffed behind my back. If there's an emergency child latch in here, it'll be behind me. Chance of grabbing it: effectively nil, might be a different story if my right arm wasn't fucked. Inventory of useful shiny occult tools: zero. Inventory of weapons: zero, unless you count my head. *Give 'em head-butt . . .*

Ow, fuck. Speed bump, traffic planners, red-hot pincers, you know the drill. It's stiflingly hot and noisy in here, and it smells bad. They won't get my blood out of the carpet in a hurry, hah! Forensics'll have a field day if . . . if . . .

Oh. For a moment there I was hanging on that pole, staring out across the gray wasteland towards a distant pyramid. There's an eye in the pyramid, but it's sleeping. I'm terrified that it's going to open and see me . . .

They're taking me somewhere specific. When they get there and open the boot of this car, I'll be in the open for a while. That's when I'm going to have to make my run. Won't get a second chance. *Observe, Orient, Decide . . .*

Boris sent me on a course on evasion and escape a couple of years back, after the mess on Saint Martin. Said it might come in handy sometime— I thought it was only going to be useful for keeping out of Human Resources' sights, but you never know. Trouble is, ninety-nine percent of the game lies in not getting caught in the first place. Once the bad guys get their claws into you everything gets a lot harder.

Harder. How desperate am I to escape? Depends. Because I'm not totally without resources; I've still got my head. *Yes, but if I start down that road I won't have it for much longer.* I'm an experienced computational demonologist; I can program zombies, plan the perfect Pet Shop Boys album . . . but running code in your head, that's a one-way ticket to Krantzberg syndrome. It's like the Queen, and her magical power over Parliament; she can veto any law she likes, but it's a card she gets to play *once*. Am I willing to risk a one-way trip to the secure wing at St. Hilda's?

Hell, *yes*—if the alternative is to be the center of attention at a cannibal cultist dinner party.

Ah. Lost it again. Roundabouts—I feel really sick. The smell in here isn't helping; need to concentrate on not throwing up. What procedures do I know that are simple enough to iterate in my head and effective enough to—

We're slowing. Too soon. Shit.

It's hard to deal the imaginary tarot cards when you're being thrown about the boot of a car that's braking hard, then turning. The road noises under me change to a crunching of gravel, which goes on interminably. Then there's a long stationary pause. Just as I'm about certain that we've arrived, the car starts moving again, bouncing slowly across more gravel. It goes on and on—if this is a stately home or a public estate it's huge. But after a brief eternity, we turn through a tight circle and then stop. The engine dies, and in the quiet I hear the ping of cooling metal. Then footsteps.

Fresh air blasts across my back as the boot lid swings open. The interior light comes on, showing me gray carpet centimeters from my nose. "Is he—"

"Yes. Get his legs."

I tense, ready to kick, but they're too fast for me. They slide something—feels like a belt—around my ankles and I can't pull them apart. Someone else pulls a canvas bag, smelling faintly of decaying vegetables, over my head. Then too many hands grab me and lift, and drop, with predictable consequences.

When I surface in the sea of pain, I find I'm lying on my left side—a small mercy. I'm not sure what I'm lying on: it feels like a trolley, or possibly a stretcher. It's cold and smells of disinfectant and it's rolling over a hard, smooth surface. I can't see: my arm is a monstrous, distracting wall of ache, I'm still handcuffed, and now they've hooded me and pinioned my ankles. *So much for making a run for it.* They're obviously taking me somewhere indoors—

Indoors?

Something tells me that, yes, we are indoors now. Maybe it's the lack of fresh air, or the echoes, or the ground beneath this trolley's wheels. We must be nearly there. I distract myself, trying to recall the transition table for Cantor's 2,5 Universal Turing Machine—the one with the five chess pieces and the board. I was always crap at chess, never really got into it deeply enough at school, but I understand UTMs, and if I can hold enough moves in my head before the gray stuff turns to Swiss cheese I might be able to code something up. *Damn it, Bob, you're a magician! Think of something!* But it all blurs, when you're in pain. Like most of my ilk I work best in a nice warm office, with a honking great monitor on my desk and a can of Pringles in front of me. I start swearing, under my breath, in Middle Enochian: cursing is the only thing that language is good for. (That, and ordering the walking dead around.)

We stop, then there's a scrape of doors opening. I bounce across a threshold—a *lift*, I think. Then we begin to descend. *Shit, a lift. We're underground. That's* all *I* need. I'm angry. I'm also terrified, and in pain, and light-headed, and dizzy. My heart's hammering.

"Are you awake, Mr. Howard?" chirps Jaunty Jonquil, the demon princess of Sloane Square.

"Nnnng," I say. *Fuck you,* would be more appropriate, but in my current position I'm feeling kind of insecure.

"Praise Pharaoh!" That's someone else: a male voice, *not* Julian. *Observe, Orient—okay, you're tentatively designated Goatfucker #3.* "What happened to his arm?"

"Midnight snack, don't you know," Julian replies from somewhere near my feet. "Is All-Highest in residence yet?"

"Yes," says #3. "You are expected."

"Ooh!" squeals Jonquil. She pokes me in the ribs, harder than necessary: "You're going to see Mummy now! Isn't that exciting?"

I realize that a "no" might offend, and keep my yap shut. I'm trying to string together Words of Command for making the undead repeat a behavioral loop—*hey, Mummy?* Visions of a can-can line of cadavers in windings bounce through my imagination. *Fool, they're going to kill you. Focus!* The part of me that's on-message and plugged-in to this very unpleasant reality game is panicking at the languid detachment that's stealing over the rest of me. He makes a bid for my lips: "Where . . . are . . . ?" I hear myself croak.

The lift grinds to a halt and I feel a cool draft as the doors open.

"Brookwood cemetery. Have you been here before? It's really marvelous! It's the biggest necropolis in England, it covers more than eight square kilometers and more than a quarter of a million people are buried here! This is *our* section—it used to belong to the Ancient and Honourable Order of Wheelwrights, back in the eighteen hundreds—"

"Quiet," says #3. "You shouldn't tell him this thing."

"I don't see why not," Jonquil says huffily: "It's not as if he's going to escape, is it?"

That's right, remind me I'm doomed, see if I care. Hey, isn't Brookwood where the Necropolitan line used to terminate? *Oh, that figures.* The cultists have built their fucking headquarters right on top of the power source for that ley line they trapped me with. And, let's face it, it's a nice neighborhood. There isn't much of a crime problem here, community policing keeps a low profile, it's dead quiet—

They wheel me out into what I'm pretty sure is a sublevel. A lift, in a mausoleum? Doesn't make sense. So this is probably a mortuary building, abandoned and re-purposed. I try to give no sign of the cold shudders that tingle up and down my spine as they roll me along a short passage, then stop.

"Greetings, Master," says Jonquil, an apprehensive quaver in her voice for the first time: "We have brought the desired one?"

I can feel a fourth presence, chilly and abstracted. I have a curious sense that I am being inspected—

"Good. The All-Highest will see you now." The voice is as cold as an unmarked grave.

I hear a door open, and they wheel me forward in silence. Abruptly, someone leans close to me and pulls the canvas bag up and away from my head. It's dark down here, the deep twilight of a cellar illuminated only by LED torches, but it's not so dark that I can't see the All-Highest.

And that's when I realize I'm in much worse trouble than I ever imagined.

MO LISTENS TO HER PHONE IN DISBELIEF. "THEY *WHAT?*" SHE demands.

"They left the paper clip attached to a book in Putney Library," says Angleton, with icy dignity. "A copy of *Beasts, Men and Gods* by Ferdinand Ossendowski."

"Then you've lost him."

"Unless you have any better ideas."

"Let me get back to you on that." She snaps her phone closed and glances across the table. An idea is taking hold.

"Who was that?" asks Panin. "If you do not mind . . ."

"It was Angleton. The memorandum is still missing. The enemy identified his tracer and neutralized it."

"You have my sympathies."

"Hmm. Do you have a car? Because if so, I'd appreciate a lift home. If you don't mind."

Ten minutes later, the black BMW with diplomatic plates is slowly winding its way between traffic-calming measures. Mo leans back, holding her violin case, and closes her eyes. It's a big car, but it feels small, with the driver and a bodyguard up front, and Panin sitting beside her in the back.

"Do you have anything in mind?" Panin asks quietly.

"Yes." She doesn't open her eyes. "Angleton drew a blank, trying to trace the missing document. But that's not the only asset the cultists have got their hands on."

"Your husband." Panin's nostrils flare. "Do you have a tracer on him, by any chance?"

"No." She doesn't bother to explain that Laundry operatives don't routinely carry bugs because what one party can track, others may pick up. "However, he has a mobile phone."

"They'll have switched it off, or discarded it."

"The former, I hope. If so, I can trace *that*." The shiny, beetle-black car double-parks outside a nondescript row of terrace houses. "Please wait. I'll only be a minute," she adds as she climbs out.

Ninety seconds later she's back, her go-bag weighing slightly more heavily on her shoulder. "Laptop," she explains.

"Your superiors let you take classified documents home?" Panin raises an eyebrow.

"No. It's his personal one. He paired it with his phone. Which is also a personal device." She belts herself in, then opens the laptop screen. "All right, let's see." She slides a thumb drive into the machine, rubs her thumb over a window in it: "Now *this* is a secured memory stick, loaded with execute-in-place utilities. Nothing exotic, mind you, strictly functional stuff. Ah, yes. At the end of the road, turn left . . ."

The driver doesn't speak, but he has no trouble understanding her directions in English. The car heads south, slowly winding its way through the evening streets. Mo busies herself with the laptop, a route finder program, and a small charm on the end of a necklace, which she dangles above the screen: a ward, taken from around her neck. "It's along here, somewhere," she says as the car cruises yet another twisting residential street, where large houses are set back behind tall hedges. "Whoa, we've gone past it. Okay, pull in here." She pulls out her phone and speed-dials a number.

"Yes?" Angleton is alert.

"I'm in Hazlehurst Road, near Lambeth cemetery, with Nikolai and his driver. Tracking Bob's personal phone. How soon can you meet me here?"

"Hold on." *Pause.* "We'll be there in fifteen minutes. Rolling now. Can you wait?"

Mo glances sidelong at Panin, who shakes his head slowly. "I don't think so," she says. "Nikolai has urgent business elsewhere." She pulls the door latch, and it swings open with the sluggish momentum of concealed armor plate. She extends one foot to touch the pavement: "I'll be discreet."

"Good-bye, Dr. O'Brien. And good luck."

Most of the houses on this road are detached, sitting in pricey splendor on plots of their own, a few down-market Siamese-twin semis lowering the millionaire row tone. It's London, but upmarket enough that the houses have private drives and garages. Mo walks slowly back along the pavement until she comes level with the hedge outside a semi with a built-in garage, probably dating to the mid-1930s. The ward throbs in her hand as she reluctantly fastens the fine silver chain around her neck and tucks it in. This is the place. She's sure of it.

She pulls out her phone, dials again, says, "Number thirty-four," then puts it away. Then she opens her go-bag and pulls out a pair of goggles. She pulls them on and flicks a switch. Then she stalks around the side of the house.

There is a bad smell from the drains out back, and the lawn is unmown. The hedge has not been trimmed: it looms over the over-long grass like the dark and wild beard of the god of neglect. The windows of the house are dark, and not merely because no lights shine within. It's strangely difficult to see anything inside. Mo stares at the flagstoned patio beneath the French doors through her goggles. They are goggles of good and evil, part of the regular working equipment of the combat epistemologist, and their merciless contrast reveals the stains of an uneasy conscience mixed with the cement that binds the stones: it's an upmarket Cromwell Street scene, she realizes, her stomach churning. The police forensic teams will be busy here later in the week, as the tabloid reporters buzz round their heads like bluebottles attracted to the rotting cadavers beneath their feet.

Mo moves farther around the house. A sense of foreboding gathers like static beneath the anvil cloud of a thunderstorm. Her heart is beating overly fast and her palms are clammy. She is certain that Bob's phone is here, and where goes the phone goes the Bob. But this is not a good place. Suddenly she is acutely aware that she is on her own, the nearest backup ten minutes away.

Well, then.

There is a quiet click as she unfastens the latches of her instrument case. Moments later the bow is in her hand, the chinrest clamped between her jaw and shoulder. The case dangles before her chest, two compact speakers exposed. There's a sticker on the back of the instrument. It reads: THIS MACHINE KILLS DEMONS.

Mo walks towards the glass doors, on the indistinct shadows behind them, and touches her bow to the strings of the pallid instrument. There is a sound like a ghost's dying wail as the strings begin to vibrate, blurring and glowing as they slice the air to shreds. "Open," she says quietly, and as she sounds a chord the glass panes shatter simultaneously and the door frame warps towards her. She advances into the suburban dining room, playing raw and dissonant notes of silence to confront the horrors within.

THE BMW IS HALF A MILE AWAY WHEN PANIN LEANS FORWARD and taps his driver on the shoulder.

"Sir?" The driver glances at Panin's reflection in his mirror.

A blank business card appears between Panin's fingertips, twin to one

Panin passed to an unwitting contact a couple of days ago. "Track this," he says.

"Yes, sir." The driver reaches back and takes the card, then places it on the dashboard in front of him. It glows faintly in the darkened interior of the car.

After a moment, they pull over, then the driver performs a U-turn and accelerates. "If you don't mind me asking, sir . . ."

"Yes?" Panin looks up from the map book on his lap.

"Do you want me to call for backup?"

"When we know where we're going, Dmitry. Patience."

"Sir. Shouldn't you have told . . . ?"

"The wolf may not bite the hound, but that doesn't make them friends. I intend to get there first, Dmitry. Wherever 'there' is."

"Then I shall drive faster. Sir." The saloon accelerates, heading south.

"HELLO, BOB," SAYS JONQUIL'S MUMMY, A SMILE CRINKLING the crow's-feet at the corners of her eyes. "Oh dear, what did you do to your arm? Let me have a look at that." She tuts over the state of Julian's first-aid—very rough and ready, a wadded-up rugby sock held in place by tubigrip, now black with clotted blood. "You really ought to have taken the week off sick: overwork will be the death of you, you know."

"Fuck off!" Fury and pain give way to a mix of disgust and self-contempt. I should have seen this coming.

"Do feel free to let it all hang out," she tells me: "It's not as if you've got anything to lose, is it?"

Damn Iris. She knows me well enough to get under my skin.

"You've been studying me, haven't you?"

"Of course." She glances over her shoulder. "You. Fetch the first-aid kit at once." Back to me: "I'm sorry about . . . that."

"Does your idiot daughter always go around chopping up strangers when you're not around?"

"Yes," she says calmly. "It runs in the family. I don't think you have any grounds to complain, given what you did to poor Gareth. Would you like me to take those handcuffs off you? Don't get any silly ideas about escaping: the guards upstairs will shoot anyone they don't recognize."

"I didn't do anything to Gareth," I say as she pulls out a key and holds it up in front of me between two black-gloved fingers: "If he hadn't meddled—" I stop. There's no point arguing. "What do you want from me?"

"Your cooperation, for the time being. Nothing more, nothing less." There's a click, and my right wrist flops free. My arm flares for a moment, and I nearly black out. "That looks painful. Would you like something for it?" I don't remember nodding, but a subjective moment later I'm sitting up on the trolley and someone I can't see is leaning over me with a syringe. It stings, cold as it goes in—then my arm begins to fade, startlingly fast. "It's just morphine, Bob. Say if you need some more."

"Morph—" I'm nodding. "What do you *want*?"

"Come and sit with me," she says, beckoning. An unseen minion lifts me with an arm under my left shoulder and guides me towards one of two reclining leather armchairs in the middle of a dim pool of light on the flagstones—*Flagstones? Where are we?* "And I'll explain."

I fade in and out for a bit. When I'm back again, I find I'm sitting in one of the chairs. There's a tight bandage on my right arm, with something that isn't a rugby sock under it. My hands are lying on the armrests, un-cuffed, although I've got sore red bands where the metal cut into my wrists. I can feel my fingers, mostly—I can even make them flex. And for the first time in hours, my arm isn't killing me. I'm aware of the pain, but it feels as if it's on the other side of a thick woolen blanket.

Iris is sitting in the other chair, holding an oddly shaped cup made of what looks like yellow plastic, watching me. She's put her hair up and changed from her usual office casual into what my finely-tuned fashion sense suggests is either a late-Victorian mourning gown or a cultist priestess's robes. Or maybe she's just come from a goth nightclub with a really strict dress code.

I stare past her. We're in a cellar, sure enough—one designed by an architect from the C of E school of baroque cathedral design. It's all vaulted arches and flying buttresses, carved stone and heavy wooden partitions cutting us off from darkened naves and tunnels. Just like being in church, except for the lack of windows. Putti and angels flutter towards the shadowy ceiling. There are rows of oak pews, blackened with age. "Where are we?" I ask.

"We're in the underground chapel of the Ancient and Honourable Order of Wheelwrights," she says. "They had an overground chapel, too, but this one is more private."

"More p—" I stop. "Were the ancient whatevers a cover organization by any chance? For a brotherhood of a different hue?"

Iris seems amused by the idea. "Hardly! They were purged in the 1890s, but nobody found the way down to this cellar. We had rather a lot of cleaning up to do, interminable reconsecrations and exorcisms before we could dedicate the chapel to its true calling." She pulls a face. "Skull worshipers."

Skull worshipers? Does she mean . . . ? Oh dear. There are as many species of cultists as there are dark entities for them to wank over. If this place has a history of uncanny worship going back a century and a half, then it's a place of power indeed—and that's before you take into account its location inside a huge graveyard, at one end of a ley line leading into the heart of London that was traversed by tens of thousands of dead over a period of nearly a hundred years. The whole thing has got to be a gigantic necromantic capacitor. "So it was vacant and your people moved in?"

"More or less, yes."

"You people being, hmm. Officially, the Free Church of the Universal Kingdom? Or unofficially . . . ?"

She shakes her head. "The Free Church aren't terribly useful over here—the British aversion to wearing one's religion on one's sleeve, you know. We'd get lots of very funny looks indeed if we went around fondling snakes and preaching the prosperity gospel—even though that sort of thing is de rigueur for stockbrokers. No: on this side of the pond we mostly use local Conservative and Unionist Party branches. And some Labour groups, we're not fussy."

Enlightenment dawns, and it's not welcome. Firstly, the Tory grass-roots are notorious for their bloody-minded independence—their local branches pretty much run themselves. And secondly, political leverage . . . Isn't the Prime Minister very big on community and faith-based initiatives? *Oh dear fucking hell . . .*

I blink owlishly. Iris leans forward, concerned. "Would you like a can of Red Bull? I'm sure you could do with a pick-me-up."

I nod, speechless. "Why me?" I ask, as a male minion—wearing a long black robe, naturally—sweeps forward with a small silver tray, on which is balanced a can of energy drink. I stare at it and twitch my right hand. He opens the ring-pull and holds the tray in front of my (functioning) left hand. I take the can gratefully, and manage to get most of a mouthful down my throat rather than down my tee shirt. As he steps back, I repeat my question: "Why did you abduct *me*? Because I'm quite clear now that this little charade *is* all about me. We've all been suckered. Iris is one of the two sharpest managers I've ever had—the other being Angleton—and she's been one step ahead of us all along. She probably swiped Mo's report, too. "Why? I'm a nobody."

"You underestimate your value, Bob." She raises her cup, and smiles over its rim as she takes a sip of something dark. I blink, focusing on it. (*That's not a cup,* I realize with a sense of detachment. *Why is she drinking from a—because she's a* cultist, *idiot.*) "You've been fast-tracked for senior management for the past eight years. You knew that, didn't you? But you're only graded as an SSO 3. That's a bit low for someone who's reporting directly to a DSS, so I did some digging. You're not being held back; it's just that the Laundry operates a Y-shaped promotion path—administration and line ranks diverge above a very low level. You're due for regrading later this year, Bob. If you pass the board, they'll make you an SSO 4(L). Doesn't sound like much, but it's the first step up from the fork into the line hierarchy, and it'll entitle you to boss Army majors around. Or police superintendents. I'm an SSO 6(A) but you'd be able to tell *me* what to do. And a year after that, unless you really go off the rails, they'll be coaching you for SSO 5(L)."

I try not to boggle openly. I haven't been paying too much attention to my grade, frankly: I get regular yearly pay raises and rung increments, and I knew I was up for promotion sooner or later, and I knew about the Y-path, but it hadn't occurred to me that I might be about to effectively jump three grades.

"I've seen your confidential record, Bob. It's impressive. You get stuff done, and Angleton thinks very highly of you. *Angleton*. You know what that means, don't you?"

I nod. My mouth is dry and I feel my pulse fluttering. "You didn't infiltrate the Laundry just to get close to me. Did you?"

She chuckles. "No, Bob, we didn't." *We. Oh holy fuck.* There's more than one cultist infiltrator in the Laundry? I swallow. "But I've been looking for someone like you for a long time. You're on track for executive rank when the stars come right. You lucky, *lucky* man." Her voice drops to a low croon as she raises the baby's skull and drains it, then holds it out for a refill. "It won't work, of course."

"It won't—excuse me?"

"Everything." She shrugs. The effect is rather fetching, if you have a goth fixation. "Go on, tell me what you think is coming up next."

Oh hell. "This is the point," I say guardedly, "where the evil cultist monologues at the captive agent and tries to convert him to her way of thinking. It never works. Does it?"

Iris shakes her head. "You're probably right, but I ought to give it a go. Okay, here's my pitch. If I thought for a moment that official policy as set forth in CASE NIGHTMARE GREEN stood a chance of success—if it was *remotely* possible that we, the human species, could stand shoulder-to-shoulder against the elder ones and build a shield against our Dark Emperor, do you think for a split second that I wouldn't go for it?" She looks at me speculatively. "*You* know just how high the odds are stacked against us. There are just too damned many people—we're damaging the structure of reality by over-observing it! And we can't kill them either, not without releasing a pulse of necromantic energy that will have every brain eater for a thousand lightyears in all directions homing in on us. The latest research"—she bites her lower lip—"it means the breakthrough is inevitable, and soon. The dead things quicken, and the harder we fight against the inevitable, the worse it will be."

She falls silent. Despondent? Or resigned?

"What you're saying is, if rape is inevitable, lie back and try to enjoy it. Right?"

She glares at me, blood in her eye for an instant: "No! I'm not into, into *enjoying* this. I'm interested in *survival*, Bob, in reaching an accommodation. Survival at all costs and ensuring the continuity of the human race, that's what the Brotherhood of the Black Pharaoh is about these days. I won't lie to you by denying that our history is ghastly, but we change with the times. Our goal is actually *your* goal, if you think about it for a moment."

Which, for me, is an *Oh hell* statement with brass bells on. It's not as if I haven't had my quiet nagging doubts about the Laundry's methods and goals, and its intermittent self-thwarting tendency to substitute circular arse-kicking routines for progress. Iris is goddamn good at what she does. Wasn't I thinking earlier that I'd follow her to hell if—

—If I couldn't hear an echo of Mo's voice, reminding me: *the things in the cultists' bodies had already eaten the blonde teacher's face and most of her left leg, but the Somali boy-child was still screaming*—

"You used a phrase there," I say quietly. "I don't think it means quite the same thing to you that it means to me. *At all costs.*" I put my energy drink can down. I've emptied it but I'm still exhausted and the pain is still lurking, just beyond the edge of my awareness. Plus, I feel drained, countless years older than my age. "Implying that the ends justify the means."

"Just so." Iris nods. "So. Will you join us of your own free will?"

I give her question the due weight of consideration it deserves. "Piss off."

She sighs. "Don't be childish, Bob. I like you, but I'm not going to let your selfish little fit of pique stand in the way of human survival." She stands up, gathers her robe around her, and walks past me. "Bring him," she commands.

Strong-armed cultists seize me under the shoulders and lift. I'm in no position to put up a fight as they frog-march me after her. "What are you going to do with me?" I call after her.

She pauses before an oak door studded with heavy iron nails. "I'm afraid I'm going to have to sacrifice you," she says apologetically, "so that the Eater of Souls can stalk the corridors of the Laundry wearing your promotion-fast-tracked skin. I'm really sorry, dear. I promise I'll try to make sure it hurts as little as possible."

The door opens before her, and they drag me down into the catacombs.

15.

DEAD MAN WALKING

THERE IS A HALF-EATEN SANDWICH SITTING ON A BREADBOARD IN the kitchen, and an empty milk carton next to the electric kettle, and to the witness in the corner of the room the sandwich is a thing of horror.

Mo stares at it for almost a minute. Then she reaches out very carefully and lifts the upper slice of bread. Lettuce, sliced tomato, and either chicken or turkey—not ham. She breathes in deeply, shudders for a moment, then moves on. Battery farmed and de-beaked chicken, not properly stunned at the slaughterhouse—that would account for the shadow in her left goggle. No need to remember the tunnel in Amsterdam, nor where it led . . .

Behold: a typical London family home. Recently renovated kitchen, dining room with French doors opening onto a patio in the garden, lounge with bay window out front, staircase in hall, under-stair closet, side door leading into garage, bedrooms and bathroom upstairs. Why the creeping dread, then?

Mo stalks the lounge like a shadow of judgment, violin raised and ready. There's a row of books on a shelf above the plasma TV. *Manage-*

ment for Dummies, *The Power of Positive Thinking*, *The Book of Dead Names*—she pauses. "What the *fuck*?" she says, very quietly. She's seen *that* one before, in the unclassified section of the archives: it's the Sir Richard Burton translation of *Al Azif*, the source text referred to by the mad pulp writer of Providence, who renamed it *Necronomicon*. It's not of any great significance—it's mostly the deranged babbling of a schizophrenic poet who'd smoked far too much hashish—but it's as out of place in a suburban living room as a main battle tank on the high street.

There's a rumble outside, as of a heavy truck. Mo glances at the window in time to see the blue strobes flickering. A knot of tension leaves her shoulders. She steps into the hallway, towards the front door, and freezes.

Lying on the carpet before her is a runner. The rug is handwoven with an intricate mandala. To an unequipped civilian it might look harmless, but in Mo's goggles the buzzing, humming tunnel of lies flickering with greenish light is unmistakable. She kneels beside it, inspecting its woolen edge. Very carefully, she lowers her bow across the strings of her instrument. Her fingers slide on the fretboard, leaving a fine sheen of skin oils and blood behind as the strings light up, cutting brilliant blue gashes in the air above the mandala. She plays a phrase that trails down into a wailing groan, then up into an eerie scream. Then she plays it again, louder. The rug smolders. Once more, with emphasis: and there is a bang, as the binding between the woven wool carpet and the place it connected to gives way.

The cloud of acrid smoke from the rug sends Mo into a coughing fit. An unseen smoke detector starts to scream as she stumbles forward and yanks the front door open. "In here!" she calls to the firemen walking up the driveway. As the first of them reaches her she holds out an arm: "I've checked the ground floor. There was a welcome mat, but I defused it: I think it's clear now, but let me check out the stairs."

"Understood, ma'am." Howe turns to face his men as Mo starts to check the staircase for surprises. "*Wait* while the lady checks the staircase. Scary, secure the garage. Len, backyard. Joe, show Dr. Angleton to the living room."

Ten minutes later, Mo joins Angleton downstairs. He's sitting in a floral print armchair with a book in his lap, looking for all the world like someone else's visiting grandfather. He closes it and looks at her mildly. "What have you found?" he asks.

"Nothing good." She peels her goggles off and perches on the edge of the sofa, then begins to return her instrument to its case. Wiping down the bloody finger-marks on the fretboard with a cloth: "Who lived here?"

"That's an interesting question. Would you be surprised if I told you these are designated premises?"

Mo's fingers stop moving. Her eyes grow wide. "No. Really?"

"It's very interesting: the Plumbers don't seem to be aware that they've signed off Safe House Bravo Delta Two as clean without inspecting it. It's assigned to one of our managers, by the way: SSO 6(A) Iris Carpenter. She's lived here for some years." Angleton's cheek twitches. "Husband and university-age daughter, a typical happy family. The family that prays together stays together: or preys, perhaps? Bob was reporting to her, and she was on BLOODY BARON. We've found our mole."

"But the back patio—"

Angleton closes his book. It is, of course, the Burton. "Yes," he says, cramming paragraphs of foreboding into the monosyllable.

"There's a bedroom upstairs," Mo says shakily. "The window frame is nailed shut, the door locks from outside, and there's a foam mattress on the floor with bloodstains on it. There's a monstrous thaum field, echoes of violent death—recently. And a dirty plate."

"Is that so?" Angleton carefully removes his spectacles, then extracts a cloth from his suit pocket. He begins to polish the lenses.

Boots thunder on the staircase. A moment later, a fireman bursts into the living room. "Sir!" He's holding something shiny in his right hand.

"What is it?" Angleton asks irritably, holding his glasses up to the light.

"Give that here." Mo reaches for it. "It's Bob's new phone." She stands up, holding it close: "Where did you find it?"

"It was under the chest of drawers in the small room. Oh, and there's a body in the garage—not one of ours." Warrant Officer Howe looks gloomy: "We only missed them by an hour or so. Judging by the blood-stains and the body—still damp and still warm."

Mo scuffs her right foot on the floor in frustration. "They've been one jump ahead of us all along, because they've been sitting in on our investigations, inside our decision loop. That's where the Dower report went. It's where that missing memo went. They've got Bob—what are we going to *do*?"

Angleton slides his spectacles back on. "I'd have thought that was obvious," he says mildly: "We've got to find him."

"How?"

Angleton stands up. "That's your department. You've got his ward, his phone, his laptop, if you've got any sense you've got an item of recently worn underwear . . ."

Mo nods jerkily. "He was *here*. If there's a trail—" She turns to Howe: "The foam mattress, with the blood. Have you taken a sample?" Howe holds up an evidence bag, its contents black and squishy. "That'll do."

"Back to the truck." Angleton waves them out of the living room, ahead of him. "I hope we're in time."

"What do you think they'll do to him?" Mo's anxiety is glaringly obvious.

"They've got the memorandum." Angleton shrugs. "I think they'll try to invoke the Eater of Souls and bind it to Bob's flesh."

"They—" Mo glares at him. "Bob said you gave him a fake!" she accuses.

"No, just a photocopy." Angleton's ironic smile is ghastly to behold. "The Eater of Souls is already taken: if they try the rite, they won't get what they think they're asking for. And I will admit, I didn't expect them to make it this far. I'm not infallible, girl."

A minute later, the driver switches on the blue lights and pulls out into the road. Behind the departing truck the house's front door gapes open, as if ready to welcome the next official visitors. But the victims under the patio will have to wait a little longer.

* * *

OKAY, SO I WAS WRONG ABOUT THE A-TEAM AND THE B-TEAM.

And I was wrong about the cultists, and what they believe.

Assuming Iris is telling the truth, there's an angle to view things from which their actions are, if not justifiable, then at least understandable. Poor little misunderstood mass murderers, with only the best of intentions at heart. And their hearts *are* pure for the goal they seek is the only one any sane—

Stop it. That's Stockholm syndrome talking, the tendency of abductees to start seeing things from their kidnappers' viewpoint. *Just stop it.*

They're frog-marching me along a tunnel towards a summoning grid where they plan to turn me into a host for a demonic intrusion from another universe, and my subconscious is trying to see things from their point of view? I'm confused—

It's a broad tunnel, low-ceilinged. Every five meters or so there stands a cultist, male or female figures in hooded black robes who hold lamps, the better to illuminate the whitewashed brick walls and the niches therein. The niches have occupants; they've been standing there for a *long* time. There's a soft, dry breeze blowing—I've got no idea how they manage the ventilation—and some of the inhabitants are pretty well preserved. The way the skin shrinks across the skull, drawing the shriveled lips back to reveal yellowed fangs and blackened tongues, almost as if they're screaming. The dead outnumber the living here, all dressed in dusty Victorian or Edwardian finery. If Iris has her way, I'll be joining them soon—or worse. When I signed the Act there was a binding promise placed on my soul: the Laundry doesn't like its staff to leave ghosts and revenants behind to face interrogation. No afterlife echoes for me.

We pass a rack of wooden shelves, bowed with age beneath piles of skulls and bundles of femurs tagged with faded labels, and pause at another oak door. One of the cultists—do I recognize Julian the shotgun-toting cannibal under that hood?—steps forward with a key. My heart's pounding and I feel feverish, and to top it all I'm so scared I'm in danger of losing bladder control, like an innocent man being dragged to his execution. I'm also angry. *Hang on to that anger,* I tell myself. Then I start trying to string phrases together in Enochian, in my own head.

If they're determined to kill me, then fuck 'em—I'm going to go out with a bang.

The dead. I can feel them pressing in around us, outside the wan light of the LED torches. Empty vessels waiting, entropic sinkholes of randomized information, all charged up with nowhere to go. These dead bear no love for the living among them: followers of a ghastly fertility cult, the spawner of unclean things—now dead and withered, they lie here where once they conducted strange bacchanalian ceremonies, watching while the austere puritans of the Black Brotherhood desecrate their tombs and reconsecrate their altars. They can't possibly be happy with the new tenants, can they?

To summon up a possessive entity takes a Dho-Nha geometry curve, a sacrifice of blood, and an iteration through certain theorems. (Not to mention a power source, but I'm sitting right on top of the necromantic equivalent of the Dinorwig stored hydropower plant: if I can't turn the lights on with *that*, I might as well give up.) I know this shit: it's years since I first did it. I can just about visualize the curve, and if I try to flex my right arm—*oh gods, that hurts*—is that a trickle of blood I feel? I start to subvocalize, trying to hold a warped wireframe image in my mind's eye: *One plus not-one equals null; let the scaling coefficient be the square root of—*

The door is open. How big is this place, anyway? The Ancient Order of Wheelwrights must have been rolling in cash. The sacrificial cortège begins to move again, and now the cultists around me begin to sing a curious dirge-like song. We're descending across broad steps—almost two meters wide, topped with dusty mattresses to either side—towards a central depression beneath a low, vaulted ceiling. The skullfuckers probably used this space for their orgies, more than a century ago; it's haunted by the ghostly stink of bodily fluids. We've been brought up to think of the Victorians as prudes, horrified by a glimpse of table leg, but that myth was constructed in the 1920s out of whole cloth, to give their rebellious children an excuse to point and say, "*We* invented sex!" The reality is stranger: the Victorians were licentious in the extreme behind closed doors, only denying everything in public in the pursuit of probity.

Now the cultists around me are breathing faster, raising their voices higher, trying to drown out the phantom sighs and moans of a thousand dead and withered seducers. I try and keep to my own chant, but it's hard to focus on suicide when all around you the ghosts of gluttony sleep so lightly.

There is a huge bed at the center of the well of mattresses: a four-poster, canopied in rich black brocade, ebony uprights supporting a drapery as ornately swagged as any Victorian hearse, with a huge chest sitting in front of its footboard. The bed alone is wide enough to accommodate half a dozen—*not sleepers,* I realize—although only two bodies lie there now, curled in fetal death, close to one side.

As the singers continue, two of Iris's minions walk up to the bed. They raise the quilt piled against the footboard, covering the mummified occupants; then they take hold of cords dangling from the base of each post and attach manacles to them.

"No," I say. "No!" Then I try to bite the hand that's reaching in front of my mouth with a gag.

"Mummy said not to hurt you unnecessarily," Jonquil explains. "So open wide, or—" Her other hand grabs my crotch and squeezes. I gasp in pain. *Bitch.* "Good boy!"

When they dump me on the counterpane a cloud of stinking dust billows out in all directions, hanging so thick in the air that I spasm and sneeze. It takes six of them to hold me down and fasten the manacles, and I nearly faint when they extend my right arm—the morphine must be wearing off. Everything blurs for a few seconds. I look up at the inside of the canopy over the bed, and it seems to me as if I've seen it before—seen it in my mind's eye a minute ago, in fact.

This isn't a bed: it's an altar. It used to belong to a fertility cult. It's been used for sex magic. What do I know about sex magic, and revenants, and summonings? *Think!*

The chorus take up positions around the bed, continuing their chant; Iris walks around it slowly, tracing a design using a small fortune in granulated silver tipped from an antique powder horn. Then she walks to the chest at the foot of the bed and waits while two more cultists produce the varied tools and ingredients for a summoning: knives, mirrors, unpleasantly molded black candles, a laptop computer, and bookshelf speakers. She is out of my sight most of the time, unless I lift my head—it's hard—but I gradually realize something else: she's using the chest at the foot of . . . the original altar, as her own summoning altar. They've put me on the *other* cult's summoning grid.

Iris is an SSO 6(A)—middle management in the administrative branch—because she's not actually very talented at magic. And I'm in the position of a man, sentenced to hang, whose inexperienced executioners have temporarily sat him in the electric chair while they work out how to tie a noose. Except magic doesn't work like that. My shoulders begin to shake. I try to get a grip on myself. A few seconds pass. I open my eyes and stare at the headboard, and flex my right arm until I nearly black out. Then, when I'm awake again, I start to subvocalize again, repeating the black theorem I started outside the door to this place.

Iris begins to chant, in Aramaic I think—something containing disturbingly familiar names. I tune her out and focus on my own liquid, gurgling subvocalization.

They strapped me to the electric chair, but they didn't notice I was wearing a suicide belt . . .

A BLACK BMW CRUISES DOWN A TREE-LINED COUNTRY LANE IN the late evening dusk. To one side, there's a fence, behind which trees block out the view. To the other side, there's a two-meter-high brick wall, the masonry old and crumbling, with trees behind it—but spaced more widely than the woods opposite. A black minivan follows the BMW saloon, which has slowed to well below the national speed limit.

"It's around here, somewhere," says the driver, frowning at the brightly glowing rectangle of card on his dash.

"It's getting weaker," says Panin. "I think"—he glances sidelong out of the window—"our man is on the other side of that wall."

At just that moment, the wall falls away from the road, as a driveway opens out. Dmitry needs no urging to turn into it; the trailing minivan overshoots, but the road is empty, and its driver reverses back up to the drive.

There's a gatehouse, like that of a stately home, and a black cast-iron gate topped with spikes. There are no lights in the house, and the gate is chained shut. Panin points at it. "Get that open."

"Sir!" The front seat passenger gets out and approaches the gate. It takes him less than a minute to crack the padlock and unwrap the chain; he waves the small convoy through, then leans in the BMW's open door as it creeps alongside. "Do you want it closing or securing, sir?"

"Both." The guard disappears again, the car door closing as the driver slowly accelerates along what appears to be a narrow and unlit woodland road. The driver spares him a glance in the wing mirror. He's the lucky man: all he has to do is stand guard over a gate tonight. What could go wrong?

"Brookwood cemetery," Panin says quietly. He uses a pen torch to read his gazetteer. "The London necropolis, built in the nineteenth century. Eight square kilometers of graves and memorial chapels. Who would have thought it?" He clicks his tongue quietly and puts the torch away.

"What do you want me to do, sir?" asks Dmitry.

"Drive. Headlights off. Follow the card until you see a chapel ahead of you, then pull over."

Dmitry nods, and switches off the headlights. The BMW has an infrared camera, projecting an image on the windscreen: he drives slowly. Behind them, the minivan douses its lights. Its driver has no such built-in luxuries—but military night-vision goggles are an adequate substitute.

Panin pulls a walkie-talkie from the back of the seat in front of him and keys it. There's an answering burst of static.

"Rook One to Knight One. Closing on board now. We'll dismount before proceeding. Over."

"Knight One, understood, over."

The big saloon ghosts along the winding way, past tree-shadowed gravestones and monuments that loom out of the darkness and fade behind with increasing frequency. Then it slows. Dmitry has spotted a car parked ahead, nearside wheels on the grassy verge, its tires and exhaust glowing luminous by infrared: it hasn't been there long.

"That will be the target," says Panin.

Dmitry kills the engine, and they coast to a silent halt. Doors open. Panin walks around the BMW, to stand behind it as the minivan pulls up behind. More doors open. Men climb out of the minivan: wiry men, clad in dark fatigues and balaclava helmets, moving fast. They deploy around the vehicles, weapons ready. Panin pulls his own goggles on over his thinning hair and flicks the switch. Then he drags a tiny, grotesque matrioshka doll on a loop of hemp string from one pocket and holds it high. Seen by twilight it appears to have a beard: and the beard is rippling. "Wards, everyone," he says softly. "This is the target. Clear it. Spare none but the English agent—and don't spare him either, if there's any doubt." He slides the loop of string over his head. "Sergeant Murametz, this is your show now."

Murametz nods, then waves his men towards the building they can dimly discern in the distance. The Spetsnaz vanish into the night and shadows, searching for guards. Dmitry turns to his boss. "Sir—what now?"

"Now—we wait." Panin frowns and checks his watch. "I hope we got here in time," he murmurs. "We must finish before James and his men arrive."

ANGLETON TURNS HIS HEAD SIDEWAYS TO WATCH MO. SHE LEANS against her seat back in the control room of the OCCULUS truck, eyes closed and face drawn. She clutches the violin case with both hands, as if it's a lifesaver; the fingers of her left hand look bruised.

"I'm not infallible," he repeats quietly.

She doesn't open her eyes, but she shakes her head. "I didn't say you were."

(Up front, Major Barnes—who is navigating by means of a simple contagion link Angleton established for him—tells the driver to take the second left exit from a roundabout. The truck sways alarmingly, then settles on its suspension as it accelerates away.)

"I had a long list of suspects. She was very low down."

"Angleton," Mo says gently, "just shut up. To err is human."

"It seems I have not been truly myself for a long time," he says, barely whispering, a dry, papery sound like files shuffling in a dead document archive.

Mo is quiet for a long time. "Do you want to be yourself?" she asks, finally.

"It would be less—limiting." He pauses for a few seconds. "Sometimes self-imposed limits make life more interesting, though."

The engine roars as the truck accelerates up a gradient.

"What would you do, if you weren't limited?"

"I would be terrible." Angleton doesn't smile. "You would look at me and your blood would freeze." Something moves behind the skin of his face, as if the pale parchment is a thin layer stretched between the real world and something underneath it, something inhuman. "I have done terrible things," he murmurs.

"We all do, eventually. Dying is terrible. So is killing. But I've killed people and survived. And as for dying—you don't have to live with yourself afterwards."

"Ah, but you *can* die. Have you considered what it might be like to be . . . undying?"

She opens her eyes, at that, and looks at him coldly. "Pick an innocent, if you're looking to put the frighteners on someone."

"You misunderstand." Angleton's eyes are luminous in the dark of the cab. "I *can't* die, as long as I am bound to this flesh. Have you ever longed for death, girl? Have you ever *yearned* for it?"

Mo shakes her head. "What are you getting at?" she demands.

"I can feel my end. It's still some distance away, but I can feel it. It's coming for me, sometime soon." He subsides. "So you'd better be ready to manage without me," he adds, a trifle sourly.

Mo looks away: through the windscreen, at the onrushing darkness of the motorway, broken only by cats' eyes and the headlight glare of on-coming cars on the other carriageway. "I hope we get there in time," she murmurs. "Otherwise you'll have to do more than die if you want me to forgive you for losing Bob."

MY ARM HURTS. AND I'M FADING IN AND OUT OF CONSCIOUSNESS. There's a foul taste in my mouth but I can't spit it out because of the gag. Iris is singing. Her voice is a strangled falsetto, weird swooping trills that don't seem to follow the chord progressions of any musical style I'm fa-miliar with. I'm tied to an altar between two long-dead corpses as the Brotherhood choral society sing a dirge-like counterpoint to Iris's diva and slowly walk around me, bearing candles that burn *dark*, sucking in the lamplight . . .

The distorted lines inscribed in the canopy above my head seem to blur and shimmer, cruel violet lines cutting into my retinas, surrounded by a pinprick of stars—or are they distant eyes?—as I keep up my lines. They don't make much sense, translated into English: the sense is some-thing like, *for iterator count from zero to number of entropy sinks within ground state, hear ye, hear ye, I open the gates of starry time for ye that you may feel the ground beneath your feet and the air upon your skin; I invoke the method of Dee and the constructor of Pthagn, forever exit and collect all the garbage, amen.* See? I said it didn't make much sense. In a particularly corrupt Enochian dialect that allows one to string together arbitrary subjunctive tenses it's another matter, though.

Standing before her altar Iris is recounting the myriad names of the

Eater of Souls, and she's *also* pumping energy into this system. She's got twenty black-robed followers and the computational hardware I lack, and if I'm lucky I can piggyback on her invocation—

Uh. I don't feel so good.

A wave of darkness sweeps over me. For a moment I can feel the bony bodies to either side of me in the bed, and they're warm and flesh-covered, almost as if they were breathing a moment ago. The tomb-dust stink is the yeasty smell of bodies from which the life departed only seconds hence. But the *really* weird thing is that I feel light, and dry, and unspeakably thirsty, a mere shell of my former self. The lines on the canopy overhead are glowing like a gash in the rotten fabric of reality, and I seem to be rising towards it. It's death magic, pure and simple. I *can* summon the feeders out of night, I can open the way for them to crawl into the empty vessels all around me, buried in the wall niches outside this temple and the holes in the ground above its ceiling, but only if I use myself as a sacrifice, thinning the wall and letting them feed on my mind. The reason cultists prize virgins as human sacrifices is nothing to do with sex and everything to do with innocence. Iris probably thought the morphine would fog me enough to lie back and gurgle at the pretty lights. Or that the training—to never, ever attempt magic in one's own head—would hold. Or perhaps it simply didn't occur to her that I'd take the Samson option. But be that as it may—

Is that what I look like?

I'm looking down on my body from above. I'm a real sight, hog-tied between two irregular mounds in the bedding, gagged, my head split open and bleeding where Jonquil knocked a handful of butterfly sutures loose, my right arm leaking into a messy stain on one pillow. Eyes are closed. I'm floating. Iris is singing and I can understand the harmonies now, I can hear her as she tries to summon something that isn't there.

"Beloved and forsaken! Eater of Souls! Lover of Death! Mother of nightmares! We who are gathered to observe your rite remember you and recall you by name! Come now to this vessel we prepare—"

I've got company up here. I can feel them gather in the darkness, blind curiosity thrusting them close, like sharks butting up against the legs of a swimmer stranded in the middle of an ocean. They're class three abominations. I have summoned them to feed on the rips and gashes of my memory that I dribble in the water of Lethe. I'm not alone up here: and they sense me. Soon one of them will taste me, take a bite of my soul and find that my memories are richly textured and deep. And then I'll begin to lose stuff. I push at them, trying to shove them towards the empty vessels that *I* have primed, but they aren't having it; I'm far more interesting than any century-dead bag of bones.

And then I feel a horrible visceral pain, as if someone has stuck a barbed knife through my umbilical.

"Come to this vessel!" shrieks Iris. *"Come now!"*

I convulse: the pain is unspeakable. And I feel the tugging. If I travel with it, the pain lessens slightly. *"Obey me! Enter the empty vessel! On pain of eternal torment, I instruct you to enter!"*

I drift down from the canopy, watching the ripples of nightmare twitch and spiral above me, still seeking. *What the fuck?*

"Enter! Enter! Enter!" Iris yodels. And as I lie on my back, looking up at the canopy above me, the pain in my guts evaporates.

What the fucking fuck? I close my eyes, and resume my gurgling, muffled invocation. *For a moment, I'd swear I was having an out-of-body experience . . .*

Then a coherent picture forms in my mind's eye.

It's like this. Iris is trying to summon up the Eater of Souls and bind it into my body where, among other things, it'll eat my soul and take up permanent residence. But the Eater of Souls is otherwise occupied right now. But Iris doesn't know this—she doesn't have TEAPOT clearance.

Meanwhile, I have just been trying to vacate my body all on my own, in order to summon up the feeders in the night, because if a bunch of Goatfuckers are trying to sacrifice me, I might as well fuck 'em as hard as I can. Again: it's not Iris's fault for failing to anticipate this, because she's never had to visit the Funny Farm. She's not really much of a demonologist. And she's such a good manager she's never had reason to see me when I'm seriously pissed off.

Here's the upshot: Iris's invocation has got a dangling pointer, an uninitialized variable pointing to an absent *preta*. But there's a soul in the vicinity, cut free—mostly—from its body. So instead of hooking onto the Eater of Souls, the *preta manger*, it latched onto *me*. So she's just spent fuck knows how much carefully hoarded ritual mojo to *bind me into my own flesh*.

Like she said: "Fatal accidents never have just a single cause, they happen at the end of a whole series of errors." Well, Iris has strung about five errors together and she's about to go down hard, because I'm about to turn fatal on her.

I open my eyes again and stare at the canopy overhead.

The feeders in the night are dispersing—but they're not going back from whence they came. They're rippling outwards, through the temple towards the walls. This body's occupied. But outside the doors, the vessels I've been prepping are waiting.

The chant continues, as do the invocations and imprecations in the name of an absent monster. I lie back and try to calm my hammering heart. I don't feel quite myself—I'm sweating and cold even though it's a summer night, and my skin doesn't seem to fit properly. It's very strange. The cultists continue with their rite, which takes some unexpected turns. There is a large silver goblet of wine, into which a hooded man empties a familiar-looking syringe full of blood—it boils and steams on contact, which is rather disturbing. Then a quorum of the chorus line start to shed their robes, and don't stop at their underwear. They walk around me naked, which is *really* disturbing because they appear to be into mortification of the flesh in a big way—even bigger than Opus Dei—with a genital focus that makes me wonder how they ever get through airport metal detectors. Or reproduce. No wonder Jonquil is an only child—

And speak of the devil's daughter: here's her mother, leaning over me— black robes covering up who-knows-what, and really clashing with her blonde rinse. Iris unhooks the gag, steps back, and throws her arms wide: "Speak, oh Eater of Souls!"

I work my jaw. It feels subtly *wrong*, as disarticulated as if I've just done hard time in a tomb and haven't noticed I'm one of the walking dead. I force myself to inhale, try to salivate, turn my head sideways (*that* feels wrong, too) and expectorate. A thin stream of spittle lands on the bedding beside my eternally sleeping companion: it's black in the torch light. *Dust, of course, because I can't be bleeding. Right?*

"Speak!" she commands me. I stare at her, and feel a nearly irresistible urge to bite her throat out. Right now I should be trying to make like I'm a freshly reincarnated Eater of Souls, but I am *thirsty* and I am *hungry* and I have just been through hell and I really don't care.

Some imp of the perverse takes control of my larynx: "I'll drink your blood," I croak, and instantly regret it. But much to my surprise, her eyes light up.

"Certainly, lord! Bring the chalice!" she shrills over her shoulder. A naked minion steps forward, bearing the huge silver goblet: it's full of what I'm pretty sure is red wine, and it smells wonderful. Iris accepts it and holds it near my face. I slurp greedily, spilling more than I suck into my mouth. It's thick and sweet, like tawny port, but also warming, as if there's a trace of ginger or chili oil dissolved in it. "In the name of the Unhallowed One, I command you to stop drinking," she says.

I freeze momentarily, acutely aware that I want to keep going, but— *she won't order them to untie me if she doesn't think I'll obey her,* I realize. And I really, *really* want to be untied. I can sense the feeders all around us, dispersed throughout the soil around the crypt, doing what they do best: eating in the darkness, consuming and corrupting and possessing the material forms that are normally denied to them. Soon, they're going to take possession of their withered husks and go looking for more upmarket digs. I don't want to be tied down and helpless when that happens—

Evidently Iris mistakes my indecision for compliance. She turns to her audience: *"The Eater of Souls obeys!"* she calls. "The first test!"

She turns back to face me, triumphant and happy. "What would you have me do to hasten the opening of the way?" she asks.

"Untie me." I tug lightly at the ropes. "Untie me." My right arm feels wrong, but so does my left—they both obey me, but feel oddly distant. *Blood sugar must be low,* I tell myself. *Or that wine has a kick to it.*

Wrong response. Iris is shaking her head. But she's still smiling. "Not yet," she says. "Not until the rite of binding is complete." *Rite of binding? Uh-oh.*

"The rite *is* complete," I tell her, hoping she'll buy it. "The blood and the wine . . ."

"I don't think so." She looks at me sharply, and I see something greenish reflected in her eyes. *Something behind me?* She turns back to her altar before I can work it out, walks towards the front of her congregation. "Bring me the sacrifice pure of heart and soul!" she calls.

Then the true horror show begins.

THEY'RE CULTISTS. WORSE: THEY'RE THE BROTHERHOOD OF THE Black Pharaoh, hated and persecuted wherever they are exposed to the horrified gaze of ordinary people.

Why?

There is a pernicious and evil legend that comes down to us from ancient history: the legend of the Blood Libel. It's a regular, recurring slander that echoes down the ages, hurled against out-groups when an excuse for a pogrom or other form of mass slaughter is desired. The Blood Libel is a whisper that says that the strangers sacrifice babies and drink their blood. There are variant forms: the babies are stolen from good Christian households, the blood is baked into bread, the babies are their own incestuous get by way of the bodies of their own daughters. No embellishment is too vile or grotesque to find its way into the Blood Libel. The most frequent victims are Jews, but it's been used against many other groups—the Cathars, Zoroastrians, Kulaks, Communists, you name it. The Romans regularly used it against the early Christians, and doubtless they'd stolen it from somebody else. Its origins are lost in antiquity, but the sole purpose of the Blood Libel is to motivate those who believe it to say: "These people are not like us, and we need to kill them, *now*."

I always used to think that was all there was to it.

But now I know better; I've witnessed the wellspring of the bloody legend and seen its practitioners in action.

And I'm still in their hands.

16.

EATER OF SOULS

MEANWHILE, SOME DISTANCE ABOVE MY HEAD, HERE'S WHAT happens as Iris's rite runs to completion:

Benjamin paces around the Chapel of the Ancient and Honourable Order of Wheelwrights, nostrils flaring to take in the sweet summer night air, heavy with pollen and sweet with the scent of new-mown hay.

Benjamin is a mild-mannered debt management consultant from Epping, and he's doing very well, thank you. He works out for half an hour every morning in the gym downstairs from his comfortable office; then he goes to work, where he helps distressed businesses find ways and means of improving their cash retention practices. He spends his evenings arranging social activities under the aegis of his local church (who the neighbors consider to be slightly odd but generally friendly and helpful), and sometimes, at the weekend, he plays with the church paintball team.

Epping is one stop down the line from Barking, which is what the neighbors would think of him if they could see him now, wearing the black cloak of a member of a very different Order, and carrying a gun that fires something more substantial than paint pellets.

Grigori, in contrast, is not mild-mannered at all. Grigori is a violently aggressive young thug from the slums of Nizhny Novgorod, born in the year of the collapse of the Soviet Union and raised half-feral amidst the wreckage of the timber and steel industries. Conscripted into the Russian army at eighteen and subjected to twelve months of brutal training, he showed a remarkable aptitude for butchering Wahhabi guerillas in the hills of the Kadar zone during the Dagestan war. Already tapped for promotion to sergeant he was instead inducted into Spetsgruppa V, "Vympel," the FSB's special operations unit, where he was taught German, Arabic, and sixteen different ways to strangle a man in his own intestines.

Grigori does not play paintball; Grigori kills people.

Here comes Grigori, crawling silently through the bushes, taking care not to place hand or foot on any twig that might snap, nor to disturb leafy shrubs that might whisper in the darkness. He pauses regularly, glancing sidelong to maintain situational awareness and positioning relative to his comrades, neither too far ahead nor lagging behind the line of advance. They use no radio; the occasional flicker of a red LED torch or the hoot of a tawny owl are more than sufficient. Grigori pauses before the open apron of the parking lot in front of the chapel, waiting for the sentry to complete his round. While he pauses, he double-checks his crossbow. The body is made of black resin and the bow sports a profusion of pulleys. It's a hunting bow, fine-tuned for hunting the kind of game that shoots back on full auto; it's totally silent and it throws a cyanide-tipped bolt that can slice through five centimeters of Kevlar armor.

Here comes Benjamin, pacing quietly around the side of the chapel. Benjamin is a good sentry. He's been bushwhacked by rival paintball players often enough to be ambush-savvy, scanning the darkness with nervous, night-adjusted eyes. He is well-equipped, his cloak concealing a small fortune in camouflaged body armor; to his belt is clipped a small pager. It vibrates every ten seconds, and if he fails to press a button on it within another ten seconds a siren will sound, loud enough to wake the dead. And he's cranked up on a cocktail of provigil and crystal meth, sleepless and compulsively alert. All-Highest has briefed the Security

Team carefully. The threat of a hostile intrusion is very real tonight, and Benjamin holds his AA-12 assault shotgun at the ready, his index finger tense beside the trigger guard.

Grigori and Benjamin are not as mismatched as a superficial comparison might suggest. Grigori's lieutenant has meticulously planned a seek-and-destroy raid on a nest of cultists defended by vicious but amateurish killers. And Iris's security chief has briefed the sentries to be on the alert for an infiltration attempt by an elite unit of special forces troops attached to a secret interior ministry department.

But as Grigori and Benjamin are about to discover, they've both been briefed for the wrong mission.

Benjamin pauses in the shadow of an ornamental buttress at one corner of the chapel, and scans the darkness beyond. There are low shrubs, and a row of lichen-encrusted gravestones, some of them leaning towards a low dip in the ground where a willow tree holds court over a circle of beeches. He sniffs. There's something in the air tonight—something beyond the efflorescences of pollen spurting from the wildly rutting vegetation, something beyond the tang of mold spores drifting from the cut ends of the lawn over by the road. His eyes narrow. Something about the bushes is *wrong*.

His pager vibrates. He peers into the gloom, tensing and raising the heavy shotgun, and tries to move his right foot forward into a shooter's stance.

His boot is stuck . . .

Grigori crouches in the darkness behind a drunkenly leaning gravestone. His nostrils flare. The ground here smells *bad*, in a way that reminds him of a mass grave outside a nameless village near Rakhata in the mountains above Botlikh. Damp ground, rainy hills, and a season of death had soured the very earth, making the nauseous soil threaten to regurgitate its charges. After a week on duty there he'd had to indent for a new pair of boots: no matter how he scrubbed and polished he couldn't get the stench of death out of his old ones.

Grigori frowns, and raises his bow, sighting on the buttress to the right of the chapel, where he is sure the sentry will appear in a few seconds. His view is partially obstructed by the gravestone, so he tries to move his left foot sideways a few centimeters.

His boot refuses to shift.

Meanwhile, on the other side of the chapel wall, Benjamin slaps his pager into silence then tries to lift his right foot again, freeing it from the root or wire or whatever he's caught on. His left knee nearly buckles. Something has caught on his right ankle. Cursing silently, he glances down.

Grigori's nostrils widen as he smells rottenness, mold, and mildew. He shifts his stance slightly as the ground softens beneath his right foot. There's a faint vibration underfoot. *Do they have earthquakes in England?* It was once like this in the mountains near Botlikh—but the vibration is getting stronger. He glances aside, and sees the ground rippling.

Oddly, none of the bells are sounding—not in this chapel, nor in any of the others.

Benjamin sees something moving in the loose soil underfoot. Adrenal glands squirt, and his pulse spikes: he unslings his gun and turns it, slamming it butt-first on the white and crawling thing below, thinking *snake—*

A second hand, less fully skeletonized than the first, pushes through the soil and grabs the shotgun's dangling tactical sling.

Grigori's nerves jangle as he sees the ripples of ground spread silently out around the chapel: he is not superstitious but he belongs to the company of Spetsgruppa "V" assigned to KGB support operations, and this is a fucking *graveyard* at fucking *midnight*. He lowers the crossbow, raising his left hand to the matrioshka charm dangling at his throat just as the earth beneath him heaves and a bony claw punches up through the grass beneath him and reaches for his neck.

THE OCCULUS TRUCK ROARS ALONG THE M3 MOTORWAY, DRIVING
south in darkness.

Major Barnes has a mobile phone glued to his ear. He's nodding unconsciously. Then he turns, looking at Angleton and Mo in the back of the cab. "Dr. Angleton, Dr. O'Brien, we have a fix."

Mo sits up instantly. "Yes?"

"That was Jameson at headquarters—DVLA have coughed up the registration details on Iris Carpenter's car. Highways Agency say it came this way earlier this evening and turned off onto the A322 at junction three. The ANPR cameras on that stretch are down, but looking at this map—what does Brookwood cemetery suggest to you?"

"Brookwood." Angleton raises an eyebrow. "Yes. Continue."

"I'm waiting for—" The major's phone rings again. "Excuse me." He flicks it open. "Yes?" He nods vigorously. "Yes, yes . . . I concur. Yes. I want you to get onto the Surrey Police control center and ask if the ASU can provide top cover. Get them to send a car with a downlink receiver round to the main entrance on Cemetery Pales, we don't have a police downlink—no, no, but if the armed response unit is on duty get them up there. Yes, I'm authorizing that." Barnes blinks at Angleton, who inclines his head. "I'm in the OCCULUS with Howe's brick; get the rest of third platoon moving immediately, I think we're going to need all the support we can get. Is there any SCORPION SCARE coverage—all right, that was too much to hope for. We should be at the gates in another fifteen minutes. Get the police to block all the roads in and out—The Gardens, Avenue de Cagny, yes, and the rest—tell them it's a terrorism incident."

When he finally hangs up he looks tired. "Did you catch that?" he asks.

Mo stares at him. "It's a cemetery. Yes?"

"Brookwood is not just *a* cemetery," Angleton informs her: "It's the London necropolis, the largest graveyard in Western Europe. Eight thousand acres and more than a quarter of a million graves."

The penny drops. Her eyes widen. "They're planning a summoning. You're thinking it's death magic?"

"What does it sound like to you? Lots of space, no neighbors within earshot, lots of raw fuel for a necromancer to work with, raw head and bloody bones." Angleton looks at Barnes. "Have you tried to call the cemetery site office?"

"Gordon tried that already. Got a bloody answering machine."

"Ten to one there's nobody at the gatehouse. Or if there is, he's one of them."

"And we've got eight thousand acres to cover, and no CCTV, never mind SCORPION STARE." Barnes's expression is sour. "No surveillance, no look-to-kill—the ASU had better deliver or they'll hand us our heads on a plate."

"What would your preferred option be?" Angleton asks softly, his voice almost lost beneath the road noise.

"If we had *time*—" Barnes grimaces. "I'm sorry, Mo. I can't afford to throw lives away needlessly by going after Bob before we're ready."

"But we're not just going in after Bob," she says tartly. "We're going in to prevent the Black Brotherhood doing whatever it is they're planning. Angleton: the Ford paper was a decoy, granted—but what can they do anyway? What kind of summoning are we looking at?"

"They can try to summon up the Eater of Souls." His smile is ghastly. "They won't get him. What they get in his place—could be anything—" His smile fades, replaced by a look of perplexity. "That's funny."

"Funny?" Mo leans forward. "What's funny?"

Angleton raises his right hand and rubs it against his chest. "I feel odd."

"Oh come *on*, you can't pull that—" Mo stops. "Angleton?"

His eyes are closed, as if asleep. *"They're calling,"* he whispers. *"The dead are calling . . ."*

"Dr. O'Brien—" Major Barnes stares at Angleton. "Code Red!" he calls, yelling at the back of the truck. "Code Red!"

Angleton leans against his seat belt, unmoving.

THE HUMAN SACRIFICE IS OVER IN SECONDS: IRIS IS THE KIND of priestess who believes in running a tight ship, and the tiny body stops thrashing mercifully fast. She lowers the bloody knife to the altar below the foot of the bed and what happens next is concealed from me.

I lie back and screw my eyes shut, but blocking out the sight of what they're doing doesn't make things better: I can feel blind things moving in the darkness, all around, scraping and scrabbling at the porous walls of the world. They're trying to get in. I invited them, and many of them have found bodies, but those that haven't—there are myriads of them. *What have I done?* I'm not sure. I'm not sure of *anything* except horror and disgust and a sense of nauseous unease at my own body. I'm lying on a bed, surrounded by corpses, at the exact end of a ley line that connected the capital with its dead underbelly, the citadel of silence in the English countryside. And they're trying to do something awful, using me as a vessel, but it failed. Just like my attempt to use the energy of my own death to summon the eaters in the night—

"By the blood of the newborn be you bound to this flesh, this body, and this will!" Iris's voice is a dissonant screech like nails on a blackboard, compelling and revolting, impossible to ignore. I open my eyes. She stands beside the bed, holding the silver goblet before my chin. It's full to brimming with dark fluid, thick and warm and amazingly wonderful to smell and I finally twig, *That's not wine.* I try to turn my head away, but two of her followers grasp me with gloved hands and push me up, straining against the ropes and brutally stretching my sore arm. "I command you and name you, Eater of Souls and master of Erdeni Dzu! I name you again, heir of Burdokovskii's flesh! And I bind you to service in the name of the Black Pharaoh, N'yar lath-Hotep!"

Then they pry my jaws open and stick a funnel in my mouth and start pouring while some bastard grips my nostrils shut, giving me a choice between drowning and swallowing.

"There!" says Iris, smiling at me as she hands the half-empty goblet to her daughter. "Isn't it so much better now?"

I roll my eyes, force saliva, and spit. I'm not aiming at Iris, I'm just trying to clean the taste from my tongue—but her smile slips. "Hey now, I didn't give you permission to do that. No spitting. Do you understand?"

I bite my tongue before I succumb to the impulse to tell her where to shove it. I want to be rid of these ropes. There are *things* waiting outside in the dark, learning once again how bones and sinews are articulated, and I don't want to be tied up down here when they arrive. Her words of binding slide over and past me, like a fishing line with rotten, unappetizing bait, but if I really *was* the Eater of Souls they'd sink into my inner ears like barbed-wire kisses. The only way out of here is to convince Iris that her little ritual worked: I'll just have to pretend. "I—understand," I croak after a brief pause, and it's not hard to sound utterly unlike myself. "Mistress."

The fat, happy smile begins to steal back across her face. "Here are your orders. You will serve the goals and rules of the Brotherhood of the Black Pharaoh. You will not attack or attempt to damage any of the Brotherhood, under penalty of the binding I hold over you. You will not reveal your true nature to anyone outside the Brotherhood without my permission. And you will inform me at once if you suspect you are under suspicion. Do you understand?"

That's a no-brainer: "Yes, Mistress," I say, looking her in the eyes. Her face has an unhealthy greenish sheen to it, as if there's an ethereal light source behind me. She's really sucking this up.

"Good." She nods to her minions. "Untie him."

They bend over the black cords that bind me, and as they loosen I feel a very strange sensation in my chest—a gathering sensitivity, an awareness of the darkness around me. The ropes, part of the ritual apparatus prepared by the Brotherhood of the Skull for their own purposes so long ago, held their own geas: it made me feel weak. But now they're gone, the sense of strangeness redoubles. I'm an alien in my own body. It's very disturbing.

"Can you stand?" Iris asks me.

"I'll try." *First* I try to sit up, using my left arm as a lever. It's clumsy and I'm physically unbalanced, and my right arm is still throbbing distantly—but I succeed. Throwing a leg out sideways I crab round, then lean forward and (with a silent apology) slide across the back of the mummified sleeper under the counterpane. Is it my imagination or do they twitch, and push back at me? I don't stop to find out, but continue, sliding my feet towards the floor. It's like standing for the first time after being bedridden with a fever. At first it takes all my energy, and I nearly black out: everything goes gray for a few seconds, and there is a buzzing and chittering in my ears. But then my head clears, and I find I feel fine. I *feel fine*: and the feeling extends beyond me, beyond the walls of the crypt, out into the damp soil and among the tree roots and into the cavities encysted in the ground, their occupants now waking from their long slumber. "I'm standing," I say, swaying slightly.

"Good." Iris turns towards the altar. "Behold, the Eater of Souls!" she says, and takes my left wrist and holds it up, for all the world like a referee hailing a winning boxer.

"What would you have me do now?" I ask her out of the corner of my mouth, hamming it up for the benefit of the audience.

"Nothing yet. But I have sent out a summons to our brethren; next month we will hold another rite, and you will open the way to the Gatekeeper. If all goes well, the Pharaoh shall walk Earth's ground again next March. Do you think you can do that?"

Silent voices tickle the back of my skull: *What would you have us do, Lord?*

I tell them precisely what I want, in pedantically detailed Enochian—a dead language with which to command dead things.

"Eater. Speak?" Iris stares at me. We're close enough that I can see that greenish glow reflected on her face. *Oh, it's me. I'm glowing*, I realize. *My eyes are glowing. I'm possessed.*

I look at her. "Iris," I say softly, "you've forgotten the first rule of applied demonology."

She stares. "How did you know my—"

"Do not call up that which you cannot put down."

She tries to jerk her left hand away from me, making a grab at her improvised altar with her right. She reaches for the blood-tarnished silver sacrificial sickle but I yank her back and bring my right hand up to catch her wrist. We stand for a second in a parody of a waltz step, and I smile at her, baring my teeth. Her expression of heart-struck terror is as pure as fresh-shed blood. Around us her followers are turning, beginning to realize something has gone wrong, as the voices at the back of my head whisper oaths of fealty to me and the feeders bend to their tasks.

I raise my right arm—painless, now—over her head, and spin her round, then gather her to my chest, with my mouth centimeters from the nape of her neck. I'm careful not to make contact with her bare skin: a strangely irresistible aroma rises from her, and I suspect if I touched her I'd be unable to control myself. She smells of *food*. "Nobody try anything!" I shout. "Or I'll kill her!" A couple of the cultists are armed, but their security guys seem to favor shotguns: not the ideal weapon for dealing with a hostage-taker if you want the hostage back in anything other than lots of little pieces.

Simultaneously there's a stifled scream, and Jonquil falters in the act of raising a knife to throw at me. "The bed!" She hiccups—yes, fear gives some people the hiccups. "Look at *the bed*!"

"Shut up—" Iris begins to say, as I twist us both round so that I can see what everyone else is looking at; then she falls silent.

A man near the back of the congregation yells: "Run for it!" He grabs his robe and legs it in the direction of the doors.

In front of my eyes, on the bed, and everywhere else I can sense around me, the dead are rising.

"ALPHA TWENTY. THIS IS CHARLIE MIKE. DO YOU RECEIVE. over."

"Charlie Mike, Alpha Twenty receiving you clear, over."

The Eurocopter EC 135 banks gently as it turns towards Brookwood. Behind it, the streetlights of Guildford sprawl across the North Downs like a gigantic luminous jellyfish, swimming in deep waters; ahead, the ground is dark and peaceful until Woking, another amber-pricked sprawl of suburbia sleeping lightly in the summer night.

"Alpha Twenty, are you in visual range yet, over."

"Charlie Mike, two miles out and closing. No lights on the ground, over."

"Alpha Twenty, roger that, we recommend Nitesun. Focus is any parked vehicle on side roads off Cemetery Pales, we're looking for a Mercedes 500SL, color silver. Over."

The police sergeant sitting in the backseat with the controls to the infrared camera is peering into his screen, searching the tree-lined darkness for any sign of life. Tracking down the straight boulevard that leads through the park-like cemetery, his eyes are drawn to a row of vehicles parked off to one side of a crescent-shaped side road. "Got vehicles," he says, tweaking the joystick to turn his camera and zoom on them. "Location, Saint Barnabas Avenue, adjacent to building in clearing to south of road—Jesus!"

The bright pinpoints of bodies are clearly visible on his camera. They're moving around in the woods northeast of the building, and a couple south of the building—and there are flares, moving fast, bursting like fireworks.

"Alpha Twenty, we see fireworks, repeat, fireworks, numerous parties, situation confused, south Saint Barnabas Avenue. Climbing to flight level twenty, over."

The ground drops away and the airframe throbs as the pilot pulls up on the collective pitch and climbs at full power. "Roy, what's going on down there?" he asks over the intercom.

"Not sure, skipper—looks like rockets—" There are dark pinpoint figures down there, what looks like a mob, but they're not showing up as heat sources. "Something wrong with the camera, damn it. There are people down there but I think the rockets are masking their body heat. Never heard of that—"

"You can use the Nitesun once we're above three thousand feet. Clear?"

"Got it. Tell me when. Jesus, that was big—they've set a tree burning. Oh Jesus fucking Christ I've never seen anything like it! Sir, there's a whole *crowd* down there, and the idiots with fireworks are aiming at them—"

"Hit the switch when ready, we need to see this."

The observer hits the power switch on the Nitesun searchlight: thirty-million candlepower dialed to maximum area washes over the churning landscape of the cemetery, turning night into day.

"Alpha Twenty, this is Charlie Mike, do you have a Sitrep, over."

"Charlie Mike to Alpha Twenty, major incident in progress. Illegal fireworks, also major crowd control issue, vegetation on fire. Center of disturbance is the chapel on Saint Barnabas Avenue but the crowd—they're everywhere. Is there an illegal rave? Request backup, major incident team, Plan Red, over."

Half a mile up the road, a red fire-control truck has pulled up just outside the entrance to the cemetery, blue lights strobing; a small army of police cars are streaming in behind it, converging from every point of the compass, breaking the amber-lit monotony of the roads with red and blue flickers. The observer in the back of Charlie Mike zooms in with his FLIR camera, focusing on the crowd, frowning.

"Skipper, I don't know how to put this, but a lot of the bodies down there—they're showing up cold. I mean, stone cold. I can see them by Nitesun, but they ought to be in hospital with hypothermia, know what I mean?"

OVER THE CENTURY AND A HALF FOR WHICH IT HAS BEEN OPEN for business, roughly a quarter of a million funerals have been carried out in Brookwood; many more cremations have been held, and many older graves have been disinterred and their occupants moved piecemeal to the ossuaries, but the ground still holds more souls than the nearby towns of Guildford and Woking combined.

The cemetery grounds are churned like newly mown fields, but no birds will chance this terrain in search of earthworms and grubs. Below the helicopter, thousands of eyeless faces look up. They stand where they have risen: strange fruiting bodies sprouting from the decay-riddled earth, in concentric circles that ripple outwards from the Chapel of the Ancient and Honourable Order of Wheelwrights. Their withered faces track the helicopter as it spirals overhead, shattering the night with a thunder of blades. Among them, a handful of warm bodies still move, desperately trying to form a defensive line around the chapel.

But one by one, the pinpoints of warmth and life are going out.

THE STROBING BLUES CAST GHOSTLY SHADOWS ACROSS THE interior of the OCCULUS truck as it sits at the entrance to the graveyard, engine idling. W/O Howe and his paramedic, Sergeant Jude, are sitting over Angleton's supine body.

"Flatline," Jude says phlegmatically. "He's breathing and his heart's beating, but there's nobody home. Might be a stroke, but if so it's a big one." Jude's specialty is trauma, especially violent trauma; he's rusty at this end of the game. "Wish that ambulance would hurry up."

"It's too big a coincidence," Mo says harshly.

"You diagnose enemy action?" asks Barnes.

"Absolutely. We're on our way to retrieve"—she glances around the cabin—"among other things, a document of binding. And there's *that*." She gestures forward, through the windscreen, at the churning night beyond the gates. "What are the odds that he'd blow a gasket right at the critical moment?"

Alan Barnes thinks for a moment, then nods vigorously. "All right, Doctor, assuming you're correct, how do you think I should deal with the situation? We came expecting to deal with cultists and a possible hostage rescue, not the night of the living dead. There are certain tactical issues to consider." He nods at the windscreen. "Notably, (a) how we get through the crush to wherever our cultists are holed up, (b) how we deal with them when we arrive, bearing in mind that our arrival is not going to be terribly stealthy, and (c) how we get out alive afterwards. I should say that the possessed are *your* department. We've got a SCORPION STARE interferometer, but that's an area denial weapon—wouldn't do us much good to burn through the walking dead and catch Mr. Howard in the sweep, would it?" He looks at her expectantly. "Do you have any recommendations?"

"Hmm." Mo squints at the windscreen. "If this truck can get close to the chapel—you've got a link to the police helicopter?"

"Yes—why?"

Mo looks up at the hatch in the roof of the driver's cab. "I need to be able to see what's going on," she says. "We need to find the center of this summoning and kill whatever's responsible. Can you give me something to stand on?"

"You're thinking of—" Alan looks at her violin case. "That's not terribly safe."

"Can you think of a better idea?" Mo bares her teeth in something not too unlike a smile. "Because I'm fresh out of subtlety right now."

"As long as we keep moving ahead, and they don't come climbing over the bodywork, it ought to get us in close," Howe says slowly. "Sir, if we ride topside with entrenching tools to keep 'em off her—"

"Very good." Barnes nods jerkily. He looks at Angleton: unconscious but breathing. "We can't wait for the ambulance," he says finally. To Howe: "Off-load him. Jude, you wait with Dr. Angleton. Howe, you want to leave a guard?"

"Sir. McDonald, you're staying with Jude and the doctor until the ambulance shows up. Once he's on his way to hospital, wait here. If the trouble overflows, leg it—we'll pick you up later. Clear?"

McDonald—short, wiry, still dressed as a fireman—nods. "Can do."

"Okay, get the stretcher and jump to it. Williams, get Dr. O'Brien's instrument patched into the external sound system. Scary, collect two shovels and get up top. Let's move it!"

Minutes later the truck rolls slowly towards the gates of Brookwood and the heaving darkness beyond, three figures crouched on its roof. Two of them hold collapsible shovels with sharpened edges; the third clutches something bone-white in her hands. She lowers her bow until it kisses the strings of her instrument. The walking dead turn to listen as Mo plays her lullaby. Beyond them, in the darkness, the screams are getting fainter.

HERE'S WHAT I SEE IN THE CRYPT:

The dusty counterpane on the altar-bed falls away as the two mummified lover-sacrifices sit up. They glow with the pallid green of bioluminescence from within, their empty eye sockets writhing with a nauseating slow-motion churn as they look around. Bony metatarsals click on the flagstones as they rise to their feet.

A bunch of the cultists are fleeing, making a dash for the iron-studded door. They don't care whether they end up on Iris's shit-list; they're more scared of the walking dead.

A male cultist, still robed and bearing one of their shotguns, is the first to show some balls. He moves into a firing line on one of the rising dead, bringing his gun to his shoulder. He aims, and fire gouts from his weapon. Indoors, reflected and reverberating from stone, a fired shotgun hammers your eardrums with spikes of compressed air as sharp as knives. I see people shouting, and Iris spasms and screams in my grip, but I hear nothing but echoes from that dreadful report. The walking cadaver's head vanishes in a spray of bone and parchment, but still it stumbles forward, straight towards the shotgun-aiming guard. He stares at it in disbelief, then lowers his aim and fires again, blasting a hole in its thoracic cavity. The truncated revenant falls, but its arms and legs are still moving. Another cultist, one of the ones who stripped for Iris's disastrous summoning, dances forward, holding up a billet of wood. He smashes it down on the twitching remains, raises it, prepares to bring it down again—

The mortal remains reach out, and one bony fingertip scrapes the inside of his calf.

I can feel what happens. The glory of satiated hunger, the sensual, almost erotic sense of dissolution as the feeder in the night moves from the parched, damaged host to this new playground of sensual corporeality, driving down and digesting its former owner's identity, submerging him in a tide of white noise.

It only takes a split second. I make eye contact with the possessed one: I recognize the glow at the back of his eyes, a reflection of my own refulgent glory. I nod at the shotgun bearer, who is sidling carefully around the bed, clearly stalking the other cadaver, and mouth *"Take him."* The syllables my tongue curls around are not English, nor any other language routinely spoken by human beings. The feeder blinks with delight at being so honored as the vehicle of my will. And then he begins to move.

Perhaps five seconds have passed since the man at the back shouted *Run for it* and broke for the door.

What Iris and those cultists who aren't fleeing see is probably something like this:

They see the Eater of Souls, newly risen from his bed, grab their high priestess and whirl her around in a deadly embrace, warning them to stand back. Then the skeletal remains on the bed sit up. One of them stands and begins to advance on the congregants. A guard shoots its head off, then blows the still-walking corpse in half at the waist. A member of the chorus bashes it twice with a length of wood. He freezes for a second—then hurls the timber at the guard's head and leaps.

The other feeder hobbles out from behind the four-poster bed. It's halfway up the stepped ring of mattresses, and it's moving towards the exit. Meanwhile, the mob of terrified cultists have gotten the door open. And that's when the *real* panic begins.

Iris is shaking but I force her to turn, holding her so that she can't look away. "This is your doing," I shout in her ear, barely able to hear my own voice. Harsh words force themselves through my larynx, words that come without my willing them: "Death waits you! You're all going to die! You have signed an oath of obedience to your dark master, and with Hell you are in agreement. Death awaits you all!"

Her congregation numbers perhaps thirty to fifty at most, with another eight to ten on guard outside. The Wheelwright dead, in contrast, number in the hundreds, and the honored dead of the Skull Brethren certainly outnumber Iris's followers. I can feel the feeders waiting outside the door, eager for the warmth they can sense within. *Wait for my word of release,* I tell them.

(Eager? Sense? I'm not sure those words are applicable to feeders. I'm not sure feeders are conscious in the way that we are—or even as aware as mammals or birds. They're bundles of rough reflexes, bound together by the strange grammars of night, more like software agents than anything that's ever had flesh. But if it walks like a lizard and breathes gouts of fire you might as well call it a dragon, and the feeders certainly seem to prefer bodies with a bit of metabolic energy and structural integrity remaining . . .)

Behind me, the first feeder completes his leap, slamming chest first onto the floor with a bone-snapping *crack*. The shotgun-toting guard is reeling from the thrown baton as the feeder lashes out and grasps him by the trouser hem, yanks him closer, and touches skin to skin as the butt of the shotgun descends with force born of panic.

In front of me, the other feeder lurches towards a robed woman. She's made of sterner stuff than the ones who are panicking, or perhaps she's just running her anti-rapist self-defense training script on autopilot: she raises a highly illegal taser, and there's a snap and a blue flare as she zaps the feeder. The cadaver collapses like a marionette with its strings cut, its rider temporarily banished back from whence it came: beings who are basically patterns of energy bleeding through from a parallel universe to ours don't respond well to high-voltage electrical noise. A femur goes rolling underfoot among the panicking congregants, triggering a rush to avoid touching it. *Wimps,* I think contemptuously. *Shoot her,* I instruct my surviving feeder.

The feeder raises the shotgun, its butt sticky with a mat of blood and hair, and tries to aim it in the general direction of the door, but its musculoskeletal control is patchy—it has taken three hosts in less than thirty seconds, all in different states, and it's confused. The shotgun pitches up as it clumsily jerks the trigger, and there's a repetitive stabbing pain in my ears as it blasts away at the ceiling above the crowd.

They've got the doors open, and they're trying to run away. *Stop firing,* I tell it, as the panicking cultists scramble for the exit. *Shut and barricade the door behind them.* I can see a hooded female, eyes staring back at me and full of hate; it's Jonquil. She mouths something—probably some variation on *I'll be back*—but she's not going to stay in a locked crypt with the Eater of Souls, even to save her mummy dearest. That's the trouble with cultists: no moral fiber to speak of.

Iris tenses as her followers leave, and it's then that she makes her bid for freedom, stamping hard on the inside of my right shin and trying to elbow me in the guts. "Let me *go!*" she shouts.

I feel the pain in my leg as if from a great distance, and the elbow in my abdomen is just a mild nuisance. "I don't think so," I say, and tighten my grip on her. "You don't know what's going on out there," I add. She keeps struggling, so I force her facedown on her own altar. "You made a really big mistake," I explain, as the feeder with the shotgun stalks after the last fleeing worshiper, and reaches for the door.

"Fuck you!" she snarls.

The feeder with the shotgun draws the door shut. *You may rise now,* I call silently to the ones who wait patiently outside, and I feel them begin to stir in their niches, shaking the cobwebs from their uneasy bones.

"You made several procedural mistakes, Iris." I don't need to shout now, but my ears are still ringing. "You tried to summon up a *preta* but it didn't occur to you to check first to see if it was already incarnate. Which it was, leaving you with an invocation and no target. So it latched onto the first available unhomed soul in the neighborhood, and it just happened to be mine. You're an idiot, Iris: you bound me *into my own body.* And you've just killed us both."

She's still tense but she stops struggling. She's listening, I think. "You've killed me, because I— You know what happens to demonologists who run code in their head? You made a big mistake, giving me time to think about what was happening. Suicide invocations are always among the most powerful, and you put me in the middle of the biggest graveyard in the country, with all that untapped necromantic go-juice. Bet you thought it would make your summoning easier, didn't you? Well, it worked for *me*. But I'm dead, Iris. I don't know how long this binding is going to hold up, and when the field collapses I'll be just another corpse."

The ringing in my ears is subsiding, almost enough to hear the muffled banging and screams from outside the door. *Oh dear, it sounds as if they want in again. Can't those people make up their minds?*

"I don't believe you," she says. "Ford's report . . ."

"Angleton arranged it. He knew we had a leak; Amsterdam proved it, but he'd already spotted the classic signs. He briefed Dr. Mike to put out a plausible line in bullshit, intending to drive you guys into a frenzy of self-exposure. I don't think he expected you to go quite this far, trying to bind the Eater of Souls and turn it loose inside the Laundry, though."

She's shivering. Fear or rage, I can't tell—not that it matters. Dimly and distantly I realize that fear and rage is what *I* should be feeling, but all I seem to be able to muster up right now is a vague malevolent joy. Ah, schadenfreude.

Fetch the taser, I tell my minion. I *could* kill her, but she knows too much. So I need to lock her down until the seventh cavalry arrive, even if I fall apart before then. And maybe get us the hell out of this crypt before the things in the air tonight get loose and come looking for me.

"How are you doing this?" she says in a loud whisper. "You shouldn't even be alive—"

"I'm one of *them*, Iris, weren't you listening? I'm possessed, recursively." *Take aim,* I tell my feeder. *You don't want this one, she tastes bad.* "Which is, on the face of it, nuts—I've never heard of such a thing—but we learn something new every day, don't we?"

I let go of her abruptly and step clear to give my minion a clear line of fire. She straightens up and begins to turn, and I realize I miscalculated as she raises her sickle. I duck as she lets fly and the feeder shoots, all at the same time. Iris collapses; something nicks my shoulder and falls off. *Stand back,* I tell my feeder. Then I walk over to the bed and collect the black sacrificial cords. The sickle did some damage, I realize, and I appear to be bleeding, but I can worry about that once I get Iris tied up.

By the time I finish binding her wrists and ankles, I'm beginning to feel oddly weak. The noises outside the door to the crypt have died down. *Go to sleep,* I tell my feeders; they crawl and writhe outside in the tunnels, happy and replete with the feast of new flesh, and need little urging to fall into a state of torpor. It's becoming hard to think clearly. I know there's something I ought to be doing, but . . . *oh, that.* I take the ring-bound black folder from Iris's improvised altar and tuck it under my arm, then I look at my patient feeder, who stands by the altar with a vacant expression, his eyes luminous in the dark. *Go to the entrance to the chapel. Open the doors. A truck will come with men. Lead them here, then sleep.*

He turns and shuffles towards the door, grateful and obedient to the Eater of Souls for granting him this brief existence. Then I am alone in the crypt with Iris. Who has begun to recover from her tasering, and tries to squirm aside as I walk past her to the bed. *"Hasta la vista,"* I tell her: "Give my regards to the Auditors."

Then I keel over on the dusty black satin sheets, dead to the world.

THERE IS CHAOS IN THE CHAPEL AS THE CULTISTS DESPERATELY prepare to defend the perimeter.

On the roof, the surviving guards—Benjamin is not among them—have taken up positions around the corners, pointing their guns out at the sea of bodies that slowly shuffle towards the building. Below them, the worshipers on the ground mill and rush in near-terror until three of their number, better organized and equipped than the rest, gather them into groups and set the unarmed to dragging pews into position to form an improvised barricade, while those who bear arms prepare to defend against the creeping wave of darkness.

Crouching behind the gargoyle at the southwest corner, Michael Digby (orthodontic technician, from Chelmsford) glances sideways at the cowled head of his *principale*, the sergeant-at-arms responsible for the coven's guard. "What are we going to do, sir?" he asks quietly.

"What does it look like, soldier?" Clive Morton (retail manager, from Dorking) studies the darkness with dilated pupils.

Digby looks back to the field of fire in front of the chapel as a brief snap of gunfire knocks over a clump of drunkenly walking figures that have shuffled out of the long shadows cast by the floodlights in the chapel doorway. "Looks like zombies, sir. *Thousands* of 'em."

"Right. And we're going to hold out here until dawn, or until All-Highest figures out how to drive them away, or we run out of ammunition. That answer your question?"

"You mean the only plan is to stand behind a few feet of church benches?"

"Beats having your soul eaten . . ."

Down below them, the worshipers have dragged the bench seats into position in an arc around the entrance and steps leading up to the chapel. Their fellows inside the building have lifted up the heavy wooden tables and tipped them against the windows, barring entry. They think they're safe, as long as the armed men on the roof can pick off any shuffling revenants that enter the circle of light. But death is already among them.

Alexei from Novosibirsk idles in the darkness behind the worshipers, lurking in the vestry where a cultist guard now lies beneath a pile of moth-eaten curtains.

Alexei is seriously annoyed, but professionally detached from the cock-up and chaos going on around him. The operation has not gone in accordance with earlier plans. He has, as expected, succeeded in infiltrating the vestibule area; the seething chaos outside, accompanied by a panicking mob erupting from the depths of the chapel, has made things run much more easily than anticipated—up to a point. But the ward around his neck is hot to the touch, smoking faintly with a stench of burned hair. And his radio has clicked three times—panic signals from soldiers unable to take their assigned places. Once is happenstance but twice is enemy action, and thrice is a fuck-up. Something has *gone wrong*, and he can no longer count on backup from Yuri and Anton. Finally, as if all of that isn't bad enough, the dead are rising.

This latter item, Alexei thinks, is deeply unfair. He's a sergeant in Spetsgruppa "V"—a professional, in other words—and when he kills someone professionally he expects them to stay dead. These walking abominations are an insult to his competence. If it wasn't for their annoying habit of infecting further victims through touch, they'd be a trivial obstacle at best; as it is, with his ward and his full-body insulated clothing, not to mention his Ostblock ballistic knife, AKM/100 assault gun, and other tools of the trade, he's well-equipped to deal with them. Except that there are *too damned many*, and they *won't stay dead*, and the rest of his team are dispersed and in trouble.

Speaking of trouble, here comes more. Most of the cultists are wearing black robes, or stupidly inappropriate army-surplus camo gear for the guards; if it's naked and you can count the ribs, it's probably one of the risen dead. Bonus points for shuffling like a stockbroker on a stag night, and big booby prize if you let it get so close you can see the green luminosity writhing in the depths of its eye sockets . . .

Alexei melts into the shadows behind the figure climbing the steps from the crypt. It's wearing a robe and shuffling drunkenly, and he's about to slide the blade of his knife between its two uppermost cervical vertebrae when he realizes that it is not, in fact, one of the possessed. Which raises some interesting questions. A moment later his gloved hand is covering the climber's mouth and his knife is at her throat. "Say nothing," he grunts, tugging her backwards into the vestry. "You want live, yes? Be silent." The cultist stumbles as he drags her into the shadows, but doesn't say anything. Alexei rolls her to the ground and has her pinioned in a second. "Where is All-Highest?" he demands, in heavily accented but serviceable English.

"Downstairs—with the Eater of Souls—" The young woman stiffens for a moment, then sags bonelessly. Alexei rises, wraps himself in the cloak that she won't be needing anymore, and wipes his knife on the back of her dress. Then he tiptoes towards the steps down to the crypt. If the Eater of Souls is lurking downstairs, he reasons, then it's very probable that what he came for is to be found there. And Alexei doesn't give up easily.

TO THE NORTH, A RED TRUCK CREEPS ALONG A DARKENED AVE- nue. Three figures sit atop its roof. One of them holds a white electric violin. Her two guards watch and wonder, entrenching tools raised and ready to shovel mortal remains off the roof should any such encroach. The truck bumps slowly along in low gear, pushing through a sea of withered bodies that sway and jostle slowly. Occasionally there is a crunch or crackle as the truck rolls over bones that failed to get out of its way in time. The driver doesn't speed up or slow down; to stop in the middle of this unnatural crowd is to court disaster, although none of the feeders has so far attempted to climb aboard the OCCULUS truck.

Down in the darkened truck cab Major Barnes rides next to the driver, peering into the darkness for any sign of ambush. He talks into his headset: "Two hundred meters in. Dr. O'Brien, do you see any sign of survivors—"

Mo, atop the cab, raises her bow. "Not right here," she says shortly. The walking dead are undirected; the grounded metal framework of the truck blocks their ability to sense those who ride within, and the warm meat on the cab roof is out of easy reach.

A crack of gunfire sounds. Mo looks round sharply as Howe grabs her shoulder. "Down!" he snaps, and she ducks as he raises his MP5 and squints through its night sights. The gunfire is coming from a chapel, half-concealed by trees and the silent army of walking corpses. There are more shots, followed by shouts and a scream, cut off short. "Shooters on the building roofline," Howe reports: "Four, no, five bodies. Defenses at ground level, barricades, I can't see anyone manning them. The crowd's thickest there. Defenders have—no, wait."

Cold flesh, bodies that do not show on infrared, have formed an abhuman pyramid to one side of the chapel. The survivors on the roof are shooting, but not at the OCCULUS truck: they have problems that are closer to hand. As one corpse disintegrates another takes its place, and the defenders have fewer banishment rounds than Brookwood has open graves. "Doc, can you do anything about them?" Howe asks. "Because I don't think we're going to get in there without—"

Mo raises her bow, strikes a shivering note from the burning strings. Howe winces and moves aside. "Give me some elbow room," she says flatly. Then she touches the strings lightly, coaxing an eerie, familiar leitmotif from her instrument. "Put this out through the PA circuit," she mutters, grimly determined.

Down below, Barnes grimaces tensely and twists input dials on the truck's external public address systems. The growing wild resonance of *die Walkürenritt* floods from the big speakers mounted to either side of the cab; the driver looks sidelong at his CO, then floors the accelerator in low gear, adding the roar of the big diesel (and the crunch of unburied bones) to the music. Barnes announces to the back of the truck: "All right, gentlemen, this is going to be an opposed entry and they know we're coming. Wards, up! Arms, up! Party time in sixty seconds!"

The risen dead are fleeing, for the most part, out of the way of the truck as it roars and bucks across the path. It's the music that does it; Mo stands atop the roof, utterly engrossed in tracking the melody. Richard Wagner, it was said, hated violinists: blood drips from her fingertips as the eerie extradimensional resonances of her interpretation of one of his most famous works drags the sound of an entire string section— and a brassy resonance echoing from the metal flanks of the truck—into being.

The truck crunches across skeletal remnants that lie in rows around the chapel, silent and unmoving. A few bodies, less damaged than the rest, lie near a minivan; others are clustered near the door to the building, which is ajar. A few less emaciated figures lie among the skeletonized forms: of these, most bear the signs of gunshot wounds.

"Back us up to the door," Barnes tells the driver. Switching to the common channel: "All right, we're going in. Standard entry protocol for mass possession. Scary and Howe, over to you. Dr. O'Brien, time to get down off the roof. You can follow with me once we've cleared the way. See if we can figure out what we're looking at."

The soldiers pile out of the back of the truck, wearing bright yellow HAZMAT suits, MP5s at the ready. The bodies are packed in so tightly around the steps to the chapel that they dash across rib cages and cloak-swathed torsos on the way to the open door.

There's a snap of gunfire from up top: two of the soldiers drop to their knees and reply with a burst of aimed fire. A black-clad figure tumbles from the roofline. One of the soldiers throws something up and over the eaves; the others take cover as the fragmentation grenade explodes.

"What's up there?" Mo tries to ask, shouting in Barnes's ear.

"Bad guys." Barnes grins hungrily. "Ah." He taps the earpiece screwed into his left ear: "Follow me." The gunfire from the defenders on the roof has stopped as he steps out of the back of the truck and walks towards the chapel entrance. Mo follows him, her violin raised. They're halfway across the ten-meter gap when a silhouette lurches clear of the side of the building and throws itself towards the major. Barnes raises his HK-5 and plants a neat three-round group in the middle of the assailant's torso; by the time Mo's bow makes contact with an eerily blue-glowing string, the fluorescence in the back of the revenant's eye sockets has begun to fade. "Bloody fans, always waiting outside the dressing room . . ." Barnes cocks his head on one side, listening. "Dr. O'Brien? This way, *now*."

They're inside in seconds, and one of the soldiers pulls the tall oak door shut behind them. The chapel hall is full of bodies, the long-dead and the fresh draped across one another in promiscuous embrace. Some of the recent bodies are naked: in the soldier's infrared vision they still glow with body heat.

"Look sharp, some of them made it to the door," Howe comments over the open channel. A couple of bodies still clutch bulky assault shotguns with drum magazines: one, wearing a distinctly more professional camouflage rig than the rest, is holding a Russian AKS-74 rifle. None of them, however, are moving. The feeders have eaten their fill and moved on.

"Trapdoor over here, sir!" One of the troops waves, pointing at a raised door.

"Secure it," says Howe. "Tidily, our boy might still be down there." He doesn't say what everyone fears: the next living soul they find in this city of the dead will be the first.

As the soldiers move in, something runs at them, out of the tunnel, frighteningly fast. There's a burst of automatic fire. "Hold that!" yells Howe, as the revenant comes apart in a tumbling rain of dust and bones. "Batons!" A pair of troops step forward, holding heavily customized cattle prods before them—electrical shock-rods, customized with signal generators to loosen the grip of extradimensional horrors on their walking hosts. There's a snap and crackle of sparks as they test their tools.

"You think he's down there," Mo says quietly.

Major Barnes nods. "Cultists. They go to ground for their rituals."

Up ahead, Scary triggers his shock-stick, sparking the terminals: he grins at Howe. "I love the smell of—"

"Don't say it, son, unless you want a week on toilet duty."

"Aw, Sarge." He steps forward, bending to follow the lead team into the cellar. "That's harsh."

There are no living bodies in the tunnel. Some of the possessed are still stirring feebly, their luminous eyes guttering in the darkness, but the flying wedge of soldiers with shock-sticks shut them down in short order: it's easier than clubbing baby seals.

At the end of the tunnel they come to an open door. Now there's noise, and the troops take up position to either side of the entrance, ready for a forced entry. But while they're waiting, Dr. O'Brien and Major Barnes arrive. Mo holds her violin, ready for a killing chord. Barnes glances at her, then waves Howe back from the right-hand side of the door. "What do you think?" he asks quietly.

"It stinks, sir. You saw the sov kit back there?"

"I did. I reckon we've got company. More to the point, we haven't found our boy yet. Could be a hostage situation."

"Shit. I'll tell Moran to bring up the snoop kit—"

Mo's eyes are hollow shadows in the darkness. "Major?"

"What is it?"

She points at the entrance with a hand half-folded around something. "He's definitely in there." She unfolds her hand, palm upwards to reveal the cracked and battered screen of Bob's iPhone, icons glowing balefully in the darkness. "Got a soul tracker on this thing. He's alive, and he's not alone—"

Which is when the screaming starts.

ALEXEI IS BECOMING ANNOYED.

He's been down in the crypt for half an hour, moving with painstaking care. The place is literally crawling with the risen dead, feeding on the dwindling survivors of the Black God Slave Cult—some of whom have barricaded themselves into the ossuary, with predictable consequences— and only sheer luck and the revenants' lack of situational awareness has saved him. They don't communicate with each other, don't raise the alarm when he lands among them and lashes out with a sharp-edged entrenching tool or shoots their neighbors with a silenced pistol firing banishment rounds. It would be good news under other circumstances, but Alexei is acutely aware that he has a serious lack of backup and a mission that under other circumstances would be hopelessly compromised.

The sounds of gunfire from up above had nearly died out ten minutes ago. Now they're getting louder and more frequent. And there's something different about them: different weapons, much tighter fire discipline. The new shooters are professionals, but they're not his squad—they're firing NATO spec ammunition.

As it is, it looks like the only way out is in; if he can find somewhere to hole up until morning, he stands a chance of exfiltrating on foot, and if he can meet the mission's core objective, retrieve the missing document, so much the better—

And everything looks like it's coming down to this corridor here, and the open doorway gaping blackly at the end of it.

Alexei glides towards the entrance, then pauses briefly on the threshold. It's a cul-de-sac, and every instinct warns him not to go in—at least, not without a couple of fragmentation grenades to clear the way. But there's a quiet sobbing sound coming from inside, a woman's lamentation. (And if the mission target is present, it wouldn't do to cut up hard.) He adjusts his goggles, then flashes his infrared torch briefly at the ceiling.

A confused jumble of impressions: bodies. Mattresses arranged in concentric rings around a pit, leading down to an altar. There's a four-poster bed behind the altar. The sobbing comes from a figure on the bed. *Sacrificial victim*, thinks Alexei. There are bodies, some new and some old: this is not a novelty. The idea of rescuing a victim from the cultists, however, holds some appeal—especially as she might know where they will have taken the mission target. Alexei is Spetsnaz through-and-through: the product of an incredibly harsh training system, ruthlessly self-disciplined, and trained as a soulless killing machine. But he's also intelligent, a misfit who was a round peg in the square hole of the regular army, and possessed of the romantic streak that leads some men into professional soldiering. Given an opportunity to rescue a damsel in distress *and* expedite his mission goals at the same time, Alexei will go for the gratitude shag. And who can blame him? It's been a hard night's work.

And so he dances down the aisle, leans over the lady tied to the bed, and—holding a knife to the neck of the man lying next to her—who just happens to be me, myself: Bob Howard—asks: "Woman, you tell, where is Fuller Memorandum? Speak now, or will cut throat of All-Highest."

I LIE IN THE GRIP OF A GREAT LASSITUDE. I'VE BEEN LYING here for what seems like decades, staring with unblinking eyes at the star-pricked canopy of black silk above the Skull Cultists' altar. I know, distantly, that I am in extreme danger; I'm in the middle of a monstrous summoning, and lying like a drunkard next to a bound but still deadly Iris while her minions panic and try to fight off the eaters outside the chapel is not a life-expectancy-enhancing situation. But I *can't* move. I don't even feel tired; I feel *dead*. Some kinds of summoning cause serious physical fatigue, possibly via a mechanism not unlike a mild form of K syndrome, and this would appear to be one of them.

The black sky above me, pierced by the flickering light of unfamiliar constellations, blows like a chill wind through my awareness. *I've seen this sky before,* I realize; *where? Oh.* Yes, the canopy of the altar-bed of the Black Skull mirrors the chill starlight that sluices across the desiccated plain surrounded by the fence of impaled corpses that I dreamed about, the fence that locks the Sleeper in the Pyramid in somnolent darkness. I'm not the only one to see that skyscape when I close my eyes, I think.

I can feel Iris nearby, her mind slowed and frustrated, defocused by the bindings woven into the ropes that trim the altar of the sex-magic cultists that used this chapel before her own people moved in. She's angry, terrified, embittered; I could almost feel sympathy for her if my right arm didn't remind me constantly of what she stands for, who she is. There are the eaters, torpid and in some cases well-fed, resting in their bony chrysalids in the porous earth beyond; and there are other human lives upstairs, some of them familiar. They're coming this way. One of them, not so familiar, is almost here already—

Something touches my neck, as a voice speaks, in a thick eastern European accent: "Woman, you tell, where is Fuller Memorandum? Speak now, or will cut throat of All-Highest."

Bastard. I'm lying here helpless and I can't even tell Laughing Boy that I'm not the All-Highest! That, and the Fuller Memorandum happens to be snugly jacketed in the folder I'm clutching to my bosom with arms like lead weights: this is not looking good. Close to panic, I try to twitch a finger or blink an eyelid—anything to reassert control over my own treacherous body.

"Untie me and I'll take you to it," says Iris, quick as a flash. "Please?" I can just about see her batting her eyelids at Laughing Boy. Then she adds: "You'd better cut All-Highest's throat before he wakes up. He was going to sacrifice me—"

I try to shout, *She's lying!* But nothing comes out of my throat. I am not, in fact, breathing, I realize distantly. *Am I dead?* I wonder. *Am I undead?* I'm not one hundred percent clear on the clinical definition of death, but I'm pretty sure that lying trapped in my own unbreathing body meets some of the requirements. I don't know about the continuity of consciousness bit, but maybe it's a side effect of the binding ritual they used. If I had my phone I could go online and google it, but zombie don't surf. I feel the knife blade move, and I really start to panic—

"*Nyet.* Is already dead. You take me for fool! Where is Fuller Memorandum? Tell and I release."

The knife is at Iris's throat; I lie beside her, paralyzed and apprehensive.

Iris's breath ratchets harshly through her throat. "The file All-Highest is clutching. Be careful, you don't want to touch his skin by accident—"

But she's too late.

Alexei, Laughing Boy, pulls the Fuller Memorandum from my hands. As he does so, he makes momentary contact with one of my fingers. And the inevitable happens, because this torpor that's come over me—the torpor associated with the summoning, and the control of lesser eaters, and with K syndrome—is symptomatic of something else: I'm *hungry*.

IN THE BACK OF AN AMBULANCE SPEEDING TOWARDS THE ROYAL Surrey Country Hospital with lights and siren, an old man opens his eyes and whispers, "*Good job, boy.*" The paramedic, who is looking at the EEG trace, glances at him in surprise.

The stroke victim tries to sit up, struggling against the straps that hold him on the stretcher. Then he frowns thunderously. "How long was I out?" he asks the paramedic. Then: "Forget that. Turn round—I want you to take me to Brookwood. Immediately!"

* * *

SECONDS LATER, BARNES AND HIS MEN COME THROUGH THE DOOR
with a strobing flicker of light bombs and a concussive blast of stun grenades. They're ready for business: they've got Mo and her singular instrument ready to suppress any residual occult resistance. But they're too late.

The screaming is mine; I'm yelling my throat out: a weird, warbling abhuman keening that doesn't stop until the squad paramedic gingerly sticks me with a battlefield-grade sedative. Which takes some time: when they find me I'm lying on a vampire prince's bed, covered in gore, with a lump missing from my right arm, and my eyes rolled up in my head so that only the green-glowing whites show. It takes them a while to confirm that I'm safe to approach; and a while longer to get an insulated stretcher down to the chamber and strap me down onto it.

Iris is sobbing, cringing away from me as far as the ropes will let her. She can't get very far, though: she's weighed down by the body of the dead Spetsnaz trooper, a black ring-binder lying on the floor beside him.

As for Alexei, he's dead: eaten by the thing the cultists tried to make of me. Their sacrifice bit a huge and vital chunk out of my soul; after the power of my death-magic ran down, I was all but inert until Alexei unintentionally filled up the hole. I don't think he intended to do that. *I* didn't intend to do that, certainly: I'm no necromancer. But when they've performed the ritual of binding upon you, trying to turn you into a vessel for the Eater of Souls . . .

You need to eat.

Epilogue

ON THE BEACH

THE MIND'S EYE HAS A FAST-FORWARD BUTTON. IT'S FUNNY: most of the time we don't think about it in those terms; but when you're trying to write down a sequence of experiences, to take a series of unfortunate events and turn them into a coherent story, the mind's eye takes on some of the characteristics of an old-fashioned videotape recorder: balky, prone to drop-outs and loss, cumbersome and wonky and breakable.

So call me a camera and stick a battery in my ear.

FIRST. PANIN GOT AWAY.

Here's what I imagine happened, around the time I was screaming my lungs out on a bed of nightmares:

In the back of a shiny black BMW speeding towards Woking—and thence to the motorway south to Dover and the Channel Tunnel—an old man opens his eyes and takes a deep breath. "That was altogether too close for comfort," he says aloud.

Dmitry glances at him in the rearview mirror. "With respect, sir . . . I agree." His knuckles are white where they grasp the steering wheel, and he is racking up fines from the average-speed cameras at an almost surreal rate. "The men . . ."

Panin closes his eyes again. "Dead. Or they'll exfiltrate. Vassily in the embassy can see to their needs. I am going home to explain this fiasco." He is silent for nearly a minute. "We nearly had it all: a transcript of the Sternberg Fragment, Fuller's memorandum on binding the Eater of Souls."

"With respect, sir, cultists are always unreliable proxies. And we did get the schemata for the violin, and we weakened the British . . ."

Panin glares at Dmitry: "Weakening the British is not the goal of the great game! Survival is the goal. We are intelligent men, not panicking rats biting each other as they struggle to escape the sinking ship. They are the enemies of our enemy, never forget that. It is the cultists' error, to imagine themselves beset by foes they can never defeat."

"Like back there?" asks Dmitry.

Panin doesn't answer. They drive the rest of the way to the Channel in silence.

SECOND. HERE'S WHAT I *KNOW* HAPPENED:

Once I woke up briefly, in a darkened nighttime room with two beds and a door and a man in a blue suit standing outside the door with a gun. The man in the bed next to me was familiar. He was asleep, and I remember thinking that there was something very urgent that I had to tell him, but I couldn't remember what it was and the file was missing—

Then the alarm went off and the medics came and they made me go back to sleep.

I don't remember much after that. Which is a mercy—the dreams were *bad*.

Mo tells me that for the first week they kept me heavily sedated—if they eased up on the chlorpromazine I started screaming and trying to eat my own fingers. She visited every day. She sat by my bedside and fed me, spooning mush into my mouth and making sure I didn't choke on it.

Angleton recovered much faster. Two nights under observation and they released him. Then he heard about me and kicked up a stink. They were planning on moving me to St. Hilda's. Angleton had a better idea of what was wrong with me and refused to take no for an answer; so after nearly a week in hospital (with my head wrapped in the pink fluffy haze of a major antipsychotic bender), a private ambulance picked me up and deposited me in the Village.

The Village used to be called Dunwich, back before the Ministry of War evacuated it and turned it into a special site. It was allocated to the wartime Special Operations Executive, part of which later became the Laundry and inherited this small coastal community with its street of cottages and decaying pier, its general store and village pub. Today we use it as a training center, and also as a quiet place for taking time out. There's no internet access, and no mobile phone coverage, and no nagging from head office about time sheets and sickness self-certification. There *is* a medical doctor, but Janet is sensible and very patient, and has seen an astonishing number of cases of Krantzberg syndrome (and other, more esoteric sorcerous injuries) over the years.

They billeted me in a tiny seaside cottage and Janet took me off the chlorpromazine, substituting a number of other medications—not all of them legally prescribable. (MDMA helps a *lot* when you're suffering from the delusion that you're one of the walking dead.) After three days, I stopped shivering and hiccuping with fear; after a week, I could sleep again without a night-light. At the weekend, Mo came to visit. I was glad to see her. She knows what it's like where I've been, to a good first approximation. We spent a lot of time together, just holding hands. It feels very strange, touching someone who's alive. Maybe in another week I'll be able to hug her without recoiling because I'm terrified I'm going to accidentally eat her mind.

(That's the trouble with this job. Sometimes it chews you up and spits you out—literally.)

Mo came back the next weekend, too. She says she's trying to get a week's compassionate leave, but the fallout from Iris's actions has been beyond earthshaking. We'll see.

* * *

I'VE BEEN WORKING ON THIS REPORT FOR A COUPLE OF WEEKS now.

This being the Village, and an internet-free zone, I'm allowed to use a computer and dictation software—although it's had its CD drive and wifi chipset removed, the case is welded shut, and it's padlocked to an oak desk that weighs approximately half as much again as Angleton's Memex. It beats the manual typewriter hands down, but when I asked if I could take it home with me, the security officer barely managed to conceal his sneer.

I suppose there are some loose ends I should tie up, so here goes:

We never did find out exactly what happened to any of Panin's men apart from Alexei, or to Panin himself: you should read my speculations with more than a pinch of salt. I can't even be certain beyond a shadow of a doubt that Panin was behind the theft of the violin report, although theft of state secrets *is* the sort of thing that the Thirteenth Directorate's parent agency traditionally excelled at. I'm assuming that the elite Spetsnaz infiltration troops assigned to an occult warfare department probably stood more of a chance of escaping alive than the cultists: but we didn't account for all of them, either. The scene at Brookwood the next morning was indescribable. I've seen the pictures. It was easy enough to close down the cemetery—police roadblocks, reports about an illegal rave and grave-yard vandalism, a handful of D-notices to gag the more annoying local reporters—but then they had to do something with the bodies. The feeders raised just about everything that wasn't totally dismembered and disarticulated. In the end, they had to bring in bulldozers and dig trenches. They identified some of the cultists—but not Jonquil the Sloane Ranger, or her boyfriend Julian.

I don't think Brookwood will reopen for a long time.

Brains has been given a good talking-to, and is being subjected to the Security Theater Special Variety Show for breaching about sixteen different regulations by installing beta software on an employee's personal phone. Reminding Oscar-Oscar that if he hadn't done so they'd have lost the Eater of Souls to a cultist infiltrator appears to be futile. Right now, everyone in Admin has joined in the world's biggest arse-kicking circle dance, except possibly for Angleton, who is shielding me from the worst of it. Because they haven't forgotten that *I've* been a naughty boy too—if it wasn't for me, they wouldn't have needed all those bulldozers at Brookfield, would they? Although Angleton *has* had a measure of success in pointing out to certain overenthusiastic disciplinarians that if it wasn't for the feeders I summoned, they'd have had the Brotherhood of the Black Pharaoh trying to open up a long distance call to the Sleeper in the Pyramid, paid in the coin of London's dead.

AS FOR THE MAN HIMSELF——CALL HIM TEAPOT. CALL HIM

Angleton, call him Sir—I haven't seen him since I woke up here, and I won't be seeing him until the Auditors hear my final report and I go back on active duty. But I have this to say:

I used to think he scared the shit out of me, but now I know better. I know what he's like, from the inside. The effects of Iris's botched binding faded fast, and I probably only borrowed a tiny fraction of his power. I didn't know how to use it properly, either. But I have been destiny-entangled before, and I know what it was like then, and I don't think it's a coincidence that Angleton was in a flatlined coma for the entire duration of my funny turn.

I also learned this much: Angleton isn't bound to the Laundry by the ramshackle geas that Fuller and his fellow eccentric occultists threw together in the 1930s. He's a free agent—or at least as free as any of us are, be we beasts, men, or gods. The reason he puts up with us? I don't know. It may be long habit—he's lived the life of an Englishman for so long now that he self-identifies as such. But I have a theory.

Angleton knows what's coming. He knows exactly what is going to bleed through the walls of reality, when the stars burn down from the pitiless heavens and our ever-thinking numbers begin to corrode the structure of reality. And he believes we're his best hope for his own survival.

Like I said: the only god I believe in is coming back. And when he arrives, I'll be waiting with a shotgun.

GLOSSARY OF ABBREVIATIONS, ACRONYMS, AND ORGANIZATIONS

AIVD Algemene Inlichtingen- en Veiligheidsdienst (General Intelligence and Security Service) [Netherlands]
BA British Airways [UK]
BLACK CHAMBER Cryptanalysis agency officially disbanded in 1929 (secretly retasked with occult intelligence duties) [US]
CESG Communications-Electronics Security Group (division within GCHQ) [UK]
CIA Central Intelligence Agency [US]
CMA Computer Misuse Act (law governing hacking) [UK]
COTS Cheap, Off The Shelf (computer kit; procurement term) [US/UK]
DEA Drug Enforcement Administration [US]
DERA Defence Evaluation and Research Agency (privatized as QinetiQ) [UK]
DGSE Direction Générale de la Sécurité Extérieure [France]
DIA Defense Intelligence Agency [US]
FBI Federal Bureau of Investigation [US]
FO Foreign Office [UK]
FSB Federal Security Service (formerly known as KGB) [Russia]
GCHQ Government Communications HQ (equivalent to NSA) [UK]

GCSE General Certificate of Secondary Education (high school qualification; not to be confused with GCHQ) [UK]

GRU Russian Military Intelligence [Russia]

JIC Joint Intelligence Committee [UK]

KCMG Knight-Commander of the Most Distinguished Order of St. Michael and St. George (honors service overseas or in connection with foreign or Commonwealth affairs) [UK]

KGB Committee for State Security (renamed FSB in 1991) [Russia]

THE LAUNDRY Formerly SOE Q Department (spun off as a separate organization in 1945) [UK]

MI5 National Security Service (also known as DI5) [UK]

MI6 Secret Intelligence Service (also known as SIS, DI6) [UK]

NEST Nuclear Emergency Support Team [US]

NKVD Historical predecessor organization to KGB (renamed in 1947) [USSR/Russia]

NSA National Security Agency (equivalent to GCHQ) [US]

OBE Order of the British Empire (awarded mainly to civilians and service personnel for public service or other distinctions) [UK]

OCCULUS Occult Control Coordination Unit Liaison, Unconventional Situations [UK/NATO]

ONI Office of Naval Intelligence [US]

OSA Official Secrets Act (law governing official secrets) [UK]

OSS Office of Strategic Services (disbanded in 1945/remodeled as CIA) [US]

Q DIVISION Division within the Laundry associated with R&D [UK]

QINETIQ See DERA [UK]

RIPA Regulation of Investigatory Powers Act (law governing communications interception) [UK]

SAS Special Air Service (British Army special forces) [UK]

SBS Special Boat Service (Royal Marines special forces) [UK]

SIS See MI6 [UK]

SOE Special Operations Executive (equivalent to OSS, officially disbanded in 1945; see also the Laundry) [UK]

TLA Three Letter Acronym [All]